A FELL PRESENCE
IN THE JAIL

Lifting in the air, the rubble rolled up into floating piles and crunched into a condensed conglomerate. A low guttural chant was beginning as Hamui worked his hand in a rigid configuration, twisting his fingers as he worked the floating rock orbs tighter, the electric blue glow in his staff's crystal brightening.

Thrusting his staff forward, one of the orbs launched at the arisen giant that was lurking towards Cray, who had finally gotten to his feet after the massive blow.

The smooth rock slammed into the cranium of the large creature, exploding into powder as the giant was forced to use its hands to steady itself from the impact.

Hamui had gotten its attention, its milky white eyes locking onto the little praven that stood with three more rock orbs ready for launch.

Another polished orb shot into its flat ape face, this ball holding together a bit better, crushing facial bone, opening up a few lacerations along its brow and cheeks.

It started to hustle towards Hamui, blasting past Malagar and Matt, receiving another blast from the last two orbs, clobbering its face into mush, a massive sunken hole on its right ocular cavity now; but it needed no vision at that point. It knew what direction the little praven was in…

Lords of the Deep Hells Trilogy

Book 2

Lords of the Sands

This is a work of fiction. All the characters and events portrayed in this book are either products of the author's imagination or are used fictitiously.

All rights reserved, including the right to reproduce this book, or portions thereof, in any form.

Copyright © 2021 Paul Yoder

Cover art by Andrey Vasilchenko

All rights reserved.

You can contact me at:

authorpaulyoder@gmail.com

Visit me online for launch dates and other news at:
authorpaulyoder.com (sign up for the newsletter)
instagram.com/author_paul_yoder
tiktok.com/@authorpaulyoder
Paul Yoder on Goodreads
Paul Yoder on Amazon

ASIN: B094HPTS8J
ISBN: 979-8715737335

In loving memory to my father, Frank Yoder,

whose last words to me were, "Your writing, you've got something special there. Never give up on that."

This one's for you, Dad.

LANDS OF WANDERLUST NOVELS BY

Paul Yoder

LORDS OF THE DEEP HELLS TRILOGY
Shadow of the Arisen
Lords of the Sands
Heart of the Maiden

KINGDOM OF CROWNS TRILOGY
The Rediron Warp
Firebrands
Seamwalker

LANDS
OF
WANDERLUST

Paul Yoder

Lords
of the
Sands

Lords of the Deep Hells Trilogy

Book II

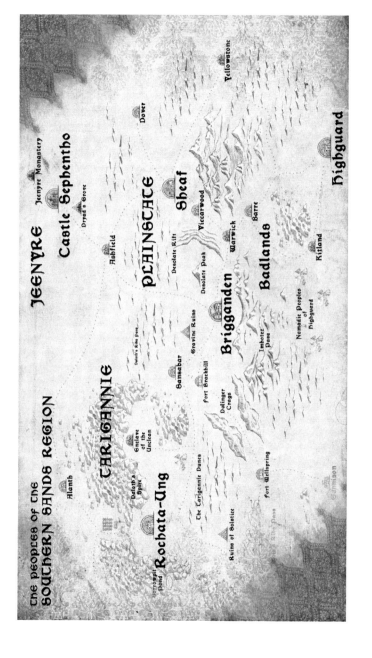

The Peoples of the
SOUTHERN SANDS REGION

JEENYRE   Jeenyre Monastery

Castle Sephentho

Dryad's Grove

Abbfield

PLAINSGATE

Dover

Yellowstone

Highguard

Sheaf

Desolate Rift

Viccarwood

Warwick   Barre

Desolate Peak   Badlands

CARIGANNIE

Enclave
of the
Unclean

Briggarden

Grovine Ruins

Sansabar

Imhotep
Pass

Nomadic Peoples
of
Highguard

Kitland

Hianth

Delroth's
Spire

Fort Brachhill

Dolinger
Crags

Fort Brachhill

Rochata-Ung

Portentual
Pond

The Carigannie Dunes

Fort Wellspring

Ruins of Solstice

Gumrison

Part One: The Wayward Trails

1

FACE OF ASH

His pulse hastened, his temple throbbing so prominently that his vision blurred with every heartbeat, causing him to shake his head to attempt to jog his recent memory back to where he was and how he had gotten there.

The ground he stood upon was a deep yellow, slick sponge-like surface. Ashen veiny vines weaved across the endless plain, plumes of spore occasionally spouting out small mouths in the network of vines.

Coughing as he rose above the mixture of ash and spore that hung low in the air, he stumbled to his feet, looking around to see a hellish landscape, one that didn't resemble his planet, Una, in the least.

"Where am I?" he slurred, voice still raspy, the spore seeming to cling to the insides of his lungs, belaboring his breath and speech.

No one answered him vocally, but after his query, he felt a presence behind him.

The throbbing in his head intensified, almost causing him to topple over as he spun around, lethargically throwing a hand to his sword hilt as he turned to face his stalker.

A withered, ten-foot-tall figure hovered in the air a few yards from him. The creature's ashen skin was tattered, thin; seeming like it was ready to split at the softest touch. Its paper-thin skin was a deathly black purple, fading to a sickly orange-yellow around its ribs and arm bones that barely had anything separating them from view.

Its face, though, was a pale yellow, speckled with splotches of ash, darkening the area just around its closed eyes, mouth, and hole where its nose might have once been.

He stood there looking in disgust as the giant emaciated limbs began to spread out, its long arms hanging outstretched as if on a crucifix, its body ready to tear apart from its own weight, even though it remained aloft, supernaturally hovering in the air before him.

He went for his weapon now, having seen enough of the grotesque display in front of him, but as he reached for the handle of what should have been his sword, he gripped onto something fleshy and cold.

Looking down, he held not a sword, but a rotten arm. Dropping the dead weight, he looked back up at the mummified giant to find it had moved much closer to him, only floating a few feet away now.

The startling swift advance set him back a step, almost stumbling over himself as the thing's soot-lined eyes and mouth shot open, revealing nothing but black cavities within—devoid of fleshy tissue.

A low croaking moan, almost indiscernible at first, issued from the gaping maw of the mummy, the sound growing louder and louder as he turned to run from the demonic being.

The sound rattled through him, instilling an inescapable feeling of doom. His limbs were becoming less and less reliable as fear continued to cinch around every muscle in his body.

He could hear the open-mouthed, drawn-out groan directly behind him. He knew the abomination's dry, cracked lips were mere inches from the nape of his neck.

That thought momentarily locked up his right leg—not for long, but just enough to pitch him forward, his shaken reflexes failing to see him graciously to the ground, as he landed hard along the web of ashen vines covering the landscape.

He lay face down in the knee-high, spore-filled cloud, attempting to force his petrified lungs to take a breath, but unable to do so, his whole body momentarily frozen as he listened to the groaning slip closer and closer towards him—and then, it stopped.

A wrung-out gasp issued from his mouth, his lungs able to starve of air no longer, intaking ashy pollen afterwards, which spurred a fit of coughing.

The spasm broke him from his petrification, and he flung himself around to see a figure standing above him, a symbol burning from its forehead of a reverse crescent that showed spikes shooting forth from it, an empty, torn eye directly below the shapes.

The symbol flashed, blinding him for a moment as he brought up his hands over his face a moment too late.

Something tugged sharply at his outstretched wrist, and then the other one, both of his unattached hands now falling back down upon his chest, the realization that his hands had been severed only now striking him as a searing jolt of belated pain shot through his limbs.

Holding his two bloody stumps close to his eyes to confirm the gruesome reality, he let out a ragged scream as blood spattered down upon him, soaking in the creases of pain and terror etched in his face.

His focus switched from his bloody stumps to the creature above him, which had changed from the grotesque giant to a six-foot figure shrouded in black, raising a curved blade, ready to cleave him in twain.

As the blade came down, the shadow and ash in the air dispersed, giving him a clear view of his executioner, and everything, all the confusion as to why he was there, came into focus as he realized that the man that now cleaved his body in two, the man many knew as *The Nomad*, was none other than himself.

2

THE MORNING SUN

"Nomad," a voice called, accompanied by the tune of a nearby songbird.

Soft shafts of light showing through lightly rustling leaves caressed his closed eyelids, the sound of lapping water gently arousing his senses.

A touch, soft, tentative, persuaded him to open his eyes, squinting terribly at the sight of the morning sun, even though they lay well covered by a healthy forest canopy.

"You sleep longer these days," was all his companion, Reza, forlornly had to say to him once she saw that he was up and coherent.

Holding eyes on him for a moment longer to assure that he was up, she stood, offering him a hand.

Closing his eyes for a moment, trying to push past the dreadful weariness that seemed to depress his whole body, even after a full night's rest, he threw his hand to Reza's and allowed her to pull him from his resting place at the foot of a large, mossy oak tree, up to his feet.

"Camp's packed up and the horses are ready," she said to him, walking him over to his stallion as a light autumn breeze swept through the grove.

They had been traveling for less than a month, but Reza had seen a great deal of change in her friend, Nomad, since their setting out for the Jeenyre monastery. He had grown tired during the day, and though he attempted to sleep at night, often his screams would wake her, so much so that she had to resort to sleeping a great distance away from him. This worried her, not just because of the mental trials her friend was going through, but also, she worried his cries in the night might attract unwanted visitors from man or beast, and with her sleeping so far off from him, she would not be there to protect him in his madness.

She had been to the Jeenyre monastery many times through the years, and she knew that they were only a few days away from their destination, which she was profoundly grateful for.

Nomad was as close to a friend as she had ever had, but he was wearing her raw. There was seemingly nothing she could do to help his continual dip into a darkness that was a mystery to both of them. The sooner they arrived at the monastery, the sooner they would find answers to his demonic condition.

The trail was easy—peaceful. Pine, oak, walnut, and a host of other pleasant trees made up the woods they trotted through. Leaves, most deep in the turn of autumn colors, were rolled by the wind down the earthen trail, only the evergreens holding the hills' true green hue up above.

The trail let out next to an expansive lake, the mist of water from a huge waterfall, hundreds of feet high, rushing past them as if desperate to escape the lake's borders.

"Ah, Nomad," she called back, having to blink her eyes from the gust of moist air from the lake. "Castle Sephentho!"

Nomad looked up to where Reza excitedly pointed. A mile or more across the mountain lake, amongst the rock walls that basked in the warm glow of the half cloud-covered sun, was a spired castle, multiple tiers of brilliant architecture, and a weaving road clearly leading up to its steep gates from the road they traveled.

"And there is Sephentho Watch," she said, pointing up above the castle to a watchtower at the peak of the mountain from which the great waterfall poured out over the lake. "See how the Kalis River cuts to either side of the tower before emptying into the Sephentho lake? They say the tower was there even before the river meandered to that spot, withstood the wear of the water, and remains immoveable and in use even many hundreds of years after being in the direct path of the river. Some think it's hallowed ground. A post that is divinely watched over, just as those posted there watch over the castle."

Smiling for a moment longer, heartened at the sight of the landmark that confirmed that they were only a day or two away from the monastery, she looked back to Nomad to see what he thought of the sight, only to find that he had nodded off, slumping over in his saddle as his stallion munched on some grass at the side of the trail.

She had had enough of Nomad's lethargy for the day.

Jumping off her horse, leading both mounts to a low-hanging tree branch close by and tying them up, she hefted Nomad out of his saddle and shouldered him over to the lake bank.

Slowly coming to as she half dragged him over the grassy knoll, she forcefully undid his belt buckle holding his scabbard, throwing his sword and loose pouches in the grass, put a boot on his backside, and kicked the dazed man headlong into the chill mountain lake.

Reza smirked for a moment, guiltily delighting in the complete, unexpected surprise in Nomad's countenance before he plunged beneath the lake's surface, realizing too late his icy fate, but she quickly began to regret her rash action as she saw Nomad's silhouette sink quite deep into the clear water.

She waited a moment longer, worry rising as to what she had done as Nomad made no visible attempt to resurface, cursing as she flung off her strapped equipment, readying to jump in if Nomad didn't surface within the next few seconds.

She looked into the icy pool of water, Nomad remaining quite still a dozen feet down or so, wondering if his condition had truly weakened him so completely as to render him incapable of springing off the lakebed to the surface. Apparently, it had, and her childishness had placed her friend's life in sudden danger.

Leaping through the air, diving headfirst, her hands parted the water as she lanced quickly to the lakebed where Nomad lay. Deftly tucking an arm around his torso, she recoiled, launching powerfully off the silt floor, breaching the water's surface.

Digging in deep, Reza stroked hard towards the lake's bank, touching down on the sloped beach.

She dragged Nomad's body ashore and quickly looked him over, placing a trembling hand on his chest and an ear to his mouth, waiting for signs of life. She stiffened as she heard him open his mouth.

"Getting out already? Not too cold for you, is it?"

Turning to look at a smirking Nomad, realizing he had played her, her look of concern shifted to indignation as she splashed a wave of ice-cold water in Nomad's face before standing up, looking away from him as she collected herself.

"I didn't deserve that," she spat out, the spite clear on her tongue.

"No, you didn't," Nomad generously agreed as he slowly got to his feet, poising to pounce at his victim's back, finishing with, "but you do deserve this!"

Reza turned just in time to see Nomad leaping through the air at her, colliding with her so hard that it took her off her feet, throwing them both far back into the deep of the lake.

Coming to the surface, Nomad treaded water as Reza furiously resurfaced, hostilely eyeing him as he chuckled, "We both needed a bath anyways."

Luckily for Nomad, he saw the slightest wicked smirk from Reza a moment before she grappled him up, thrashing him around in the water as he responded in kind, the two, for the most part, playfully trying to dunk the other, splashing, and exchanging blows underwater.

The birds in the trees, perhaps due to the ruckus the two were causing, all fled at once, and it was a sign that, even amidst their roughhousing, was not lost on the playful pair.

Their play now over in an instant, both looked to the trees, then down to the trail they had come from and listened as the sound of footfall preceded a band of armed, scruffy-looking men.

Nomad and Reza exchanged a concerned side glance as they began to swim back to the shore, all mirth from their swim now completely washed away, seeing the patched and ragged robes and openly worn weaponry inherently pointing to shady motives.

They stopped swimming as the lead man held up a loaded crossbow and said, "Not a stroke further, me loves."

Looking around at the group who now finished meandering over to the edge of the trail, Reza and Nomad counted seven, all in drab, ratty apparel, holding knives, short swords, clubs, or rods, each oddly appearing horribly forlorn as they looked upon the two treading water.

Both their gazes came back to the leader, the only one with a crossbow and a wide grin.

He was slightly sunbaked; his skin showed a great deal of wear and abuse, though his features didn't appear to grant him the likelihood of being much over thirty. Holes in his skin, where piercings might have been, pocked his ears, eyebrows, and nose. His smile showed a few gold teeth in his grin, and a number of dark tattoos lined his chest and arms.

Looking him up and down, Nomad and Reza silently assessed their options as they waited for him to make the next move.

The man smiled, looking at the two, then back at their horses and stash as his grin widened.

Without another word, the telling click of the crossbow catch releasing the loaded bolt cut through the silence, sending Nomad and Reza diving headlong off to either side, the whizzing bolt skipping harmlessly between them, digging angrily into the water for a few feet before starting to float back up to the surface.

"Damn it! Where's me bolts? Darrell, throw me another!" Reza heard as she resurfaced, looking over to Nomad who was still underwater, moving fast to the bank where she had pushed him in.

She knew they only had a short reprieve from the crossbow as the scoundrel reloaded it. She needed to get to shore to deal with the leader; the rest in the group already seemed ready to bolt just from the missed shot.

After taking a few strokes towards the shore, she noticed the leader's gang now looking the other way, all seeming to be scared stiff by whatever, or whomever, it was that approached the group from behind.

She looked over to Nomad who was just getting up out of the water at the bank far off to the side of the road, wondering if not Nomad, then who was threatening their robbers so terribly.

The latch click of the crossbow caused her to put the question out of her mind as the leader leveled it directly in line with Reza's head.

"Not a step further, love," he whispered, then shouted, "By neither of ya!" causing Nomad to stop in his tracks on the road, dripping wet, still in all his travel clothes.

"J-J-Jans," the lackey next to the boss stuttered out, putting a trembling hand on the scar-enriched arm of the lead bandit.

Shrugging the weak man's hand off, the leader looked over momentarily to see what his crony was nagging about.

The distraction was Reza's opening, and she lunged towards the man, swatting the crossbow away from her just as an iron rod came down on the side of her head, disorienting her for a split second before the leader spun around and slammed a foot into her gut, launching her back into the water, out of the fight.

Nomad was dashing towards him a moment later, but the gang, though preoccupied with another figure rushing up behind them, was still aware enough to confront Nomad, weapons ready.

Ducking under a swing from the closest flunky wielding a club, he snatched a hand that held a rusty knife from another, cranking on his wrist until the knife fell to the ground. Nomad slammed an elbow into the one holding the club, sending him down, badly dazed, then shoved the knife wielder off the trail and into the lake.

A second knife, followed by a hand, came in seemingly out of nowhere, latching onto Nomad's neck, holding knife point dangerously close to his chin, putting a halt to the scuffle.

"Eh, shit!" the bandit leader said between heavy breaths, trying to steady himself after the lively, though short, uprising. "You don't want to be doing that again—I assure you—or a bolt in your eye ain't going to be the biggest problem you've had all day."

Nomad looked down at the knife blade the man held to his chin, eyebrows now raised by the man's quickness of hand.

"An arrow in your rat skull won't be the biggest problem you've had today either if you don't release that man this moment."

Everyone's attention turned roadside to see a tall woman, yew bow drawn and pointed at the leader, with long, brown and white hair shimmering as the autumn sun kissed it. Her striking green eyes were frosted with a silver sheen. They were eyes Nomad knew all too well.

"Well, well. Aren't you a lovely specimen," the bandit who held Nomad said, not seeming overly worried by the tall woman aiming an arrow at him. "Name's Jans. Gold Tooth Jans, as me mates call me. What's yours?"

"Arie," the woman simply said.

"Ah, proper name for such a lovely lady. Arie, I don't suppose you'd shoot me seeming's how this good-fer-nothin' you're fixing to save is directly between us, and no matter how good a shot you are, it'd be a foolish risk to take. So, I suggest you keep on your way, and we forget about this whole intervening," the tattooed man said as he slid the knife he held at Nomad's chin to his neck, keeping a dangerous amount of pressure on the blade, allowing Nomad no chance at slipping out of the hold without Jans' quick hands finishing him.

Eyeing the man a while longer, Arie let out the breath she was holding and lowered her bow.

"Fine. You win," she said coolly as she turned and casually began down the road towards Castle Sephentho.

"Smart lass," the bandit softly spoke, looking back to Nomad and Reza, then called to his flunky to fetch his crossbow for him.

Just as the man he had called Darrell was handing him the crossbow, an arrow came thudding into Jans' outstretched hand with enough force to twist him around slightly, allowing Nomad wiggle room to safely slip out of his blade's threatening reach.

The arrow had thrown Jans off for a split second, but the distraction was enough for Nomad to throw a haymaker jab directly for Jans' unguarded face.

The thud and pop of flesh and bone violently colliding sounded clearly throughout the crowd, and Jans went down instantly, going unconscious before even hitting the ground.

Scooping up Jans' dropped knife, Nomad stood up, settling into an offensive stance to face the rest of the riffraff that stood dumbfounded trying to make sense of the quick takedown of their leader.

Slowly backing away at first, with nervous glances over to Arie who was now walking towards the group, bow drawn, they turned and ran back the way they had come, leaving their leader to his own fate.

"Better tie that one up before he wakes. A rogue *that* quick with a knife is not one you want on the loose after you've ruined his day," Arie said, walking up to Nomad as she tossed him a small length of cord.

Nomad snatched the knot of cord and got right to work on securing Jans, not wanting another knife to his throat any time soon.

Reza came out of the lake, shivering by the roadside from the freezing water that clung to her, a bit dazed to see Arie, whom they had left weeks ago back at Sheaf.

"There. He's bound," Nomad said, standing up, smiling as he looked to Arie, a look of welcoming relief easily showing as he went to her.

"It's good to see you again," Nomad mumbled into the crook of her neck as he embraced her.

"That's cold!" she let out, struggling to distance herself from the drenched man, which spurred Nomad to lift her up in his arms, nuzzling her. Reza let out a slight chuckle, seeing the man that had seen so many dark moods of late happy and spirited for the first time in weeks.

3

WOUNDS FROM THE PAST

A hasty knocking on the door followed by Reza's voice declaring, "The sun is up," broke the silence in the sleepy inn hallway.

She fidgeted with her pack straps as she waited for Nomad and Arie to stir, leaning against the wall as she finally heard a moan, rustling covers, and a foot touching down in the inn room she stood waiting at.

Reza idly studied the quaint, but carefully crafted workmanship of the doorframe she stood before as the morning sun crested through a window to the side.

After handing over Jans to the castle guards the night before, Nomad, Reza, and Arie had spent the evening there, which happened to be the only inn outside of the castle proper.

Though Nomad and Arie had stayed up and had a few drinks at the inn's little bar, chatting deep into the night, Reza had bought a room for herself and went to bed early, still not sure how she felt about Arie's surprise appearance the day before. They were so close to the monastery that Reza wasn't sure if Arie would add anything to the group now other than act as a distraction to Nomad and the mission, which was to get Nomad cured of his terminal condition.

The door opened, jolting Reza out of her reflection.

Nomad came out into the hallway, heavy bags under his eyes, his pace dragging, but all packed and ready to move out.

"Arie said she'll catch up with us later in the day. If you're so eager to head out, we can start up early I suppose."

"Nomad…," Reza mumbled, bringing up her hand to his face as she studied a thin, subcutaneous black vein that ran up through his cheekbone to his eye that wasn't there the day before.

"Let me see your back," Reza ordered, forcibly turning Nomad around before he could argue the point.

A few dabs of black spots speckled his shirt over where his wound was, and as she pulled uncomfortably on his collar to peek in past his harness, peeling back the bandage she had placed over the wound, a rank heat assaulted her senses, causing her to tear up and cover her nose, looking down at the splayed flesh as a fuzzy, fungal-like blackness seeped and oozed large droplets of dark liquid into the bandage.

She reflexively let go of Nomad's shirt, causing him to lurch forward slightly from the release, already beginning to button up his collar tersely, starting to resent the abrasiveness of Reza's mannerisms so early in the morning.

She gagged unexpectedly as she covered her mouth with her hand, bending over slightly as she attempted to forget the vile smell and wretched sight she had just witnessed.

"It's always the worst at night," Nomad said, so softly that Reza had to hold still just to hear him.

"Come," he said after a lingering moment that seemed to instantly weigh him down more than he had already seemed, "the sooner we make it to the monastery, the better—for us all."

As they broke through the last remaining treeline up the mountain path that led to the Jeenyre monastery, Reza pointed up at the jagged mountains before them and said, "There's the Jeenyre mountains. The monastery is not too deep within them. We'll easily make it there before nightfall at this pace."

Receiving no answer from Nomad caused her to glance back at him, finding him preoccupied with something in the woods behind them.

Arie leisurely strolled out of the woods and went to Nomad's side, making a brief greeting before looking to Reza, waiting for her to lead them onwards.

"The trail can be tough on horses, and they'll be safer back at Sephentho for now. Hopefully the trek isn't too rough this time of year. The cliffside passes can get dangerously icy and narrow," Reza called back as she started forwards with the two in tow.

Taking a deep breath of the chill mountain air, Reza rounded her head from side to side, cracking her neck before stepping up the pace, hoping to make good time on the trail for the morning.

They only traveled a minute or so more before Reza began to slow, her attention trained on a shape ahead along the trail side. Turning back to the others, she saw that Arie was already studying the same dark shape along the roadside a few hundred yards up the trail.

"What is it?" Nomad asked, knowing that out of all of them, Arie possessed the keenest sight.

"A man. Seems to be alone. Strange attire, though—perhaps foreign."

"Foreigners are known to seek out the Jeenyre monastery. It's not exactly a widely renown saren monastery, but there are visitors from distant lands that pass by from time to time," Reza added.

"Well," Nomad sighed, "let's just hope it's not another ambush. Be on your guard, just to be safe."

The three walked silently up the trail, the minutes ticking past as they closed the distance between them and the lone roadsman. As they came close enough to make out details of the stranger, Nomad slowed, hesitant to continue forward.

The man's face was mostly covered by the brim of a flat, conical-shaped straw hat, laced with silk under his chin to keep it firmly atop his head, immovable amidst the light breeze. A golden-red, pleated half-sash adorned his right arm, chest, and lower body, bearing a satin white and amber undergarment underneath the striking overcoat. The whole ensemble, though extremely well made, seemed trail worn.

Nomad knew what peoples the wanderer belonged to, and a swell of trepidatious emotions flooded his senses.

His apprehension was easily felt by his two comrades. Arie and Reza both laid hidden hands close by their weapons.

"Far from home, you've wandered," Nomad spoke as the group stepped up to the stranger's small, single-man encampment.

The foreigner, who kneeled on a straw mat at a low, compact table, got up at the sound of Nomad's voice, and walked over to the pot that was affixed over the small campfire. Handling it with care, he walked back over to the low-standing table and placed the pot atop a bamboo mat, producing two teacups from the folds of his garments, gesturing for Nomad to kneel across from him.

Nomad hesitated at first, everyone silently waiting for his move. Arie and Reza could almost feel the tension on the breeze from Nomad's petrified inaction from the foreigner's presence, and they knew now that something about this stranger struck deeper with him than just the threat of another highway bandit attack. This person, this culture, held some heavy weight upon their friend.

Moving slowly to the straw mat, as if he were moving to a chopping block in chains, Nomad ducked under the wide, oil-papered umbrella that was affixed over the table, shadowing the two men.

Nomad now kneeling, the man began to pour a green tea into each black ceramic teacup, placing the teapot back on the bamboo mat afterwards, motioning for Nomad to have a sip before gracefully taking a sip from his.

Nomad spoke in his native tongue, leaving Arie and Reza out of the now private conversation.

"You hail from Silmurannon, that is plain to see, but those colors—I do not know of any house they belong to."

Putting down his cup, the stranger, whose face was still partially covered from Nomad's view by the brim of his hat, whispered, "That is because after our house's slaughter, I was the remaining family member, and I added red and amber to our banner, signifying the death and end of our great house."

Tilting the brim of his hat up to allow Nomad a clear look at the stranger's face for the first time, Nomad's grasp on the teacup loosed, dropping the cup which spilled its contents across the table.

"Yozo…," dripped from Nomad's lips, the sight of the man's familiar face completely freezing Nomad in place.

"Yes, Yozo," the man tiredly replied. "The same Yozo that looked up to you as his older brother-in-law. The same Yozo that watched in disbelief as you selfishly, brashly led a war to which his sister was sacrificed. The same Yozo that watched his brother-in-law leave when his wife's family was in dire need, watching as his family was slaughtered—impaled and lifted from the ground to watch them struggle and then rot atop their own weight. Yes. The same Yozo—Hiro."

A sudden, searing pain in Nomad's back caused him to pitch forward, bracing himself across the table, scattering the scalding hot teapot and mats everywhere. As the man, self-identified as *Yozo*, deftly backed away from the table before the tea could splash upon him, he could see and hear a hissing, bubbling eruption of black liquid spring forth through Nomad's clothes from the wound on his back.

Arie and Reza both rushed to Nomad's side, but a curved sword, strikingly similar in style to the one Nomad wielded, was out and between Nomad and the two women before either could reach him.

"You do not interrupt tea," Yozo coolly said in broken callatum, eyeing both Arie and Reza, sizing them up before turning back to Nomad, who silently trembled through a painful spasm along his back.

"Take your time," Yozo said in his and Nomad's native tongue. "Recover your strength, but I will have a duel out of you before you leave this camp, brother."

Nomad's spasms ceased after a few deep coughs. Black flecks covered his hand as he brought it away from his mouth, and he kneeled there inspecting the ink-like substance that had come from within him.

"Nomad, we need to get you to the monastery," Reza said in a harsh tone, stepping once again towards him.

Yozo's blade flashed up towards Reza to stop her from advancing, but Nomad's blade, just as quick as Yozo had drawn his, was out, deflecting Yozo's threatening sword tip away from Reza.

Shakily getting to his feet, Nomad held his sword unnervingly steady in comparison to the rest of his haggard body.

The slight tinge of surprise Yozo showed at the sudden movement was slowly replaced by a grin as he brought his sword back to center, touching blades with Nomad as he sidestepped to the right, forcing Nomad to step right as well.

Sliding his blade up Yozo's, Nomad grunted as he locked into an overhead sword stance, leaving his lower body open to attacks.

Yozo's grin faded, seeing the extremely aggressive and desperate opening stance from his dueling partner, and waited for Nomad to make his move.

Even through the harsh wind and the intensity of the moment, Nomad heard the slightest notch of an arrow several yards behind him.

"Arie! Don't interfere," Nomad gruffed, keeping his eyes locked on Yozo.

Trusting that she would obey his wishes, Nomad concentrated, crowding out the burning pain in his back that was making it hard for him to breathe, focusing now completely on the maneuver he was readying himself for.

He came in at Yozo, right leg and sword point leading, thrusting directly for Yozo's face.

Instead of attempting to deflect the powerful thrust, Yozo sidestepped Nomad's attack, returning the thrust with a low slash, cutting open Nomad's right leg, opening a fresh, bloodless half-inch slice.

Nomad, not even seeming to notice the strike, chopped down towards Yozo, twisting his body to realign with his opponent.

Barely ducking under Nomad's diagonal swing, Yozo came up and jetted past Nomad, pulling his sword along Nomad's torso as he passed him, cutting past most of his leather and cloth.

Turning around, this time Nomad had taken note of the nasty wound Yozo had landed. Clutching his side, blood finally starting to seep to the two cuts, Nomad flung blood from his hand, gripping his sword once more and let out a blood-curdling yell as he came in again towards his opponent.

Yozo struck Nomad's sword tip, guiding it to the side while simultaneously tripping Nomad in the midst of his frenzied charge, sending him to the ground in a bloodied heap.

The dull *twang* of Arie's bowstring sounded, and Yozo fluidly dipped to the side as Arie's arrow flew past him.

Yozo took one last look at Nomad, seeing that he was not moving from the place on the ground that he had collapsed, and then to the two women.

"Get him the help he needs," Yozo softly said, breaking eye contact and taking a seat once more at the squat table, seemingly not concerned with the group of three in his camp any longer.

Reza dashed to Nomad's side, inspecting Nomad's two wounds as Arie kept an eye on the dangerous foreigner.

Hefting Nomad's limp body up in her arms, Reza noticed that he was unconscious. As Reza carried him out of the camp, Arie directed her over to an uneven bed of moss at the base of a large shrub a safe distance away from the deadly stranger. Laying him down, Reza rustled through her pack for a long strip of clean bandage, easily finding the clean cut to Nomad's right thigh, beginning to wrap it tight.

"The other cut seems mostly superficial. No time to properly treat either wound, just needed to stop the bleeding. We need to get to the monastery *now*," Reza said, picking him up and over her shoulder, starting off to reconnect with the mountain trail that led to the monastery.

Yozo finished cleaning up the mess Nomad had made of his tea, picking up his teapot and took a seat once more. He watched—like a hawk eyeing a mouse—as Arie and Reza struggled to carry Nomad towards the base of the mountain until they were no longer within sight.

4

TEMPLE GROUNDS

The main cathedral double doors burst open, letting a gust of wind and snow angrily shoot through the pews of the great hall.

Lightning cracked, illuminating three figures in the doorway for a moment before the dark veil of night abruptly covered them again.

"Lanereth!" Reza's frantic voice was cut short as another crack of thunder rumbled through the dark room.

A figure moved hastily towards them from the shadows, unveiling her face as she approached the travel-warn trio. Reza fell to her knees upon seeing that she had found the one she was seeking, laying Nomad's still body before her, quietly weeping.

The woman looked briefly to Arie before kneeling down to place a hand on Reza's back who was slumped over Nomad's body.

"Reza?" a wispy, thin voice said, concern easily showing through the tall figure's inflection as she looked down to regard the man Reza had fallen over. "Bring him hither, quickly."

Arie helped Reza to her feet and shouldered half of Nomad's weight as Reza began to slog along behind the tall figure, halfway dragging Nomad, trying to keep up with the woman Reza had called Lanereth.

They didn't have to carry Nomad far as the tall woman entered a nearby room and brushed aside a centerpiece of a wreath of laurels, helping to lay Nomad's limp body down on the oak table.

Placing a hand on his forehead, closing her eyes, Lanereth took in a deep breath and slowly released it, eyes trembling in pain after a moment. Arie and Reza eagerly waited for the woman to reveal what she thought of Nomad's health.

She issued a sharp intake of air, hissing as she released her hand from Nomad's flesh, recoiling and holding her hand as if she had just been stabbed.

"What? What is it?" Reza shouted, latching onto Lanereth's arm.

Lanereth ripped free from Reza's grasp and snarled, looking Reza crossly in the eye. "What evil have you brought to this sacred place, child?"

Clutching a silver gleaming amulet dangling from her neck, Lanereth closed her eyes and began praying out loud. A heavenly tone filled the room quickly as her prayer began to increase in volume. She declared loudly certain key phrases which began to have an impact on Nomad's body.

Arie began to take heart as Nomad's body twitched, then grunted, thinking he was coming around as Lanereth revived him, but Reza knew the prayer she now gave. It was no prayer of healing; it was an exorcism that she now performed.

Nomad's head shot up, eyes wide, and let out a bloody roar, deafening Lanereth's prayer for a moment before she raised her voice so loud that it seemed there were other angelic mouths assisting her chant.

Nomad strained to get up, but he seemed restrained by some unseen force. His muscles now bulged, his eyes filled with blackness, and he bled slick, dark ooze from his wounds, mouth, and eyes. He screamed out in pain and rage.

"Lanereth, wait! You're hurting him!" Reza called out, but Lanereth was so carried away in her zealous chant that Reza's cry fell unheard.

Arie pushed Reza aside and slugged Lanereth on the jaw, easily knocking the elegant woman to the ground, silencing her chanting prayer.

"Wait! Both of you!" Reza yelled, pushing Arie back while getting between her and Lanereth who had recovered and now bore a look of indignation so wrath-filled that Reza knew retaliation was not off the table.

"Leave these sacred grounds," Lanereth hissed, a chill quiet unnervingly settling in the room.

"Lanereth—" Reza started but was cut short by a blinding white light that burst in from the hallway, followed by two pairs of quiet footsteps.

"High Priestess, do you require aid?"

Only Reza was able to see through the blinding light emanating from the two soldiers' hands, and only she knew the significance of their position as High Guard and the caliber of their skill.

"Oh, she'll need aid—" Arie seethed, moving to Nomad to guard him.

"No, Arie…," Reza ordered, turning now to address Lanereth. "I will remove this man from these grounds *if* you promise to talk with me after he is removed."

Lanereth paused to consider Reza's offer for a moment before seething out, "Get that *thing* out of here."

Arie waited not another moment, hefting Nomad from the table, carrying him as Reza led her through the door, the blinding light making it almost impossible for Arie to make her way through the building.

Departing the light and leaving the monastery gates, Reza and Arie found a large fir tree with a low-hanging skirt of branches just off the path. The snow, even with the wind's aid, didn't quite make it under the great tree's boughs, and Reza quickly began to construct a bed of needles as Arie lowered their comrade's body down amidst the dead foliage.

"Should have never come here," Arie spat.

Reza barked back, "You're right, you *shouldn't* have come here," then stormed back to the monastery grounds without giving Arie another chance at a retort.

She immediately regretted her last remark as she marched back through the monastery gates. Though she did not get along with Arie very well, she knew that she would take care of Nomad now, and she knew without her help these last few miles, she would be collapsed with Nomad's cold body quite a ways back.

Opening the doors once more to the cathedral, Reza stepped in, seeing a sitting figure she knew to be Lanereth, her superior.

She walked down the aisle, emotions awhirl, remembering the years of close tutelage and reverence towards the woman that had, without consideration for the victim, almost put an end to her close companion.

In the end, her oppositional emotions had drained her, and she sat next to Lanereth with a heavy sigh, not sure where to begin her conversation with her former teacher.

"You have been disconnected from the sisterhood for a while now—too long, I fear. Your judgment has become clouded, it seems."

Lanereth's words, though few, carried a great deal of weight for Reza. She had been gone many years now from the monastery, or from any other saren. She wondered now if her sojourn into the world had worn poorly on her character.

"Sareth is an exacting deity and does not forgive missteps easily. You know this. To bring a corruption so black into her grounds willingly...this is a grave offense, one I will need to commune with Sareth to learn a recourse for—"

Something inside Reza snapped. She fell easily back into her readily provoked temperament, cutting Lanereth off. "I need no recourse for this. Nomad, that one so corrupted now, was not so long ago a hero, defending the peoples of the Plainstate valiantly, and selflessly risking his life to save others, myself included, multiple times. He is a man Sareth would approve of without reservation, I am sure of it. I came here seeking help from Sareth—from you—but what were we greeted with? Banishment without any chance at an explanation. Perhaps it is you whose judgment has become clouded since last we met."

Her words, she could tell, shocked her former guide, and for a moment, memories of years gone by of her bouts and heated disagreements with Lanereth flooded back. It was the same look of disappointment mixed with indignation etched upon the face of her superiors that accompanied much of her interactions in her early years, being passed from monastery to monastery, High Priestess to High Priestess, each all but giving up on her stubbornness and nonconformity.

Lanereth eased back in the pew and regained her composure, calmly admitting, "Perhaps I did jump to judgment too hastily—*but* only because I have learned that when it comes to true corruption, you don't give an inch and you rarely have a chance to hesitate when dealing with it. Your friend that you brought in, whatever he was, well, it is not what he is now."

"Nomad has changed over the past few months," Reza said, her soft voice barely audible above the storm's fury outside. "It has not been easy for us to watch him changing before our eyes with no methods to cure him of his sickness."

Lanereth considered Reza's tone as she spoke of the man she called *Nomad*. She knew Reza cared for him, never hearing her speak so reverently of anyone before.

"I have confronted devils in high ranking with their dark lords in the past, and he, I feel, has not only been marked by one of these entities, but has passed through the threshold to becoming a powerful tool to the enemy."

Lanereth was trying to be compassionate, Reza could tell, but her words were all but easing her mind. Reza continued to press, "There must be a cure for him. I owe him my life. It's my duty to find it if possible."

Sighing heavily, Lanereth furrowed her brow, considering her words for a moment before taking a hard look at Reza. Reza's fierce countenance seemed to soften Lanereth a bit more, perhaps seeing that there was no convincing her otherwise to discontinue pursuing her damned quest.

"Tell me how he came to be cursed," she resignedly mumbled out.

Reza lowered her head and let out a held breath, thankful that Lanereth seemed ready to listen.

"He was stabbed by an illimoth blade—"

"Gods!" Lanereth forlornly chuckled, placing a hand over her face, coming to realize how hopeless a fight her pupil had chosen to take up.

"There is a way to reverse what sickness has taken root, I know it. We saw Henarus, a prophet of Hassome, greatly reduce the amount of taint that had set into Nomad's body not but a month ago! I know Sareth can do much better through the hands of one of her key handmaidens like yourself," Reza blurted out, desperation thick in her voice, more so to try to convince herself than the one she spoke to.

"Henarus is a great man—one in high favor with his god. I've served beside him in years past, and even for a High Priestess like myself, he is a competent peer to me. And you say he failed to completely remove the curse, and that was a *month* ago," Lanereth softly said, adding almost in a whisper, "You are so young, Reza. So sure you know exactly how things are or should be, but so often unaware of how things actually are. You have much to learn."

Straining to hold back her tongue at Lanereth's last remark, she pressed on, "You must be able to remove this curse, and if not you, someone else in or outside of our faith. I cannot believe this is an irreversible curse. There's always an answer, now please help me to know where to look if you don't have it."

A quiver in Reza's voice betrayed her stern countenance, and Lanereth stopped to consider how deeply devoted to this cause—to this man—she was. She had never seen Reza emotionally attached to anyone, not to her peers, not to any of her race, not even to Sareth herself. This *Nomad*—even without knowing much at all about him, she knew, through Reza's appraisal, who had a critical eye above all else, to be an extraordinary individual. One even perhaps worthy of a saren's protection.

"I can tell you care for this man a great deal, and I would help remove this curse if I could, but he has passed through the threshold of no return. He no longer is human. If it was illimoth steel that drew his blood, then it seems that he's already completed the transition to become a tool of Telenth-Lanor. He is lost. You'll deepen the hurt you feel at his loss if you continue to seek to make him whole. We need to put his body and spirit at rest. You need to honor what he would want you to do for him now. There *is* no return for him."

As Lanereth spoke, Reza began to clam up, seeing that Lanereth did not intend to fight in the cause she was committed to.

"You give up as soon as you're met with the least bit of opposition," Reza mumbled.

"I remind you, though I'm sympathetic to your plight, I am your High Priestess and your senior, Reza Malay. You do not speak to authority like that."

Within an instant, Reza shifted back onto the defensive. "Inevitability and fate are masters over you. Regardless if the odds are slim, if it's the right course, I take that path. That's the difference between you and I. High Priestess or no, a saren stands for good. That man *is* good. For you to cast him aside without any effort to help him after all he's done in selfless service diminishes you."

For a moment, Lanereth seemed on the verge of lashing back at Reza, but her features slackened. Placing a hand over her eyes once more, she sighed out, "Oh Reza. What am I to do with you?"

Reza was ready for a fight, but Lanereth seemed so tired just then, so worn out and done with fighting her on every point between them.

"Lanereth, please. If you can't help me, at least tell me where I can go to get some answers. I'm not going to stop until Nomad is back to normal."

"You'll find, even if he was miraculously cured from this taint, that he will never know 'normal' again," Lanereth replied, looking to Reza, who resolutely waited for more information on her companion's condition.

Looking up hopelessly at the cathedral's ceiling, Lanereth continued, "He is indeed beyond the redeeming touch of any goodly influence, that includes Sareth, but…."

Reza leaned in closer, eyebrows raised slightly in anticipation, finally feeling Lanereth was ready to level with her.

Lanereth went on, "It may be theoretically possible for a curse so powerful to be reversed. I've never heard or read about a single case of those inflicted with illimoth poisoning ever breaking free of its pull after they pass through the threshold of life to death, but if it were possible to reverse it after that point, you would need the one who the curse serves to unbind the curse, or for the master to die.

"With illimoth, though, it's only a substance extremely powerful servants of Telenth possess. That you apparently encountered one of these servants and lived seems unfathomable considering how unskilled you are as an unpracticed saren, but I suppose it speaks volumes as to just how far your sheer tenacity can take you. You never let barriers stand in your way, no matter how impossible they seem to be to overcome—"

"Yes, but we destroyed Lashik. He was the one that stabbed Nomad, so he would have been the master that needed to be killed, right? Why is the curse still present?" Reza hurriedly interjected.

"No, that's not how illimoth works. If you had spent more time in tomes and less seeking field work, you might know all of this. Illimoth steel is bound to a High Lord of Telenth. They are sort of an avatar, or representative of the lord of ash here on Una. Extremely powerful, they come and go, influencing here and there the tides of war and eras. These are the powers *my* superiors work tirelessly to contain. High Lords can lend the illimoth weapon to their most trusted, and usually powerful, servants. The binding of the victim then is to the High Lord, not the servant. That has to be the case here. Your Nomad is bound to a High Lord, not to this *Lashik* you speak of.

"The arisen lord…," Reza whispered, thinking back to the hulking knight that had almost snuffed her out with no effort at all that night which seemed so long ago.

"You…know of this High Lord?" Lanereth asked, worry seeping into her voice.

"If it wasn't for Isis," Reza paused, fondling the now ordinary ring she wore that once housed the protective spirit, "I would have died in his clutches that night."

"You faced a High Lord? Reza, this is no small matter. Why did you not report this to the sisterhood immediately?"

"Why do you think I am here, Lanereth!" Reza snapped. Regretting her hasty retort, she responded quickly with, "I'm sorry. I just—this whole thing, it's frustrating to feel like an ant compared to the forces we face. We were so ill-equipped to face that monster, even his second, Lashik. Without a number of incredibly skilled allies and last-minute miracles, we would have surely fallen by our efforts alone."

"My dear, this is not a fight for you," Lanereth said, overlooking the immediate disapproving scowl Reza wore at the statement. "You have played quite a part if you indeed aided in vanquishing a second to a High Lord. I'm beginning to piece together some recent events down in the Tarigannie region. There's been wars and rumors of evil forces at work there. It seems the sisterhood needs to pay closer attention to that region in the days to come, and I will see that we provide aid and investigate this growing shadow further."

"I will lead that investigation," Reza stated, looking Lanereth in the eyes.

Lanereth scoffed, looking sideways at Reza. "You said it yourself, Reza, you are but an ant next to the awful power of a High Lord. What makes you think you are prepared for a task so important as this? We will let the sisterhood decide who is capable of such a mission."

Reza knew how long timelines were for intervention missions within the sisterhood, and she knew Nomad did not have that kind of time. She needed to press Lanereth's hand, or risk losing Nomad further to Telenth's influence.

"I'm going, with the sisterhood's blessing or not, and Sareth will be with me," Reza said, conviction heavy in her voice.

"You go on this mission, and we will not see each other again. You don't go for any high cause dedicated to Sareth, you go for this man—and you will die for this man," Lanereth said. Reza knew by Lanereth's tone, she was not bluffing, and that scared her.

"Go with me, Lanereth. We could defeat this High Lord and secure peace for the people of Tarigannie."

"Against a High Lord, I can only briefly defend and delay. Such a foe is beyond me. I know, I have faced one in the past—*one*. A

Submagis of Jezelethizal, Lord of Rot, the equivalence of High Lord of Telenth. I was young then…." Lanereth paused, searching the past with her distant eyes. "One time I have stood in the presence of an avatar of one of the six evils, and I could but last minutes in her presence. So twisted and potent their power is, even their aura is enough to unhinge their enemies—I could not alone hope to defeat a High Lord, and your presence there would make no difference."

Reza sat. Lanereth allowed her to ponder on her words in silence, the rush of wind outside clattering at the structure doors.

Slowly getting to her feet, looking to the front of the large room at the marbled statue of Sareth momentarily, Reza said in a quietly determined tone, "Then attend your council and do nothing. I'll bring that son of a bitch down myself."

Reza turned and walked down the aisle.

"Reza," Lanereth said, a heaviness in her voice, "I don't condone your decision, but if you're going to chase after this High Lord, then I won't stop you. The most I can do is offer you some advice. Whoever this Isis is you spoke of earlier, the one that protected you from the High Lord, if you want to stand even the slightest of chances at surviving another encounter with the enemy, make sure to have them with you at all times."

Reza, standing in the middle of the aisle, rubbed a finger over the old silver diamond ring, fighting an internal battle. She was so frustrated with Lanereth, but she knew, through all their disagreements, Lanereth was the one High Priestess that tolerated her to any extent. She alone seemed to care about Reza in her faith. She knew parting on somewhat good grounds would put her conscience at ease later down the road.

"Isis—she's gone now," Reza reverently said, remembering tenderly the shared plight and interactions she had with the spirit inside the ring she now wore.

"Oh—I'm sorry," Lanereth tenderly said, getting up to walk to the grief-stricken woman.

Reza recovered quickly, brushing off the forlorn look she wore for a brief moment, attempting a casual tone. "At least I think she's gone. Not sure she was ever really there to begin with, at least physically. It all could have been a spell—but I think she was real."

Lanereth gently held Reza's arm, attempting to comfort her. More than a little bemused by Reza's strange chatter, she asked, "What do you mean? Who was this Isis? A spell you say? Was she not a real person?"

Taking her ring off, Reza cleared her throat and handed the silver hoop over to Lanereth, allowing her to inspect it while she explained further.

"I found it in a tomb, an old place, centuries old. The ring, at first when I put it on summoned an apparition of a grieving woman, Isis. She was some sort of royalty, a queen of her time. Her husband sacrificed her and magically bound her through a hex to this ring. She said the hex was old and the magic was almost all spent by the time I found her, so in the fight with Lashik and his master, she used up the last of the ring's enchantment to save me from—a very unpleasant fate."

Lanereth, who had stood there slack-jawed, mumbled, "Astounding," turning the ring over and over in her fingers, gazing endlessly into the faceted diamond that still glimmered with an unusually bright sparkle.

"I think you're wrong, though," Lanereth said in a hushed voice. "A residue of that hex still remains. I can see it. Yes, as you said, old magic is right. I wish you had spent more time in books, girl, but nonetheless, come. The Gaia's altar may just kindle some of that flame that once burned so bright."

Grabbing Reza's hand, Lanereth rushed to the doors, opening them to a blast of wind and snow. Reza didn't feel the cold though, only the burning feeling of renewed hope in regaining a lost friend.

5

GAIA'S ALTAR

The dark of the night mixed with the storm of snow and wind made it hard for Reza to navigate the overgrown path to the spot on the cliffside, which rarely saw visitors.

"The altar shouldn't be much further," Lanereth said, her soft voice almost getting lost on the wind.

"Why is it so far out here again?" Reza asked hesitantly, feeling as though she should know the answer, not sure if Lanereth had lectured her on the use and purpose of the altar before.

"It was a gift from a very old ally, an arch druid of Farenlome. The stone has to be kept in a place of seclusion, or rather, offset from structures and cultivated grounds. Its uses are limited, and it is out of the way, so for this reason, this path and the altar are not visited very often."

Reza, trying to keep up with Lanereth's quick step, asked, "Limited in what way? It was hardly discussed at all in my studies."

"The druids draw their magic from arcane currents, whereas we draw our power from a divine source, our heavenly mother, Sareth. She is more liberal than most lords of the heavens, but still, we have no power without her allowing us to use it. The druids, however, can freely tap into the arcane currents of Una at will, without even the permission of Farenlome, the goddess they worship.

"It is this distinction that makes using the Gaia's altar artifact that they gifted to us tricky. I've been taught from the druids to see and manipulate the arcane currents, but as you know, we do not condone mixing with other faiths, especially in terms of mixing magic. I was given special permission in order to nurture a relationship with our allies as well as to have a bit of utility since there are benefits of having access to arcane ways.

"I'm not a master in their ways by any means, but I might know just enough to help refill that ring of yours with new life. If Isis is still in there, I might be able to call upon someone who can arouse her spirit once more."

Lanereth slowed and pulled aside a curtain of vines, showing a ledge, the grey blizzard hiding how high up they actually were.

In the center of the slab of granite that they stepped out upon was a stone, cracked and etched in frozen moss, a symbol long ago carved deep into the center of it. The symbol was simple enough. Reza understood what it represented, and she had seen the same symbol in connection with the druids before. It was a circle with crescents on the outside, representing the sun and moons. Stars were scattered over the circle; within that circle was a smaller circle with a fire in its center.

Both now looking down at the rock, Reza asked, "That smaller circle with the flame, is that Una?"

"Yes," Lanereth spoke, "that is our world. Farenlome is said to be the heart of our planet, and without her constant flame, Una would become a cold and uninhabitable place. She is a very integral part of our existence."

The wind whipped the two's clothes violently, causing Lanereth to clutch at her loose robes. Looking to Reza, she held out a hand.

"The ring," she said as Reza pulled it from her finger, handing it over.

Looking it over once more, Lanereth clutched it to her chest and kneeled down upon the stone in silence, seeming to go into some meditative state.

Reza was still as could be for the first few minutes, but after a while of standing in the cold, Lanereth not appearing to be performing any sort of ritual, she went to huddle next to a bush on the cliffside of the curtain of icy vines.

Just as she was getting settled, Lanereth got to her feet, stepping back. A green sprout appeared from the base of the altar.

The sprout grew impossibly fast, winding and twisting upwards until it slowed to a stop at Lanereth's waist. A bud near the top grew and then opened to reveal a red and white flower blooming towards Lanereth.

The strange, vine-like plant stopped its miraculous growth just as suddenly as it began, and Lanereth placed the ring directly in the center of the red-white flower. It began to close immediately after, until the ring was consumed within the flower's petals.

Though Reza saw nothing, she began to feel a heaviness. Not uncomfortably so, but an impactful presence, her senses going numb and her soul opening to accept the old spirit that now graced the spot they lingered at.

The wind died to a light breeze, the snow falling almost straight down, and Reza thought she saw for a moment the snow fell upon an invisible object, hovering above the ground next to Lanereth. Only after a few seconds of strange stillness did the snow and wind begin to bluster again.

Almost as suddenly as the presence had come, it began to depart, relinquishing Reza's physical faculties back to her. The flower began to open once more with Isis' ring brightly aglow momentarily before whisking off with the breeze that started up again.

"Take it," Lanereth whispered, gesturing to the ring.

Reza, speechless still from the strange experience, got to her feet a bit shakily, and made her way over to the ring, plucking it from the flower, the petals and plant wilting somewhat as she did so.

"Was that Farenlome that was here?" Reza asked in a whisper.

"No, no," Lanereth said, somewhat amused at Reza's inexperience on the subject of deities. "That was an old spirit though, a grandchild of Farenlome. He has been with me since the druids charged him to me, to stay in our lands, to watch over us, and to give me tutelage in the ways of Farenlome and this precious gift, Gaia's Stone."

Reza did not reply, still awestruck at the encounter. Lanereth continued, saying, "I suppose now is not the time for a class. Go on, put the ring on. Let's see if old Quehuar met our plea."

Reza's heart fluttered, hesitation of hope still holding her hand back from trying the ring on. She missed Isis, and if she did not come back to her now after hope of having her constant companionship returned, Reza felt that the loss would be worse than losing her the first time.

"Go on, Reza," Lanereth prodded, placing an arm around the young saren's shoulders.

Turning over the ring, just as she had done when she had first found it, Reza traced the worn inscription along the ring's underside.

Whispering the line she knew now by heart, she closed her eyes and put the ring back on her right ring finger.

"Sa-ahlorn tulleip—decant ethül-long." The cryptic words hung in the air momentarily before she spoke to them again in her tongue. "Our love shall bind us—in this life, and the next."

Hot tears flashed to her eyes as she was overcome with a burst of spectral teal-white light that shot out from the diamond atop the ring, the surrounding cliffside now set aglow in its ghostly light. The swirling snow whizzed past her tear-streaked face like shooting stars.

She felt a familiar presence—one that had been with her through difficult times. Isis was present then, visiting her—lovingly communicating with her soul.

The flurry of light and energy bubbled, then dissipated, letting Reza's hopeful heart slowly down. She had been expecting Isis to come back to her in spirit form, but as the wintry calm of the cliffside began its gentle breeze back up with no further signs of change from the ring she wore, her spirits sunk.

"Is the ring made whole?" Lanereth asked, worrying that from Reza's expression the rite had not been given Farenlome's blessing.

"I felt so at first—" Reza stopped, considering the ring that was now on her finger. "But she is not here as she used to be. Something's different."

There was a silence between them as the wind picked up, the biting cold seeping into their garb doubly so now that they had enjoyed a reprieve from the storm momentarily.

"The gifts of Farenlome are not always easily discernable," Lanereth whispered to Reza, clearly seeing the disappointment on her former student's face.

"Come, the cold gathers along this cliff," her mentor said. She guided Reza back through a curtain of frigid vines, the two silently pondering the meaning of Farenlome's blessing and the ring.

6

DEMON IN IRONS

"Another ale," Reza slurred, holding up a hand until a freshly filled mug was placed in it.

Rarely did she drink, and to her recollection, never had she been this drunk, but for some reason, that night, she had lost reason to care. Perhaps it was the hopelessness of her newly charted mission, or perhaps it was the company she kept, a half haltia she didn't care for and a half-dead friend that had been unconscious for three days now.

She realized that even with the odds being overwhelmingly poor in locating and destroying the Telenth High Lord, having to lug around an unconscious body while doing the impossible had quickly dampened her resolution to save her friend. There *was* no hope of achieving what she had so adamantly told Lanereth she would do, and the reality of that was beginning to set in.

Slipping the mug out of Reza's hand, Arie paid the waiting barmaid a gold strip for her running tab of drinks and faced down her seething companion.

"That was my ale. And by the way, I'll not have you pay my way! You owe nothing to me, and I nothing to you, and that's how it'll stay," Reza blurted out, causing a patron or two at the surrounding tables to sneak a glance over at the two bickering women.

"That's it. You've had your fill. I'm starting to see you'll cause us all trouble if you have more, and the Sephentho castle guard is not known for their tolerance for ruckus foreigners."

Grabbing her hand, Arie jerked Reza to her feet, all but dragging her out of the bar, disheveled platinum hair bobbing frantically as Arie led them down tight alleys back to the inn they were staying at.

The moonlight fluttered in through the breezy tree above the inn's façade as Arie held Reza up, saving her from tripping right into the doorframe. Adjusting the bulk of Reza's weight, Arie opened the door with her other hand, leading them inside.

The front room was dimly lit, but the candle on the front counter clearly showed the terrified features of the innkeeper who looked at the two women as though they were there to end him.

Arie considered asking what the problem was, but Reza's gut lurched, the saren holding unusually still for a moment before Arie realized what was happening.

"Damn girl," Arie cursed under her breath. She dragged her nauseous companion back to her room, unlocking the door and finding the bedpan just in time.

Holding her hair back for her, patting her on the side as she finished expelling the rest of the intoxicant, handed Reza a rag as she poured a large glass of water for her to wash out with.

Reza groaned, knowing she had gone too far that night and now not wanting to deal with the consequences, the cold weight of hopelessness slowly creeping back into the corners of her consciousness.

"I'm going to check on Nomad while you—clear your head," Arie said, the strain in her voice clear now.

Fishing out the key to her room, she unlatched and opened the door, freezing in place as her eyes scanned the room for Nomad.

"He's not there," Arie blurted out as she rushed back to Reza, who had sobered up a bit after vomiting.

"What—" Reza began, trying to catch up to the meaning of Arie's statement.

"He's not in there," she stated again, looking quickly down the hall before rushing into her bedroom momentarily, showing up at Reza's door fastening her dagger belt.

"I'm going out to look for him," Arie said, already rushing off down the hall to the front desk. Reza stumbled after her.

The innkeeper, seeming to have calmed since their entrance, still looked on edge as the two barreled into the room. Arie urgently asked, "Did you see the man we came in with leave recently?"

The pale man quickly nodded his head, pointing out the front door. "There's something not right with him. His eyes—"

Arie looked to the side in momentary confusion, then glanced over at Reza whose head bobbed a bit, holding back a hiccup.

Letting out an exasperated sigh, Arie ran for the door, not bothering to wait for her inebriated companion.

"You'd better stay in your room. I'll find Nomad," Arie yelled back, rushing out the door just as Reza made it to her.

"I'm coming," Reza shot back, leaving no space in her voice for debate.

Arie tore down the street, looking down the alleys as she made her way to the castle village's main street. Reza, though off-balance, managed to stay in tow.

A scream and a horrified gasp sounded further up Main Street towards the castle, spurring Arie and Reza headlong towards the commotion.

Rounding the corner, Arie slowed, trying to figure out what exactly she was looking at. Reza, however, seeing a figure that resembled Nomad standing before two locals who stood frozen in front of him, rushed towards him. Arie yelled for Reza to wait, but Reza easily ignored her companion's promptings.

"Nomad!" Reza blurted out, sprinting towards the dark figure.

Nomad slowly turned to face Reza who was coming towards him, the frightened couple taking the moment to bolt off down an adjoining street.

A glint of red in Nomad's eyes caused Reza to stumble to a halt right before him. His hands clamped around her arms, holding her firm as Nomad's pallid visage looked down on her worried face, his mouth splitting into a wide, unnatural grin, black sludge seeping through the cracks in his teeth, all while empty eyes with a sheen of crimson, like that of an animal's in the dark, bore down on her.

She tried to break his grasp, but it was locked like steel. She saw then that something was horribly different about Nomad. Something that with but a single look told her that he saw her now not as a friend, but as prey.

He clinched down on her arms harder, tightening his grip as he gazed at her.

Mewling quickly turned into screaming as Reza felt her bones under enough pressure to snap at any moment.

"Hiro!" Arie shouted, using his given name.

The tightening stopped, and his grin faded, some level of recognition seeping in as Arie slowly approached the two.

The inner castle gates opened down the street from them and the sounds of soldiers in armor clamored towards them.

"We need to go, now," Arie harshly whispered to Nomad and Reza, grabbing both of them, attempting to haul them off down the street to the outer gate's exit.

Nomad swatted Arie's hand away, a feral snarl making it clear that he was not in the mood to listen to her orders.

"You! Turn around, *now*!" the lead guard yelled, three other armored men with iron maces following close behind.

Nomad hesitated for a moment longer, starting to ease up on Reza's arm, looking off to the side in contemplation, fully ignoring the shouting group of guards that continued to approach.

"In the name of the king, I order you to turn around, or we will attack," the lead guard shouted, stepping within striking distance from Nomad, brandishing his iron capped staff.

"Last warning!" the guard growled, lining up a shot with his weapon.

Arie and Reza pulled on Nomad frantically to move out of the way of the incoming assault, knowing that once a blow was struck, their night would become unconditionally worse.

Nomad stood still like a monument of stone.

The iron cap smacked solidly into the back of Nomad's head with enough force to crack a skull, a sickening impact jolting his head forward for a moment.

Nomad's red eyes went wide, his gaze snapping to the assaulter behind him. He glared at the man with bloody intent.

Nomad ripped away from Arie and Reza and snatched the guard by the neck, easily lifting him in the air, pausing a moment before throwing him to the ground in a heap, the snap of a bone splitting the otherwise quiet night.

The three other guards did not wait to jump in as more guards began to rush to the scene from the castle gate, the night shift apparently informed of the unusual scuffle happening along Main Street.

Nomad was about to pounce on the fallen guard when a mace slammed into the side of his head, delivering another, what should have been fatal blow. The ball of iron nudged Nomad a step to the left before he switched targets, now aware of the other three guards coming at him with maces swinging.

He sidestepped the second guard's attack just in time, having to readjust his movement a moment later to attempt to get out of the way of the third attacker's mace, which did land on Nomad's shoulder, but not solidly enough to matter to the red-eyed horror.

Curling his fists, Nomad sprung back in at the three guards, snapping his fist into the side of the first guard's helmet, knocking him off into the gutter. Without a pause, Nomad threw an uppercut at the second guard, hitting him beneath the chin strap, blowing him off his feet for a moment before landing unconscious on the ground.

The third guard swung again, attempting to land another hit on Nomad before his focus turned to him. Nomad rolled with the hit again though, and the solid ball of iron only glanced ribs as Nomad brought a leg up to kick the last guard back. The guard stumbled around as he backpedaled, trying desperately to keep his footing as reinforcements began to show up.

His eyes grew more wild, more crimson, visibly enough to halt the approaching castle guards in their tracks a good ten feet away from the menacing stranger.

The twang of a crossbow sounded just before a bolt whizzed in, thudding into Nomad's upper chest, sinking half the shaft through just above the man's lungs.

Worried murmurs began to sound through the ranks as Nomad took a step forward, not fazed by the bolt stuck in his body in the least.

Two more crossbows were raised, trained on Nomad, ready to shoot, but the guards never got their second shot.

A warm hand pressed softly on Nomad's marble-like skin as Reza, drawing energies from deep within, began to unleash her inherited power of healing. She blacked out almost instantly after a wild scream of pain and fell back into Arie's arms.

Nomad stumbled forward, grunting as he tried to shrug off the searing touch of his former comrade. What was once a touch of divine healing now crippled him, locking up the muscles in his racked back, contracting until the pain forced him to scream out like a wild, tortured beast, loud enough for all of Sephentho to hear.

His screams were cut short as a dozen iron clubs came in on his unprotected body, beating the consciousness from him.

"Seize 'em! Seize all of 'em!" the captain shouted, rushing in with the rest of the guard.

7
A GRIM SENTENCE

Slitting an eye open, Reza peeked out at her unfamiliar surroundings, her battered brain attempting to catch up with where she was and how she got there.

It was dark, to the point where the only thing she could make out was a torch on the wall through the bars. Reaching down, she felt a cold shackle bound around her ankle, and with the constant drip of condensation coming down from the ceiling and the far distant wind echoing through corridor after corridor, she was beginning to piece together where she might be.

Placing a hand on her head caused her to recoil momentarily before lightly inspecting once more. A large contusion just above her brow, and the pounding headache that began intensifying, brought to mind the events that likely landed her here in jail.

Nomad had gone on a rampage, and after he had fallen, mostly due to her healing touch, she had been knocked cold by one of the guards.

From her side came a low voice, "I'm surprised you're up so soon. After all that alcohol, excitement, and punishment, I was figuring you'd be out the rest of the night."

Reza turned her squinty gaze to Arie who was a cell over from her, also shackled and shivering slightly.

"Arie, what's happened?" Reza hoarsely mumbled out while rubbing her noggin.

"The guards locked us up in here a few hours ago. They were pretty gentle with me considering what they did to you and Nomad," Arie said, wincing at the knot just above Reza's brow.

Reza looked around the jail once more, trying to get a clearer sense of her surroundings. There was no one else, aside from Arie, in their wing of the jail that she could see.

Turning back to Arie, Reza asked, "Nomad—what did they do with him?"

"I don't know," Arie replied in a sharp tone, pausing a second before continuing, "Once they clubbed him unconscious, they dragged him off first. My guess is they're still dealing with him, or they'd probably already have questioned us by now."

Reza sat back against the cold, damp stone wall, trying to push past her headache to consider her options with the current situation. With nothing immediately clear coming to her, she gave up, closed her eyes, and tried to rest.

She didn't get shuteye for long, however; the urgent footfall of someone in armor marching towards her cell roused her from her half sleep.

"Who the hell are you two and what are you doing in the company of that demon?" the captain from earlier said in a cutting tone.

Reza rubbed her face, trying to wake up again while Arie remained silent, waiting for Reza to give the answers the man was there for.

"Multiple witnesses say you had been seen with him earlier. He's calming down now but he had my men hard-pressed most of the night just to keep him restrained in his cell. We had to triple up on the shackles he's so damn strong. So, I ask you again, who are you people, and what is your business in Sephentho?"

Reza dropped her hands to her lap. Though the man did not know her, Arie did, and she could tell how absolutely exhausted the girl was. Rarely did she not have a drive to what she did, but there, in that jail cell, she seemed as though, perhaps since the first time Arie had known her, she had given up on something.

"Yes, he was our companion. He was a good man, once…" Reza whispered out. She looked down to the floor, silent once more.

Arie, though she didn't care to be the one to answer the questions, saw that she would have to speak for them or risk having the captain prosecute them for withholding information.

"His name is Nomad. He was cursed a few moons ago and we've been traveling to priests since then to try and have his curse removed. He hasn't harmed anyone up till this point, though I understand he seems dangerous."

"Seems dangerous? I've got two of my guards in the infirmary from that scuffle in the streets, one's in a real bad way too. Not sure if he's going to pull through. Look into that man's eyes and tell me he's not a demon."

Reza did not move, a true picture of pity, while Arie broke eye contact with the captain, wanting to argue Nomad's case but knowing the captain had the truth of it. Nomad had indeed fallen a great ways since their time at the monastery.

Seeing the worn and beaten women silent in their cells softened the captain's features momentarily. He took in a deep breath, attempting to relieve some of the pent-up stress that had built up from the night's events.

"Look, neither of you gave us trouble last night. In fact, it seemed as though you were trying to calm that beast of a man you were traveling with at your own peril. I have no further reason to hold you here, so I'll have a guard gather your belongings and see you out. If…" the captain hesitated for a moment before awkwardly continuing, "…what you say is true about that demon being a former friend of yours, I'm sorry for your loss. He cannot be permitted to roam neither our streets, nor the countryside. He's unhinged. I'm sorry."

Arie could tell, in terms of military men, that the captain seemed a genuine fellow, and though she appreciated his kindness, she knew he was more likely to sentence Nomad to execution than dungeon time.

"What will you do with him? Nomad isn't our former companion, he's our companion *still*," Arie pressed, more than a little desperation in her voice at the thought of what might befall Nomad in the coming hours.

"Death would be too kind for servants of the devil…whatever devil it is he serves. Our priests will find that out tonight. Tomorrow at trial, I suspect the judges will call for his execution," the captain said before walking off, leaving Reza and Arie to reflect in quiet a moment before a guard arrived with a few of their personal items and unlocked their cells. He led them out to the streets before setting them free.

Arie looked around, seeing a few townsfolk gawk at them briefly before moving on with their routines. Looking to Reza, who was still sulking and exhausted, she grabbed the saren's hand and toted her back to their inn, making their way through the streets in silence.

Walking past the two low-hanging trees on either side of the front door to the inn, Arie led Reza into the front room of the establishment. Fishing out the keys to their room, Arie sighed, "Alright, let's get you in bed, you look like hell," as they started back to the hallway that led to their rooms.

"One does not simply tell Reza Malay to do anything," a familiar voice warned from the bench by the window of the sitting area.

Both Arie and Reza looked over to see their former traveling companions, Finian and Cavok, in dust-covered trailcoats, sharing a pipe.

Reza barely glanced Fin and Cavok's way before snatching her room's key from Arie and headed off down the hall, leaving Arie to deal with a confused Fin, as Cavok took another long toke of the cheap ragweed he had been tending to.

"What was that all about? I know she's not big on hellos, but gods, I at least expected some manner of recognition."

"Fin," Arie started, considering how much to tell him and how to deal with Reza's current state. "Nomad is to be tried and most likely executed tomorrow. You're not going to get a nice *hello* from Reza right now. Give her some space."

"Executed?" Fin's eyes widened. "Well that's a harsh sentence, how'd he get himself into that situation? What happened with you three?"

Arie scanned the sitting room briefly. The innkeeper wasn't there currently, but just to be safe from prying ears, she grabbed Fin's arm and led him down the hallway to her room. Cavok slowly got up to follow behind them. Fin waved Cavok to hurry up so they could close the door to the hallway.

Once the three of them were in the room, Arie began to answer Fin's question in a hushed tone. Ragweed smoke already filled the small bedroom as Cavok kicked back in the corner chair and Fin and Arie had a seat on her bed.

"Well, there's a lot to the story, but suffice it to say, Reza's people weren't able to help. In fact, it almost came to blows at one point. They were convinced Nomad is a lost cause. While I don't think that's true, he—" Arie paused, trying to pick her words carefully to not overly concern Fin. "He has been losing himself to this wound with each passing night. It's not looking good at this point."

"Even the sarens can't heal him?" Fin whispered, his gaze drifting off to the window, watching the tree leaves shimmer in the morning breeze.

Not having anything reassuring to say about that, she continued, "We arrived here two nights ago. Sometimes we can't get through to him. His eyes go black. He mumbles in his foreign tongue, and neither Reza nor I know what he says most of the time. Last night his eyes were red, somehow they were lit! Almost as if on fire, like a dark ember. He made his way into the streets, and we met him there, and he…well, he attacked us along with anyone else that moved to confront him. The city guard did not take the situation lightly. They jailed Reza and me and just let us out this morning, but the captain said that they plan to bring him to trial and most likely will execute Nomad within a day."

"Tried here in Sephentho? That's not good. Their judges are known to be brutal. This is not a place you want to get tried," Fin said, looking back to Arie.

Arie got up and snatched a wine bottle from the nightstand, uncorking it before adding, "Reza has not been taking all this too well. She may be close to giving up on this whole thing. I don't know her well enough to say, and maybe it was just a really rough night, but she's starting to shut everything out." She took a swig of wine, giving Fin and Cavok time to think the situation over.

After a while, Cavok knocked his pipe against the table, fingering the remaining ash on the floor, breaking the silence with his deep voice. "Let's jail break 'em."

Fin gave Cavok a sideways glance, mulling over a reply to his comrade's suggestion. "I don't enjoy skulking around castles. Cities are one thing, lots of places to hide and get lost in, but castles are made to keep things in or out. A jailbreak would be far from easy, even for you and me."

"You getting old, Fin? You've been in and out of jail since I've known you so many times that *I've* lost count. C'mon, it's Nomad. It might not be simple, but we can handle it," Cavok said, stretching out in the chair.

"You two okay with being felons, huh?" Arie pointedly asked, looking both men over.

Cavok answered for the both of them. "It's never ideal to burn bridges like this in regions, but if it means bailing a friend out of trouble, you do what needs to be done."

Arie locked eyes with Cavok, thinking on what Cavok was proposing they do, and asked after a moment, "What if Nomad's too far gone into the dark? What if he's not worth the risk at this point? If we get caught trying to bust him out, we're all headed for the chopping block."

Cavok licked the smoke from his gums and responded without blinking, "We owe that man our lives."

The two stared hard at each other for a few tense seconds before Fin let out a long sigh.

"Alright Cavok, you bloody hero. I'll get to devising a plan. Alls I can say is that Nomad better be happy to see us."

8

THE RED

"He's calmed down from the night before or I wouldn't allow this visit; but, if he is tried and sentenced for execution tomorrow, then it is custom here that we allow farewells by loved ones," the guard said, casually leading Arie and Reza along the golden-lit corridors of the ground-level cell.

Reza, still in a state of despair, didn't respond or even seem like she was paying attention, but Arie was doing her part to play along, asking as many questions as she could to find out more about where they were keeping him.

"Thank you, he was a good friend of ours until that curse was placed upon him. He's not been himself lately. I hope this visit helps us get some sort of resolution in this unfortunate circumstance," Arie said, with as much concern in her voice as she could stand to invest. She knew they needed the sympathies of the guards if she wanted to get good information out of them.

"So, I hear he was giving the guards a hard time last night?" she tentatively probed, seeing how talkative the guard was willing to be with her.

"Yeah. Oh yeah," the man chuckled. "Took a crew of five of us just to strap him in a few pairs of irons when we first got him in a cell. Even with three sets of manacles, we've got two guards on watch at all times since he's straining the anchors when he really gets into a fit. So far he hasn't responded to any questioning."

"I see," Arie said, mulling over the information the guard had divulged. Fin and Cavok could use that when planning their jailbreak, and though asking the captain to have one last visit to see their ill-touched companion had mostly been a smokescreen to obtain location and information of where they had Nomad held, she genuinely did want to visit with Nomad to assess where he was in dealing with the corruption that had hijacked his body and mind.

As they rounded a corner, she noticed the guard glancing sideways at her and Reza, sizing them up almost with a predatory look. She knew her and Reza were attractive specimens when it came to men in the region, and though Reza never thought to use that fact to her advantage, Arie thought it senseless not to. She doubted this guard, or the captain, would have treated them as respectfully as they had if they were ugly or dressed in peasant's garb. Wealth, power, and beauty were inescapable high-value tokens in the game of life. Tokens that could be cast aside; or used when the stakes were right.

"Here we are," the guard said as Arie and Reza clung to the cell's iron bars, looking at their visibly exhausted companion.

Nomad seemed a different man from the night before. He lay on his back amidst a sea of iron links, three chains per limb binding him loosely down. He rested uneasily, twitching in his slumber, eyes closed but squinting from time to time. He was paler than they remembered, most of his color gone from his darker, foreign complexion.

"My god, he looks awful," Arie whispered, holding her hand to her mouth. "May we go in to see him?"

The guard looked uneasy. "We had a terrible time getting him to calm down. He's still dangerous—"

Placing a hand on the guard's chest piece, Arie moved in closer to him. "This might be our last goodbye. Please, let us at least have a moment with him."

The guard shifted uncomfortably a moment before looking to the other two guards on duty there at the cell. She only hoped their escort held command over the other two sentries there.

Looking to the two men, nodding his head for them to follow him, he unlocked the cell door and whispered, "Five minutes, no more. I'll be right around the corner down the hall," before walking back the way they had come, leaving Reza and Arie alone with Nomad.

"Hiro," Reza softly spoke, moving towards him. Arie curiously waited for Nomad's reaction.

Reaching a hand out, Reza was just about to rest it on his shoulder when he snapped out of his tentative slumber, eyes flashing with a red glint, issuing a low snarl as he took in Reza and Arie.

At first, he just seemed tense, ready to snap at Reza, but she made no move, waiting for him to calm, whispering, "Lanereth warned me that there's nothing left of you in there to save—please show me that's not true. We want to help you, but only if there's still someone in there to help."

His snarl didn't change, but Reza proceeded to place her hand on his arm. To Arie's surprise, he did not withdraw or lash out at Reza.

His features slowly began to melt into a tired slump, eyes going from red to black again, leaning forward as Reza caught him and cradled him, his torso heaving. Reza pulled him in tight as he let out a heavy breath.

Reza smiled, rocking them both slowly, as Nomad said his first words in many days, "The red—my thoughts—not my own…."

She had stopped rocking upon hearing him speak. Though she held him close, there was no warmth coming from the spasming body she held. He had been dealing with a terrible pull to darkness, she knew, and she wondered how long he would be able to hold out before he was completely enveloped in it.

"We're here for you, Hiro. We'll come back for you tonight. Hold out till then—" she whispered, pausing as she could tell through his grunts, he was trying to respond to her.

"No…not tonight. Red. Endless red—" A jolt of pain racked his side as he contorted out of Reza's hold, balling back up on the cell floor as he tried to deal with whatever internal torment had regained its grasp upon him.

"Time's up, girls," the guard said as he rounded the corner.

Reza stood up and joined Arie as they took one last look at their friend, writhing in a ball on the floor accompanied by the constant *clink* of rustling iron chains.

"Come," Arie whispered to Reza, "we got what we came for." She turned away from a scene she could no longer bear to watch.

45

9

IRONS RENT

The small table in Arie's inn was cluttered with parchment, drinks, food, tools, and hands sorting through rough-drawn maps of the jail the girls had drawn out for Fin and Cavok to work out their plans of a jailbreak.

"You say he was coherent when you saw him? He talked directly to you? About what again? His exact words. It didn't sound overly lucid," Fin quizzed through puffs of his pipe, looking at the route he agreed with Cavok on, which they'd be using to get to Nomad's cell.

"Drowning in a sea of red, blood, hate. Something to that effect. It sounded like he's struggling with the call of Telenth, but he was with us for a moment. He let Reza hold him for a while," Arie replied. Reza nodded in agreement.

"Hmm," Fin let out, looking to Cavok with a bit of concern in his eyes. "We'll need him *with us* for more than a moment on escape. We can't be dealing with a struggling Nomad if we want to escape quietly. Cavok, do you have any ink to help with sedating him? I didn't bring any poisons or potions with me for that sort of thing."

Cavok took off his glove and slid up his sleeved tunic enough for the group to see a rising moon tattoo that Arie and Reza did not recall him having before; with the ink looking fresh, they suspected he had gotten it within the last moon cycle.

Arie traced the raised lines of black and purple ink that ran along the strong man's veined arm. "Beautiful, but I fail to see how a tattoo is going to help silencing Nomad if he struggles with you during the jail break."

"Do you remember Metus' obscure present to Cavok? That strange token? Cavok cashed it in for a new set of tattoos. Not just any tattoos, hexweaved ink inscriptions. They are costly." Fin sighed, a bit of jealousy showing in his admiring gaze. "Probably the most expensive gift Metus gave to any of us. There are few artists in any nearby regions, and the art is somewhat of a dying practice, but rumor has it, hexweaved tattoos can mimic spells if called upon by the host. Cavok has been testing some of his inscriptions out on the road with me, and I've got to say, though at first I was skeptical, our friend here has reached a whole new level of dangerous."

Cavok pointed to the rising moon and said, "This one can put people to sleep. It works. I put Fin out a few times with it."

"You did what?" Fin shot back incredulously, getting a smirk from Cavok, the large man replying with, "Had to test it on someone."

Arie let Fin finish his grumblings before asking the two, "So you have your route in and out established?"

Fin directed his attention back to the task at hand, still a bit annoyed about Cavok's non-consensual testing practices, and answered Arie. "Yes, yes. Seems straightforward enough. Since he's on the ground level, we'll be making our way in through a barred window. The prison courtyard is guaranteed watched, so we'll slip past or take care of the night watch beforehand.

"After we're in, we'll take out the two guards standing watch over Nomad and break him out, returning the same way we got in. From there, you two," Fin said, pointing to Arie and Reza, "need to already be out of the castle walls, waiting for us with horses ready for a long run that night. We'll more than likely be trailed once they find Nomad gone.

"We'll do best to cover our tracks, but I expect somewhat of a chase. Castle Sephentho is known for their tight justice system, and they won't let a jailbreak go unpunished. It may be a rough couple of days as we move to outwit and outdistance them."

"We'll have our things packed and horses bought within the hour," Reza said, getting a look from Fin and Arie, since, until that point, she had remained silent since her return from seeing Nomad.

"Yes, getting out of this inn would be good for both of us, I believe. We'll spend the evening outside the city walls in wait for you. We'll have a fire lit a mile outside the castle walls," Arie added, nodding to Reza in approval.

Fin took a long drag on his pipe, taking the plan all in, blowing the smoke out atop the jail-sketch parchments. Picking up the bundle of fine rope and a satchel of pebbles, he patted his large companion on the shoulder and went to leave the room, stopping at the door before mentioning on his way out, "If by midnight we're not out, you two pack camp and head back to Sheaf. There's no sense staying to watch Nomad's *and* our execution."

"Always one for melodramatics," Cavok said under his breath. He got up once Fin was gone, creating swirling trails in Fin's smoke.

"We'll be fine. See ya tonight," he said, smiling, patting Reza on the back, then turned to follow his friend out of the inn.

Things were quiet that night, few night watchmen had been in the streets, and only a lone sentry stood inattentively watching at the jail wall. Fin wondered if this was normal for Sephentho castle. He had been through there once before, but it was years ago, and he was not paying much attention to the law enforcement activity levels at the time. In fact, he remembered very little of his last visit due to the number of intoxicants that had been involved during his stay.

"Come." He waved to Cavok, slinking along through side alleys close to the jail's wall. The two men breezed through the shadowed streets like quiet alley cats, each step decisively avoiding any street rubbish that might give their presence away.

Both were donned in black now. They had bought a few goods from the market before sundown; among the items were black cowls and tunics.

Fin came to a halt at the edge of a shaded alley, looking down both walls for roundsmen before running up to the ten-foot-tall wall, easily scaling its rough crags, peeking over the top to get an idea of what they were up against.

It was slightly foggy out, making it a bit difficult to get a real take on the scene, but from what he could see, the courtyard seemed to match Arie's description of the one where Nomad's cell looked out to. It was large, a good two city blocks of space. It looked like most of the yard was reserved for some type of chain-gang mining operations, chiseling stone for various purposes. Fin briefly wondered if this was a main source of stone exports Sephentho was known for. Endless free labor. The more they could jail there, the more they put into the city's coffers.

"Damn bureaucrats," Fin breathed under his breath, looking back to the alley, waving for Cavok to follow. A moment later, the large man clung to the ledge along next to him.

"Only one guard watching the courtyard, over there in that small corner tower," Fin said.

"Is he at attention?" Cavok whispered, knowing Fin had the better eyesight.

"Looks like it; we'll need to sap him. You ready to use that tattoo on someone other than me?" Fin asked, a bit of salt in his voice.

Cavok simply nodded, dropping down to hug the wall and made his way over to the corner tower. Within a minute, Fin saw the guard slump onto his sitting stool. Soon after, Cavok hopped back up to hang on the wall once more next to Fin.

A bit winded, the large man whispered, "Alright, should be out the rest of the night. We ready to move to the courtyard?"

Scanning for guards one more time, Fin nodded, then hoisted himself over the wall and landed down in the stone-filled courtyard, Cavok dropping next to him.

There was little light, most coming from the steaming clouds of fog catching light from the surrounding lanterns and torches of the city, making it dimly glow. It was just enough to light their path while keeping them somewhat hidden as they picked their way through the courtyard to the jail wall.

A hellish yell echoed from within the jail a ways down from them, followed by a horrendous jangle of chains. Fin turned to Cavok and exchanged confused looks.

"What the hell was that?" Fin whispered, not sure if they should go and inspect or proceed with finding a barred window to break in through.

Before he had a chance to think twice about their path, another primal scream came roaring closer to the courtyard as they could now see hands on the bars of one of the jail cells windows.

The two men watched in shock as the bars, along with part of the cell wall, were ripped inwards, a plume of dust bellowing out of the now exposed cell.

Nomad, eyes aglow in a deep crimson, leapt out of the jail cell wearing a few cuffs and chain links along each limb, with a large iron strap around his torso.

Like that, he was gone, rushing through the courtyard and bounding up the ten-foot wall.

"Shit," Fin cursed. "We need to leave town right now," he slurred out as he bolted across the courtyard, climbing up another section of the ten-foot wall. Cavok followed Fin's lead.

The jail burst to life just as Fin and Cavok got over the wall, the courtyard now bustling with shouting voices. Atop the jail wall, boots rushed this way and that. Voices in the streets sounded the alarm, and the whole town of Sephentho began to light up, the militia on high alert and organizing.

"Maybe *that's* why we saw so few on shift outside. They were more busy dealing with what was on the inside," Cavok said as they halted a moment in a trash alley.

"Yeah, probably right about that. Well, it doesn't seem Nomad needs our assistance, and even if we could get to that maniac, I doubt even your sleep spell would calm that one down now," Fin replied, peeking his head out of the street corner to get a read on the area of town they were in.

"They'll be closing the castle gates if they haven't already. Good thing I brought this rope. We'll need to get over that wall," Fin said, waving for Cavok to follow and stay close as the two ran through side streets, avoiding the majority of the commotion along the main streets of the city.

"He's on his way to the gates, boys! Lower the porte! Spearmen, ready up!" Fin and Cavok heard a booming voice, many blocks over, call out.

"Well at least we know where he is," Fin said as they came to a stop at the castle wall. "Damn, he's not making tonight easy on anyone, though."

"Com'on," Cavok grunted, locking his hands together to give Fin a boost up the fifteen-foot wall.

Cavok easily flung Fin in the air. Fin grabbed onto the wall's ledge, hoisting himself over onto the patrol path.

Unloosing the rope from his pack, Fin threw the end over to Cavok, leaning back, anchoring himself in place while his companion practically lunged up the wall on the rope.

"Oi, who goes there!" a voice called out, a guard rushing to the pair of black-cloaked skulkers.

"We're part of the scout party the king's sending after that madman," Fin said, in as steady a tone as he could manage after the exertion he just went through of holding Cavok's weight as the man made his way over the ledge.

"Stay where you are!" the man yelled, not seeming to buy Fin's bluff.

"You stay where you are," Fin snipped back, helping Cavok to his feet.

"Hold him back!" a distant cry sounded. The commotion at the city gate turned the guard's attention away from Fin and Cavok momentarily. It was long enough for Fin to rush the man, elbowing him hard on the back of his head and knocked him cold to the ground.

Fin adjusted his cloak and tossed Cavok the rope to set up for their descent down the castle wall.

10

NIGHT HUNT

"Put the fire out," Arie said, eyes on the city gates, seeing that the portcullis was now closing and that there was a commotion happening along the parapets.

Reza covered the small fire in dirt, extinguishing its flame immediately. The low fog bank helped to conceal the remaining smoke.

"What do you see?" Reza asked, knowing that Arie's bloodline of half haltia granted her greater eyesight than Reza had.

"I see Fin and Cavok along the wall, but Nomad is not with them. They're clambering down the wall now," she said, squinting, shifting her attention to the movement at the gate. "There's a gathering at the gate, the portcullis is lowered. No—wait. It's being raised again. I don't know what's happening there, but the place is buzzing with activity. We need to see if we can rendezvous with Fin and Cavok and figure out what happened."

Reza looked to the horses she had bought earlier that evening and asked, "You think the castle's militia is going to be out on the road? How are we going to keep hidden with four horses?"

Arie stilled a moment, considering possible answers to Reza's question.

Leaping onto her mount's back, she hastily issued orders. "I'll take a horse, find the boys, and bring them here. You take the other three horses off the trail a ways, stay hidden, and wait for us."

Arie was gone within seconds, and in the silence of the night, Reza could begin to hear distant voices yelling out towards the castle. She didn't have long to break the camp down.

She quickly shoveled more dirt atop the campfire and bundled up their packs, strapping them to the horses. Looking along the road, she found somewhat of a break in the foliage, trotting the horses through the underbrush until the road was barely visible through the trees. Tying the horses to a tree, she stood in wait, hoping for Arie's quick return with Fin and Cavok.

After a bit, the horses quieted enough for Reza to listen once again to the voices on the air. They were still quite a ways off towards the castle, and they were less frequent now. She could only guess as to their meaning, though. She felt so blind. What had happened with Fin's plan? If Arie said that Nomad wasn't with them, well, where was he then?

The sound of footsteps took her from her thoughts. Someone was on foot, racing down the road. Peering around the tree she had racked the horses to, she slowed her breath, waiting for the footsteps to pass by her.

A blur through the trees came into sight down the road, a slight rustle of iron links, and then, Nomad's face, eyes streaking crimson, wounds visible along his torso and arms, dark blood slicking off as he ran.

A sharp clang of iron sounded, hinges breaking under impact and strain, and shackles flew into the brush off to the side of the road as he worked at his many cuffs; and then he was past her, off down the road, heading south out of the mountains.

All of it came together for her suddenly. Nomad had broken out of jail, with or without Fin and Cavok's help, and the castle was very aware of it, judging by the amount of commotion she still could hear in that direction.

"They must be on his trail," Reza breathed, unleashing one of the horses from the tree.

Looking one last time back towards the castle, hoping to soon see Arie, Fin, and Cavok show up, she mounted her horse and made her way to the road, taking off after Nomad.

She hoped Arie would be able to find the two spare horses, but she didn't have time to wait around. Nomad might not only outdistance the city guard, but them as well if she didn't keep track of him.

She spurred her horse on, knowing that within a minute or so, she'd catch up to him on the road, and she prayed he'd be able to recognize her as friend, not foe.

"So all that commotion at the gate was because of Nomad?" Arie questioned as she trotted her horse alongside Fin and Cavok.

"Oh yeah. Had a small platoon chasing him down, and one at the gate ready for him. I doubt they were able to stop him from breaking past the gate patrol. He moved like a bat out of hell," Fin explained between breaths, both Fin and Cavok having to sprint to keep up with Arie's horse.

Making their way through the thick of the forest was slowing them down. Arie had to trot her horse around felled trees and thickets multiple times as they caught each other up on the situation. What starlight that did shine down through the canopy was being diffused further by the fog that covered most of the woods.

"Then he must have broken through. On my way over here, I saw troops on the road. It did take a while to find you two in the woods off-trail. I'd guess they've made good time on their way to hunt down Nomad. They had horses. I don't suspect Nomad was on one."

"Speaking of horses," Fin cut in, "I know Cavok wouldn't mind it, but I can't keep this pace forever. Maybe you should go ahead, and we'll catch up as quick as we can. Nomad might be run down sooner than we'll be able to make it to his aid at this rate."

Arie trotted past two hitched horses calmly waiting for Reza, who, unbeknownst to the horses, was not returning for them.

"Well…that certainly is convenient," Fin said as he came into the clearing.

"It's not convenience, it's planning," Arie said. "Though, Reza should have been here. I bet she's on the chase ahead of us."

Unhitching the horses from the tree, Fin and Cavok mounted up and followed Arie, who was now headed to the road, kicking her horse into a full-on gallop as soon as she made it to the wide dirt path.

A slight breeze picked up, pushing the fog into swirls along the dark road by the lakeside. Starlight was not enough to illuminate much of the scene below on the road under the oak canopy where a red-eyed shadowy figure turned to hiss at an approaching woman atop a white horse, who pulled up to a halt just before the defensive man.

"Hiro! Please, I know you're in there, please, fight it!" Reza called, jumping down off of her horse, coming up to him with a hand held out.

He snarled, hackles raised, and ripped off the trail and into the woods, leaving Reza quickly behind.

"You there! Stay where you are!" a voice called from a ways down the road, breaking Reza's gaze away from Nomad. Six or seven guards on horseback rode towards her through the fog.

Grabbing a satchel from her mount's rigging, she slung it over her back and—though every fiber of her warned her away from rushing into a lightless forest with a feral predator—dashed off into the woods after Nomad, getting a glimpse of his red eyes as the rest of him was black and grey, blending in well with the dark woods.

The woods were thick and following Nomad's trail was no easy task. If her garb wasn't so sturdy, all the snagging on branches and bushes would have quickly derobed her, but she was following Nomad's wake, and he had trailblazed somewhat of an opening for her to stumble through.

She could hear the rustle of troops behind her, roadside. Steel on flint sounded as torches were lit aflame, their light dancing through the thick woods as she pushed onwards in the direction Nomad had gone.

She could see Nomad caught on something up ahead, and getting closer, she noticed that he was all wrapped up in vines. He was ripping through them, uprooting bush and roots, but it was costing him distance as Reza leapt over a trodden brush, catching up to him quickly now.

"Hiro, please, wait! I'm here to help you!" Reza cried, rushing up to him and grabbing one of his arms, trying to turn him around.

Letting out a lion's roar, Nomad did turn around, but it was to bat Reza to the side, slamming her so hard that she was launched a few yards over bush and vine, chest slamming into a tree trunk. Memories of the arisen king slamming her as he had that one night months ago flashed through her head, blackness befalling her as she went unconscious.

11

BACK WOODS SCUFFLE

"Reza, hey!" a voice called, causing her to open her eyes. Everything was dark and blurry at first, with Arie's face slowly coming into view.

"Hiro!" she called out, trying to get to her feet, but instead dipped into Arie's arms as she began to wobble backwards.

"Reza, slow down. Tell us what happened," Fin said, helping to hold Reza's off-balanced weight.

Steadying herself a moment, looking around, she noticed where she had engaged Nomad at in the thicket of vines, then noticed the trampled path passing through that area as though a whole group of people had recently tromped that way.

"The soldiers—looks like they got ahead of us," Reza said through gasps of breath, feeling her chest bruised where she had slammed the tree.

"Yeah, no kidding. At least their trail won't be hard to follow, and if they're close on Nomad's heels, then we should still be able to track him down. Lucky we saw you, though, you are a ways off the trail over here. You alright?"

Reza held her ribs and began walking back towards the fresh trail in the thickets, resisting the urge to grunt through the pain. Arie could tell Reza was shrugging off what was likely a nasty bruise or fracture, but Reza toughing through her injury did make things easier for them, since they didn't have time to stop and take care of her.

"Fin and Arie, make sure we don't lose him. Reza and I will catch up with you as soon as we can," Cavok ordered tersely.

Without a word, Fin and Arie nodded and sprinted off through the woods after the destructive wake of the soldiers. Reza was about to protest Cavok's command but let it go, seeing that the two were already out of sight.

Cavok didn't speak another word as he marched behind Reza, letting her head the trail at her pace, the two following the now very well-trodden path.

It had taken Arie and Fin less than an hour to catch up to the Sephentho search party, and though they considered circumventing the group to track down Nomad first, they decided against that as it was very thick woods, and there was a possibility of losing the trail or being detected by the search party if they did.

The night wore long, and the morning sun soon showed through the treeline as the search party began to slow down, orders being barked as the group scuttled frantically in an outcropping up ahead.

"He's coming around on you, sir! Watch out!" one of the guards shouted as Arie caught a glimpse of what she assumed was Nomad flailing out at the same captain that had released her from jail the day before.

Swords and stud-covered cudgels were brandished, swinging to keep Nomad at bay as the seven guards encircled him by a tree.

Arie looked to Fin and waved him to come closer. The two were not but a dozen or so lunges to the scuffle, but the thick overgrowth covered them well enough that she doubted they would be seen by the engaged guards.

"What's the plan?" Fin asked, huddling next to Arie, both well hidden behind a full holly bush.

She watched the guards a moment longer as they smacked Nomad with their clubs, a few slashing his arms as he lashed out. It seemed the guards would have the upper hand in this fight, Nomad's usual tremendous strength flagging the longer the scene went on.

"Nomad's going to need some help. I'd like to not kill those guards if possible, but that's going to take some extra care. You comfortable distracting them while I pick them off at range?"

"Hmm, seven against one? You better be good on your word about helping with that bow. And you better not hit me in the heat of it, either."

Without answering, Arie was off through the woods, bow out, searching for a perch where she'd be able to pick her targets with ease.

Shaking his head at the recklessness of stepping up to seven armed guards on his own, he unclipped four of his bronze throwing daggers, and after taking a stabilizing breath, stepped out from the bushes and walked towards the harrying guards who continued to mutilate a flagging Nomad.

"Sir! Someone in the woods!"

Turning around, the captain considered the new approaching threat.

"Damn," the captain grunted, having looked up at the approaching stranger just as Nomad came in and knocked the man down, pushed back by a flashing short sword just before descending upon the prone man.

"Bron, take care of him," the captain barked at the man who called out Fin's arrival.

Fin held his hands up nonthreateningly but continued to approach the group, who were having difficulty even with an extremely exhausted Nomad.

"Leave, now," the man the captain had named Bron said in a deep, threatening voice. The man was large, not quite as big as Cavok, but close, and Fin knew he didn't want to get in a brawl with the brute, so he came to a halt ten feet from him.

"I said *leave*!" Bron yelled, brandishing a nasty studded club, approaching close enough to Fin that he had to backstep or risk being within the man's threat range.

"I think it's you gentlemen that need to leave. Though I doubt you'll heed my words, I'll at least give you the courtesy of a warning. We have you surrounded, and you're harassing our man," Fin said in a voice that held a lethal edge, now lowering his hands to hover over his unbuckled daggers that glinted a bright, warm red-gold in the morning light.

Bron, Fin could see, was no novice to warfare. A fool would scoff at potential bluffs like Fin just issued, but Bron made no confident chuckle, instead eyeing the surrounding woods quickly to check if there was any merit to the seemingly lone wanderer's claim.

Raising his cudgel, Bron rushed the distance between him and Fin in a flash, but after the second stride, just as he raised his club, a whistling arrow shrieked through the woods, punching through the large man's arm, tip coming out the other end of his bulging bicep.

Fin grabbed the faltering man's wrist, twisting around to deftly place his feet within Bron's wide stance, and threw the off-balanced man head over heels into a thorny holly bush, scratching him up as he wriggled around to try and right himself.

The encounter had not been overlooked. Two of the other guards rushed over to engage Fin, making no small talk as a swordsman and another cudgel wielder came right in at him.

Fin turned, flicking both wrists, once, twice, and out came his polished bronze daggers, flipping point over handle towards the two guards. The first two, though they hit their target, stubbornly bounced off the uniform lamellar chest piece. The following two daggers, however, found home in exposed flesh, sinking a few inches deep into the swordsman's thigh and one directly into the hand of the club wielder, tacking the stick to the man's hand.

The volley of daggers caused a moment of hesitation in the two attackers' step, but the charge continued after they realized the wounds weren't fatal. The guard with the club made it first to Fin, swinging the now bloodied club at his head, attempting to slam Fin unconscious.

Fin, hearing a rustle in the bush behind him, dropped low and sidestepped to the left, juking around the attacker and tripped him as he stumbled past. He fell into Bron who, was poised to lunge at Fin from behind, now forced to help steady his comrade.

A short sword came point first at Fin, spurring him to twirl to the side of it, gripping the man's sword arm, rolling with it extended over his shoulder and snapped the man's arm beyond the ability to bend, dislocating it. He let go, moving past the screaming man towards the next two guards that now faced him.

Two more arrows came screaming into the fray, one thudding into the cudgel fellow's leg as the other narrowly missed Bron, who ducked out of the way just in time.

The whistler arrows had, by this point, garnered the rest of the guards' attention, and the sight of three bloodied guards over by Fin, and a few of them wearing claw marks and bruises from Nomad's demonic grip, did little to reassure the captain's confidence in the quickly waning odds of him getting his troops safely home to their families that night.

"Alright! Hold your fire! Let me tend to my men and we'll be gone."

Things were still for a moment, even Nomad recognizing an agreement was being struck just then. Fin brushed fingers over his swept hilt dagger, eyeing the group and kept track of those on the ground to his right and those standing to his left.

"Alright," Fin said in an unusually calm voice, "take your men and leave us be. Don't attempt to regroup and hunt us or there will be no parley next time."

With gritted teeth, the captain let his quarry be, waving for his men to gather Bron and the others, leaving Nomad completely exhausted, breathing heavily slumped against a tree base.

"If you ever return to Castle Sephentho, orders will be to kill on sight," the captain hissed out as he led his men back through the forest the direction they had come.

"Well ol' boy," Fin mused, taking a look at a hacked up, heaving Nomad, "you've sure seen better days, haven't you?"

Usually the one to bring light to a dim situation, even Fin this time seemed saddened by what rotten circumstances fate had decided to unleash on his good friend.

12

THE ANCIENT GROVE

"They saw us, but didn't pursue," Reza said, a bit confused at the situation.

"We just whipped their asses. They'll not be interested in any run-ins till they get back to their castle and get reinforcements," Fin answered, turning back to take note of the two stragglers as both Reza and Cavok finally caught up to Fin and Arie.

Pointing to Nomad as he finished collecting his two thrown daggers from the bushes, he caught Reza and Cavok up on the situation.

"Nomad's exhausted and in pain. Not sure if he's aware of who we are just yet, but we'll need to figure out what we're going to do with him soon. He's catching his breath now, but who knows how long that'll be for."

Arie jumped down out of a tree beside the two newcomers, walking into the clearing and said, "You made it just in time. Those guards just left naught but a minute ago. We were waiting to see if they were going to return before dealing with Nomad."

"By the looks of it, I'd say he's already been dealt with. We should see about staunching the bleeding," Cavok said, moving in to inspect Nomad's wounds.

Wait, don't get too close—" Arie started, but Cavok was already kneeling next to Nomad, who, for a moment, snapped out of his internal struggling to take note of the large man reaching out for him.

Nomad backhanded Cavok's arm so hard that it off-balanced him. He fell over as Nomad scrambled to his feet. Hanging onto the tree for balance for a moment, Nomad eyed the group of watchers for a split second, then sprinted away through the tall field of grass.

"No—" Arie started, holding a hand out towards Nomad. She rushed off out of the clearing and into the field after him, the rest of the group running to catch up with Reza limping in the back, trying to not fall too far behind.

Fin caught up to Arie quickly enough, and the two trailed Nomad closely. Though he was sprinting recklessly headlong into the obscuring grass fields, he was badly injured, causing him to stumble often. Reza was having a harder time catching up, and Cavok held back to make sure they didn't leave her behind.

Bursting through the wall of grass that ended at another forest treeline, Nomad tumbled down a knoll, streaking the moss-covered forest floor in red-black blood.

Splashing into a small stream beneath a springhead, Nomad went to stand, slipping and thrashing in the spring a few times before he was able to get to his feet again.

Looking back, he saw no signs of his pursuers. He started forward again, stumbling along the mossy carpet of the heavily shaded forest grove he had fallen into, going deeper and deeper.

Arie and Fin stalked silently to the side, keeping up with him, waiting for Cavok and Reza, who were taking an awfully long time to catch up. They needed Cavok's muscle, they knew. If it came to a wrestling match, neither of them wanted any part of Nomad's ferocity. They felt Cavok might be their only chance at subduing him if it came to that.

Nomad halted, dead in his tracks, and Fin and Arie stopped as well, though why Nomad had come to a halt, they weren't sure.

"A darkness, you bring to my grove," a calm voice whispered, which would have been passed off as the breeze or the soft rolling of the creek if Fin and Arie hadn't been so still and silent.

Nomad stood deathly still, looking off to the side. Fin and Arie concentrated on what Nomad was looking at, their eyes widened, as a human-shaped sapling slowly moved towards Nomad now.

Nomad growled, crouching, ready to spring at the tree-like figure, but Arie stood up, shouting, "Nomad, don't!" distracting him as the figure raised its arm.

Vines sprung up and latched around his legs, holding him in place long enough for thicker roots to sprout and blur to life. The roots pulled him down to the ground, lashing him to the soil along a knotty grandfather tree, its gnarled trunk moving slightly to pin Nomad fast in place.

As Nomad thrashed and squirmed, the roots bore down harder, sinking him further into the rich soil, partially burying him until, at once, he stopped, dropping his head back while heaving, trying to catch his breath, only able to loll his head from side to side as he struggled to stay conscious.

Turning its head, the tree-like figure looked towards Fin and Arie, then to Cavok and Reza who came rushing into the grove, taking cautious note of the stranger as well as Fin and Arie coming down from the knoll across the way.

A light breeze playfully ruffled the treetops above, dropping a few acorns along the moss carpet before Arie stepped towards the treekin and asked, "Are you…a dryad?"

The feminine figure's skin slowly morphed and shifted, bark, leaf, and vine making up what seemed to be living clothes or armor. Her face seemed like a detailed wood carving by the hand of some long-forgotten master.

She looked at Cavok and Reza, and then over to Arie and smiled, her plaited, vine-like leafy braids shimmering in the sun that broke through the canopy momentarily with the breeze.

"You have knowledge of my kind? This is rare these days," the figure said, her voice an intricate weave of earthy and airy notes.

"Though, haltias *have* long been friends of the soil, root, and all green things. Why do these children hunt a tainted one?" she said, walking towards Arie now, her steps seeming like a blur of forest growth. Everyone in the grove was mesmerized by the spectacle, all speechless at merely the sight of her stride.

"H-he—" Arie stuttered as the treekin closed the gap between them, "is our companion, inflicted as he may be. We are trying to help him."

"Help, she says," and the dryad's smile faded as she turned back to consider Nomad. "No. This one is beyond reclamation. This child's fate is sealed in ash and shadow."

"No," Reza firmly interjected, stepping into the conversation. "There is a way to reclaim his soul, and we've vowed to see the black taint purged from him."

The figure did not turn to face Reza but walked past Arie and into a tree next to her, phasing her body into the bark and disappearing, startling the group a second time as she phased from a tree back into the grove behind Reza. "You think to slay a devil? Reckless. More will be added to the Ashen One's numbers."

Reza turned around to face the illusive treekin who had gotten so close that she was but inches from her face, the slight oaky scent of vanilla now enveloping her.

Though she wanted to take a step back, the figure much too close for comfort, Reza firmly held her ground, intercepting an oaken hand that was slowly rising up towards her. Even though she firmly gripped the dryad's wrist, it continued to rise easily until the clenched wooden hand rested between the two at chest level. All the while she stared unblinkingly into Reza's eyes, a smile on her nymphish face.

"Give your hand to me, child," she whispered, only loud enough for Reza to hear.

Reza pulled harder at the dryad's wrist, trying to budge it, but it was as though she were trying to move a firm oak with deep roots tying it to the earth. Giving up on controlling the thing's wrist, she went to step back, but found that roots had slipped around her boots and clenched tight the moment she went to move.

Branches sprouted out from the dryad's sides, latticing itself to Reza's form, knitting a living net around her, weaving in and through her legs and arms, not actively restraining her as of yet, but Reza now had no doubt what was a comfortable net of wood and vines that enveloped her could at once secure her tight in place.

"Your hand, child," the dryad issued once more, her tone holding less of her previously wispy playfulness.

Cavok stepped forward, chest heaving, and the quickly mounted aggression Cavok exerted was palpable in the air. Though she couldn't see him, Reza felt Cavok was about to trounce the dryad.

"Stand down, Cavok—for now," Arie called, seeing things were beginning to escalate.

Reza awkwardly felt the trellis-like vines inch their way around her every body part, continuing to thicken. She saw no other options at that point.

Hesitantly, Reza brought forth her other hand, tore her gaze from the wooden face inches from her nose, and looked down, moving to hold out her hand in front of her, doing as the dryad had asked.

She held her oak hand over Reza's and began to open it, causing

Reza to flinch as something cool and gritty sprinkled onto her skin. The wood hand moved away, and Reza saw that she held soil in her palm.

"This is the fate of all who live in the cycle of life. It is your fate, the fate of your friends here, this forest's fate, and even my fate. In that way, we are all kin. But," she said, now looking towards Nomad, who writhed in the hold of the old grandfather tree's roots, "it is not that one's fate. He is no longer in the cycle. The lord of ash only takes—never gives back. None of his children, even in death, help to renew life on this planet. They are not fit for compost or peat. They only deplete what life remains within the cycle."

As the dryad had talked, the webwork of vines had receded from Reza, and she once more looked back to the dryad's deep lavender irises.

"Let—me go!" Nomad breathed out, the tree trunks weighing heavy on his chest.

Everyone looked to him now, even the dryad. Reza moved warily past the treekin and kneeled at Nomad's side. The roots were pressing down on him so heavily, she doubted anyone else in the grove in his position would still be drawing breath.

It was the first time since her visit with him in the prison that she had heard his voice. Hearing his voice kindled the flicker of hope she had for his returning to them.

"Nomad, do you recognize me or know where we are?" Reza asked in a tender voice.

Nomad looked to her, his eyes clouded, bloodshot, but not an angry red as they had been previously.

Straining his head and torso around to get a bit more space to breathe, Nomad managed to squeeze out, "South—to Tarigannie. I need to go back! Let me go!"

Reza turned and looked to Arie and the others who had moved up to join her.

"What's in Tarigannie?" Arie asked. Everyone was now huddled around him, getting more information out of him in his last two sentences than they had the last few days.

"The black blood—calls to him. It's ripping my mind apart! I need to go to him!" Nomad writhed with such intensity that the group took a step back, not knowing if the large roots were enough to contain his outburst.

"Black blood, calling to him, Tarigannie—you think he's speaking of Lashik's master, the arisen lord?" Fin asked, looking to Arie and

Reza. "Lashik is dead, and the arisen lord took off after the battle along the road to Warwick. That cursed wound of his could be drawing him back to the one that cursed him, or the next closest thing."

"This one is drawn to whatever abomination that represents Telenth-Lanor currently here in Una. Lashik, the arisen lord, are these disciples of Telenth?" the dryad asked, appearing behind the group suddenly, once again awkwardly close to Reza and seemed to ask her the question directly.

Cavok moved to position himself between the two, obviously not liking the tree sprite's centering in on Reza. Though his show would have been intimidating even to the roughest of men, the dryad didn't turn to consider him once, instead continuing to hold eye contact with Reza.

"I—don't know for sure, but we think that perhaps the arisen lord is indeed an avatar of Telenth. When I first encountered him, there was no disputing his power and presence. He was…like nothing I've ever faced," Reza responded, taken aback by even revisiting the memory of the arisen lord.

A thrashing from Nomad shook Fin and Arie's attention back to the man buried in the ground, but Cavok remained solidly fixed between the two women, Reza's eyes glued to the dark lavender orbs peering into her soul.

"Few have witnessed an avatar of the Deep Hells and survive to speak of such. There is a curiosity with this one. More than that, I feel the touch of Farenlome has graced you recently. What is this blessing you carry upon you?" the dryad said, moving even closer before Cavok stepped in, placing a warning hand on the slender branch that was her shoulder.

"I sense it, an old magic wrought from the earth by the hand of an ancient one of Farenlome," she said, now looking to Cavok to consider the large man.

Fin and Arie both looked to the strongman and dryad, practically feeling the amount of tension that sparked between the two. They all knew Cavok didn't get riled up unless he meant to deliver good on his threat, and currently, he appeared plenty threatening.

"Oh!" Reza exclaimed, drawing everyone's eyes, instantly breaking the rising tension. "I know what earth magic you're speaking of," she said, shuffling through a side pouch momentarily before producing Isis' ring.

"A member of my faith recently brought this before an altar

dedicated to Farenlome," Reza explained, the ring completely captivating the dryad as well as the others.

Though she didn't touch it, the dryad bobbed her head around the ring, inspecting it from various angles. "Rarely does Farenlome or her children offer such a generous bestowment of life energy…curious." She paused, seeming more interested in Reza the more they talked. "Why do you not wear it? I sense a strong protecting power within it," her oaky voice crooned.

"I—do not know how long the enchantment will hold. As I understand it, the longer I wear the ring, the faster—Isis' presence fades," Reza hesitantly answered, still not sure if the dryad before them was in fact friend or foe.

"You say there was a presence within it?" the dryad asked. "I sense no spirit within."

"Isis possessed this ring. She spoke with me often. Are you saying she's no longer attached to this ring? But Farenlome blessed it," Reza said, worry seeping into her words.

"Farenlome is the god of nature. It is unnatural for spirits to linger here in this realm. They belong elsewhere. If there was a spirit within, Farenlome may have very well released her from her artificial prison."

Reza looked devastated. She had not even said farewell, and to think she had left her back there on the cold cliffside.

Seeing how distraught she was at the news, the dryad attempted to comfort her. "Farenlome would have not done this against her will. She is a gracious god. If there was a task keeping this *Isis* of yours here, or if she had desired to stay within that ring, she would not force her eviction."

Reza contemplated the dryad's words, narrowing her eyes and gazed upon the mesmerizing dryad's wooden facial features, lost in thought for a moment as she contemplated Isis' unannounced departure.

Deciding it was not the time to overly linger upon Isis, she asked, "You say there's great power still within it, a protection? Might you be able to tell me more about that? If Isis is not there to give the aid, where does it then come from?"

"Farenlome converted what magics were there with a repurposed power. I know it is a source of protection, to guard the wearer from harm; though, I would need to commune with Farenlome herself to fully understand the nature of that ring. I would but say, wear it. It was a gift freely offered from our Mother. Do not take it lightly. It was meant to protect you along your way for some higher purpose," the dryad said, weaving her words along, mesmerizing all listening.

"You seem to know more about this ring than any I've come across. I might ask you more on the subject if we had the time," Reza spoke, then looked back to Nomad and added, "but we have pressing matters to attend. Hiro's hold on sanity wanes more and more each day. We have very little time to accomplish the impossible task of slaying the arisen lord to cut his blood bond."

"Yes, well you four would have scarce a chance to contend with Telenth's finest. This is a god's chosen we speak of, after all. The one beneath those roots there," she said, pointing to Nomad, "is, for all intents and purposes, forfeit to Telenth's beck and call. He seems bound to return to his master—" the dryad said, finishing as though amid an intriguing thought.

Arie took the pause to question the woodland entity. "You say we stand no chance at defeating this avatar and releasing Nomad from his bonds. How do you know what we are capable of? How are you to say for sure we stand no chance when you don't even know us? We have overcome a great many challenges before together. Perhaps the gods are on our side."

The woodland figure continued to pause, standing so still that she might otherwise be mistaken for a delicate carving, then her lavender orbs shifted slowly to Arie, considering her questions a moment before answering. "Your strongest among you is no match for my strength," she said, grabbing the man's hand that still rested on her shoulder and twisted his arm out of the way with little effort. Cavok grunted as he strained to resist her press, giving inches all the while.

"Those who might be blessed by the power of gods have little knowledge of that power," she continued as she looked back to Reza. "And those who might aid their friends stand on the sidelines, indecisive," she finished, looking back to Arie and Fin.

She released Cavok's wrist, waiting a moment to assess if he was going to re-engage with her. Cavok seemed willing to let the dryad continue her point, which she did.

"I am but a lesser child of Farenlome, one of countless. There is little special about me. Even the name the elders gave me upon my rebirth denotes my frivolous nature—Leaf. A leaf matters, yes, but not alone. If I, a lowly *leaf* could halt you all here and now, what chance do you stand against a god's chosen?"

The group stood idle, each considering the question posed. Even Nomad calmed a moment to rest half-buried beneath the old tree.

"We may be individually weak, relatively speaking, but you of all of us should know, together we are strong. It's not just us four that fight for Nomad and against Telenth's finest. We have friends; some who are not here, that will heed our call for aid. Those that have influence and power in the region, some that hold high office in the realm of the enchanters, those that can help us hunt down our quarry. We stand in favors of many benevolent gods and goddesses. We're not going to be facing the arisen king alone," Reza calmly stated, slipping on the ring of Isis. "We stand against Telenth and his minions with powers that far surpass us—even you would not stand a chance against the movement we will rally together."

Leaf, noting the ring along her slender finger, considered the saren's words carefully for a moment while everyone waited for her answer. After a moment, she whispered, "Farenlome has deemed you worthy. In truth, this is all I require. Whom you stand against or with, means little beside this. I wonder if perhaps—there may be more to your gang than meets the eye, as one should know, the eye may often deceive the true nature of things."

Sighing, her eyes slowly shifting to Nomad covered in sweat and dirt, hair tousled and slick against his skin, Leaf said in a burdened voice, "Still, you wish to save the unredeemable. Telenth is a mighty foe. Your band and I have a common enemy. He is despised by Farenlome's children and all living things. Knowing that an ancient one has already aided your mission causes me to consider seeking the council of the sisters. Perhaps there is more to this than what I initially suspected. My sisters will provide us with a clearer answer."

"Sisters?" Cavok asked, concerned that there might be more treekin hiding in the grove, seeing firsthand that just *one* could give them more than enough trouble.

"Calm, large one," Leaf said, smirking at Cavok, her fairy-like demeanor slipping back easily enough. "I and my sisters mean no harm to you. In fact, we may be able to further aid you, if you are willing to grant me time to call them forth, that is," she finished, looking to Reza for an answer.

Reza was taken aback. A moment ago, she was borderline being assaulted by the dryad, and now she was offering to call in the aid of her family for their cause.

"Take the dryad's offer, Reza. My people knew to never refuse them. Ill luck falls upon those that don't come to their aid when called on." Arie, who wasn't usually overly concerned with folktales, was feeling quite differently about this one.

Reza looked back to Cavok and Fin for approval, but neither seemed to have an answer ready, though it was clear that Cavok was displeased by the dryad's presence. The choice lay at her feet, it seemed.

"This council you mentioned, would we be required to be present and where will you hold it?" Reza asked after a moment of contemplation.

"The inner garden. It is but a little ways further in the grove not far from here. I would only admit *you* there," she said, slowly pointing a wooden finger at Reza. "It is a sacred place, and though we usually allow no outside sprouts like yourselves, considering the circumstance, I think my sisters need to witness you and your ring for themselves when making their decision for aid."

Reza was not particularly scared of traveling deeper into the woods with the dryad, but she was still unsure if accepting the dryad's help was in the best interest of ultimately helping Nomad. The dryad did have him roughly pinned down, after all. What if the council decided not to aid them and ordered Nomad expunged? What then? At the least, her friends would be watching over him while she was away.

"I will go with you to the garden," Reza sighed heavily, turning to her companions as she added in a finite tone, "I'm trusting you three to watch over Nomad. Keep him safe. I will be back as soon as possible. We move out when I do."

"You got it," Fin replied. He took a seat a respectful distance from Nomad and the grandfather tree, seeing that they'd be staying there for a while.

"Don't linger for too long. Those city guards and their friends just might come back to give us trouble after how we dealt with them. Best not to stick around these parts longer than we have to," Fin added, taking out a knife and a sharpening stone from his pouch.

She nodded her head, considering the advice of her friend. Fin out of all of them knew the mentality and motives of law enforcers. She trusted his judgment on the matter without reservation.

Leaf, intently watching the group, silently assessed everyone's responses. Slowly turning, she guided Reza past the boughed archway of two oak trees, leading her deeper into the shady forest that stretched endlessly before them, the treetop canopy becoming lower and the smell of soil becoming heavier the further they walked the old path.

13

COUNCIL OF SISTERS

"You are a saren, correct? I feel the residue of many lives upon your soul," Leaf chatted as they casually made their way through the sleepy woodland trail.

"Yes," Reza replied distantly, transfixed now for the last few minutes on studying the strange moving form of the woody dryad. She pulled her fixation from looking at the back of Leaf's unreal form.

"This garden is young, comparatively to my kind, but even so, it has stood guarded by dryads for a millennium now as the oaks in which we hail from began to become the predominant tree here. Only a handful of outsiders have been allowed here, and half of them were saren, the other half, haltia. The two peoples share a respect for Farenlome and her ways."

"Yes, Sareth holds friendly ties with Farenlome and often shares knowledge and magicks with her children. It has been a mutual boon for our people," Reza confirmed, sounding as though she were reciting text from a study book back at the monastery, feeling more than a little pang of guilt at how little she knew and had paid attention to her studies and her people's ways during her upbringing.

Leaf held aloft a branch that hung low in the path to allow Reza to pass under, quietly in thought as she considered Reza's heritage.

The two women stepped into a clearing; moss, pools, and small lazy streams blanketed the floor of the forest with moss-covered, winding oak boughs constructing the low-hanging canopy that shaded most of the open area. There was little that made sound there. The occasional ruffle of leaves high above and the quiet trickle of water below seemed muffled. It felt like a sacred place, even to Reza, and she at once suspected this was their destination.

Yes, this is the garden," Leaf said, smiling at Reza's awed expression. "It has been a long time since our last visitors here. Come, have a seat while I call my sisters."

Leaf lifted a hand over a jutting island of soil amongst the shallow pools and river, and slowly up came a webwork of roots, interweaving and forming what looked to be a delicate stool. Reza looked to Leaf and approached, testing it with her hand, then took a seat, finding it to be quite sturdy.

Reza waited patiently now, watching Leaf walk a little further into the garden, past a few mossy pools until she reached a ring of trees, softly touching each, whispering silent words, reaching into its trunk and pulling her melding wooden hand back out.

After melding with the last tree, she turned and came back to Reza. She stood next to her, looking back to the trees, waiting patiently as the sounds of the forest slowly crept back in to fill the hush of the place.

Minutes passed by, and Reza shifted in place more than a few times. She had the sole constraints of dealing with a physical body, at least one made of flesh and blood, unlike Leaf. She was considering breaking the silence and asking Leaf what they were waiting for when something began to grow out of one of the trees.

It was slow at first, but then, the knot of wood protruding from the grand oak's trunk began to take shape and form. Before she could tell what shape the mass of wood was forming, another tree began the same process; this one a slightly different hue of wood, but the size and shape seemed similar.

A few more trees began to groan and protrude, and soon the whole circle of trees seemed alive with movement, each harboring forms that were molding into figures much like Leaf's.

Reza's expression was a look of wonderment. She doubted few mortals had ever witnessed such a sacred procession of the heart of the woods. She couldn't recall of any record even describing such an event.

Each of the figures' features became more defined and delicate as they separated from the trees they had spawned from. Soon, all nine dryads were walking towards the group, lumbering and creaking at first, but becoming more limber with each step.

Encircling Reza now, all ten dryads, including Leaf at the center of the ring, stood looming over their guest—and lucky Reza felt to be a guest, as the sight of the dryads would have been the sight of doom had she wandered into their brook on her own, uninvited. The thought alone was enough to cause her to tremble.

A guttural clicking sound began to resonate from one of the dryads, and Leaf responded in kind, creaking and mutely popping in what Reza guessed was a form of communication between the treekin.

One among them stepped forward, speaking in a low, groaning voice. "We hail from many lands all across Yuna. Some of us are young, some very old. We are all descendants of Farenlome, some distant and not so distant. The one you know as Leaf had called us here on your behalf. I would know who you are before we discuss your need."

The one that spoke was a darker grain than the rest, and she had dark green sprigs and buds. Reza looked to Leaf briefly and answered the dryad addressing her.

"My name is Reza. I'm a saren knight currently on a mission to kill an avatar of Telenth."

She felt it was brief but was not sure how much more of an introduction the dryads required.

Each of the dryads looked from Reza to Leaf, now waiting for an explanation from their sister.

"Farenlome has seen fit to bless her recently. An ancient one renewed a powerful enchantment upon her ring. This fact alone gives me reason to believe the mission she is on may require our aid, for their numbers are weak and small currently, and though Reza has spoken to me of allies and plans in which to expunge Telenth's chosen, I fear the strength of their foe may be too powerful for them as it stands. I consider bestowing her a portion of the life sap."

Wood creaks and chirps started up again after Leaf's last statement, sending a wave of excitement through the ring of dryads.

"Gifting the sap of the dryads is a decision not to make lightly, Leaf!" the dark oak dryad almost hissed, garnering nods and headshakes from the other treekin. "It would take not just from you and your grove, but all within the sisterhood and their connected groves. One has not bestowed this gift to a mortal for well over a thousand moons!"

"Their need and cause are great. I would not have suggested the gift unless I deemed it prudent."

"The sap collects slowly, and the health of oaks across the land wanes for a season. It would be a difficult time for us, but mostly for Leaf and her grove as the sap is renewed," one of the lighter oak dryads whispered suddenly in Reza's ears, providing her with a bit of context to the mysterious speech the council was wrapped up in. Though she had just met Leaf, the apparent consequences did set a good deal of guilt in her heart, even though she had not even been the one to ask for the dryad's help.

"I didn't know, Leaf. You don't need to risk yourself for us—" Reza started but was cut short from a side-eye and a terse reply.

"I do this for the cause you are wrapped up in. It is Farenlome's will, and I will see her will realized. If I deem to aid you, you *will* be aided."

Leaf's usual fairylike tone had turned fierce. Reza knew better than to rebut her, surrounded by her kin in the heart of their sanctum. She sat with hands on her lap as if an obedient child wishing not for a second reprimand.

The garden was silent for a tension-filled moment before the dark oak dryad said to Leaf in an exasperated tone, "Most stubborn of all our kind—most mercurial. Leaf, you and your woods will suffer the drain more than ours. For us, a few trees may die due to sickness, for you…."

The elder paused, leaving off on the depressing train of thought. All waited for her to continue. "We will do what we can to support your grove in its time of need. I can tell, nothing we can say will change your mind on a matter such as this. If it is indeed our great Mother's will to impart with these mortals the precious blessing of the forest to help them accomplish their quest, then she will surely answer our prayer and imbue you with a measure of her essence which should be potent enough even to bring low an avatar of Telenth-Lanor, that great corruptor."

At that, Leaf's crinkled brow eased, and she seemed once again to return to her whimsical self. Bowing to the dark oak, she crooned, "Thank you, Tulanae. Being the oldest child among us, having your support eases my mind. Though sometimes I know you think I heed not anyone's advice, I do—hence why I called you all here. Even begrudgingly giving your blessing shows there is some faith and wisdom in heeding a call I suspect is true."

For Reza, interpreting the treekin's expressions was difficult, but the look Tulanae gave Leaf seemed to be one of exasperation with her younger sister.

"This…blessing. I will not treat it lightly, I assure you," Reza added, seeing that the others held a great deal of doubt for Leaf's support for their cause.

"I suppose that is all we could ask of you. We would hold you to that vow," Tulanae said after a moment of silence. She turned to Leaf, adding, "And of you, be careful, Leaf. After the sap has been given, the winter's chill will bite deeper into your wild woods. Call upon us as need arises. If this truly be Farenlome's will, you will have the support necessary to see through the season of frost."

Leaf nodded graciously, switching their speech from callatum back to the creaking moans of treekin, and left Reza there to listen to the haunting sounds of the forest and trees for some time. The day in the sleepy grove wore slowly on.

14

THE STRAY HOUND

"We have no idea how long this *Leaf* intends to keep Reza occupied, or even where they were headed. I don't like it. It's been over half the day already," Fin said, throwing down a botched leather braid he had been working on for his pack and looked to Arie for a response.

"Yes," she muttered, seeming conflicted with the whole situation. "My people generally have positive relations with treckin, but, for the most part, I did not grow up around them. I admit, I'm not sure if we can trust Leaf," she said, pausing again, thinking on the matter further. "I would need more time with her to know of her true motives. This all happened so fast. Now is not the time to put our faith in strangers."

"Heaven knows we need all the help we can get, though. This is a fool's errand we're on," Fin voiced, looking at a worn-down, deathly ill Nomad who had been feverish since earlier that day, still buried under the roots. Since Leaf's departure, the tree had not moved once.

Cavok had been still the past hour, deep in meditation, Arie and Fin figured by the looks of it, but now they noticed that his eyes were open, and he was staring intently out past the trees the way they had come.

Fin slunk to a wide tree almost unnoticed, even to Arie's keen eyes, noticing that he was contoured to the back of the tree. She focused on what he was holding; though, oddly enough, she was not able to discern what was in his hands, almost as though her mind refused to see it.

She was about to follow Fin's lead when she noticed a figure standing at the knoll top. His features were concealed by the light from the grassy field behind as it shown past him and into her and Cavok's eyes.

Slowly, the stranger walked down out of the sunlight and into the shaded grove. Arie let out a gasp as he did so.

"Yozo…."

Cavok slowly got to his feet, no weapon in hand but still remaining a terribly threatening sight to the average traveler's eye.

"How did you find us?" Arie inquired, a hint of worry apparent in her voice. With how winding their trail had been over the last few days, she realized that to find their trail, it meant his intent would have had to have been paramount, making sure to track their every move hourly for the last week or so since they had seen him along the road. A man whose whole focus doggedly remained glued to their whereabouts for a week straight was no man to be taken lightly, she knew, and with how he had dispatched Nomad so easily last encounter, her worry was well warranted.

"It seems whatever you did to him up in that monastery got Hiro moving again; though, whatever possesses him now, does not seem to render him coherent," the foreign man Arie knew as Yozo said as he casually strolled down the hill of moss and grass.

Cavok went to intercept the approaching man, but Arie called for him to stop.

"Wait," she said, the tremble in her voice causing Cavok more pause than the word itself. Keeping an eye on Yozo's sword hand lightly atop his hilt, Arie hefted her bow and addressed the foreigner. "We give you one chance to explain yourself. You are a skilled duelist, I have borne witness to that, and so I would have us avoid conflict here if possible, but think us not novices to battle."

Arie waited for an answer from the man, ready to nock an arrow at the first signs of aggression. She knew they had no margin of delay with Yozo.

Yozo's eyebrow rose, a smirk flashing before he responded in broken callatum. "Threaten me with muscles…" he nodded to Cavok, "and arrows?" nodding to Arie. "You've tried that last we met. If I wanted, I could handle you both without effort, even with the help of your sneak behind that tree over there. But my purpose does not involve you three. Hiro must pay for his sins upon my family…our family."

Fin quietly stepped out from behind the tree, realizing his cover was blown, and responded to the man's ramblings, "If your quarrel is with Nomad, then it *is* with us. We will protect him with our life. If you are here for Nomad, you may not have him. If you plan to fight us to get to him, then let's go. If not, be on your way. We have pressing matters."

Yozo's grip tightened on his hilt for a moment, his smirk turning deadly flat, eyes darting from one foe to the next, calculating.

Tension in the grove ramped suddenly. Arie began nocking an arrow; Fin slipped a hand to a line of throwing daggers; and Cavok's muscles went taut, straining in anticipation. The tension mounted to a tipping point, just before Yozo relaxed his grip, letting out a sigh as a distant yell broke the silence.

"What was that?" Arie blurted out, relaxing her string as Yozo let his hand slide off his sword hilt.

"Sephentho's scouts are on their way. I thought I could get to you sooner than they, but it appears they were not leisurely about their pace." Yozo sighed once more.

"We need to get Nomad and move. We've stayed here much longer than I had liked," Fin insisted, moving to a buried, exhausted Nomad and started to work on digging him out.

"Wait," Arie barked, not liking that Fin was letting his guard down with Yozo still a threat in their presence.

Looking back to Yozo, she questioned, "How many scouts are on their way?"

Yozo tilted his head, trying to get a better listen as the sounds of commotion could be heard in the grass field above, and said in a low tone, "Five, but they are not the problem. The troop they scout for holds thirty-five as far as I could count. I do not know how far behind that troop is but dealing with those scouts would delay us for too long."

Arie looked to Fin and Cavok, not sure where they stood currently—Yozo's presence complicated the situation further.

"I wish to settle things with Hiro, but now is not the time. Get him out of here or risk having Sephentho's might upon us all here and now. I can give you only a few minutes. Use that time wisely."

Tipping his wide-brimmed hat, Yozo turned, and just before

rushing back up the mossy knoll, he added, "Just know, I will be back to collect my dues. Hiro will answer for his transgressions."

Arie watched the foreign man for a moment as he disappeared through the tall grass and headed straight for the noise of the scouting party. She turned to see that Cavok and Fin had already begun the task of getting Nomad unearthed.

The great tree's roots gave them no rebuff this time, and with a bit of dirt removed and one great yank from Cavok, Nomad's ragged body was wrenched from his earthen, wooden prison. Fin tightly wrapped the unconscious man with steel cord around the arms and torso, clipping it to itself to bind the man in case he awoke to his usual ill-tempered self.

"At the ready! He's in the grass!" the group heard from above in the field. A scuffle ensued, though luckily for them, the melee did not sound as though it was getting closer currently.

Looking back for a moment through the dark woods into which Reza had followed the dryad, Arie went to help Cavok hoist Nomad's exhausted body over the tall man's shoulder.

"What about Reza?" Cavok huffed, adjusting to the weight.

Arie looked back once more, still not sure if they should search out Reza, and risk getting deeper into the strange woods, or head off to the west and attempt to reconnect to the highway after losing their pursuers.

"I'll find her," Fin said easily, patting Nomad on the back. "You two just get this one safe back to Sheaf. It's maybe a two-week journey from here at a clip. Get some mounts when you can. With Reza's healing attempt for Nomad failed, I'm not sure what other options we have, if any. At least in Sheaf we'll have safe harbor while we figure this whole mess out."

"Sounds good," Cavok gruffed, starting off immediately to the west along the treeline.

Fin called after Cavok as he left, "Keep an eye out for that Yozo fellow. He seemed like trouble. And I know how you like to push your luck with trouble."

Fin let out a smile as he watched Cavok lope off, grunting back at his long-time friend's unnecessary worry, and gave Arie a hearty reassuring pat on the shoulder before turning for the dark woods.

"Hey," Arie called to Fin, causing him to pause once, halfway turning back to her. "Watch over her. You damn well better not make us wait for you there long."

Fin issued a flippant smile and salute before heading through the oaken boughs that led him down the shady woodland path, hoping the trail led to Reza.

15

BLOOD IN THE TREES

A calm breeze blew in through the green canopy above, drifting a sappy bitter smell down to the garden floor where Reza sat, listening to the council of dryads chatter in their creaky treekin speech.

Just when she was about ready to interrupt the drawn-out communion, badly wanting to get back to her group at that point, Leaf turned to her and spoke once more in their language. Tulanae stood supportively by her sister's side as she made her announcement.

"We have come to some conclusions. Most more than likely don't concern you directly, but I feel it best to keep honest with you of our motives in helping you on this mission of yours.

"This unfortunate 'Nomad' friend of yours. He is the key to finding the avatar of Telenth. He will lead you to his master, and as long as Nomad does not know of your plans to use him, he will not be able to give your plans away. Telenth will draw him back home while you use him as a lead to strike the avatar. It is imperative that nothing is mentioned of this around him, or you run the risk of exposing your path to the Ashen One."

Reza had listened carefully to Leaf's ploy. She supposed she had figured to do the same; allow Nomad to lead them to the arisen king and then dispatch the warlord. She realized now, though, it was the default course of action. She did not have an actual strategy on how to best approach their goal.

Leaf's scheme seemed sound. She guessed Telenth had some kind of connection with Nomad, as he had babbled dark words regarding the lord of ash before in his sleep. If he did have some way to check in on Nomad, perhaps there was a way they could feed the dark lord some misinformation. She had no idea if they would be able to out-clever a god, but they could try.

She nodded after a moment and agreed with Leaf's reasonings.

"I will let the others know we need to be careful about letting any important information slip around Nomad."

"Good, see that you do," one of the other dryads said. The grove of treekin leaned in on Reza and got a nod out of her, even though she was already in agreeance.

"Give me the ring," Leaf said, holding out her wooden hand. Reza deposited it in her palm without hesitation.

Leaf held it forward, and the other dryads circled around it, each lowering their leaf-covered heads to shroud the gemmed ring, making it difficult to see what was happening within the canopy of hair.

Tears glistened from each, one by one, and though she only saw the fluid briefly, the light-amber and spring-green colored drops fell onto the ring's gem, melting into it, giving it a liquid-like shimmer within.

The dryads broke the circle. Leaf slowly handed the ring back to Reza, admiring her handiwork a moment before it slipped from her grasp.

"Now this trinket has not only Farenlome's blessing, but ours as well. You hold a very rare gift with this ring. Cherish it. Keep it safe," Leaf whispered as she locked eyes with Reza.

"As a saren, you have the power to heal. This blessing of living sap can provide any number of powers to the various children of Una. For the children of Sareth, however, it will provide you with more essence to draw upon when exerting your people's power. Whereas before you had to balance your own life energy to heal the wounds and sickness of others, now, you may call upon what collective life we have bestowed upon you through this ring to help sustain you beyond your natural limits.

"This blessing we rarely offer. I have paid the price not just with my blood, or the blood of my sisters, but with that of my whole grove. Use this blessing wisely in this war you bring to Telenth, or—there will be consequences."

Reza shuddered. She wanted to ask in detail how she would know when an appropriate time would be to call upon the blessing, or even how she was to tap into the power within, but the eldest dryad broke the silence first.

"Reza," Tulanae said, not quite as fluent in callatum as Leaf was, her tone a bit harsher, "go back to your people on the edge of the grove. Gather them and leave this place."

"I will. Thank you," Reza said, getting up from the root seat and bowed to the intimidating line of delicate, living trees. She headed back through the trail she had come, eager to meet back up with her friends and leave the increasingly oppressive grove.

Reza had been hustling her way back through the small forest path when Fin came flying down the trail towards her.

"Fin! What's happened?" Reza asked, seeing the urgency in his look, knowing he would not have come this far into the dryad's forest unless necessary.

"Sephentho forces are here looking for Nomad. Cavok and Arie took him and left. We need to leave these woods, now—"

Fin was cut short by a baleful breeze and a shadow rushing past them the direction Fin had come.

"What was that?" Reza questioned. The trees bent low, feeling much too oppressive for either of their liking.

Turning to head back, both began to run down the trail towards where Nomad had been buried, the forest constricting the archway of boughs as they ran.

There was another shadow, trees undulating for a moment, then a ripple of green shot past them on the trail. Shadowy figures darkened the claustrophobic woods as the two of them had to hunch low as they exited the forest trail just in time, the foliage now shrouding the path that was just there moments before.

A man's scream, then another yell sounded out somewhere just outside the treeline up the knoll.

"Reza, come on. We need to go," Fin whispered, grabbing her wrist, tugging for her to follow his lead, another scream sounding closer as a man in armor came running into view down the knoll into the grove.

He saw them for a moment, making eye contact with them, desperation in his eyes, then tripped over a root, tumbling head over heels down the grassy hill. He got wrapped up in a tangle of spiked vines as he fell, one looping around his neck, wringing taut as he came close to the end of the decline, the thick barbs ripping every inch of skin away from his neck as his makeshift noose hung him at the bottom of the slope. He now wore a crimson splattering of a necklace, blood gushing from the noose.

Reza looked up the hill to the treeline, which now seemed smeared with blood, morphing shades floating in and out of the dark places in the foliage, guardsmen's bodies being tossed and played with, though it was very hard to see the predator that hunted them.

A firm yank on her wrist from Fin and the two turned and ran the other way, not giving that godforsaken grove another glance.

Part Two: Assembled to a Cause United

16

MONSOON FOR THE LONE ROAD AHEAD

"Oh my god! Didn't think I'd ever be so happy to see endless desert!" Fin exclaimed, kneeling in the sand to take up handfuls of it, letting the grains filter through his clenched fists. Reza tussled his hair as she walked past her melodramatic travel companion.

"Let's hope the others are on the same path back to Sheaf. Can't believe we haven't come across any signs of them yet," Reza said, a slightly subdued note in her voice as she walked ahead, leaving Fin there, kneeling in the sand.

"Come, Fin," she said in a smooth voice, some distance ahead now. He watched her slowly saunter into the sunset with the backdrop of the orange and purple dunes stretched out for miles ahead of them.

He slowly got up, dusted himself off, and started to catch up with his old travel companion, idly reflecting on the long and lonely road they walked, strangely feeling sure they were not destined to meet back up with Cavok and the others on the road to Sheaf.

The dunes of the Plainstate stretched out for miles, and Fin knew it would be many days more before either party would see the red walls of Sheaf.

"If not on the trail, we'll see them back in Sheaf," Fin said confidently, catching up with Reza who had slowly made her way ahead of him along the first dune in the cooling desert. The sun was almost lowered below the dunes now, distant, heavy storm clouds hovering over the horizon.

She remained silent on the subject. As they crested the first dune, seeing the open expanse with nothing and no one in sight for as far as he could see, his thoughts turned over on themselves again and again on ways things could have gone bad for the other group.

He missed Cavok.

The night was cold, much colder than the nights had been amidst the woods and soft soil hitherto. The transition from high mountains and lively woodlands to steppe and then to desert had been quick, only taking them two days to make it from foothills to endless dunes. It was a beautiful, and impressive, shifting of scenes.

"Fin," Reza called, snapping him out of his private reflections while curled up in his blanket at the fire's light, "come here. You're being unusually quiet over there by yourself."

Fin looked up, seeing Reza's open arm, beckoning him to join by her side near the fire's warm glow.

She seemed in better spirits the last few days than she had been. Perhaps she had needed some time away from Nomad—surely she had needed that—but it was something more. The ring she wore seemed a warming presence to her, softening her mind, her mood.

"Come," Reza beckoned again, smiling invitingly, a smile Fin felt as though were from a distant time.

Slowly getting up, stretching out his bones, Fin sauntered over to Reza, snuggling into her open arm as she draped the blanket she wore around him.

"Rare indeed are the nights that you share an embrace with anyone, even those you're closest to, Reza," he said, pulling a flask out and taking a draw while he waited for the fire to warm him.

Reza ignored his observation and took the flask from him when he handed it to her. Though he meant for her to share a swig of the high-proof alcohol, she capped it and stashed it instead, leaving a very disappointed, long-faced Fin under her wing.

"Guess I can't expect too much change from you at once. Ever the party-pooper," he said, lightly jabbing her in the ribs and got an expected, though still painful, sharp jab back, depositing him out of her welcoming blanket.

Fin looked a little more than mockingly hurt by the gesture. "I need that flask back, Reza. I'm leaving soon, probably tonight."

Reza smirked at Fin's retort, but when he saw that she wasn't taking his comment seriously, he pressed, "I mean it, Reza. I'm heading out tonight and damn it if I'm heading into the desert alone without a bit of goddamned liquor!"

Reza's smirk faded as she saw he was not just being facetious.

"You're heading out? Why? Where?" Reza asked, brows now furrowed.

Fin stood up, looking to the ring that seemed to glow with a life force of its own in the night's light, and then back to Reza.

"You're set on helping Nomad, it's clear. You actually plan to face this *arisen king, lord, avatar* or whatever—that monster that forced us to abandon Bede that horrible night—" Fin hesitated, the mere mention of Bede causing him to close his eyes in hurtful recollection before continuing. "You are amassing a crew, it seems. And we are returning to Sheaf. I'm assuming you will enjoin Metus to lend aid to your cause."

"And what? Would you not have me attempt to save Nomad? You speak of *my* plans. Shouldn't this be *our* plan, or have you given up on Hiro?"

Fin smiled, happy to see Reza's old flame of stubbornness and hot temper still within her.

"No, no, Reza. That's not what I'm getting at. I'll join back up with you at Sheaf, like Cavok, Arie, and Nomad will. If it's a special force you're looking for, I know someone who would be worth having on our side. He owes me one—well, a few—but if he comes through for us on this mission, I'll let him off the hook in terms of our debt. He's not too far out of the way. I should be back at Sheaf soon after you three arrive."

A distant rumble of thunder rolled through them, a light, moist breeze ruffling their hair and garb.

Reza looked to the dark, fast-approaching clouds on the last-light horizon and asked, "We're still so far out; you sure you're going to be alright traveling alone?"

"I've been able to handle myself so far. Spent most of my life alone, on the streets. Don't know why now would be any different. Besides, you're the one I worry about out here alone. I had to think long and hard to come to this decision. But you made it to Jeenyre caring for a flagging Nomad; I think you'll be able to handle a few days' travel without me. Who knows, maybe you'll meet up with Cavok and the others on the way," Fin said hopefully. "Hope I'm right about all this. I think it'll be worth our while. You'll see once you meet Blind Bat Matt…" Fin ended with a chuckle and gathered his things, looking to the rainfall they could now see. "Not getting any sleep tonight, judging by the monsoon that's coming our way. Might as well start walking. The sooner I make it to Sansabar, the sooner I'll be back at Sheaf to a nice, relaxing hearth and banquet."

Reza, standing there wrapped in her blanket, struggled for words for a response, but the speed of the storm clouds was pressing any arguments she was trying to formulate away, and Fin had already gathered his things and bent over to plant a kiss on Reza's cheek before charmingly tipping his wide-brimmed traveler's hat at her.

"Safe travels," he said, pausing, struggling to finish his thought. "I'd hate the thought of something happening to you on the road, so stay safe and be smart. If we had the time, I'd see you to Sheaf and then head for Sansabar, but with Nomad how he was…time is short."

"Why not just send a messenger for Matt once we're in Sheaf?" Reza questioned as Fin watched the rain line approach.

"He wouldn't listen to a messenger. Hells, not even sure he'll listen to me, but I think it'll be worth my effort," he said with a sigh, his breath smoking in the sudden cold snap. "Tell everyone I'll be there quickly as ol' Matt's legs will allow us to be. Might want to pack some things up in that leather bag if you don't want them wet. Rain should be hitting us any minute now. Farewell, Reza!"

"Fin!" Reza called out, the crack of thunder nearby drowning her voice out. "Be safe!" she yelled after him, but the wall of rain a few hundred meters out was already dampening her voice.

Fin didn't seem to hear her last words to him, or if he did, he didn't respond. He was already headed off into the wall of rain that swept across the sandy dunes.

17

THE WRETCHED TREK

"Hold!" Cavok urgently whispered, raising his hand to halt everyone from heading over the next dune, the beckoning for Arie to make haste and join him at the lip of the dune's crest.

She had just made it to Cavok's side when he let out a curse. "Bugger's over the ridge already. There was someone far off a few dunes over. Seemed to be alone. Keep those keen eyes of yours that direction in case they show up again."

He watched along the dunes a moment longer before continuing. "We'll take a break for now to make sure we don't connect with any trouble. I'll watch that louse and make sure he keeps his distance with Nomad. He's been getting bolder lately."

The two turned and locked eyes with the foreigner who had been loosely traveling with them since they had split up in the oak forest weeks ago.

Yozo was out of earshot, a good distance back from where Nomad stood idle, covering his head with Yozo's own wide-brimmed hat to keep from literally burning up. Any skin that got exposed had begun to boil within moments of contact with direct sunlight.

"Cavok," Arie whispered, trying to be a bit more discreet than her companion, "we need him. Without his hypnosis, or whatever it is he does, we'd stand no chance at containing Nomad. I know it's hard for you, but don't chase him off yet."

Cavok didn't answer, but Arie could tell that he was considering any alternatives to having Yozo continuing to work his ritualistic magic on their friend. She assumed he couldn't think of any as he got up and walked to Nomad to check on him instead of moving to chase off, in Cavok's own words, 'the parasite.'

Cavok stooped under Nomad's wide brim, taking a peek at the state of his comrade. A champ of teeth and a snarl quickly warded Cavok off; backed up slightly as he considered his edgy friend's temperament.

He gave a hard, long look at Yozo who stood thirty feet back, glaring at Cavok with cold, focused eyes. He knew that look—that stare. It was the stare of a predator; one that was not processing emotion or concern for others, even oneself—only processing how to eliminate one's target. It was a look he knew so well because he had often given the same look to his enemies. He knew the look of a killer intimately—because he was one himself.

"You," Cavok boomed needlessly; Yozo was already clearly paying close attention to him. "Do your witchcraft."

Yozo waited a moment, whether to defy Cavok in a small way or to consider approaching Nomad while the hulk loomed close by, it was not clear, but he did begin to walk towards the two, spanning the scorching sands, coming up a whole two heads short next to Cavok's height.

The two stared at each other a moment longer, exchanging murderous looks as heat waves swirled around their sweaty brows, the sounds of desert locusts chittering in the distance. Yozo broke eye contact first, looking to Nomad and adjusted the dusty grey cloth that wrapped his whole body, checking his skin for signs of pestilence and blistering.

Cavok watched as Yozo unstrapped a foldable parasol from his side kit and handed it to Cavok, then kneeled down and took out a tin container from one of his backpacks. Cavok extended the well-made parasol and held it over Nomad to shield him from direct sunlight while Yozo began to gently lift Nomad's prison shirt, revealing his necrotic scar on his back where he had been stabbed by the illimoth blade.

Yozo inspected it for a moment, keeping his thoughts to himself, then went to pop open the tin container's lid and dipped a finger in a gel-like substance, drawing a symbol encircling the wound.

Nomad growled at the touch, quivering slightly, but Yozo began chanting in a language Cavok did not understand, though knew it to be Nomad's people's language, having heard his companion speak it a few times before. Humming in a trance-like tone, Yozo slowly traced his middle finger over the now dried gel, igniting it in a faint green glow, heavy black fumes seeping from the flame.

His chanting grew louder, and he swept the flames out in one motion, dropping Nomad's shirt, moving around to face him. Plucking a powder from the tin, he brought it before Nomad's face, which was currently a dazed grimace, then snapped a finger over the powder, producing green flames atop it, lighting it up in an elongated flash. Yozo blew the grey smoke in Nomad's face.

Nomad, at first disgruntled by the puff of smoke, began to ease up, relaxing his shoulders, his posture starting to slouch as Yozo closed up his case and finished his chant. He looked to Cavok once more, cracking his neck both ways before snatching his parasol from him and walking back to the spot where he had first been summoned.

"Cavok," Arie called down from atop the dune, "whoever you saw is long gone. We should get moving again."

Cavok took one more hard look at Yozo and then grabbed Nomad's arm, prompting him forward. They slowly made their way up the sand dune with Yozo a constant ten yards behind them, the small group slowly making their way through the barren desert, the only other person they had seen in a week now being the one they just avoided.

The day had been exhausting for the whole crew. Even Nomad seemed actually asleep, perhaps for the first time in days. They had double-timed their pace once the stranger had passed their trail and they had not stopped for a break the rest of the day and late into the night.

The moon was low and thin, the stars providing the only real light along the sandy carpet. They hadn't bothered to set up camp, throwing their supplies down and setting up Nomad beneath Yozo's sun parasol in case the sun rose before they did so to avoid him getting burned without their knowing. Cavok had drunk the last of his spirits he had brought for the journey and was slouched over on his side, chest heaving, though making very little noise while he slumbered. Arie was out, both keeping watch and hunting scorpions in the cool sands, gathering what would be their snacks for the following day.

Yozo had disappeared late in the day, which was a relief to both Cavok and Arie.

The strange man had shown up only a day after they had departed the dryad's grove. Nomad had given them a great deal of trouble after recuperating somewhat, his demonic strength returning in degrees, so Cavok had resorted to binding their friend. They had not known what they were going to do, since making it back to Sheaf with Nomad fighting them every step of the way seemed untenable.

Yozo appeared around that time.

He had walked into their clearing, not even Arie aware that their perimeter had been intruded upon. He held surrendering hands up and simply said, "I can calm his demons."

They sat beside him as he administered his ritual and were both shocked to find a great change over Nomad. The rest of that day he had been docile, manageable, compliant, though in no way coherent other than to walk in the direction he was pointed in. Cavok did not like it. He called it 'black magicks,' but it was the only way they could foresee making it back to Sheaf without fighting with an entity that possibly would grow stronger the longer they traveled.

The three had made a kind of pact, though very little had been said between them. Cavok and Arie had allowed Yozo to follow them to keep Nomad zombified, and Yozo stuck close for what dark reason Cavok and Arie could only guess at. As Arie filled Cavok in on their first encounter when Nomad had still been himself, Cavok's disposition grew instantly cold towards the foreigner.

Nomad's chest slowly rose and fell, indicating life at some level. The deep sapphire glitter of the starlight reflecting off countless sand grains gave the slightest indicator that Nomad was not alone under the parasol's silken canvas.

A shifting in the sand, the noise so soft it could have been attributed to a desert bug or rodent, preceded a black shadow that slipped over Nomad's limp body.

Yozo's ice grey eyes shone brightly in the darkness, two calculating gems of hate, peering down on his long-standing grudge. He hovered there, hunched over his kinsman's vulnerable, drug-riddled body, silently taking in the sight, mulling over his options.

A gleam, bright against the black backdrop of the parasol's shade, shone as a stout knife came into sight beside Nomad's face.

"You thought you could escape our land, our people, run away from your failures…." the man whispered, barely mouthing the words. The knife slid up along Nomad's cheek, slicing open the ashen skin, draining dark blood from the incision.

"You started a war and then left us at the mercy of our enemies."

The knife slipped deeper into Nomad's skin, puncturing through his mouth, just below the jawbone. Nomad's eyes lazily opened, a slight grimace accentuating his features.

"Yes," Yozo grinned, twisting the knife blade into Nomad's gums above his molars, carving into the ivory roots before jerking the knife out of the gaping cut he had made.

"Open those eyes. I wanted my revenge on you to be pure, for you to have full faculty of your mind so that you could properly comprehend your disgrace. I wanted to beat you fairly at the peak of your skill—but it seems—" he said, looking down at the exposed skin of Nomad's face, "there is little hope of that becoming a reality now. You are lost."

The blade tip plunged just under Nomad's collarbone, slitting a line that filled with black blood that gleaned like oil in the starlight as Yozo continued, lost in his own speech now.

"Perhaps this is a fitting end of your legacy. This is, after all, all you ever were. A demon who fed upon the good of those around you. Leading them into shit, asking your loved ones to answer for your sins."

Perhaps his voice had risen above a whisper at some point, or perhaps Cavok could sense his slithering presence, but what Yozo had not expected was how silently and quickly the large man could move. Either his carelessness or his underestimation of the fierce man would cost him that night.

Cavok snatched Yozo by the wrist, controlling the knife point, bringing it out of Nomad's chest forcefully. Yozo's other wrist was quick at work, snatching another hilt, drawing it just as Cavok grabbed his other wrist. Though Cavok was fast, Yozo had managed to get the blade out and stuck it into Cavok's thigh.

It would have been a deathblow had Cavok not secured the wrist when he had. The blade slid out an inch, blood oozing forth with the extraction. It was not gushing, however, and with that, both men knew the fight was practically over. Yozo stood no chance against the muscle of such a brute.

Cavok brought both wrists up, forcing Yozo to his feet, dropping the blades as the strain on his wrists threatened to give under pressure. Cavok snapped Yozo's wrists up further than the man was capable of yielding, a ripping sound slowly issuing as his tendons began to tear from the bone.

Yozo kept quiet, though his wide eyes belied the pain he was in. He was struggling to backflip out of Cavok's grasp, but Cavok held him too close to allow him room enough to lift his legs up between him and the brute.

Cavok grabbed the back of Yozo's neck and stepped in. He pounded Yozo in the face with an elbow, knocking the man senseless, sprawling him out in the blue sands. Cavok was mounted on top of the man before he had a moment to collect himself.

He rained down blow after blow to the man's once delicate features, shattering his nose and dislocating his jaw within the first few hits.

Yozo attempted to put up a defense, not knowing where blows were coming from, but at least having enough sense to know to put up a guard; but after a few more elbows broke through, his feeble attempt at a guard dropped, leaving him open for the raging strongman to beat his head in, caving in eye sockets, breaking his jaw, and blowing out teeth, leaving bloody smears all the way up his arms, from fist to elbows as Cavok began to slow, seeing the man had been unconscious for some time into the assault.

"Cavok!" Arie yelled, rushing up over a nearby dune, dropping the small stack of scorpions she had found and skewered as she ran towards the bloody scene.

"What in the world happened!" she frantically let out.

Cavok ignored her, slapped Yozo's limp face to the side, letting out the blood that had pooled in his mouth so that he wouldn't choke, heavily breathing, "You're not allowed to die just yet. We need your filthy magic still." He stood up, looking to Arie who was rushing over to the two downed, bloodied bodies.

"Arie, Nomad's bleeding. I'm no healer," he added, lumbering off into the night, figuring Arie would watch over Nomad now, in case by some miracle Yozo managed to rouse enough to do harm to him.

Blood covered the sands in frightening amounts. The shock of the scene greatly unsettled her, her hands trembling as she searched Nomad for wounds.

Rushing to her pack to grab what few medical dressings and supplies she had brought for the journey, she cursed Cavok openly, who was no longer around, in disbelief at the horrifying scene she was rushing to handle.

"Cavok! You fucking get back here and *help me*!" she screamed as she put pressure on Nomad's chest wound to feebly attempt to staunch the flowing black blood. His bloody mouth was gashed open, leaving an exposed jaw seeping ooze as she worked on his other wound.

Her cries were in vain. Cavok didn't return that long, wretched night.

18

QUIET NIGHT IN SANSABAR

The sun had just gone down, and no one was in sight at the rickety gate along the town limits. Though Sansabar looked deserted and ready to turn belly-up any year now, Fin knew how hardy the people were here, having visited its worn dirt streets many times over the years living in Tarigannie.

With no guard to approve his entrance into the town, Fin strolled right down the main street, trying not to look too nosey while looking for someone who might be able to give him a lead on where his friend was staying.

He was gathering some curious looks from the few locals that were out in the street or sitting out on the front porches of their stores.

It had been a long journey, nearly a week since he had split up with Reza and the others. He had traveled fast and made very few stops.

"Hey, Johnny," Fin called to a boy running past him towards a group of kids playing night games down the way.

"I ain't Johnny! I'm Tim," the kid yelled, looking back only for a moment to correct the strange adult.

"That's right, hey Tim, hold up, I need your help. Looking for Blind Bat Matt. You heard of him?"

Tim turned around, clearly irritated that his time with his friends was being held up by a chatty adult.

"Yeah, I know him. Whatdoya want with him? I never saw you round before," Tim said in a whiny voice, loud enough to draw the attention of a few porch watchers, the exact opposite of what Fin was going for with fishing a kid for information.

"Timmy, I'm just looking for Matt. Just point me in the right direction, then you can go play with your friends," Fin said, trying to keep his voice low, hoping the child would follow suit.

"I ain't Timmy! You can't keep me from going to play with my friends! Think you can force me to tell you where people are, not if my dad has anything to say about it. And he will if you keep talk'n my ear off!"

Fin rolled his eyes, throwing his hands up in defeat to the eight-year-old who stamped a firm foot down. Fin looked around to find all the townsfolk in earshot giving him a hard, distrustful look.

"You always were shit with kids," a grainy old voice sounded from down the street, causing Fin to spin back around to see a familiar, silver-haired man, crinkly white eyes wincing, looking in Fin's general direction.

"Good job making a scene, boy. I swear, the only talent you had was deftness with those blades you pack around. Didn't you pick up any tact since you been on the road?" the black-rag clad man said, stepping out of the shadows and looked to the gawking kid that had stuck around now that things had gotten somewhat more interesting.

Matt reached behind his black tattered robes and lifted a few coins from them, a flash of copper shining dully in the moon's dim light.

"Tim, who be the girl ye got eyes for? Tell me who ye fancy and these three coppers are yours."

"Lissa Hardingwood," Tim said instantly as he watched the coins start to disappear from Matt's knuckles, back into the black folds, halting a moment while Matt stared hard with his cloudy eyes at the boy to make sure he wasn't fibbing.

"Honest, she's the prettiest one in this dump, she got me heart. For three copper that ain't no lie, I swear," the boy answered, manners remarkably improved since dealing with Fin.

In a flash, Matt flicked each of the coins in the air to the boy, little hands snatching them up deftly before the boy bolted off without another peep. Matt stood there with a disapproving look on his face directed at Fin.

"See, he wouldn't tell his own mum that he's got an eye for Lissa Hardingwood. Treat kids like they're adults, and you'll get kids that reply to you like adults. Treat them like kids, and you'll get kid responses. I should know best; I been trying to treat you like an adult for years against my better judgment of what you actually are. Tim there takes a better hint than you do most the time."

Fin was taken aback, forgetting how difficult the old man had been with him and Cavok. He knew, though, even with all Matt's rough edges and age, he was wise, and cunning, beyond even his years.

"I'm in a bit of a pickle—" Fin started, but Matt interjected with a gruff, "Course you are, why else would you be here look'n for me? Cut to the chase, boy, and buy me a drink while you're at it."

"Matt, this is important. Like, *important* important. It's not just about me and Cavok this time," Fin chided, walking now with the shrouded blind man down the street to the dimly lit rundown saloon.

"Where is that overgrown oaf? You two always been inseparable," Matt mused, ignoring Fin's urgent warnings as he made his way slowly up the saloon bowed stairs.

"Cavok should be close to Sheaf right now," Fin answered. He was not sure how to explain and tie in his friend's location with the crisis he was trying to explain to the old man.

"Open that door for me, would ya?"

Fin obliged, creaking open the swing gate and ushered Matt into the saloon. A healthy rank of cheap ales and sour wines permeated the room.

"Matt!" the barrel-bellied man with a handlebar mustache behind the bar shouted, leaving Fin to wonder if the greeting was a friendly one, or a threat.

"Geric, I'm here to pay my tab," Matt slyly winked, patting Fin hard enough on the back to make him take a step forward.

"I'm not here to pay your drinking tab, you slick weaseled—" he started, but Matt cut him off before further insults could be flung his way.

"If you came here to tell me something, we're going to have a drink—I can't listen to you sober—and if we're going to have a drink, we need to pay off my bill in order to do that."

"I only have enough on me for a few drinks," Fin shot out, exasperation starting to show.

Matt stared hard to the side of Fin, squinting as though he was looking right at him. "Pay the man my tab. I'm buying drinks tonight if you want to talk."

"God damn it, you're insufferable," Fin murmured as he walked up to the bar and had a seat on a stool.

"How much does this ol' crook owe ya?" Fin asked, pulling out a side pouch with some copper and silver in it jingling around.

"Fifteen," the burly man grumbled, arms crossed.

"Here," Fin said, picking through, slamming copper after copper down on the wood countertop.

"Silver, not copper."

Fin let out a frustrated sigh and tossed the whole purse to the man. "That's somewhere around that amount. That's all I'll be paying at least."

The stout man opened the pouch, poked through its contents for a moment before stashing it behind the bar, and asked Fin, "Wine or beer?" His voice softened ever so slightly.

"Something stronger than that. I have a feeling I'll need it tonight," he answered, grabbing Matt's rags, pulling him to a seat next to him at the bar.

"Beer for me," Matt said, trying his best to maintain some level of dignity from all the ire being directed at him.

Geric uncapped a brown glass bottle and slammed it in front of Matt, then uncorked a green bottle, took a whiff, nodded his head in approval, and poured the clear liquid in a fat, hazy snifter, sliding it over to Fin.

"I'm only servin' ya because of your friend here, Matt. No more tabs for you, I'll have coin up front before any more service here," the bartender said. He grabbed the coin purse Fin had given him and stepped back into the back room, leaving the two alone in the dimly lit room.

"Alright, you all settled now? Got your little drink, finally ready to have a little chat with me?" Fin asked, more than slightly perturbed at that point.

Taking a long sip of his spruce beer, letting out a satisfied sigh, Matt nodded his head, perkily agreeing, "I'm ready."

Fin took a deep breath. He needed to collect himself. Matt was getting under his skin, and he had been talking with him no more

101

than five minutes!

Taking a swig of the drink, he swirled it a moment in his mouth before swallowing.

Gin. Not his favorite spirit, and not a great gin at that, but having been without drink for two weeks now, it was more than a welcome offering.

He had eaten and drank very little the last few days, and he could feel the alcohol hit his system instantly, a light headrush relaxing his thoughts and stress. All of the travel's cares seemed to sluff off his shoulders as he eased back and breathed deep once more, collecting himself before having to continue with Matt.

"You sure needed that," Matt remarked, looking up, staring at nothing, but listening to Fin's breathing.

"Yeah, Matt—it's been tough. Me and Cavok, we got into some real shit the last year or so. Not the normal hijinks you used to know us for. A real 'end of the world' tangle. We're gathering anyone we think could help. We need you with us. Me and Cavok," Fin said. He looked at his drink a moment longer before taking another swig, "We're nothing next to what we're facing."

"Well," Matt garbled between quaffs of his beer, "I didn't train you two boys for nothin'. I figured somewhere in both of you there was a nugget of potential. What are you tangled up in?"

"Yeah, well it's a long story. You know Reza? That saren we've been tagging along with?" Fin said, looking down at the legs of gin on the hazy glass.

"Yeah, what? She got you into religion? Those sarens tend to be overzealous—not to mention, over *pretty*. You fell for her?"

"No," Fin said flatly, ignoring Matt's jest. "We took a mission to find out what was happening in Brigganden. We liberated that city, but in the mix, one of our friends got cursed by an Illimoth blade. He's turned rotten. Not himself no more. He's drawn to an avatar of Telenth. That avatar is the lord of the arisen that took that city. He's on the run or hiding. We're not sure where he is, but he needs to be stopped, and our cursed friend is going to lead us to him. Brigganden is only a slice of what he's capable of. This whole region is in unwitting danger. Our little force is growing, but we're still under matched to face him. We need your help, Matt. This whole nation is on the line."

"Any payment involved, or is this just a 'hero' kind of job?" Matt probed, looking to the back room. They could hear the clink of glasses and plates sloshing around as Geric began washing the day's dishes.

"I'm not sure yet. I mean, last time we helped with this issue, Sultan Metus compensated us. I'm sure there's someone that's going to pay us this time around as well. What it really comes down to is saving Nomad and stopping the arisen lord before he can ravage the countryside. You've heard of what happened to Brigganden, I'm sure. That's going to be every city and town from here to the neighboring regions if we don't stop him now."

Fin waited for an answer, watching Matt intently as Matt emptied the last drops of his spruce beer on his tongue.

"Not really feeling it," Matt finally said, satisfied that there was no more beer in his bottle.

"What? Matt, the Plainstate is at risk, Brigganden already fell to this monster, and Tarigannie is next! You trained me and Cavok how to take care of ourselves out in the world because you said it was your way of making a difference out there, your little contribution. That maybe someday we would go on to do great things.

"Now I know we haven't really done much good; actually we kind of done the opposite, we got in a lot of trouble for a long while there, but since joining up with Reza, well, this is the first time I feel actually involved in something bigger than a reward, something that could make a real difference in people's lives, and now you're telling me when one of those real 'hero moments' pops up, *you're* not feeling it?"

Matt sat back, looking uninterested now that the beer was gone. He snapped back at Fin with, "Tarigannie may be in trouble and all, maybe even the whole continent, but believe me when I tell you, I don't give a damn. What I care about right now is what I'm involved with, and that's keeping this new group of idiots alive. They're young, and they're full of ideas, but that's about where you and Cavok were when I trained ya. The world can wait. It's always in danger, or at war. Someone's always a threat, and it always turns out, eventually, even if it's a couple hundred years, it always turns out whether you get involved or not."

Fin shot the rest of the gin in one go, forcefully let out a fume-heavy sigh, and placed a disappointed hand over his face. Had he left Reza on the road for this? His friends needed him, and if he came back empty handed….

An old, wrinkled hand patted him on the back. Though Matt couldn't see Fin's exasperation, he could surely hear and sense how crestfallen he was; regardless of if it was indeed Matt who had gotten

Fin into his sour mood.

"Fin…" Matt said in a hushed voice, "I'm gettin' there in years. Not sure I'd be much help to you or your crew at this point," he admitted in a quiet voice, his usual spunk receding as he leveled with his former pupil.

Fin looked at the old rag man, studying his rickety frame for a moment. Matt had indeed aged since last he had seen him. It was the first time Matt had brought up his age as an excuse, and that thought was more than a little sobering for Fin.

Matt turned around, looking to the door as Fin began to hear frantic footfall running up the saloon's porch. Throwing the swing doors wide, a large man, bigger even than Cavok, to Fin's surprise, came rushing in.

"That weren't no bandit troop at the old fort, there's arisen camped there. They jumped us, snagged everyone, shackled 'em. Comon', Matt, we got to go get 'em," the man spouted out, catching his breath afterwards. The bartender came back in the room to see what all the commotion was about.

"Arisen you say?" Matt said, his eyebrow raised in thought.

"Yes. Dead as they come. Up, walking, taking orders from a wicked-looking fellow. Not sure, but I think he's arisen too. Mighty pale. We got ambushed, least they did. I was out scouting the perimeter while they were back at camp. By the time I got back, they were already surrounded. At least twenty of them. Thought it would be best if I came and got you."

Matt had slipped out an old pair of brass knuckles, gouged and well-rounded, and was fiddling with them, flipping them through his boney fingers.

"Aye, probably best you did," Matt said, staring off through the still swinging door. He patted Fin on the back. "Fin, you better had not jinxed us with all that talk of arisen earlier. Show us the way, Cray."

Matt got up, stretching out as Fin remarked, "Us? Matt, we don't have time. I've got to get you to Sheaf now!"

Matt cracked his neck with a loud pop and looked dead in Fin's eyes, betraying how blind he really was, and replied, "If you need me, you have time. Save my boys, and we'll talk about Sheaf and this arisen lord. Till then, use what good sense and skill I trained into you and help me out. I'm not as young as I used to be; sounds like we'll need an extra hand or two for this one."

Fin stared hard at Matt's timeworn face and softened. The man had been like a father to him and Cavok, had taught them and honed their skills. He raised them rough, but it was a hard world that they inherited, and Fin was grateful for what guidance Matt had given them early in life. It was probably due to Matt's care that they survived through that merciless start of life in the city streets.

"Alright, Matt. I'll help you. You had better be there for me and Cavok after this, though."

A slow, wicked smile appeared on the old man's face as he placed his hood up to drown him in a dingy shadow. Throwing his shoulders back sharply, his rags popped behind him, a bit of dust coming off their folds.

Geric shuddered slightly as Matt's ripped physique showed clearly now at his readied stance.

They started out of the saloon, Matt almost smacking right into the doorframe just before Fin readjusted him to walk out the door without incident.

Letting out another long, frustrated sigh, Fin shook his head at the unnecessary delay he had just signed on to.

19

CLANDESTINE ARRIVAL IN SHEAF

She laid the folded silken desert outfit gently down on the newly dusted dresser top. Next to it lay his sword and other personal belongings Reza had gathered before Nomad had lost himself. After standing, looking into the dresser's mirror at herself for some time, noticing how tan she had gotten over the past few months which stood out in contrast against her platinum hair, she sat down to take a moment of silence on Nomad's bed.

Sultan Metus had kept their rooms cleaned and empty since they had left. It had been a kind gesture, though since arriving a few days prior to, she was feeling the pangs of worry and loneliness as no signs of any of her group's return had been announced.

She had briefed Metus on the status of their journey and the severity of their mission and her intentions going forward. She had asked him for help, for him to join their cause, but he had remained unusually quiet and vague with a response. He wanted first for the return of Arie and Cavok and to see Nomad for himself before addressing her call for action. And so, she had been resigned to wait, and rest, both her body and mind needing the reprieve.

She had visited Nomad's quarters quite a few times over the past few days to sit in silence and reflect on the path that lay before them, and to reflect upon her seemingly lost friend.

She had needed the distance from him, she now realized as he continued to spiral down the self-destructive tear he had been on. This did not make her miss him any less, however.

She had told Metus about the destruction and confiscation of the outfit he had had made for Nomad, and suggested something even more durable for next time, and Metus had conscribed the same tailor to immediately set upon making a double-lined, double-stitched outfit, similar to the first, for when Nomad next needed sturdy clothes.

The tailor had just finished the outfit and delivered it to her for safekeeping that morning, and now it lay amongst his other belongings that Reza hoped he would someday come to use and appreciate once more.

A knock at the door brought her out of her reflections. An older man's voice said in a low voice, "Miss Reza, Sultan Metus is calling for you."

Getting up, she made her way to the door and opened it, seeing that it was Garik, the serviceman that Metus had assigned to Reza's group. He was a nice, quiet old fellow. Seemed solid enough a guy, and never pried. Knowing how good a judge of character Metus was and to what caliber of character he surrounded himself with, she was sure he could be trusted at least to some level.

"What is this regarding, Garik?" she asked, closing Nomad's door, locking it behind her.

Looking around to make sure no other residents were in the courtyard, he leaned in to whisper, "Lady Arie arrived moments ago. She's requested a special unit to secretly escort Sir Cavok and company into the palace to keep one of your members discreetly housed. We've made the arrangements but were told to gather you upon their return."

"And Nomad is with them?" Reza asked, excited by the news.

"Yes—he is with them," Garik hesitantly admitted, uncomfortable with the subject, she could tell.

"Let's waste no more time here then," Reza told Garik.

Taking a few side passages Reza was unfamiliar with, the two made their way to the entrance of an underground structure.

Unlatching and opening the building's large, iron doors, Garik offered Reza to go first, which she did. Garik closed and locked the doors from the inside afterwards.

"I've never been here. What is this place?" Reza asked quietly, once they were on their way down a hallway with a few off-shooting corridors.

"I see no reason why you would have known of the foundry. It's a small one, compared to some of the ones I've seen out in the world, but it suits the palace's needs. We produce heat here for various purposes. It's a central furnace, our best blacksmiths use a set of forges here. We have a steam room that delivers steam to some of our more neoteric projects and systems.

"Aside from the foundry, we keep a single holding cell here. We only use it for high-priority persons. It's a secret to all but a few of the senior staff, supposedly. You know how word travels in a court. It should be a suitable place though for your Nomad friend. Lady Arie said he needed to be out of sight and bound, so *the cavity* will have to do."

'The cavity' surely didn't sound pleasant to her, but Reza knew firsthand how uncontrollable Nomad could be, and how dangerous he was on the loose.

The sounds of the forge were slowly becoming more noticeable the deeper they went into the subterranean structure.

They entered a large, open room holding all sorts of piping, crucibles, gears, carts, and tracks; heat workers were scurrying about, performing various jobs, completely ignoring Garik and his guest, fully engaged with their respective heat-sensitive tasks.

It was fascinating seeing all the various trades working so interwoven in one place. Glassblowers were carrying rods of molten glass from the furnace to corners of the room to mash and twirl into various shapes and color patterns; metal casters were pouring molten alloys into molds; blacksmiths were laboriously pounding out lines of bright steels and irons; and a bubbling set of huge copper vats and glassware held boiling liquids, steam piping through tubes through walls into other rooms.

The foundry's main room was busy, but organized, and not overcrowded. It was a place Reza thought she'd much like to return to tour again sometime in less pressing circumstances.

The deep bellows whooshed and whirred in rhythm, fueling the molten flames of the central furnace that spanned half the length of the back wall. It was noticeably hotter in that room, though the ventilation ductwork installed in the ceiling and floor seemed to cut the heat by a remarkable degree to what it should have been.

She stared fixedly at the furnace a moment longer. At first hard to distinguish, what looked like a large, yellow-brown, compacted brick of material, upon closer inspection, Reza could see was a various mash of desert foliage, all compressed into a form-fitted brick of biomass fuel for insertion into the furnace's fuel shoot.

The production line and intelligent designs surprised her, especially since she'd been in the city for years and never once had heard of, or visited, the place where so much work was done.

"This way," Garik softly said, taking her attention away from the workspace and directed her through a dimly lit side tunnel. They left the heat of the burning room behind, the tunnel walls quickly muting the sounds of industry within a few turns.

"Rarely do we use this cell. The last time was when holding a council member from Tarigannie during a brief war. It was more a dispute, really. That was nearly ten years ago." Garik's deep voice droned as they drifted through the dim tunnels, passing only a few side channels that were not lit.

A bright glow of torches lit the threshold up ahead. The door at the end of the tunnel was framed in iron, and as Garik produced a key and unlatched it, Reza could see that the thickness of the door was as wide as her hand. Though not made completely of iron, the door had a heft to it that seemed to indicate the wood was filled, be it with sand or something heavier; she doubted even Nomad's demonic power could punch through it.

The room was domed, and large. Many familiar faces were there, though greeting her was not their first concern—Nomad took the center stage.

He looked wilder than ever. His eyes left streaks of red in the air, an unnatural glow and a demonic aura flickering about his crown. An invisible madness billowed from him, striking prudent caution and fear into those tasked with containing him in the heavy, steel shackles locked tight around his limbs, torso, and neck.

He was ferociously attempting to break loose of his bonds, snapping at his captors, threatening any who dared get close. And there was blood—quite a bit of it too. After her gaze drifted to a bloodied and wounded Cavok, she wondered if most of that blood was his instead of Nomad's.

"Cavok!" Reza cried, startled by the scene she had walked in on. She moved to go to support the beaten and battered man.

"Reza," Cavok acknowledged with a weak smile, attempting to rouse spirit enough to abate her concerns over him.

"It has been a long two weeks," Cavok said, tiredness thick in his voice. His one line spoke more to her of the trials he had been through than probably even a full-length explanation.

Cavok leaned on a guard for support, attempting to move as little as possible as Garik let a doctor and nurse in through the big door. They went straight to Cavok, seeing where they were needed. He had scratches up and down his body, and horrific bite marks and deep bruises speckled his tanned skin. He favored a leg, keeping as much weight off it as possible.

Surely she had seen him with more grievous wounds, but Reza didn't know that she had ever seen the man this exhausted in all the time she had known him.

The doctor immediately ordered the guard to lead Cavok out of the cell and into the infirmary wing in the palace complex, and the small group began to leave.

Cavok paused as he passed Nomad, looking him in the eyes. He wound up and slugged the chained wildman directly on the nose.

"One for old times' sake, friend," he said, a satisfied smile gracing his cut lips, before the guard pulled him rather roughly out of the room, following the doctor and nurse.

Nomad sprung to life again, renewed in his thrashing routine. No one spoke until Sultan Metus attempted to excuse Cavok's behavior. "Looks like he took enough licks to deserve that shot."

Reza looked around, taking note of everyone present now that Cavok was out of the room and with Nomad seeming secure enough to reduce her worries over him breaking loose.

Sultan Metus was there, flanked by two guards, the same personal escorts she had seen accompanying him most times he was out and about over the past few years. Prophet Henarus stood tall and stern to the side of the room with an assistant or cleric of his own, watching Nomad like a hawk. Arie was there, looking terribly sleep deprived and haggard, but standing on her own. Leith, Arie's sister and personal assistant to Sultan Metus, was between Arie and Metus. A disheveled fellow slunk in the back of the room within the shadows, crowblack hair fallen over his face. There were four guards tending to Nomad whom Reza suspected were the prison guards. And then there was a woman and a girl standing between Metus and Henarus, looking quite out of place. Reza did not know them, though they looked familiar enough; she could not place where or when she would have met them.

"Two weeks we've been separated," Reza said, shaking her head in sympathetic disbelief. "What happened to you three, Arie?" she questioned, realizing the horrendous truth of the matter just by the sight of her, Cavok, and Nomad.

Prophet Henarus stepped up, shaking his head as he said, "There is no time for a retelling of things already past. There is a sickness here in need of purging. Reza Malay, Sultan Metus called me here to aid in a healing, but you are a child of Sareth, with a heritage having a long history in healings. Your kind are best known for your ability to cure even the most dire of wounds and illnesses. We're all here to aid you in drawing the sickness from our tormented friend. If we don't act now, those bonds he wears will be broken eventually, and he will escape into the city, and all the death and destruction that follows will be upon our heads—upon your head."

All focus that had been upon Henarus' commanding voice, now turned to Reza for her answer. Everyone there had been gathered to ensure Nomad's containment, but they also were there to gather solutions and ensure that Nomad would not rattle himself or his chains apart and escape, making all their works thus far, in vain.

"I—a healing, now?" Reza stuttered, looking to Arie, Metus, and then back to Henarus as she searched for an answer to a very complex demand.

"He would overtake me, for sure! I've tried healing him of this taint, back when it was less prevalent, back when he still remained coherent as the Nomad we all knew. Now, to attempt a healing, it would take much more than just my life essence to take on that amount of corruption. I would be dead even before making a dent upon his ailment."

A powerful yank at his chains briefly redirected everyone's attention to the steel anchors that strained at Nomad's pull. He had silenced after Cavok's slug, but that did little to soothe everyone's concerns over the chained devil.

"Perhaps you would be overtaken alone, without focus. What if I were to help you to focus your inherent healing abilities?" Henarus probed, his harsh tone a bit softened now, hoping to help with an answer to the problem of Nomad's salvation.

"A focus…may help. I, as most of you know, am not the most devout among my people. In fact, when it comes to healing, I rarely attempt it. There's a balance to it that is dangerous, if not lethal, if you do not correctly account for the flow of aether. There are many factors to remain in control of, and the flow of energy often comes and goes quickly, not giving you time to consider how much to give and when to shut it off. You're not just syphoning your life energy to theirs; you're also taking on a portion of their pain and suffering. Energy, at least in theory, cannot just be made up, though it can be traded, my health for your health. It's—" she stopped, fumbling for words to finish her explanation. "It's a complicated gift. One I was never good at, and if I am to be honest, one that I always feared using."

"We all have fears, Reza. This is nothing to be ashamed of. We are, however, in need of a healer right now. And though Hassome, praised be his name, is a great god, one of peace and clarity, healing is not his holiness's main offering to his followers. I also have attempted a healing upon our cursed friend here, and I know firsthand how limited I am in removing the blackness from his blood.

"What I can offer, though, is focus and lucidity while you perform a healing. Hassome shows us the way, lends us understanding of our own potentials, and helps us to explore, amplify, and master those blessings for good we each have within us. No other god may grant a better blessing of concentration and flow than Hassome, Reza. I believe in you. More importantly, I believe in our deities. Sareth will be with you, and so will Hassome."

Metus placed a reassuring hand on Reza's shoulder. He had not even had the chance to catch up with her. It had been months since her departure. Much was left to be shared between the two, stories and reports, but now, Reza needed support more than anything.

Henarus had definitely made the case for a healing from Reza. It seemed their only option at that point if they wanted Nomad pacified. Reza laid her life on the line for healings for Nomad before, though this time, she was worried the risk was much higher. The chance that she would lose herself in Nomad's endless darkness was, in her perspective, almost an inevitability. She had never had a blessing from a priest of Hassome, and though Henarus' words were spoken with such conviction that that alone seemed convincing, she still was not comfortable with everyone prodding for her to perform a healing.

"Even with added guidance, I believe the amount of aether needed to heal Nomad is beyond what I have to give. Even if I give my life in a healing, he passed the gates of life long ago. He remains living through unnatural means. He would require more than one person has to offer in order to bring him back from the grave. I don't know much of my blessing, but I do know this without doubt. I will die if I attempt to heal him on my own, even with perfect focus."

A low grunt issued from Nomad as he ripped on his restraints. The bolts holding down the chains attached to his right hand shattered the stone they were fastened to, coming loose as the four guards jumped him, trying to hold him down to stop his attempt at breaking his bonds.

"It's only a matter of time before he breaks free. He's too strong to restrain. He will make his way to his master and cause a great deal of destruction and death in his wake," Arie said, exhaustion and resignation deep-set in her voice.

"Cavok somehow resisted him, fought him, day and night. I did what I could, but his raw strength is unmatched. The days were calmer, but the nights. My god, the nights were the worst. He wouldn't stop fighting us. We had help at first, Yozo—" Arie said, looking to the sullied man in the corner of the room, who dropped his head lower to obscure his face at the remark.

"He would perform a ritual that deadened Nomad's will. Soon, he ran out of incense essential for the rite, and we were left to deal with him in his raw form. He's an unstoppable force, at least for the likes of us. A healing is the only option. You *cannot* deal with him in his current state for long."

The jangle of chains persisted as the guards struggled with Nomad, who bucked like a wild stallion attempting to be tamed. One had a full-on rear naked choke, his bicep bulging around Nomad's neck to close off blood and air to his head. A normal man would have succumbed to such an attack within seconds, but Nomad showed no signs of slowing, even as the three other guards wrestled with his arms and torso to try and pin the heaving man.

Reza felt a pull to the ring she wore, a light constriction around her finger, as if the ring began to be weighed down with a hefty aura.

She had half forgotten about Leaf's blessing upon the ring of Isis that she wore. It was shrouded in mystery still, but Leaf had mentioned that it was bestowed with life essence, enough to aid her during her healing rituals that she might be sustained by the life that Leaf and the others imbued the ring with.

She had given strict warning to only use it wisely, to help bring about the downfall of Telenth. Surely now was one of those times, but…however she might call upon the ring's powers, she had not yet made an attempt to do so.

She needed time to prepare, they all did, and Nomad was not

going to otherwise give it to them. She knew now was not the best time to attempt to uncover the secrets of her empowered ring, but there were few other options available to them. She needed spirit aether, and Leaf had said that the life sap could provide her with just that. Nomad was the key to the movement she had taken on, and without any other solutions to calm his raging spirit, all that she and the others had fought for, might very well soon begin to unravel.

Reza was frightened at the thought of placing hands on Nomad once more and tasting of his overwhelming suffering. The last time she had, it had injected despair directly into her soul. She had felt strong before all this, self-sufficient, but facing this showed her how very small and ill-equipped she actually was. It was the worst of times for her, but the thought came to her of Nomad going through that pain every moment of every day—she couldn't stay her hand if she could relieve a measure of that suffering. Nomad didn't deserve his fate. With help, she might be able to turn the tides in this insurmountable war of his.

"I'll do it. Nomad would have done the same for me—it wouldn't have even been a question, with or without help."

A tension released in the room, even Nomad stopped struggling, panting laboriously with the weight of the guards that were atop him.

"We'll clear the room to give you privacy. The last thing you need are distractions," Metus said, waving everyone but Henarus to follow his lead out of the cell.

"I can help too," a small voice interrupted, drawing everyone's attention to the teenage girl that had, until then, been silent.

"Elendium has shown me that I'd help this man in visions. I've seen that I can help. Many interests have aligned here. Please let me play my part."

Though most looked concerned, knowing the danger of getting too close to Nomad in his frantic state, Metus looked to the woman the teen was with. After a nod of approval from her, Metus returned the gesture, coming to a silent agreement on her staying to help.

"I might be able to help as well," came a voice from the shadows.

Yozo still had his hair down over his broken features, but he took a step forward, explaining, "Not for the healing, but a chant. It has seemed to calm him in recent weeks, perhaps that will give you all time to get close to perform the healing."

"Good, then you four, plus Henarus' cleric, will stay with Reza—" Metus started to declare, but Yozo cut him short.

"—I require something in return, however. It should not be an issue if this state is a just and respectable one, one that has some semblance of justice to it."

"And what is that?" Metus asked.

"This man," he said, pointing to Nomad, "has committed war crimes in his homeland. I have been pursuing him for years now to bring him to justice, only catching up to him now. I demand a nonpartisan court to be held. He has evaded justice for far too long. He is clearly not in a coherent state to respond to his crimes, hence why I did not kill him outright when first catching up to him, but if this healing works, the deaths he is responsible for must be answered for.

"If you would lend me your court and judges that we might have a hearing that justice may be meted, the voices that cry from the dust may finally be made at ease, and I—" Yozo broke, a gravel in his voice betraying what composure he outwardly shown, "might be able to finally rest from this godawful task that was placed upon me."

Metus considered Yozo for a moment. "Fairness and justice know no better home than here in Sheaf. These are serious allegations you place upon our beaten friend. I cannot promise you a trial yet, with the state he's in. We have no idea if he will come around to his mental faculties once more, let alone his reasoning and memory to answer for such claims against his character, but if Nomad is indeed a war criminal in your country, then this would change things.

"I can offer to you that we will hear your full story out, and if I and my councilors deem it, and Nomad is healed back to some state of reasoning, then, due to the impractical nature of you extraditing him back to your homeland so far away, we may have a trial here.

"With or without your help here and now, I would still be bound to at least look into these allegations as Nomad has been under my care and service in the past, and those in service to me are usually vigorously vetted. He has been a rare exception to that due to Reza's vouching for him, though now I see, I should have still done my due diligence with looking into his past."

Yozo bowed low, Metus' promise clearly affecting him.

"Guards, Arie, Leith, Ja-net, let's give them the room," Metus ordered. The group headed out, Garik closing the door behind them.

20

THE PURGE

There was a moment where all the group could hear was the hum of the industry, far back through the tunnels, the pounding and rumble of the foundry barely discernible.

That moment ended as Yozo began chanting in a deep, gravelly voice in Nomad's own tongue. Nomad, recovered slightly after his short rest, suddenly yanked so hard on his chains that the block of steel anchor they were connected to uprooted and went flying in front of him, almost hitting Reza. Everyone stepped back away from him as he began thrashing the impromptu chained mace about, threatening any who came within his circle of reach.

Yozo's chanting droned deeper, louder, and Nomad turned, shooting a murderous glare at his countryman.

Nomad shook his head, not sure whether to try to cup his ear to lessen the chant or attempt to launch an attack with the chain and anchor.

Yozo stepped forward, coming closer, Nomad immediately whipping the anchor around, launching it towards Yozo with deadly speed.

Yozo ducked under the taut chain, stepping even closer with the dodge, his hair now flowing away from his face, showing the gruesome totality of how mangled it was.

Reza could now see, as she had guessed as much, that it was indeed the man that had gashed Nomad so horribly at the base of the Jeenyre mountains. She was not capable of much sympathy for him, but the sight of his mangled face struck her, as she had seen him before being disfigured so badly, some of the wounds still seeming freshly bruised and inflamed.

She would have to wait for a later time to ask Arie or Cavok about how he came to be disfigured, and how he came to be a travel companion of theirs.

The deft man slid under another attack before stepping into reach, opening with a slam to Nomad's temple. Perhaps he could have reacted fast enough had he not been weighed down with more than his own weight in steel, or if he had more than one free arm to resist, but he had neither, and the blow, cleanly delivered, stunned Nomad for a moment, giving Yozo a sliver of a second to jab downward into the divot just above Nomad's collarbone, instantly producing a pain-induced roar from Nomad.

The others watched in astonishment as Yozo set his feet wide apart, basing himself for an assault Nomad was not in the right mind to see coming.

Grabbing Nomad's free arm, he slugged him just below the chest, continuing with a volley of blows to the lower abdomen, ending with a sharp thrust of his elbows inside Nomad's thighs. Nomad was stunned, swaying slightly as Yozo slipped under the still secured chains, getting Nomad's back. Now that he had latched on with one arm over Nomad's free shoulder, and one under his chained arm, he renewed his droning chant directly in Nomad's ear.

There was a rally of resistance from Nomad, but to the bystanders, it was clear the assault had taken a toll on his fighting spirit.

A minute went by, the chanting continued, and Yozo rode out the worst of Nomad's resistance. Nomad now only offered weak attempts of escape, his eyes beginning to lose focus, drifting into a hypnotic state.

Yozo looked back to Reza and the rest, nodding through his mantra, telling them that they were clear to begin their rituals.

Reza began calling to her innate healing abilities, reaching for the source of her saren powers. She felt something different there than usual. The ring pulsed, and as she drew into herself, she could feel another's presence—a life energy that was freely lending itself to her. It was a warm, green glow that flowed through the ring, weaving up her arms, deep in her vascular network and into her chest, filling her with vigor. An added brightness entered her body.

As if on cue, Henarus, his cleric, and the young girl began whispering their prayer, their canticle interweaving with Yozo's, each petitioning their respective sources for aid.

Henarus' hands began to glow a fuzzy light blue. He held one aloft, pointing to the heavens, and hovered one over Reza, his fellow clergyman doing the same. Light was drifting down upon her, and it felt as though an eye of understanding that had been there all along without her knowing it began to sleepily open, awakening a state of flow so pure, all fear of failure began to melt away into nonexistence.

Though the young girl's voice was tender and much lighter than Henarus and the others, her purity shown through in a crescendo of a chorus-like note, more voices present than there physically should have been, a warm, golden white light entering the room lighting up the dark corners in a flood of peacefulness and a feeling of rightness that Reza had not felt since her days spent in supplication with Bede. A light so pure that no evil might withstand the assault of that presence for long.

To Reza, it was as though she was caught up in a whirlwind of positivity and endless pure love. Feeling each spiritual note of all united deities with perfect clarity was almost too much for her to withstand.

For Nomad, it seemed like the full weight of hell had been brought to bear on his twisted body. He contorted under Yozo's grasp, this way and that, still in a drugged state, but writhing in searing pain, nonetheless. He seemed shackled and racked by the chains of hell, and she had not even laid hands upon him yet.

Reaching forth her hand, no hesitation to allow her to waver, she soothingly held the crown of his head, getting a jolt of pain from him instantaneously, but the flood of green and white energy soothed the mental throb directly after, blunting the onslaught of darkness as Nomad shook, his eyes rolled deep up in his skull, stretching his jaw beyond what his frame would allow as he let out a howl from beyond.

There was so much to sort through, so much to take in. Normally, it was so overwhelming, she felt as though she had no control over the process, taking in pain and torment and offering uncontrollable amounts of herself all at once, with no filter. Now, however, she felt as though the process had been slowed down, or that she had been sped up, giving her the chance to sort through what to focus on and in what order.

He had so many injuries, some that should be fatal, but the same black tar that held him to the befouled call of Telenth also held him together beyond his own mortal limits. To remove the tar, she would also have to heal his fatal injuries as well, or he would be healed only to die of natural causes.

The ring injected another surge of energy into her, prompting her to move forward with syphoning out some of the webworks of Telenth, banishing the darkness from Nomad's polluted mind, opening his eyes, clearing the red haze that had settled in there for the past month.

A gasp of air and a gush of blood immediately ejected from Nomad's dislocated mouth, a heaping volume of black and red liquid spewing all over the floor in front of him.

The black webs seemed endless, and Reza knew she would not be able to clear them all. She did not linger on that thought, acknowledging the truth of it, moving on to grasp as much mental trauma as she could. She drew as much in as she could with the buffer of the familiar light of Elendium and the shared life force of the living sap.

Wounds opened up, massive slits appearing along his skull and arms, and deep pools of sickly blood drenching his rags as she tore at the walls of corruption in Nomad's soul. The gash in Nomad's back opened, disgorging volumes of black sludge onto Yozo. He held tight, refusing to let go as Nomad continued to convulse and break apart right before their eyes.

Another hellish scream released from his blood-caked lungs, the exorcism at a fever pitch now.

The ring committed one more wave of its aether before going dark to her, and Reza felt the shield of Elendium begin to fade, giving way to the clawing demons at the walls of Nomad's soul. She had to finish her healing before she was overtaken. She was about to stand alone against the full brunt of what resided within Hiro's shackled body and mind.

Having done what she could to reduce Telenth's influence within, she turned her remaining energies to his physical health, which was fast on its way to the lychgate.

Nomad yelled once more, though this time, no hellish undertone sounded behind him. It was a scream of agony, but it was the scream of a mortal.

She had so little time, she knew, and she surged her life into his, recklessly now, the ghostly light of Henarus, the last remaining light, quickly began to leave her, leaving her alone to deal with her task.

"Sareth!" Reza shouted the name of her god in hopes that her simple plea would be heard.

Nomad's wounds began to quickly stitch back up, the white-blue skin that had marbled over the loss of so much blood, beginning to regain hue once more. Nomad's face, once lacerated beyond recognition, began to come together, his jaw snapping back into place. Another gasp, ragged, but deep, rattled his chest to full capacity before letting out a hacking cough. He struggled to breathe as he lurched forward, attempting to sit up, and Yozo allowed him some guided autonomy now.

Reza lost control, her life seeping freely from her without her consent into Nomad. The chanting had stopped, and as Nomad lurched forward, Reza's grip on his skull released, abruptly ending her spiraling connection.

Helping hands caught her just in time before she slammed to the floor, everything turning to black, with whispers of distant demons following her into unconsciousness.

21

AWAKE

"Reza. Hey there, you awake?" Arie's voice called to her, cutting through the veil of sleep just before consciousness.

She groaned in response, not able to quite comprehend words just yet, still struggling to break through the haze of sleep.

"Good. Take your time. You were out for a good while. We've been waiting for you to come around," Arie said, patting her on the shoulder as Reza started to sit up on her elbows in bed.

"Arie, what happened?" she said, rubbing her eyes hard. She yawned as she blinked awake, taking inventory of herself and the situation.

"Here, it's chilled coconut milk," Arie said, handing Reza an earthenware cup filled with a cool white liquid. "You were out for four days, almost five now. The sun is setting in an hour or so. The first day after the healing ritual, you were touch and go. The doctors didn't know if you were going to make it or not, but late that night, your heartbeat, temperature, and breathing started to rouse and remain consistent."

Reza gulped at her milk, so thirsty it hurt as it went down her throat. She knew better than to gorge herself so quickly, but she was so parched that her instincts made her throw caution to the wind.

"Nomad," she said, putting down the cup, catching her breath, "has he recovered at all? I remember—a great deal of blood. Oh god—" she gasped, memory quickly catching up to her of the moments just before everything went black, awash in a tangle of demonic laughter and pain.

Arie embraced Reza. Though she had been outside of the room upon the healing, she had come in afterwards to help carry Reza to the hospital ward where she had been cared for, and there had been blood...*lots* of blood. She knew that whatever Reza, Nomad, and the others had gone through during that ritual had been akin to spending a brief moment in hell. She had heard the howls and screaming and chaos from within. She knew that Reza *should* be rattled from participating in such a traumatic experience.

"It was more than just your vitals that worried the doctors; you seemed stuck in a bad dream. You sweated through that first day, crying, struggling with something only you could see. Henarus came, as did Terra, that young girl that was present with you during the healing," Arie mentioned, not sure if Reza had officially met the young girl yet.

"Henarus had said you had some kind of feedback from Nomad, that your spirit had been *singed*, so to speak, by the corrosion of Nomad's curse. He prayed over you and seemed satisfied once you got over the initial troubles that day that you'd be fine, but still, I do not envy what you bore witness to looking into Hiro's mind and soul. I can't imagine how dark that place must have been before the healing."

Visions of dark things crawling, scratching, slowly making their way up to her came barreling back all at once. Nomad's mind, drowned in blood red. A red doused in rage and pain, the clawing things skittering everywhere. She had only been there a few moments, and even then, she had, for the most part, not been there alone. Elendium acted as a barrier there with her. But for the amount of time she had been there, it had been a confusing pit of despair, spiteful sharp things whirling, raking, searing.

Even as she breathed now, she remembered how hard it was to breathe then. The feeling of ash in her throat, in her sinuses, in her lungs. It had felt as though she had fallen in a sea of ash, falling deeper and farther away from clean air, inhaling it all, but still being allowed to live somehow. So many sensations all at once, it was hard to keep track of it all, and that, for her, made it that much more difficult to find a way out. She had no chance to focus, to escape.

"Yes, I remember now...," Reza voiced, staring off as her thoughts ran amuck with dark imagery and painful memories.

"Nomad," Arie prompted, bringing Reza's attention back to her, "he's doing much better now. He's close to his old self!"

"*Close*," Reza repeated, that one detail standing out starkly to the rest of what she had to say. "He still has the curse then?"

Arie's attempt at changing the tone of conversation to a more positive note, withered. Sighing slightly, she nodded her head. "That wound on his back is still open and bleeding black. He's maybe reverted to where he was before we set out to Jeenyre." She paused for a moment before catching herself slipping into her own thoughts. "He's back, though, for now. You can go see him soon enough."

She looked down to the quilt upon her lap in bed, taking everything in, almost in shock that Hiro, who had been the focus of her life these past few months, was in a better way than he had been.

"We would have never gotten him here if Cavok hadn't of been with us."

"Us? Oh—Yozo. He joined up with you three? He was dead-set on killing Hiro," Reza replied, scooting back to lean on the headboard of the bed, starting to feel fatigue setting in from holding herself up for so long.

"He's been causing a lot of trouble," Arie said, shaking her head, considering what to complain about first.

"He tried to kill Hiro one night. He might never attempt that again—outright at least. Cavok made sure of that, for better or worse."

Seeing that Reza was getting lost in her cryptic comments, Arie looked up, resetting, starting back at the beginning for Reza.

"He showed up when you were with Leaf in the woods—it's a long story, but Yozo followed us and started performing rituals on Nomad, making him docile so that we could actually get some traveling done. We had been traveling so slow, and Castle Sephentho scouts trailed us all the way to Ashfield. We were planning on buying horses there but had to head off trail to lose the scouts. We knew he was a threat to Nomad, but we needed him to keep Nomad compliant.

"We kept watch on him at all times, but he was sneaky, very hard to keep track of. I guess one night Cavok caught him hurting or about to kill Nomad, and so...Cavok did what he does, beat the living shit out of him. I mean, he thrashed Yozo so badly, well, I guess you saw his face in the prison cell."

Arie took a moment to collect her thoughts, her recollection of that night still raw. "He was almost dead by the time I showed up to deal with the mess Cavok left. He was gone the rest of the night, leaving me to worry and attempt to keep both Yozo and Nomad alive. There was so much blood."

She stopped, took a deep breath, then moved on with the story. "He's only been in a room twice together with Cavok. When we were in the jail cell, and the other night when we all had a council. It almost ended in disaster. He drew his sword after Cavok said something demeaning, and they were at each other's throats. Metus almost banished him right there and then, but gave him a warning, and the two are not allowed within sight of each other from here on out while in the city walls.

"He's also been hounding Metus about a trial for Nomad. He's just a lot to deal with right now, but other than him and Cavok, we're all just happy Nomad is up and about, and now you too," Arie said. Reza could tell the relief in Arie's voice was genuine regarding both their revivals.

"I'd like to see him," she stated rather than asked. She tested her strength, starting to sit up in bed, swinging her legs over the side.

"Hold on, Reza," Arie said, holding a hand to her chest, "I need to get the doctor in here to check up on you. Patience. And besides that, we've been waiting for your awakening to hold a council of war, one without Nomad present.

"I'll get the doctor. You wait here until you're called for. I'll notify everyone who's coming to the council."

Reza paused for a moment, considering the implications of a war council as Arie rushed out of the room, leaving her alone. The warm breeze blew in from the open window. The fresh air felt good, her lungs taking it in, affirming to herself the ashen death that she had experienced was all in her head.

She stood up, a bit shaky at first, but after having righted herself, she started to ease into some stretches there in the center of the room in her patient garments.

The doctor came not soon after, commending her for her form, even after a short coma. He was better than most of the medics she was used to, not ordering her back in bed and shoving medicine at her or prodding her in all sorts of places to perform tests.

After a quick checkup, he was satisfied that all she needed was to take it easy the next few days. He had a meal, drink, and a change of clothes brought to her. He left her shortly after so that she could finish her stretches until the meal came.

The greasy, cracked pepper chicken thighs were a welcome sight—her body hungered for dense foods—and the small loaf of the buttered hefty nut, seed, and dried berry wheat bread was gone all too quickly. There was a half cup of wine that loosened her up more than she thought it would, and she downed another cup of light coconut milk.

The meal, and more than likely, the wine, had gotten her in better spirits. She took some time after her meal to wash up at the wash basin that was in the room.

A servant waited outside her room while she cleaned and came in directly after, checking her clothes to her body type with the small wardrobe she had brought with her.

The clothes were too fancy for Reza's tastes, most not all too practical for use, but she ended up picking out a white, wide-sleeved blouse with a black tapered overcoat that hung down at an angle to her knees. The boots and gloves were extraordinarily soft suede, and minus a few cluttering embroidered designs, she thought the wide belt and sandy half mantle to be nice touches to the outfit.

On the way out, the fitter greeted Arie as she came back in to see Reza doing much better than when she had left not an hour before.

"My my, you cleaned up neatly," Arie said with a smirk, approving of the choice of clothing Reza had decided to go with. Arie smoothed down the ruffles along her sand-colored mantle.

"I could have just gotten my old clothes to wear, I didn't need to be given new ones," Reza said flatly, never the one to enjoy the thought of receiving gifts or things for free.

"They're washed, but your old clothes took a beating on the trail. I still need to get someone to patch them up."

"Don't worry about it. I'm clothed, I guess that's what matters," Reza replied, shooing away Arie's fiddling hands, taking a seat on the bedside, still a little weak from the days that she had been out of it.

"So a council, you say? Who's attending? Has Fin made it back yet?" she asked, yawning, still a bit sluggish from the extended sleep.

"Yes, the council. Everyone but Nomad should be there. Fin hasn't showed up yet. I was going to ask you about him. He had said he was going to be watching after you—hopefully everything's alright with him. Cavok is more than in a sullen mood about it all, especially with Fin unaccounted for.

"We've all been waiting for this meeting, so really we're just waiting on you. You feel up to it this evening? That's when Leith said she wanted to schedule it. That will give us enough time to brief you on the details. She'll be wanting to speak with you as soon as possible—Metus too. He's been pulled many ways with all this and trying to run Sheaf."

Though Reza wanted to visit Nomad, meeting with all parties sounded prudent. Nodding her head in agreement, she wrapped her arms around Arie, embracing her for a moment, whispering, "Thanks, Arie, for sticking with me."

Arie was slightly shocked by the sudden gesture, a hug very out of the ordinary for Reza. It was nice to see her give room for a bit of heart for once.

"I'm realizing that each other—we're all we have," Reza said, sitting back in her bed, looking more at peace than Arie ever remembered her being. "That's why we've got to do what we can for Nomad right now. The gods came through in that cell for us that day. It seems we really do have their blessing to go ahead with our course. I actually think we might have a chance at breaking this curse once and for all."

Arie smiled in return, though, to Reza, it seemed she was just returning the sentiment. To have hope for a happy ending at that point after seeing such horrors seemed destined for disappointment.

22

COUNCIL FOR THE WAR TO COME

Arriving in the conference room with Arie, Reza found her scabbard and a pouch of her personal belongings set neatly on the large war table Arie had sent for a bit earlier.

Buckling and looping her sword belt along her hip, tying her pouch along her waist sash, she took out and put on the ring that had once held Isis' spirit within.

Though she no longer felt the woman's comforting spirit, or saw the blue mist swirl about her, illuminating the dark places as it once had, she could feel the ring's power radiate from within, an earthy, raw power lurking just beneath the surface, ready for her to tap into its aether wells upon need.

There was a light knock at the door and Leith entered the room, followed by a chatty Yozo, who seemed in a much better mood than usual—as often was the case when he was in Leith's company, Arie noted.

Leith's and Yozo's attention turned to Reza and Arie, the two

127

newcomers hesitating before quietly attempting to finish their conversation.

"Reza, it is good to see you on your feet. You had us all worried," Leith said, a slight smile on her usually stern face.

Reza nodded, accepting the greeting, though her attention was upon Yozo.

Reza addressed him directly, images still fresh in her mind of how he had sliced Nomad open on the road those many weeks ago. "You share lineage with Nomad, do you not?"

Though his mood had been brighter than usual in Leith's presence, it soured slightly at the mention of Nomad. "To my misfortune, I do."

"It should be no misfortune to be tied to one so honorable as Nomad. He has done much to serve this land and the people that live here," Arie interjected, who seemed more fed up with the man than anyone else in the room.

Yozo's demeanor continued to turn. "With respect, you do not know him as I do. Whatever honor he has shown *this* nation was not present back in our homeland. He did not show honor when dealing with his own people—his own family."

Reza answered for everyone with her reply. "With respect, Yozo, you do not know him as we do. Though you may know his past, we know his present, and in the end, the present—here, now—is where our true identities lie, not in the shrouded tapestries of our past lives."

Yozo did not have a response to their rebuttals, but his mood did not lighten on the subject, leaving the rest of the room awkwardly silent as more footsteps sounded outside, signaling the entrance of more attendees.

Sultan Metus entered, his two sentinels standing guard outside; Ja-net, Terra, Henarus, and a strong jawed, smartly dressed gentleman filed in afterwards. Metus went to have a seat at the head of the council table, instructing all to follow suit.

Everyone settled in at the long hardwood table and the room quieted as Metus began to lay out a roll of parchment that he had brought with him.

Leith, sitting next to Metus, held pen and parchment, ready to jot down notes of the meeting. He whispered a few private words into her ear, meriting a nod from her and a quick response, then Metus turned his attention to the rest of the table, flashing a warm smile to Reza as he made eye contact with her. He cleared his voice and began to address everyone present.

"Thank you all for arriving in a timely fashion. You are all here for the sense of duty you each feel in protecting not only this kingdom, but the regions all around from a common threat of evil that plagues these lands. Telenth and his followers—even his most powerful followers—have no right to our lands, and we will fight for our way of life, freedoms, and the safety of our people to the last. You are some of my finest allies—our first line of defense, and for that, you will ever have the Plainstate's thanks.

"It does sadden me to see some of these seats empty, which brings us to the task of explaining their absence. Reza, most here know why Nomad and Cavok were not invited to this meeting, but I'll explain their absence once more. Nomad refused attendance. He has not expounded upon his reasoning, but we are respecting his wishes."

Reza nodded her understanding, replying, "I might be able to explain for him, though I'm only guessing as to his motives. A dryad in Jeenyre has made me aware that the curse of blood Nomad is under ties him to Telenth's servant, the arisen lord that harried these lands not but a year ago. This link possibly grants him awareness of Nomad's surroundings, conversations, and perhaps even his thoughts. We'll need to be cautious of what we say around him, and even more cognizant of how we go about enacting our plans from here. Perhaps Nomad, in some way, knows this, distancing himself from us to protect us."

"I see," Metus considered, reflecting on the news a moment before continuing. "Cavok is not here tonight, and you'll forgive my frankness with speaking on the matter," he directed to Yozo, "because he and Yozo have been ordered to keep their distance from each other. We will have no more incidences as we did the other night, and Cavok is still recomposing himself after the trials of the road here. He's been disallowed visitation to Nomad as well, at least until I can see a degree of peace from him. He's been awfully agitated. A visit from you, Reza, might do him good when you feel up to it. He could use a friend, and as we are short a Finian, you would be best to fill that role I think."

Reza agreed, voicing that she'd see him soon after the meeting.

"Speaking of Fin, you had mentioned that he had split from you on the trail a few weeks back. What is that about?"

"Yes, Fin had a friend in mind to recruit to our cause. He took off right after we passed by Ashfield in the dunes. I was hoping he'd arrive here soon after us, but it has been, what, over a week now? He said he was heading to Sansabar. Even with that adding many more miles on to his journey than we had left on ours, he is a swift traveler. I was hoping he'd make up the difference, but it may be that it could be a few weeks before his arrival."

Metus considered the information quickly, privately adjusting his plans accordingly. "Fin might miss this operation if that is the case. I hope not; perhaps he'll show up today or we'll meet him in crossing on the road, but time is of the essence, and I have plans to move out very soon. At the very least, I will leave instructions for him upon his arrival here if we do happen to be gone before he gets here."

Reza jumped in before Metus could continue, feeling as though she was missing some information everyone else was privy to. "Operation? Arie mentioned to me that you all have had meetings while I was asleep. What did I miss?"

"Of course, forgive me for jumping ahead. Leith, why don't you run through our previous meeting's notes with Reza briefly?"

Leith shuffled around a few papers she had brought with her, sorting through the stack quickly before clearing her voice.

"Arie, as well as Cavok, and Yozo to some extent, have informed us of the happenings of your trip to Jeenyre, and the unfortunate results you've had with Nomad and his curse. It seems that there's more at stake here than just his soul. The pull of his curse is strong. We believe that this denotes that the one he is drawn to is an equally powerful force in this realm. Nomad's strength he had been given by the curse, before the healing, was unmatched by anything we've seen.

"This development, and your efforts to gather allies to combat this dark force, deems that the forces of the Plainstate become involved with whatever power holds Nomad its hostage.

"We propose a hunt for this force, led by, against my advisement," Leith said, her tone biting in disagreement, "Sultan Metus himself. As Nomad is clearly drawn to this unknown master, we intend to follow him to the source of his curse to dispatch the unwelcome presence from our lands."

A low rumble lightly shook the windowpanes and shelves as Leith finished her summary, as if the one she spoke of executing took umbrage at the speech.

The room darkened slightly as the sun hid behind a grey, heavy curtain of clouds. A light tapping of rain pattered along the wall and windows of the palace as the group sat solemnly there in session.

Reza shook her head. She wanted to, more than anyone, believe it would be as simple as Leith had made it sound, but she had to speak up.

"You make the task seem straightforward—as though this is a mere mortal you face, as though he were a king of a neighboring land. With all due respect, this enemy is like no enemy you've fought, Sultan Metus."

Her comment rustled a few members at the table, but they quieted when Metus replied, "You forget, we've faced this enemy before in battle and claimed victory in the battlefield. I do not underestimate who we face. Telenth and his chosen are terrors of our realm, of almost mythical power. The plan, though simple currently, requires finessing, hence why we're here once more, to go over every detail before we sign on to this duty, that all might be able to execute their role without confusion.

"It is a monumental task to step up to, but I do believe in our own allies strength. I do believe that even Telenth's incarnations might meet an end at our hand if we stand united."

Reza, along with everyone in the room, was reminded of Metus' acumen in persuasion and speech. The perfectly timed pauses, heartfelt tone, his delivery, were all flawless. If she had not faced the arisen lord personally, she would believe that their merry band could take on any horror Telenth sent their way.

"Reza," Henarus said, voice stern as ever, "I understand how you feel about this foe we all face. Without facing him in battle, it is hard to comprehend what sort of power we are dealing with. You have met him, up close. You have witnessed the futility of contending with him on an even playing field. I too have had this unfortunate experience. Near Warwick, the forces of the Plainstate faced him a little less than a year ago.

"You remember it was us who fought his forces off, pushing them south, into the Badlands. I locked eyes with him, and I did tremble. His might cannot be understated. Even myself, a prophet of Hassome, knew how badly outmatched I was to his wicked might.

"Though we struck down his army, I knew that if he wanted to continue the fight, it would be our whole army against him, and I do not know if we truly would have won that engagement. I believe it was of his own free will that he chose to head south, to recoup his losses and to regrow his fell army from scratch.

"If you feel we underestimate our foe, I assure you, we don't. That is precisely why we are mounting an assault on him so hurriedly. We've not a moment to lose. And if we fail, by all reports we've received, it seems that the peoples of the Southern Sands region may be lost to the worshipers of Telenth, and that would be a horrible loss—a genocide of epic proportions."

The tone grew dark, not just from the stark contrast of Henarus' delivery as opposed to Metus', but the rainclouds outside had darkened, a heavier rain smattering the wall and the roof, thunder crackling closer now, gently rumbling the building often.

"Henarus speaks the truth of the matter," Metus agreed. "This agent of Telenth, he is no lackey. There are whispers of him being an Avatar, Telenth's representation in the flesh in our realm. Avatars are precious to the gods that they serve and have a keen connection to their respective deities. If this were true, then we deal not with an independent threat, but with an enemy that is directly tied to an eternal entity, one of the original intelligences. His resources, strengths, army, may all possess a depth that we do not appreciate on face value.

"However, if this entity were to be an Avatar, even Avatars have a history, individual uniqueness, and in turn, a weakness. Having as much information as possible on the head of this army that we face is crucial. For that, I have invited Bannon to the table today. He is my wartime general and is trusted with the recruitment, training, deployment, gathering intelligence, tactics, etcetera, for all of Plainstate during times of war. He has some reports to share with the council regarding our enemy that might be of some use."

The uniformed man took the cue promptly, nodding his head before launching into his report of their target.

"Of his origins and even his name, we don't know much as of yet; though, the peoples of Highguard, our southern regional neighbors, are calling him Sha'oul—"

Reza murmured as she stared blankly at the mahogany table, "Hell raiser…."

The general halted for a moment before confirming Reza's comment. "That's right. Some of the older settlements in Highguard still speak ancient tariganniean. This is what they refer to him as.

"He's been raiding the nomadic peoples of the Badlands, by all reports creating a living nightmare for those unfortunate enough to be in his path. We've questioned refugees from the Badlands and Highguard and many of the stories are similar. Sha'oul and his forces enter a village by night, slaughter who they can, and leave by morning's light. Those who have returned often find no bodies. It is assumed the bodies of the deceased are what make up his army, much like what we were dealing with here in the Plainstate.

"He's growing his forces once more, and not just with standard arisen, but there are rumors that he's creating arisen out of wild beasts to fill out his army—quadspire boar, dolingers, waste worms, sand drakes, and others.

"Judging by the villages that he's raised, his path seems to be heading up through Imhotez Pass towards either Tarigannie or Brigganden once more, though, with his recent defeat at Brigganden, and with it bustling now more than ever with all the refugees it's been getting, I doubt he'll be coming back for seconds just yet with it being so well manned and fortified.

"I'm guessing his eventual target will be Tarigannie, first her smaller towns and settlements, then perhaps one of her forts or even taking Rochata-Ung by surprise if they move fast enough.

"Though their military might is great, they are highly divided right now due to the ongoing rift in their internal politics. With so many factions vying for power, they would be at a great disadvantage when it comes to unverified outside threats. They might work with each other if a known peoples were said to be attacking, but, if you recall, even our state was skeptical when we heard of the arisen army's presence. They may be slow to respond.

"I don't know how much intelligence gathering Sha'oul may be doing, but if he probed his potential targets' weaknesses even preliminarily, Tarigannie is ripe for the pickings under their current regime.

"Their military might cannot be discounted, though. What they lack in camaraderie and unity, they make up for in harshness of military follow-through. Their army is constructed of vicious warriors, many of whom are criminals themselves. They often take no prisoners of war unless it deems useful for them, and they have a well-connected underground information network. If Tarigannie is Sha'oul's target, he may find her people more resilient than expected at face value."

Bannon finished his report, leaving a moment for all to consider the current situation as they were aware of it.

"The Tarigannie people, they may prove to be a useful ally if we can enlist them to our cause. This is a communal threat to all local nations, after all," Terra said in a soft voice, posing the thought to the group.

Leith shook her head, replying, "Mayhaps some of the smaller establishments of Tarigannie, but their people are a hardened people.

Rochata-Ung, their capital city, is governed by a corrupt council. I highly doubt that they would preemptively wage a war on an army that has not proven to be a direct threat to them. There's no chance they would come to the aid of a neighboring nation unless they somehow stand to benefit from it."

"Their leaders are extremely difficult to deal with," Metus added, rubbing his smooth chin as he reflectively pondered aloud. "I've tried reaching out to them in the past, lightening tariffs, criminal extradition, offers for an ambassador exchange program or even establishing an embassy in each other's capital—all attempts to establish an easier peace with them has proved fruitless. They have made no efforts or shown interest in strengthening our national relations.

"That having been said, Terra may be right. We need to at least give them a chance to reject our offer to help form a unified front against Sha'oul and his forces. At the very least, we could but offer them a warning. Maybe they make no efforts to meet him on the battlefield, but perhaps they would remain at battle ready nationwide, ready to answer any attacks on their people."

"An emissary could be there in just under a week, give or take a few days, depending on the weather," Leith supplied.

"No," Metus dismissed. "Our company would be the one to deliver the news, myself personally at its head."

Leith let out a heavy sigh. "I have advised against that line of action from the first time you mentioned it. An extremely dangerous military operation is not a place for the sultan of a nation—"

"—Though I appreciate your concern, Leith, I am aware of the risks, not to my safety, but to the success of this mission. If we fail to put down Sha'oul's warmongering ways…call it a gut feeling, but I fear all is lost if we do not get out ahead of this threat.

"Thoughts of his shadow have been gnawing at me ever since running him off. By all accounts, what we dealt with all those months ago seemed like an aborted, half attempt at a conquest. It had barely gotten underway, and without the valuable information from Reza and company, we would not have had the preemptive opportunity to staunch the warpath he intended leading up to Sheaf. I doubt he will be caught off guard, as he was before, this time around. And the fact that he immediately changed course and began raiding the lawless Highguardian nomads, who have no information network to help give them warning, is a testament to Sha'oul's military shrewdness.

"He was only known to us before today as lord of the arisen. We have never faced arisen here in the Plainstate, at least on a military scale, and it is beyond many generations since the history books and legends say that our land had to stand against the focus of a lord of the Deep Hells. When their eye is fixed, nations tremble and collapse.

"We have all the evidence we need to declare this for what it is, an attack on the peoples of the Southern Sands region. We are, relatively speaking, a small region, a simple-wayed people, and not with the greatest resources or manpower to contend with a god's hand. I would best serve this effort on the front lines, and I would not have even my trusted advisors bar me from lending my arm, my strength, to the cause. We're all in this together, and that includes me. Our fate is joined.

"This, it seems," Metus said, looking to all present at the conference table from all different sects and nations that were present, "we all understand to some degree. Destiny had drawn us together, here, in this room. Let's answer her call clearly. We all have a part to play in the weeks ahead."

The rippling pattern played off the rain-pelted windows, casting waves of shadows along the grand conference table, the room hushed besides the rolling thunder outside.

Though many had comments regarding Metus' speech, Bannon was the first to respond.

"I still do not feel sending you into the heart of Rochata-Ung to be wise. Perhaps an emissary. Do you really need to be within the city limits? You would be making my task of protecting you extremely difficult."

Metus flipped through his documents, finding a letter among them. He held it up and explained, "I received this one month ago from my steward of Brigganden. He informed me that Zaren and Jadu took passage to Rochata-Ung in order to take advantage of the better equipped facilities within the enchanters guild there to accommodate Jadu's insatiable growth in the art. It seems he's taken to enchanting faster than any pupil Zaren has ever trained, and Zaren is the head of a prominent order of magic. His authority and understanding of the hexweave is unmatched. He's surely the most senior member of the high magics that I've ever personally met, and I've held audience with many magicians. If he is this impressed with Jadu's aptitude, then we need to see about recruiting them both for this mission.

"This is another reason I am so set on visiting Rochata-Ung first, before we set out to find Sha'oul, and it is why I intend to be there to ask him personally. Zaren is not the kind to heed the call of ambassadors. I need to be there to plead our cause."

"Having master Zaren and Jadu in our company does little to ease my concerns for your visiting Rochata-Ung," Leith sighed, the mere thought of the pair exasperating her, "but you have the final word on the matter. If it is your full intention to lead this expedition and visit the city, then I would at the least ask of you to allow Bannon to oversee security of our visit."

Though Bannon didn't reply, he nodded his approval to the notion.

"Of course, that would be most appreciated. Hopefully the visit will not take too long. Once we have warned the council of the impending threat, urging them to head up the offence with us in the coming war, and entreated Zaren and Jadu to join our cause, we will straightway hunt down Sha'oul. With Nomad's help, perhaps finding him will not prove too difficult.

"How we proceed from there I expect to be the difficult part. Gods willing, the forces of Tarigannie will be by our side and an opportunity to strike the arisen army will present itself. If not, I am leaving Leith in charge in my absence here in Sheaf. We will have our military at ready to move on a day's notice to call for a mobilization of troops to come to our aid.

"From there we will strategize the best line of attack; though, if Tarigannie is not onboard at this point, they will not like having our army in their lands. Even if I mention it beforehand during our conference with them, they may consider it some sort of scheme.

"We may need to leave them to their own means of defense if they stonewall us. Though their misfortune could ultimately cost us in the end. If they were to be conquered by Sha'oul, he would, in effect, have a whole nation of newly recruited arisen at his disposal. The negotiations will be key, hence why I insist on being there to lead them."

Leith put down her quill and parchment and addressed Metus, "As long as you leave Bannon to do his job with security and heed his council, I would be more at ease. As for seeing to the affairs of the Plainstate in your stead, I would be more than willing to see to the day-to-day and will make preparations with the captains to ensure they are ready to head out upon notice."

"Good, good," Metus said, considering the formulating plan so far. "Though I will lead our company, I will have you oversee the execution of orders when it comes to the troops. Is this agreeable?"

"That is fine. I'll see to the troops as you, I assume, will have your hands full with overseeing Nomad as well as commanding any not within the ranks of our stationed soldiers. Speaking of which, who will be joining as an auxiliary unit?" Bannon asked, asking Metus in specific, but opening the table to any suggestions or volunteers.

"I have no interest in joining this company," Yozo said, a note of annoyance in his voice.

His comment instantly distilled an awkward quiet in the room.

Arie, seeing no one wanting to address the contentious man, asked, "Yozo, though I admit we would not have gotten Nomad here without your rituals, you also attacked him, and would have killed him had Cavok not intervened. That you have a mixed past with Nomad is clear. Your hatred of the man is plain, so my question is: why are you still here? You want your revenge with him? You know what company you are in. We are no enemy to Hiro. This room is filled with his deepest friends. What is it you expect from us? Sympathy? Understanding?"

"I was promised that Hiro would stand and answer for his crimes, and by the sounds of it, there will be no trial any time soon. I had hopes in Sultan Metus to deliver on his word, to bring a criminal to justice."

"You will watch your words when speaking of the sultan," Leith rebuked, and to everyone's surprise, the order did seem to calm Yozo for the moment, causing him to sit back in his chair awaiting an answer from Metus, having nothing else to add.

"I have given more thought to the matter of Nomad's past, and to be frank, Yozo, I have concluded that now is not the time to hold such an investigation.

"Much has come to light over the past few days, and a great charge has been placed at our feet—perhaps the greatest we will see in our lifetime. To slow our plans down to pursue recompense for what your people may have suffered at Nomad's hands I think is a dereliction of the more important duty. I will look into his past, if any of us survive this mission, after all this is over.

"Until then, we could all use an extra hand in confronting Sha'oul. You've handled Nomad at the peak of his madness better than anyone. You would be compensated for your service—"

Yozo's face contorted as he slammed his hand on the table, cutting Metus short. "—I do not want money. I want vengeance!"

The tension in the room escalated immediately, Bannon standing at ready in case Yozo meant to carry on further. Seeing the room at odds with him, Yozo settled himself once more, spitting out, "It is clear I will not get it here. You risk your lives for a murderer. You don't wish to save this land from evil. You just want to hold to what corrupt power you already hold here. I'm done wasting time with this council."

The room was dark, and the downpour was constant against the palace walls as Yozo stood and stormed out into the hallway, breezing past the two sentries who peeked in to make sure all was well within the room before returning to their post. They watched as Yozo exited the building, a floor below, out into the monsoon's fury.

"Shame. I know he has the deepest contempt for Nomad, but he proved useful, and could have proved helpful to our mission. Though I suppose, at the least, Cavok will be pleased," Arie said, breaking the tension in the room as she took a calming breath.

"Yes, it is a shame. Though I sense a great deal of darkness and anger in him, I think there's a decent person deep down," Metus mused, stroking his chin in thought. "But we have no time for dallying with those who are not fully committed to our cause. Asset, or liability—no use in considering which Yozo *would* have been now.

"Let us return to matters at hand. Bannon will lead the company of soldiers. Since we're keeping the numbers low and manageable for swift travel and low upkeep, I motion we employ the Hyperium for this mission. As most of you know, they are my personal division. I have seen to it that they received the finest training, and as their number is one hundred, their size may suit our current need perfectly. What say you, Bannon?"

Bannon replied without hesitation. "I would have no other division for this mission. A fine choice. And who will be in the auxiliary unit besides Nomad?"

"Yes, let's go through the charter of who all will be joining this company, aside from those already declared enlisted. I'll take lead; Nomad will be with us, of course. Arie and Cavok as well as they already have experience in handling Nomad—if in fact he does start to relapse as we're on the road. Reza, I'd like you by my side as the lead commander of my two personal guards. You have the most field experience with the enemy we face, and I'd like your voice present on matters. Henarus, how many clerics will you require? It is a religious foe we deal with after all, we'll need divine aid to combat their demonic forces."

"One cleric and myself should suffice," Henarus answered.

Metus was slightly taken aback, not expecting such a conservative answer. "Though we're traveling light, to have so few members of the faith sounds under precautious."

"Our faith is one of clarity, not combating the evils of the Deep Hells. We can aid those who do, however. We have one already assigned to the party. Reza is a saren knight. Their order has a long tradition at casting light into the dark, ridding the world of the otherworldly evils that constantly attempt to gain a clawing foothold here in Una," Henarus offered.

Reza seemed uncomfortable at the remark, even more so with Henarus' confident stare.

"And there's one other," he said, looking to Terra, the whole room centered now on her and her mother.

"You are suggesting Terra join us?" Leith questioned, unconvinced. "She is a child still. To send her on a journey so dangerous is folly."

Others at the table shared Leith's reasoning, but Reza intervened before the conversation could go further. "Henarus is right. She could help, greatly. I know the power of Elendium. Bede called upon his light many times in the past," Reza stated, giving Terra a look of confidence, similar to the look Henarus had given her. "If his presence the night of the healing is any indicator of how close she is to her god, then she has potential beyond any I have come across in her faith, perhaps even Bede. I vouch for her to come if she is willing. Who are we to refuse her?"

Leith's expression was one of doubt as she argued against the two. "There are hardships present in this journey that I doubt a young one can handle, and I worry about adding any unnecessary burdens to our already difficult task, but it is not my call to make, that decision lies at Sultan Metus' discretion."

Metus looked to Terra, then to her mother, considering the council's input.

"I was the one that sent word to you of your mother's death, Janet, and I was the one who allowed your presence in our assemblies and secret rites, Terra. I did so at first out of respect for Bede, who was a fierce defender of our people and lands, but when I saw your favor with Elendium, I began to wonder if the fates, or gods, were bringing you here at this time for a divine purpose.

"I believe, Terra, that you have a role to play in the upcoming events. I know your church is going through difficult times, internal corruption running rampant. Though you hold no recognized office in your faith, I believe Elendium will choose who he will, regardless of the clergy's designations and structure. Though you're young, if you promise to pitch in and carry your weight, and you truly wish to join our cause, I would welcome you to our band—that is, if your mother approves."

Metus' invitation was met with smiles from Terra, and her mother, Ja-net, who gently voiced a few words in response. "Terra had had powerful visions from Elendium since youth. I've known she was destined to play a great role in Elendium's wishes here in Una. Though I do not possess as strong a connection with the father of our faith, I do know this is where she should be—with you all.

"Please take good care of her. She is my only child and means more to me than life itself—" Her voice began to choke, emotions attempting to halt her speech. "May she serve beside you, Reza, as firmly as her grandmother did. Bede will be with her, and I know she will always be with you. She cared much for you, Cavok, and Finian. I think you three knew her better than we did towards the end."

Reza bit down on her lip, having to break eye contact with Ja-net to control her emotions, which were still fresh concerning Bede and her passing. Arie reached out, placing a comforting hand on her back in support, attempting to comfort her through her bittersweet resurfaced memories of her dear friend.

"We shall all look after her as though she were family," Metus kindly said, drawing the attention away from Reza to save her discomfort.

He issued a hopeful breath, feeling plans were finally solidifying and coming together. "Then it is settled. We add Terra to our company. Strong and varied are the alliances we have converging on this most important mission. I look forward to working with you all and seeing the threat that Sha'oul poses to each of our peoples soon shattered.

"Now, every day that goes by is a day that Sha'oul harasses the people of Highguard and moves closer to Tarigannie. I propose we set out by tomorrow evening. We should be able to finish our preparations for the road by then and make it to Viccarwood by midnight. Any opposed?"

Knocks on the table came as the gathering agreed to the proposed plan, and Bannon added, "I will begin immediately to ready the Hyperium. Shall we all meet in the great hall tomorrow at noon to head out?"

"The great hall? Yes. That would be an appropriate location for a departure feast. We'll need our strength for the road, and it has been a long time since we've gathered to break bread there," Metus said, smiling at the resolution in the direction they had charted.

It had been many, many years since he had been out traveling the countryside, a life of adventure and daring having been a foreign daydream to him through the years of routine, though equally important, legislative oversight. He knew their path was one of dire risk, but he admitted to himself, the thrill of it all had roused a wanderlust that had remained dormant within him these many years that he had held the title of sultan.

23

COMPANY IN THE RAIN

The rain rushed down upon Yozo with such force, the cloak he wore was fully soaked within moments after exiting the palace, adding pounds onto his clothes as he trudged through the obscuring storm, seeking a path to his apartment to the side of the courtyard.

After grabbing his things, he'd leave these walls and never return. The sultan of this land held nothing but his own self-interest, Yozo had learned, and he would not be any closer to finishing his forsaken task of bringing Hiro to justice for all the wrongs he had allowed to befall his—their—family.

He had shown mercy to Hiro upon first meeting him those many weeks ago; though, perhaps it was not mercy that stayed his hand in cutting down Hiro where he stood. If he was to be honest, what caused him to hold back that day on the road was his need for Hiro to suffer the consequences of his past.

It had been clear upon their first meeting Hiro's mind was compromised, and he doubted that Hiro had been able to reflect clearly on the guilt that Yozo intended to instill in him. He wanted it to burn Hiro, like the pain of his actions had caused Yozo's life to burn all those years.

Though it wasn't yet night, the evening was drawing to a close, and the heavy rain clouds stretched all across the sky, with only a few patches allowing sunlight in through their dark folds. The red sand washed over and through the stone brick path, dyeing it a dusty vermilion, draining downhill like blood staining the walkway.

A voice, close, quiet, but not imperceptible, called to him.

"You come back here…or go after Nomad again…and I'll kill you."

Yozo stopped in his tracks. He was not one to be snuck up upon. He had perfected the art of stalking, escaping, skulking, keeping from being noticed. He knew the voice which spoke. He knew it because he had almost been beaten to death by him not long ago, his wounds not completely healed, and his face most likely permanently disfigured. He was the only other man he hated more than Hiro, though he was not afraid of Hiro….

He turned to face his stalker. Cavok, with no shirt over his muscled frame and tattooed body, was looking down at his clenched fist rather than at Yozo, rain matting the tuft of crow-black hair above his forehead, water, like tears, weeping down over his eyebrows, nose, and chin.

There was no anger in his voice, or wicked glee, only a calm resoluteness that was jarring, even to Yozo who had received death threats more times than he cared to count.

The tattoos along his forearm began to glow a dull blue, like flowing ice running up and down his flesh, pumping into his hand, steam rising from his clenched fist before the vapors flickered out, absorbed in the heavy rain.

For a moment, Yozo considered drawing his sword, but the notion passed quickly. He knew of no other outside of his homeland that could beat him in a draw. His swiftness and technique had yet to let him down on the open road in the past years. But with this one, he dared not challenge—not yet at least.

"I will not be returning…as for Hiro—" Yozo paused for a moment, considering how wise it would be for him to finish his statement regarding his kinsmen, "—I make no promises."

"I do," was all Cavok had to say, releasing the glow along his sleeve of tattoos, slowly turning, walking back down a dark alley amongst the apartments, sheets of rain obscuring him within a few steps, leaving Yozo on edge and alone.

If he was to deliver his revenge to Hiro, Cavok would need to die. Sooner or later, they would have no civilities left between them, and

Yozo feared that he might not yet be up for that duel.

24

A THOUSAND SHADES OF THE SUN

The three were drenched in sweat. The night had been cool, chilly even, but upon the rise of the morning sun, their fast pace began to exhaust them.

The Tarigannie sun was known for ending the unprepared travelers in its endless dunes. Luckily for them, the trip to Fort Branchill was not that far off from Sansabar, and there was somewhat of a trail to guide them there.

Though there had been downpours in past days, there was a crystal-clear sky this day, and the smell of the desert dunes awash from constant showers lent a pleasant fragrance to the air, though that smell was becoming increasingly harder to appreciate through the stench of their own odor.

The bright sun glittered off all the grains of sands, acting as miniscule mirrors, all seemingly pointed directly at them, blinding them, making it difficult to keep their heading straight. For the most part, they simply followed the weathered trail and trusted that they'd show up to their destination before long.

A vulture swooped past them, startling Fin and Cray, Matt the only one to not bother following the bird's flight path. He already knew where it was headed.

Ahead in the far distance, past a mirage pool or two, stood Fort Branchill, buzzards flocking there from miles around. The stench of the place drifted a mile or so to alert Matt of the stank of corpses, though it would be a few hundred feet more before the scent registered with Fin and Cray.

"I hope that smell on the wind isn't your friends, Cray," Matt croaked, taking out his canteen to gulp down a few mouthfuls of water.

"They were seized not too far from here. I assume the fort is where they were taken. If they're not there, well...maybe we'll find some clue as to where they were taken," Cray reported, staring fixedly into the blinding horizon, hoping to see a sign of his friends. "God damn it! I should have followed them instead of coming to get you— I knew that halfway back to Sansabar. What if we lose them! What if Malagar, Wyld, and Hamui are lost for good because of me! I'd never forgive myself!"

"Hold it together," Fin said, patting the large man on the shoulder, attempting to lend some support to the man's guilt-racked mind.

"Aye, do as Fin says," Matt agreed, the two at least outwardly quieting Cray's worries.

Fin patted himself down, checking all his gear to make sure he was ready for an assault on the old fort.

He had been to Fort Brackhill before as a squatter. Not for very long, but it had proved a nicer camp than the barren dunes.

In times of war, it was a strategic location for Tariganniean troops to base out of, but since war had not raged in Tarigannie for many years, all military was either stationed at Fort Wellspring or Rochata-Ung, with only the occasional temporary occupation of Fort Brackhill. As a result, it was a location that was known to house wanderers, drifters, or the infrequent bandit tribe.

He knew that if in fact an arisen troop had taken up station in the fort, they would have a good defensive structure as their advantage. The sparse landscape surrounding it left little cover to conceal their approach. If they had sentries, it would be easy to spot their advance.

"What's our approach, Matt? They'll be spotting us before long if there's an arisen troop there in that fort. I doubt the cover of night is going to help. Those things, from my experience, see just as well in the dark as in the day," Fin voiced, now finished checking his straps and pouches to ensure that they were all secured.

"There was 'bout twenty that took the others that night you say, Cray?" Matt asked, stroking his chin in thought.

"Yeah, 'bout that many. That was just the group that showed up at our camp."

"Fin, you fought arisen, you say? How dangerous are these things?" Matt queried, pinching Fin's elbow for a response.

Fin pulled his arm away. "Not much of a threat, the troops that is, but the leaders, some of them get nasty. Most of them know a bit of magic—annoying magic at that. Once I got hit by a blast from a wand that numbed my whole side—"

Matt interrupted Fin's rambling answer. "—Yes, yes. Expect a few zealots, got it. If they're there, we'll be spotted from the road for sure. We could at least attempt for an undetected entrance from the east and scale the wall."

Fin considered the line of attack for a moment and made a suggestion. "How about the west wall instead. The dungeon and jail cells are on that side. If they're keeping your friends secured, that's where they'd keep 'em."

"Ah, you know this place well, Fin? West side it is. Hope you two don't mind a bit of sand in your boots. Let's get off this trail and come around from that direction then," Matt agreed. The three of them all trekked off the trail into the dunes, making their way slowly ever closer to the fort.

The walls were well covered, slits along them allowing sentries to have a good view of the desert without exposing much of themselves. It took until they were close up for Fin to notice that there was the occasional movement within the fort.

"I make two on this wall. There and there," Fin whispered, pointing to both ends of the wall. "They don't move unless they have to, so it's hard to tell, maybe best to plan for three. I say we scurry up the corner over there on the south end and take out that guard first, then make our way into the dungeon entrance below. Matt, you want me to go first, or you?"

Matt cracked his neck, popped his knuckles, and whispered back, "There will be plenty of skulls to go around, it seems. You take point, boy. You know the layout better than us anyways."

With their approach and formation settled, Fin nodded, clapping a reassuring hand on Cray's shoulder. Telling Cray to follow behind him once he gave the signal, he took off sprinting through the troughs of the dunes, trying to, as much as possible, keep his approach concealed from the fortified turrets.

The guards seemed unaware as he slinked from dune to bush to dune. It was a difficult approach, and he knew how well a vantage point the fort walls offered, but either to his skill as a sneak, or their ineptitude as sentries, no alarm had gone off as he hugged the fort wall with his back. He could no longer see Matt and Cray from where he was. That would change when he began scaling the wall. After the first guard was taken out, he'd wave them forward.

Scooting over to the edge of the fort's south side, he peeked around the corner—no guard stood at the south gates that he could see. Shielding his eyes from the noonday sun, looking up the fifteen-foot climb, he picked his route of jutting stones to scramble up.

Fin came into Cray's view halfway up the wall, and as Cray peered through the sagebrush him and Matt were hunkered down at, he detailed the scene for Matt as Fin soundlessly managed up the wall, pausing just next to the place where Fin had said there was a guard stationed.

"Sounds like he's about to make his move," Matt mumbled, placing a hand on Cray's shoulder to get his attention. "Soon as he goes for it, we need to get moving, because either way, he takes the guard out or doesn't in time and the alarm goes up, he'll need us at his back quick. Ready, Cray?"

"Yes," Cray offered, his heart pumping loud enough for even Matt to hear.

There were few sounds for Fin to pick through, the endless desert breeze brushing against the only structure to impede its wanderless path for miles and miles. He waited to hear the clink of chainmail on cuirass, locating where his target was on the other side of the wall, then swung up and over the lip of the parapets, coming down beside a man in armor.

He didn't take the time to identify the finer details of his target, plunging his knife that he drew midair deep into the neck of his victim, slitting through his spine, a spark of blue popping off as the standing corpse instantly fell limp. Acting quick, Fin grabbed ahold of his target to let it down quietly to the ground.

Looking down at the thing's face, it was clear now that all that Cray had warned them about was likely true. The rotten face of a person—man or woman, it was hard to tell from the bloating—lay lifeless on the ground, maggots spewing out of the slit wound on its throat, causing Fin to unconsciously swipe clean his dagger twice along a piece of cloth and throw an elbow up over his mouth and nose as he looked into the fort to assess the scene.

His location was somewhat out in the open, the courtyard visible down below. He could see glimpses of other arisen down by the south gate. Thankfully they were looking to the southern road.

Waving for Cray to move up, he considered relocating the corpse on the ground. A second glance at the rotting face and the gore oozing from its pinched, bloated body attempting to escape its armored shell, and he decided against touching the monstrosity.

He looked down to the other sentry on his stretch of wall. Fin could only see his back half, and as of yet, he seemed inactive.

It appeared that his location was not within any of the other guards' sight, but all they needed to do was take a step this way or that way, or even turn around, and he'd be spotted. Luckily for him, the arisen in the fort seemed content with attending to their post with unwavering focus. He just hoped they didn't do post shifts too often. He had, after all, seen movement earlier before scaling the wall.

It was sooner than Fin had expected when he heard Cray making his way up the wall face. Fin helped ease the large man over, and Matt snuck over directly behind him. He worried all the movement was going to alert someone, but there was no way around it. With a group of three crowding around on an exposed wall top, their only course was to get moving to where they were going, fast.

He crouched over the ledge, hanging for a moment before letting go, landing quietly. He looked around from his new vantage point. Finding it clear, he waved Cray down. His descent wasn't loud, but compared to Fin and Matt, the heavy footfall, even with Fin attempting to ease his weight, was noticeable, and the three quickly rushed into the doorway that Fin waved them into, hearing movement by the gate as they made their way into the cool shadows of the fort's many rooms.

The alcove led them to a heavy door Fin knew to be the dungeon entrance. Testing the handle, he found it open and led Cray and Matt inside, barely closing the door before a loud crash caused Fin to cringe, turning to see Cray had slammed an arisen's head into the stone wall, its skull and brains now smattered all along the hallway.

"Maybe you could be a little *louder* next time!" Fin hissed, peeking out the door they had just entered to check for movement. "Outside seems quiet enough," he whispered and rushed down the hallway towards the cells to check on any other guards before Cray could get to them.

"Outside's not quiet," Matt said, pulling Cray over to the door, ordering him to hold it closed.

"Fin, find out if those boys are here and bust 'em loose. We'll need backup," Matt called. Fin was already off down the hall, tossing a dagger at the throat of a stumbling arisen attempting to make its way towards the intruder.

The dagger landed off-center, sticking into the spongy flesh of its contorted face, affecting its advance. It lurched towards Fin, which he easily ducked under, getting around the mockery of a person, hooking a leg around it and pushed it forward to trip it as he rushed past.

The guard smeared against the wall, fumbling to regain itself; by the time it did, Fin was deep within the dungeon complex. It got up, beginning its mindless journey to hunt down the fleety intruder.

"How thick do you think this door is?" Cray asked, an axe head immediately answering him as it splintered through a slit in the door next to his shoulder.

Matt slid on his brass knuckles, stretching out his arms and legs, popping his joints loudly as he calmly gave Cray orders.

"Use your foot and hands to jam the door at its corner, Cray, you're going to get slashed holding it with your whole body like that. Give me half a minute, I'll be limbered up by then."

The moans and scratching outside the dungeon door began to amplify, repeated slams on the door making it difficult for Cray to pay attention to his mentor.

"They were on us so fast! I thought the plan was to sneak in and sneak out?"

"That *was* the plan. Maybe if it was just me and Fin, we'd be in and out by now. I still need to teach yer fat ass how to keep quiet though," Matt grumbled, twisting his neck almost completely back.

Hopping lightly from toe to toe, Matt shook loose his upper body and announced, "Alright, I'm ready for 'em. Hope that was enough time for Fin to try and find your compadres. You ready for a fight, boy?"

Another axe head slipped into the beaten door, breaking open a large hole as it left. Cray jumped back as a sword jammed through it immediately after, threatening to stick him.

The five arisen that had been working on breaking the door down slammed it wide as the first two came in, sword point leading the way. Cray stepped back, drew his two short swords, and parried the point into the side of the wall, hacking the dead-man-standing solidly in the neck, severing what flesh was left on the corpse. The other stumbled over his fallen ally just as Cray turned to dash back behind Matt.

A heel slammed into the jaw of the closest arisen, snapping its head sharply back, sending it barreling into the other approaching armed guards.

"I'll keep 'em busy. You go see where Fin's off to," Matt ordered, his feet shifting slightly, entering a stance Cray knew to be as a defensive one.

"I can't leave you here alone. You go, I'll hold them off."

"Damn it boy!" Matt spat, kicking the knee in on an arisen who stumbled over the congestion in the hall, crumpling it in on itself. "You think I'm going to get far running through that dungeon? Need ya be reminded that I'm blind? Get! Do as I say!"

Cray hesitated for a moment longer before Matt turned with his dead eyes and gave him a murderous stare so chilling that the next thing he knew, he was rushing off the direction Fin had gone to get help.

25

A BITTER DEPARTURE

"Off the road, rat!" a sweaty, portly wagon rider yelled, whipping his horses to speed up, causing Yozo to trip forward, dropping some of his belongings to avoid being run down in the lower streets of Sheaf.

He collected his things with a sneer on his face. He despised the looks he was getting from the others in the street, either due to his foreign heritage, the disfigured face he was recently given, or simply because that's what people did here—looked down in disgust on those who were in a rut.

He quickly stashed his purchased flour, rice, and prickly pear vodka back into his satchel. He was lucky his spirits and water had not spilled; the two cost him a great deal. He didn't care to spend what coin he had left on replacing the commodities.

Someday he may attempt to set his nose properly, or even search out someone to help correct the fractured, poorly mended facial bones to return his appearance somewhat to what it used to be, but now was not the time for that. He would wear his mutilation as a reminder—a reminder of the one who had given it to him, and a reminder of Hiro, who had caused him, in the first place, to leave his homeland all those years ago.

How he would pay them both back, he wasn't quite sure of yet, but one thing was certain, Hiro had enough allies currently to ensure his safety.

If Yozo was a master of anything, though, it was patience and timing. He had waited all these years for the proper intersections of fate in which to deliver justice to the one who had ruined his family's lives; he could bide his time a bit longer.

He knew where they were headed, he knew their plan, and he knew their goals. This was a tremendous insight that the others would not consider or prepare for—all, except for Cavok.

Receiving more dirty looks from street-goers, he slid his hood over his head, letting down a fan of silken hair over his face. If the locals cared so much of how he looked, then let them not see him. He knew how to disappear. Those who took upon them the life of the road have to adopt that skill fast.

His thoughts returned to Hiro, which helped him to ignore the hostility from those around him. He often thought of Hiro. In a way, he kept him going. The rage he felt when he considered his slights fueled him forward—gave him focus.

Coming to the gates of the city, he passed under them without even meriting the eyes of the guards high above him on the wall.

He would wait for Hiro's merry little band to putter themselves out in conflict with this Sha'oul they worry so much about. He would be in the wings, ready to make his move if the opportunity permitted. If he could find Sha'oul's army and keep his distance, Nomad would not be far from him. He witnessed the pull to Nomad's new master firsthand. He did indeed seem helpless to ward off the call.

He looked back on the sprawling city, considering the lights as they flickered, renewed for another cool, spring night. The place stood out in stark contrast to the dark, barren road ahead of him, leading him to Brigganden.

26

ASIDE A HEARTH ON A RAINY NIGHT

She admitted to herself, she was afraid to see him. No matter how well Hiro was doing, no matter how distant his curse was, he would eventually revert, and what hope she had regained in his remission would all come collapsing in on itself.

Not even stopping at her apartment, she had come straight to his door. She needed to see how he was getting along.

Knocking gently, Reza huddled under the eaves as the nonstop rain kept pouring down in the courtyard.

The door opened. Nomad, seeing that it was Reza, warmly smiled. He looked tired, dressed in loose, comfy lounge clothes, the soft cotton tunic and kurtis contrasting with Reza's soaked court clothing.

"Come, come," Nomad said, welcoming her in, closing the door behind her. The warm candlelight and small hearth in the room turned everything a hazy amber.

"Lady Reza, good to see you up," sounded a familiar voice from the corner of the room.

Garik got up from his seat, walking to join the two at the door.

"This was the last night I was to watch our young lad to make sure he recovered well," Garik said, firmly patting Nomad's shoulder. "He's doing well, and if you want, you can take over for me for the evening. I'm sure he's sick of my company. I've bored him for days with stories from my heyday."

"I…suppose I could stay with him," Reza stuttered out, standing there dripping wet.

"I'll make sure there's a guard on duty in this complex just to be safe," Garik said, tugging on his brimmed storm hat before nodding to them both. "Nomad. Lady Reza." He left them, quietly closing the door behind him.

Nomad enveloped her, hugging her tight, her wet outfit and hair soaking into his dry, soft clothes.

"Your presence was the first thing I was aware of when the red mist faded. You have no idea how relieved I was when you came to me. It was…an inexpressible relief. I will forever be in debt to you."

"Hiro…I'm getting you wet," she said, standing there, arms out, trying not to soak Nomad.

"Ah, forgive me," Nomad said, slightly embarrassed by his forwardness, releasing her.

"Let's get you dried off. Here," he said, grabbing a set of harem pants, a smock, and a towel for her from the dresser. "These might fit you. They're a bit small for me, though they look comfortable enough."

He left for the back room to allow her privacy as she changed out of her drenched outfit and into a dry one.

She peeled off the layers of clothes clinging to her body. Flopping them in a heap, she wrung her hair and slicked the water from her skin, grabbing the towel to pat herself dry before putting on Nomad's dry change of clothes.

She could have used some dry smallclothes, but under the circumstances she supposed she would go without as she wasn't going to ask Nomad for a pair.

Opening the door, wringing out her wet clothes outside, she took them over to the washroom and opened the door on Nomad. Squeezing around him, she flopped them over the side of the tub as he helped her spread them out.

Reza idled on the last garment, thinking of what to say to him. She turned to him in the cramped room.

155

"Hiro, I—um. I'm not sure where to start. I'm glad you're back with us. You put us through a lot…" She trailed off, trying to put into words her heart.

"Ga! It's not *you* that put us through it. It's that damned Sha'oul—"

Nomad cut her off, holding a hand gently to her mouth. Lingering a moment as she silenced, he slid it down to her hand at her side.

"I need a rest from those thoughts, at least for one night. He's stolen the last few months of my existence. Not just the waking moments, but in my slumber as well. I wish only to be in your company tonight, not his."

She felt foolish—selfish—bringing up her tangled knot of troubles to him the very first moment she had time alone with him in weeks. Though they both were hurting and dealing with difficult troubles, she knew that he needed her strength and comfort at that time much more than she needed his.

Reaching around him, she embraced him, his warmth seeping through the layer of clothes between them. It was a nervous hug. She had never had a knack or desire for intimacy, but as his arms smoothly wrapped around her in return, the tension melted from her slightly shivering frame.

She had peered into his vision during the healing, and she had been awash in the searing pain and duress that he had been subjected to constantly over the past months. She could only imagine how he felt now, to be free of control and from having his senses hijacked. He was able to feel the warmth of a hearth, the pleasantness of a quiet evening, the loving touch of a friend.

He placed a hand on the back of her damp head, placing his nose to her hair, smelling the desert rain that had a slight floral note mixed with her scent.

A head rush of feelings and emotions dizzied her as his warm hand slid from her hand to the curve of her hip.

She wasn't sure what was going through Nomad's head at that point. She hadn't been expecting this from him. They had been close, dear friends, but never intimate. She had very little experience in that area, and the rush of implications were too much for her to sort through just then.

Breaking away, she headed back to the main room and sat on the bedside, her breathing shallow as she tried to get space to consider the situation.

Nomad stayed in the washroom for a few moments, giving Reza time to collect her thoughts. He strolled in after a minute to sit on the bedside beside her.

"I—am sorry. I should not have been so forward," he whispered, softly patting her hand. He flopped back on the bed, arms wide, letting out a sigh to release some of his tension.

"Hiro—" Reza softly spoke, but after a moment of silence, instead of continuing her thought, she laid back on the bed on top of Nomad's arm and curled up beside him.

Hesitating a second, Nomad draped an arm around her there on the bed, holding her next to him. The flicker of the fire pit cast its comforting glow upon them as they shared each other's company in silence, other than the soft crackle of the popping wood and the steady drum of rainfall outside.

It didn't take more than an hour for Reza to succumb to sleep, her body badly needing it from the day's events, her breathing shifting to a deep, steady rhythm.

Nomad brushed her now dry hair out of her face, smiling as he looked upon her sleeping features, experiencing the bliss of the quiet moment beside his closest friend in all of Una in quiet solitude.

27

A FELL PRESENCE IN THE JAIL

Fin slammed the rotting skull through the jail bars, the mushy bones easily fracturing into pieces, smashing through into a pool of gore in the empty cell.

"Fin!" Cray called, coming down the dark hallway from the entrance.

"Where's Matt?" Fin replied, turning to see that Cray was visibly shaken and somewhat out of breath.

"He stayed behind, told me to tell you to find the crew, bust them out, and get back to the entrance to help him."

"Great," Fin murmured, then yelled to Cray, "Help me find your gang."

The two burst through the adjoining jail block, coming in on a group of arisen lurking by the cells. Fin was the first to move, sweeping his leg under a hefty arisen, yanking on its wrist to send it toppling over. Cray followed behind to behead the thing with his short sword, hacking at the back of its neck until it severed.

The next guard was on alert, and Fin had to duck and dodge to the side to get out of the way of its heavy swing in time, backing up to dodge the follow-up swing from the lumbering corpse. Luckily for Fin, Cray had taken notice of the scuffle.

Lunging the ten feet between him and the arisen, Cray hacked at its outstretched arm, lopping it clean off. By the time it took note of the dire wound and turned to face the new threat, Cray had swung the other sword blade directly at its neck, slicing halfway through the thick meaty stalk of rotting muscle and bone.

Fin returned the favor, slamming a wide gouge dagger into the back of the last arisen's neck, severing its spine, instantly dropping it to the stone floor.

"Nice...hacking," Fin said, attempting to compliment Matt's young one, but it came off sounding more sarcastic than anything.

Cray didn't notice, seeing his two comrades locked up in the cells at the far end of the room.

"Malagar! Hamui!" he cried, rushing to their cell doors, jangling the locked door, attempting to rip it open.

"Cray, stop. I got the door," Fin said. He snatched the jailer's keys from off the wall and opened both doors up quickly. He handed Cray the keys to help unlock his friend's manacles, looking briefly to the third person in the line of cells, noticing that it was an arisen.

"Mal! Matt's in trouble. We've got to go, now," Cray urgently said, undoing his cuffs. The tall haltia rubbed his wrists after being freed, sorely getting to his feet to help Cray with Hamui's locks.

"Matt's taking on all those dead things by himself?" Malagar calmly asked, helping Hamui to his feet after Cray unlocked the smaller cuffs set around the heavily robed praven's wrists.

"Yeah, just down the hall a ways—"

"—I know you," Fin said, cutting Cray off mid-sentence, sneering at the animated bones gazing at him from within the locked cell.

"And I, you," the skull's jaw creaked as a hiss issued forth barely discernible words.

"How...do you know an arisen?" Cray questioned, pausing for a moment, helping Malagar to the door they had entered from.

"This wanker took some very important items from me. Almost got the best of me a year or so ago back in Brigganden when it was under the control of his master. Be glad I don't have time to deal with you just yet," Fin spat, his contempt for the thing clear and unveiled. He called to the others, "Matt needs us. He's not indestructible you know."

"Release him. He's coming with us," Hamui said in an uncompromising tone.

Fin scoffed at the little praven, thinking it some sort of odd jest, but Hamui held out his little gloved hand for the key from Cray.

"You're serious, little one?" Fin asked incredulously.

"Call me *little one* again and I'll see to it you sire no younglings," the inexpressive praven threatened, adding once more, "Keys, now. He's coming with us."

Fin, seeing this was no jest, reiterated, "The thing is clearly not alive, if you haven't noticed. Arisen are under the control of their master, and their master is a warlord hell-bent on ending all life in this region. Why in hell's sake would you want that thing released?"

"He's—not like the others. It seems he possesses his own will," Malagar answered.

Fin threw up his hands, giving in, "You want that monster for a travel buddy, whatever. The trouble he's going to cause is on your head though, and I'll end him the moment he steps out of line. I don't have time for this. Matt needs our help."

Cray needed no further convincing, agreeing that Matt was in great danger the longer they lingered there. Tossing the keys to Hamui, Fin didn't wait around for the three to follow his lead, sprinting through the rooms and corridor looking for Matt, following the sounds of battle.

The crack of a skull sounded, and an armored body clanged as it slumped down against the wall as Fin rounded the bend. Seeing a heap of bodies lining the hall in front of Matt, Fin looked past at the host of dead still waiting to advance.

"Duck!" Fin shouted to Matt, which he did just before an arrow whizzed overhead.

"Fall back, Matt. More archers are lining up!" Fin shouted, tugging out dagger after dagger from a long sheath along his hip, hurling them into the advancing arisen. He moved to the side as Matt jogged past him back into the jail. Fin covered Matt's escape as the two narrowly dodged a volley of arrows that came flying down the hallway, bouncing further in past the two.

The ground shook and the walls rattled, and Fin turned to peek at what was rushing their way.

The entrance of the building had been blocked out by some mass. He only caught a glimpse before seeing two giant hands reach in and rip the top of the doorway apart, the hallway coming down around some of the arisen that had been pursuing them.

The structure shuddered, but Fin, grabbing Matt's hand and led him at a sprint to the jail cells. They made it to the jail's entrance room just as Cray and the others showed up, Hamui and Malagar having finished rearming themselves, rushing to meet them.

There was another smashing sound, and the jail shook violently, settling dust from the wooden roof overhead showering down upon them.

"That is their giant. It seems Denloth is taking no chances with you escaping," the skeleton beside Hamui hissed. Another slam, closer this time, shook the building more, a billow of dust from the open door spewing into the room they were all in.

Everyone began coughing, and the room, previously dimly lit from the slits in the ceiling beams above, was clouded out by the dust, blinding them. Matt grabbed Fin, pulling him back with the rest of the group just as the doorway blew apart, stone, dirt, and splintered wood flying everywhere.

Half of the roof was gone, and most of the wall that had been on the other side of the room had been leveled. The sun shone defiantly down through the plume of dust that had been kicked up, a giant figure, fifteen-foot tall, looming in the dark cloud it had created.

An arrow flitted through the dust, skipping off the wall between Cray and Fin.

Fin scrambled up a broken rafter beam, running along it, leaping atop the side of the blasted wall that opened up to the patrol wall above.

He could partially see the thing now for what it was. As the skeleton had said, it was an arisen giant. It seemed to be a construct of multiple bodies, its tight bluish-black sickly skin well past the rotting phase, as though it had been baked dry at the height of its putridity. Its hulking structure appeared to have been stitched onto the frame of a mammoth gorilla, its bloodshot, milky white eyes gazing haplessly up at Fin, a slave to the powers that bound its once primal nature.

He needed to get the hulk away from the others. If they continued to run further into the jail, it would simply follow, blasting the fort apart until they were cornered. As long as the dust cloud hung around, they would be fighting blind, and he figured the giant didn't need much precision to land a lucky blow with how massive its club arms were.

Blowing a shrill whistle, loud enough to even attract the attention of the archers far beyond, a few stray arrows flying in his general direction, Fin pulled a dagger from his side and tossed it into the face of the beast. The point barely pierced through the thing's hardened skin, hanging from its cheek.

It looked at him for a moment longer, as if considering if Fin merited his attention or not. It was the first quiet moment the group had had in the past few minutes. The silence broke as the giant lifted its huge foot, stepping towards Fin, lifting its arms to slam through the wall he was perched on.

Fin jumped early, as to not be caught in the blast, but the moment his foot left the stone, a whirl of events ensued.

A battle cry from within the jail sounded, ferocious, loud, and clear. Cray brought down his swords, landing meaty hacks upon the flesh of the giant, severing both tendon and sinew. It started to lurch off balance and fell forward, slamming short of the wall top as it toppled early.

It was then, with his focus on the fall of the giant, that a missile split through the gloom. He took notice of it a moment too late, the arrow piercing into his shoulder, throwing off his composure mid-flight. He fell below the fort's wall line, removing him from the whole chaotic scene as he landed on the slope of a sandy dune, his plans to lead the giant out of the fort ruined in an instant.

"Shit!" Fin yelled, pushing himself up with his good arm, looking back at the wall that shook slightly as the giant rumbled around on the other side of it.

Holding the shaft of the arrow sticking out of his right shoulder, he ripped it straight out, screaming, allowing himself a moment to work through the pain and assess if the point had split an artery or not.

The wound was a sharp pain, and sand had gotten in it, but minimal blood issued forth, and as he got up to head back to the fight, guards that had been along the walls, watching his escape, had already began to come around the fort, rushing to his location.

"Cray, I'm gonna kill you if we make it through this," Fin grumbled. He drew a dagger with his good hand covered in sand, gritting his teeth as a team of arisen ran down the dunes, spear points first.

The dust was settling somewhat by the time the giant collapsed against the wall, most of its left knee tendons severed, largely rendering its left leg useless. It flopped over on its side, looking with its dead, white eyes at the small creature that continued to harass him with cutting hacks, slowly dismantling his frame.

Cray had scored a vital hit with his first few attacks, felling the beast with the blows to its knee, but now vital targets were out of his reach, and the slices he was opening along its flanks didn't seem to be worth the effort he was dumping into the assault. A massive backhand slammed him across the room, back to the entrance of the tunnel as the beast began to rouse.

Arisen flowed into the room over the rubble that had freshly settled, stepping over Cray as they came at the group on the far end of the room.

Chaos ensued, the cornered group fanning out, each taking targets as they came. Matt stood out front, easily side kicking and pummeling the closest guards, not too affected by the obscuring dust, other than sharing in the coughing fits everyone else was suffering through.

The skeleton that Hamui had insisted be released stepped up, scooping up the closest guard and tossing it against the cell bars. It snatched the sword up and began hacking at the next oncoming arisen.

Malagar took a stance similar to Matt, striking at the joints of the armored arisen that flooded in the room, snapping heads back, and tripping the others as they rushed by him for other targets.

A shout and a burst of wind issued from Hamui's outstretched hand, clearing the air and arisen in front of him. Chanting another mantra, he shot forth his crystal-capped staff; a strong gust of air cleared half of the room of the particles still floating in the air, toppling the arisen as well, Matt and Malagar standing firm.

Cray shook his head, coming to, his eyes quickly finding the giant just as it ripped its useless lower leg violently off, the sound of tissue rending gratingly sounding in everyone's ears.

Slowly getting up, the giant half kneeled, resting its weight on its broken knee, holding its severed leg as a menacing club, looking to the little one that had caused it so much trouble.

Cray expected a primal roar, but the thing just stared at him with its soulless eyes and began slugging towards him, club raised, threatening to smash the life out of him if it was able to land a hit.

Stone, grit, and sand started rolling along the jail floor back towards Hamui as the hissing skeleton slashed down those arisen that tried to get close to his smaller counterpart.

Lifting in the air, the rubble rolled up into floating piles and crunched into a condensed conglomerate. A low guttural chant was beginning as Hamui worked his hand in a rigid configuration, twisting his fingers as he worked the floating rock orbs tighter, the electric blue glow in his staff's crystal brightening.

Thrusting his staff forward, one of the orbs launched at the arisen giant that was lurking towards Cray, who had finally gotten to his feet after the massive blow.

The smooth rock slammed into the cranium of the large creature, exploding into powder as the giant was forced to use its hands to steady itself from the impact.

Hamui had gotten its attention. Its milky white eyes locked onto the little praven that stood with three more rock orbs ready for launch.

Another polished orb shot into its flat ape face, this ball holding together a bit better, crushing facial bone, opening up a few lacerations along its brow and cheeks.

It started to hustle towards Hamui, blasting past Malagar and Matt, receiving another blast from the last two orbs, clobbering its face into mush, a massive sunken hole on its right ocular cavity now; but it needed no vision at that point. It knew what direction the little praven was in.

It lumbered forward as its right ankle was severed, Cray slashing up along its exposed lower half, hacking at the meat on its lower and upper leg simultaneously with his twin short swords.

Large sections of its calf and hamstring bunched up and became undone as Cray stopped it short of his comrade, disabling its locomotion at that point but taking another blind swat from the ape's large hands.

Slamming up against the giant's large mass, pinning Cray long enough for it to get a solid grip on his torso, the ape dragged him up in front of itself as it flipped over onto its back, holding Cray above it with both hands.

It grabbed Cray by his head and stomach and began pulling.

Hamui yelled at their arisen ally to help, and with his sword, he chopped at the thing's neck, beginning to split its feral, dead hide open, but the giant's brute strength began to work, wringing and popping Cray's neck loudly. His head ripped clean off, clutched in the giant's hand just as the skeleton chopped through to the large beast's spine, exploding a flash of dark light that blinded and deafened Hamui, Malagar, and Matt, blasting the skeleton back atop of Hamui.

The group had no time to let Cray's beheading sink in as a purple bolt of crackling electricity split the settling dust, clearing the room as it sizzled up any particulates in its path, heading straight for Matt, who turned to look blindly upon his impending doom.

A pendant, gleaming gold against the high sun, intersected the bolt, just before impact, held by the skeletal figure. The pendant ground the bolt's path to a halt, slowly absorbing the energy, angry tendril after tendril sizzling the charm into a red-hot rattle in the skeleton's hand.

With the spell squelched, all eyes turned to the direction from which it came. There stood a dark, robed figure, skulls adorning his many tattered hanging sashes. A spectral purple glow drifted about him, shifting from images of skulls and anguished faces—a display to his foes of his ominous might.

"Denloth," the skeleton said, eyes locked with the figure that stood on the other side of the fort atop a wall. A moment later, the figure was gone, and the rattle of more arisen coming their way brought Matt and the ally arisen back to the fight at hand.

Malagar and Hamui didn't hear the clash of steel on steel or the smashing of bones from Matt's blows, but stared blankly at the unmoving body of their comrade, devoid a head and spine that was buried in the large, clenched palm of the beast that lay under him.

Part Three: The Road to Tarigannie

28

THE OUTCAST

The bells pealed from the white watchtowers above, which were just being lit as the night came on in the market district of Brigganden as Yozo sprinted in and out of the crowded intersection, fleeing for his life.

"Heretic!" the call sounded. Men in white robes screamed, rallying others in the area that wore the same white uniform, all converging on his location.

He had been singled out by one of the locals for his facial deformity and accused him of being a sinner. He hadn't understood the connection, and by the cruel manner of the young man, he figured he was just being a target of harassment simply out of youthful amusement, nothing out of the norm for him since he had left his homeland all those years ago, though no less annoying.

The persistent harassment had gained the attention of the white robes, though. And when questioned briefly about some god he did not know the name of, he had replied, "Fuck your god," a retort that had elicited quite the response from all those within earshot, even silencing the jocular youth.

That little interaction had ended his shopping trip, and stay, in the city early.

"Shit!" Yozo cursed as he dropped some of the desert fruits he had just purchased, small gourds and melons tumbling into the street from his bag he now cinched back up as he rushed down an alley, getting out of the crowded highway.

The white robes were persistent and everywhere. Leaping off the side of a building and up a wall, he rushed along its spine as he located the nearest gate leading out of the blocked-in city, momentarily getting ahead of the alarm. He sped through the gate just as the guards began to hear the shouts from the white robes far behind, running after him, off the trail and out into the desert sands.

Looking back to keep an eye on the slowing guards, he sprinted as best he could in the shifting dunes, headed towards the foothills of the nearest mountain range.

The guards puttered to a stop, giving up their chase quickly, seeing that there was no chance to catch, at least on foot, the swift man.

The white robed men caught up with the guards, explaining the blatant account of blasphemy.

"We were running him down for blasphemy?" one of the guards incredulously questioned, getting a worrying look from the other guards and a menacing look from the white robes.

The group of enforcers stood, looking at the foreign man run for his life over the distant sand dunes, another guard trying to deescalate the situation.

"Don't worry, he's headed for the Imhotez mountains," the guard nervously chuckled, trying to reassure the robed figures. "I hear that's where the arisen army is. That man is good as dead where he's headed."

The group headed back to the safety of the city as the sun completely faded away over the horizon.

As Yozo turned, a mile between him and the damnable glowing city now, he spat one last curse at the wretched culture that had consistently derided him.

Looking to the sandy foothills that led into the low mountain range, he figured some travel off the trail might allow him a reprieve from harassment along the highway and perhaps would give him a chance to replenish some of his food supplies. Often, he had noticed, wildlife and game were more abundant amidst the ridges, canyons, and foothills. Not only that, but with the elevation, he'd be able to keep track of Sultan Metus' company.

As the night grew darker than usual, clouds covering the stars in the heavens, he began to hear creatures of the night calling—screaming.

At least with animals, they make no pretenses about the fact that they want to kill you, he thought, not minding the dying calls of prey deep in the crags of the mountains he was headed towards.

29

A DARK NIGHT IN THE WHITE CITY

Guards looked down from the tall towers at the gates of the city as Metus' caravan came to a halt in the dark. Rain plinked off countless shields, helms, and tabards as Bannon stepped out front to greet the gate guards. Neither party wore smiles or otherwise showed interest in exchanging pleasantries.

After a lengthy conversation, the gate guards moved to the side, waving up top to signal for the large doors to be opened, allowing the regiment entry.

The old door creaked, straining to open as its sixteen-foot height slowly lumbered wide. Bannon signaled for the troop's advance, hundreds of feet sloshing through the muddy road to enter the vast city's main highway.

The streets were empty, and for how late and miserable the weather was outside, it was understandable. Only the watchtowers were populated, the Brigganden city guards peering down from the white, sandstone chiseled spires, hooded lanterns aglow with some sort of white chemical light, resembling a phosphorus glow, casting an unnatural hue upon the cityscape they walked through, the white light contrasting with the ink-black wet night.

Metus and company had been placed in the middle of the line, where they were best protected by the Hyperium troops; an unnecessary precaution, Metus thought at first, but as the group entered the unusually quiet city gates, the new Brigganden troops ominously looking down upon them, the only sound other than the oppressive rain being a pig brought to slaughter somewhere nearby, Metus was glad for Bannon's foresight in which he ordered the tight formation for entrance into the ally city state.

"What happened to the regiment you sent months ago to help with the retaking and reconstruction of this place? I don't see a single banner or uniform from the Plainstate," Reza whispered to Metus as their group quietly marched through the sleeping city in the midst of a downpour.

"After turning over the city politics to the returning Brigganden functionaries, the new information flow has been...more arduous to procure of late," Metus said under his breath to Reza, eyes from the many towers ever upon him especially.

Shrouded in a soaking wet hood, Nomad marched up beside Reza, whispering a few words into her ear before slinking back to his position beside Henarus and Terra.

Bannon called for a halt as they approached the inner court's gate and waited for it to slowly open.

Metus turned to Reza and asked, "What did Nomad have to say?"

"He suggested," she began, pondering a moment the advice before relaying it to Metus, "that we order the men to not sleep while here, even if we must stay in this city overnight."

As the troops up ahead began moving further into the dreary, dark city, more guards posted along the inner court's walls, watching the foreign troop in silence like owls in the night, Metus responded, "That...sounds like prudent advice."

<hr />

The audience with one of the high judges had been coordinated quickly, and no sooner had Bannon secured lodgings for the troops in tents in the large courtyard than Metus and his select troop had been shown to the hearing room.

A black-robed, litigious looking man sat high atop the judges' benches, bookended by two clergy in white ceremonial robes. The judge scrawled upon parchments with no concern that Metus had arrived, while the clergy stared down at the group coldly.

After a few minutes of scrutinous reading and writing, the frail man in the black robes looked up at the two city guardsmen that had led Metus into the hearing room, barking "Report," at the senior guard.

The guardsman stood at attention, giving a brisk, customary Brigganden salute with hand clenched upwards across his stomach. "Aye, your lord magistrate. Sultan Metus and company arrived with an attachment numbering one hundred strong this evening. Upon their request, Sultan Metus wished to exchange words with available city leadership before departing on the morrow. This is my report."

The thin man with sharp features looked down to Metus for the first time since his entry, eyeing him harshly and looking over those he had brought with him—his two personal guards, Reza, Arie, Cavok, Henarus, and Terra.

"Ah, Sultan Metus," the judge softened at the recognition of royalty, "my apologies that the other two high judges are not available for your audience, but the hours are late, and judge Gibben and Niratt do hate to clock in hours past sundown. To those who might not know me, you speak to judge Hagus. What might I help you with this evening?"

Sultan Metus bowed his head, forgiving the absence of the other judges, explaining. "No apology necessary, judge Hagus. I am here under no schedule and ask you forgive me of my impromptu visitation to the great city of Brigganden. I would have sent word, save for the expedite nature of our mission. The fact that you welcome my sizable troop at such a late hour unannounced speaks volumes of your openness and trust in our relationship.

"I hope my men's camp for the night here will not inconvenience the legislative members here in the inner courts. If we are a bother, we can camp outside the city walls for the night upon your request—"

The judge waved his bony hand, interjecting with, "—It's no problem at all. The courtyard is yours for the night."

Metus bowed, giving thanks to the judge's hospitality. "Very good, you have my thanks. There is one other reason for stopping here before we head west to Rochata-Ung. Not but a year ago was Brigganden brought low due to an unprecedented arisen invasion. Even in the months following their defeat, their commander and

172

army was pushed to the south lands.

"Unfortunately, it has come to my knowledge that they have been busy at rebuilding their army, and another threat of invasion is looming on the horizon. We are shoring up our nation's defenses and advise Brigganden to do the same—especially by the southwestern wall. We have word that the Imhotez mountain range is their present position, though, I cannot say for sure if they still remain there as of tonight.

"Prepare for the worst. The arisen army has proven its lethality in the past. We hope to sound the alarm to this threat in Tarigannie to help harden its defenses and perhaps come to an alliance to deal with this communal threat. The same offer I extend to Brigganden."

"The arisen army will not come back to Brigganden. If they do, they are fools," the judge confidently stated. "After returning to rebuild this great city, we, the judges, pledged to the people that an arisen threat would never again bring low our way of life. As you know, it is not just manpower and the size of an army that can stop the arisen. It is the aid of the divine that ultimately wards off the scourge of the living dead. We secured an agreement with a sect of followers of Elendium, a prominent god that directly opposes Telenth, and many of the other lords of the Deep Hells. They have given demonstrations of their great power and standing with their god, and our people's safety has been secured."

As the judge spoke, Metus was keenly aware of the transfixed eyes from the two robed men in white beside judge Hagus, both having watched *only* Metus the whole conversation.

"Though we would like to assist you and the people of the Tarigannie region in the fight against the arisen, you must understand the state we are in, only having just begun the true rebuilding of our large city. We must tend to our people before we can consider tending to another's."

Metus took a moment to consider Hagus' stance on the matter. His reports had not indicated a revival of religion. That having been the case, he figured this was a recent development. Alternatively, the leadership of the city was keeping the new clergy presence a secret.

"Though Elendium followers are few in the Plainstate, he is a well-respected god in our lands. What authority presides here? A faithful cleric, one Bede of Hagoth, was our representative for many years—"

The man in the white robes on the judge's right, abruptly entered the conversation. "Bede was known to us. A wayward follower not recognized as holding a status any longer. She came with many apostate questions in her last visit to the Valiant synagogue. Saint Fiuray stripped her of her rank afterwards, cutting ties so as to rout out the sin of corruptive thought before it gained a hold in other fellow believers."

Terra looked to Metus, the rest of the group behind him murmuring at the disrespectful condemnation of their beloved departed friend.

"There will be silence. The High Judge and Sultan Metus have the floor," the other white-robed man said in a curt tone.

"You say you follow Elendium. What rank do you hold in the church, if you don't mind my asking?" Metus questioned, attempting to defuse rising tensions.

"You stand before a Bishop of the Most High God. I represent Elendium for Brigganden, and it is my duty to see his will fulfilled," the man, who appeared to be in his late sixties, proudly said. Metus quickly followed up before the man had a chance to puff up his chest anymore.

"And your name, good Bishop?"

"Bishop Tribolt."

"I admit, I am somewhat perplexed at the presence of the church in this setting. Forgive my naiveté on the subject, but I did not know the church was involved in the judicial system at all in the cities they reside in. Is this a new practice being adopted by the faith?"

The judge responded, "Bishop Tribolt is our honored guest at court, upholding the law of god to ensure the people of this city remain worthy of Elendium's aid. Our people welcome the faith with open arms. To keep the laws of god is a small price to pay for security of our lands and lives."

"Citizens of Brigganden are required to keep these laws, not just followers of the faith?" Metus questioned, concerned for the drastic turn his neighbor nation had taken over the last few months.

"In order for Elendium to grace this city with his presence and protection, they must keep his laws; it is a prerequisite of his grace," the priest to the left answered.

"What is a law without consequence? Do you have punishments for those who do not follow these laws of Elendium?" Metus probed, having a sneaking suspicion that he already knew the answer to his question.

"The punishment varies from crime to crime, but yes, we are enforcing violations of such offenses against his holiness. They are, to be clear, simple guidelines, hardly even a hindrance to Brigganden's normal going-ons, but it is expected for all to attend worship and inform themselves of the commandments of Elendium, or render themselves subject to the courts of the church."

"Courts of the church? What of this court? Is this not the court of the people?" Metus asked, beginning to become a little heated at the thought of what the judges deemed sensible in the face of the threat of the arisen.

"You ask many questions, Sultan. Careful you do not overstep your welcome. Your people may come and go this night, but should you be visiting our city again, we will expect you to abide by the church's law or we will not forgive your trespasses again," Bishop Tribolt tactlessly snapped, the threat clear and in the open.

"I—" Metus said between a heavy breath to calm himself, "will consider your words. A treatise on the rule of law would be helpful if I could get a copy before we depart. It's imperative I keep up to date with neighboring customs and rules of governance so as to respect those states we have interactions with."

The Bishop simply nodded his agreement in reply, the judge clearing his voice, refocusing their conversation.

"It is understood that your audience here tonight was to affirm the arisen threat at our borders, to give us due warning of our communal enemy. It shall be recorded, and your troop will be granted a one night's stay in our judicial courtyard. Afterwards, you will clear the area and be seen out of the city. Does this notation accurately reflect tonight's audience and is there anything else you may want added to the record, Sultan Metus?"

"Your summary well reflects our meeting. Thank you, High Judge," Metus said, bowing once more to show his appreciation.

The judge snapped the small pinch gavel, signifying the end of their meeting. With that, Metus, along with his company, were seen back out into the pouring rain in the dark of the night—many new concerns having been freshly added to his already troubled mind.

30

A MONUMENT TO GREAT DEEDS

The cleanup of the remaining arisen troops had not been easy, Hamui and Malagar having been in shock at the sight of their brutally dispatched teammate, Cray.

Fin had come around the gate entrance once the group that had followed him beyond the walls had been dealt with. Matt and the arisen that had aided them had subdued what arisen remained in their area, with Fin getting the jump on the three archers that had been harrying them the whole fight. He had been especially vicious in dissecting those three who were responsible for maiming him.

They had looked for the one Hamui's friend had named, Denloth, but found no sign of him anywhere in the fort, though Fin had pointed out tracks leading to the southeast, heading to the Imhotez mountains.

Hamui and Malagar were sitting under the pavilion in the fort's courtyard, sipping leisurely from their water skins, Matt conversing with the slither-tongue fellow that had helped them in the heat of battle just an hour before. They halted their conversation as Fin strode up from the internals of the fort, rubbing the pain out of his freshly patched right shoulder.

Having finished his survey, Fin announced to the group, "No sign of your buddy, Wyld. If she is here, chained up, I couldn't find her. I bet that Denloth guy you mentioned took her with him. There's a few tracks that lead to the mountains."

Fin ignored Hamui's and Malagar's downcast, listless demeanors and pressed the animated skeleton, now that it was clear they were, at the moment, out of danger.

"Now who the hell are you? It's clear you did your part to help us back there, but why? Your allegiance is defined by your appearance, you infernal, godforsaken abomination. I, for one, have had enough of your kind to last me a lifetime."

Matt gave Fin a disapproving look, and the arisen had no chance to respond to Fin's words as Fin turned to Matt, flippantly replying to his gestures. "I know that look, Matt. Don't you dare take his side, you blind fool. You don't even know what this thing is yet, do you? Touch him, find out for yourself—"

Fin saw Matt's open palm a fraction too late, Matt's hand landing a clean slap just before Fin could block the strike. Fin fumed, but held back, clenching his fists at the old man who looked ready to welcome a return assault, confident he'd not be able to land a hand on him.

Matt turned to Hamui and Malagar, who sat watching, glued to the scene. "You kids never learn, even after you're all grown up and moved on. You watch your tongue with me, boy, always. And right now, whatever the hell this man be, human, saren, haltia, praven, *arisen*, a bloated cow for all I care, he proved a comrade during the most difficult time to prove oneself, on the battlefield. He saved Hamui; hell, he even saved me. I heard what went down, I was there—unlike you."

Fin's emotions flared at the old man's words. If there was one person that could break him down, it was Matt, and at that moment, Fin hated him so much for it that he had to walk away, for fear of honestly assaulting him.

"Malagar, Hamui, go get Cray ready for burial," Matt called, still looking in Fin's direction.

Fin turned, waving an exasperated hand as he yelled, "You're going to make them handle their friend's body? I'll take care of the body. For god's sake, look at 'em," Fin said, chuffing, darkly humored for a moment, realizing Matt was blind and that he couldn't see their expressions. "They're in shock, Matt. That they're fresh, it's obvious. You know why I wasn't there in the fight? I was leading that monstrosity away from all you sitting ducks. We were trapped; I was leading the beast out of the fort. He was taking the bait when one of your nitwits charged in like a hero—"

"Cray *was* a hero. You will not take his last triumph away from him," Hamui solemnly challenged.

Fin pointed at the jail, shouting back, "Does that look like a triumph to you?"

There was no answer, and Fin collected himself, realizing his temper was getting the best of him. He threw up his hands, surrendering his point.

"I'm sorry for your loss," he said, the bluster gone out of him now. "I'll take care of Cray. It's easier to bury those we don't know well."

"No," Matt interjected, "let them gather their friend's remains. They'll have to lay to rest a dear one someday. Better it be in training than out on their own."

"My god, Matt," Fin sighed, done with the whole thing. "You two can come to help if you wish," he said to the two under the pavilion. "I'm going to recover his body and get him prepared for burial. Try and stop me if you dare, Matt."

Matt let Fin go, and Malagar stood up, helping Hamui back to his feet. The two followed Fin back to the jail to extract Cray's body from the clutches of the giant ape, leaving the arisen and Matt alone in the court.

The sound of the three clambering over rubble could be heard in the background for a while before Matt mumbled to the arisen, "He's a good kid. Obstinate, a real deviant, but his heart is in the right place. I suppose that's why I took him under my tutelage when he was a young orphan. Hate to see that bright shine get snuffed out in ol' Rochata."

A loud rockslide caused them both to turn slightly, making sure the boys were safe.

The arisen slowly began to explain to Matt as they stood there in the dust-filled court, "You are blind, I feel it needful of me to tell you, your friend is right about my condition—"

"What, that you're a dead man standing?" Matt finished for him, smiling. "I hear no heartbeat from you, nor breath. I've never met an arisen before today, so in terms of *us*," Matt gestured between them, "you've got a clean slate with me. It seems otherwise with Fin. You could be everything he claims you are. Make sure to prove him wrong, and you and me have no issue."

The others were well into the jail by then, far enough away that only the occasional distant voice made it to Matt's ears.

"What's your name?" Matt softly asked.

"Dubix," the skeleton whispered, leaving it at that.

"Well, Dubix, I don't know how you came to be imprisoned here, or what your plans are next, but with your condition," Matt said, patting Dubix's hollow frame, "few, if any, will take kindly to you showing up—well—anywhere.

"Hamui seems to have taken a liking to you, and he can be a powerful, loyal friend. Malagar seems to have no complaints with you either, so if you wish, you may travel with us, though our path, I see, just got a lot more dangerous in the days to come. You watched out for us in that battle, let us return the favor," Matt chuffed.

Dubix looked at the old blind man for a moment before looking over at the demolished jail where they had sprung him from. Turning back to Matt, he hissed, "You may regret welcoming me as you have."

Matt's smile faded slightly as he answered, "Regret at extending a hand to someone, I can live with."

"Look, Matt. I know it's no place for him, but we're burying him in rubble in the jail. Hamui is etching a monument for him right now," Fin said, the strains of the day showing in his voice. "If Wyld has any chance of rescue, we're it, and their trail isn't getting any fresher. You know how it is, a good wind will make it near impossible to pick up on that trail out here. And god damn it, Matt, if you argue with me about this, that's it, I'm done here, and you can rot in hell for all you put me through over the years."

"*I* put *you* through?" Matt scoffed, turning to face Fin as he made his way back to the courtyard through the rubble that had almost come down on them earlier that day. "So, does that mean you're comin' with us?" Matt asked, smiling as he felt Fin join the circle.

Sighing, Fin nodded. "If you're chasing that Denloth character, then yeah. He seemed like no common underling, correct me if I'm wrong," Fin said, with a fair bit of snark directed Dubix's way.

"Denloth…is a match for me. He is of the upper ranks, it is true," Dubix confirmed.

"I came to you to get your help in the upcoming war on the

179

arisen. If you're already headed that way, well, even better. I wish Cavok and Reza were here, but as you yourself taught me, it's more important to be flexible to the whims of the fates than to be rigidly pursuing your schemes."

"Well then, looks like we've got ourselves a recon team. Those arisen won't know what hit 'em," Matt crooned, rubbing his weathered hands together.

After a moment, as the soft desert wind blew through the courtyard, Matt added, "Let's help finish Cray's grave and pay our respects to the boy. Shame. He had the same thing I saw in Cavok. Strength, but a heart under all that muscle. He was tender in a few areas, but given time, I think he would have been something. Tarigannie lost a fine man this day. He died saving his friends, though, and a more honorable death, you won't find."

Fin placed a hand on Matt's arm, leading the hunched over man through the rubble, and the three made their way to the jail where Cray was buried.

31

A RESPITE ALONG THE WAY

The clouds had followed them all that week of travel, the troop only seeing the Tarigannie sun a few times over the slow traveling days.

Sultan Metus had kept their detachment at a leisurely pace so as not to out-distance the larger Hyperium company. The larger the company meant the slower the travel, and even the elite Hyperium was not immune to mount and equipment issues.

A sickness had run through to a few of the troops as well, and the pressure from a brisk pace had been decided against, as Bannon suggested to add a day to their travel plans as they took the road from Brigganden to Rochata-Ung.

Metus had no qualms of the slightly more leisurely stride, and neither did the dolingers that bore them across the sands.

The road was long before them, and though they had left Brigganden the morning before, they still had one more day of travel to make it to Sansabar at their current pace.

A few drops of light rain showered them off and on, keeping them damp though not soaked. The usual barren desert dunes were sprinkled with a few hints of vegetation in flatter areas, scraggly desert flowers, prickly ocotillo bushes, or various cactuses beginning to bud and bloom with the consistent rainfall of the past few weeks.

The occasional splash of color had made traveling more pleasant, and Nomad felt, aside from their dire mission, the morale of the troop was gratifyingly peaceful.

He looked to Reza, who had remained by his side throughout most of the trip. He could feel that she worried over him. She was always there at night to calm his night terrors and visions that woke him without relent. He would soon need to camp away from the rest, he knew. He hated thinking of keeping everyone else up as he screamed and moaned throughout the night. Reza, no doubt, would insist on camping with him as she had on their journey to Jeenyre weeks ago.

He looked over the caravan of friends, most well-known to him, though some like Sultan Metus, and especially Terra, he had not had much time with.

Terra was simple enough a person to figure out. She seemed very genuine, and aside from her youth and naiveté, he could feel the reasons for her presence there were pure and true. She clearly felt a duty in aiding in the stoppage of Sha'oul.

She strolled alongside the ever-stoic Cavok. She was often by his side. The odd pair seemed so much a contrast, but he had witnessed good come of the unlikely friendship that had begun to develop between the two.

Cavok had come out of their recent adventures calloused and more on edge than ever. Even to Nomad, he had troubles loosening up to him of late, and Nomad could hardly blame him. He had some awareness of the terrible struggle he had put up in fighting Cavok, and he doubted many could let go those beatings so readily. He knew Cavok would someday get over their recent bouts, but he suspected it would take time.

Now Cavok had to deal with Terra's optimism and good heart, and that was a positive force that, even after just a few days on the road, had begun to wear down the walls of building rage he had built up over the last few weeks.

Reza had refused to leave Nomad's side for most of the time. He knew she was worried over him, and he felt uncomfortable and guilty at the burden he was to the group. And there was good reason to worry about his gradual transition, which was already beginning anew. He knew this time where he was headed, and that was killing him.

"You alright?" a concerned Reza asked, nudging her dolinger up close to his, the group at a slow trot along the highway towards Sansabar.

He nodded, trying to shake the constant worry and thought of doom that hung over their mission in his mind. He had been deep in thought of it all the whole day, worried of the outcome.

They had told him they were to travel to Rochata-Ung to find Zaren, who may hold a solution to fully curing his curse. They were headed that way, though he felt something else was in the plans that everyone else was in on but him. He did not see the need to travel with a large regiment of troops or with Metus, for that reason, but he trusted the crew that surrounded him, and did not want to press them for information, though the worry of unknown plans and kept secrets did weigh on him.

"Let's take a rest and let Bannon catch up. We're getting a bit ahead it seems," Metus said, steering his mount over to the clump of bushy desert palms and sand grass tufts off the trail.

There were no complaints from the group. Though the journey thus far had been moderately paced, they had taken fewer breaks than some of them would have liked. A few more days, however, and they would be at their destination, which was a welcomed thought to most of them, but especially Nomad. The sun had not been kind to his aching back, which had begun to flake and split in the location he had been stabbed so long ago now.

Luckily for him, the sun was beginning to calm for the evening. It was a few hours away from setting, but it was casting a few vivid pastels across the dunes, foothills, and budding plant life now. A cool breeze blew through the little cove of vegetation they were nestling into for a water break, refreshing the group almost as much as their drink.

"Cavok. Not rum," Arie quietly scolded as the large man placed a flask jar with caramel-colored liquid in it to his lips.

"We were rationed it," Cavok replied, as though that answered Arie's concern soundly.

She gestured to Terra close by, who was too busy getting off her dolinger to notice the conversation, Arie giving him a wicked eyeing.

Cavok rolled his eyes, let out a displeased huff, and corked the flask, stashing it back in his pack roughly, going for water instead. He got down to help Terra, who had somehow entangled herself in the gangly, dog-like beast she had been dismounting from.

The heart of the thicket looked dark and damp, covered by yellow, pollen-filled brush. He half desired to seek seclusion in its canopy, just to get out of the direct sunlight; but the number of scorpions and fire ants that probably infested the plumage of dead fronds caused him to hesitate. Instead, Reza pointed towards a bowed palm tree that cast a large shady spot in the sand, and the two tied up their mounts to gain respite in the cool shadows. The others did the same, fanning out in the area.

"I think we'll need to start bandaging your back again. I can see a black stain coming through your shirt," Reza said in a subdued tone, getting some medical supplies out of her pack.

He stripped his shirt off, revealing his wound to her. She had been checking on it each night and morning, and she had said it did appear to be getting progressively worse. That it had entered the bleeding stage was frustrating. He knew that marked the beginning of the urges and impossible nights. He doubted that he would, from then on, be getting much sleep, at least during the night.

She dabbed a clean cloth into some alcohol, resting the cool, stinging cloth along the outsides of the agitated split in his skin that had formed over the day. It was small now, not but two inches, but he knew it would grow to cover half his back eventually, effectively killing him and giving his body over to his former master, the lord of ash.

She finished cleaning the wound; unraveling some fresh bandages, she placed one over the laceration and began to wrap the long one around his torso, helping to keep the cloth snuggly over the cut.

"You have sacrificed more for me than anyone, Reza," Nomad quietly said, looking out at the bright yellows and oranges of the landscape.

The statement lingered. Reza finished her task with the bandage slowly, resting a hand on Nomad's shoulder. His hand came up to feel the warmth of her skin, brushing along the back of her hand and wrist.

Feelings had slowly begun to numb once more. His connection to his senses were starting to blunt, the throb on his back leaching away his vibrancy. He could feel her softness, but barely. The sensations of life were waning.

The somber moment hung in the air for a moment longer before approaching footsteps in the sand slowly moved the two apart, Nomad putting his shirt back on and Reza sitting back in the shade, seeing that Metus and Arie were on their way over to them.

"How's the back, Nomad?" Sultan Metus asked. The two newcomers took a seat in the sand beside them.

Nomad nodded with a weak smile in reply. In truth, the speed of his curse's return was quicker this time around than last, and it worried him; but, at least for now, he was in good company, and his mind was still mostly his. He could not complain.

"Well, we're going to be coming up on Sansabar in an hour or two. We're naught but two days out from Rochata-Ung at this point," Metus finished with a smile, happy with their time and the ease of the journey thus far.

"I'm sure you're thrilled to have Jadu's constant chatter in our group once more," Nomad said, smiling mischievously at Reza, souring her mood instantly at the thought of putting up with the talkative praven's antics once more.

"He had better have learned to hold his tongue around me. His incessant prattle was straining me beyond my patience."

"Asking Jadu to hold his tongue is like asking the sun to stop in place," Nomad chuckled, knowing how much Jadu could obliviously get under Reza's skin by just being his jovial, chipper self.

"You forget, Reza. Jadu is supposedly quickly becoming a powerful enchanter. You may find it difficult to subdue him with threats as you used to—well, *attempt* to do," Arie added, smiling at the obvious distress Reza displayed at merely the prospect of sharing company with Jadu once more.

"Magic or no, if I order him to shut his trap, he had better do it," Reza crossly announced, getting a chuckle from the others.

"A dangerous combination you two are. Hilarious to watch, but dangerous," Arie laughed.

"Indeed, and poor Jadu is completely unaware he is engaged in a battle of wills when Reza puts the heat on him. He is a guileless and happy little soul." Nomad smiled. "It will be good to see him again, before…."

Nomad left off before finishing his thoughts in regard to the decline of his condition. The others seemed to know where he was headed, regardless, as the convivial moment quickly passed.

The four shared a moment of silence, gazing across the pastel-colored dunescape before rousing the others to finish their journey before nightfall.

32

RETURNING IN DEFEAT

Streaks of shadow and light ripped across the desert, unnatural sounds jerking, sounding off discordantly with silent pockets in-between. The fever-like spectacle sent wildlife scurrying in fear as the streaks began to consolidate into two figures, one in shrouds, and one in light leather armor.

The robed figure walked out of the dissolution of reality that he had been walking through, a ring on his finger burning a neat violet. The ring began to cool, turning back into a dark, lustrous obsidian before the man turned his head to gaze for a moment the direction in which he came.

Denloth had left what remained of his troop behind, more than likely to be picked apart by the small troublesome group that had shown up at Fort Brackhill the previous day. He had perhaps erred in taking prisoners of the ones he had. They seemed like nobodies, not even associated with military or the local government in any way, but they had proved themselves a worthy threat during their raid, and they had successfully beaten him that day. All he had gained was one prisoner—one the others had referred to as *Wyld*.

He looked back at his only traveling companion. She was an

indigenous race whose population had dwindled under the more 'civilized' people's rule of law. He could understand her name due to her kind being known by most others as a wild people. Language was not common among them; when one did attempt speech, it was crude, and their understanding of higher thought seemed hindered, not truly on par with the rest of the recognized races of the land.

Her kind had many names by the Southern Sands region, some older, some newer, but most referred to them as kaiths. They were known for their natural fur coats, slitted pupils, and sharp fangs. A bestial people, closer to earlier evolutions of the other races, kaiths posed a great threat when provoked, their speed and power outmatching any opponent in their weight class.

He had spoken with her, before hypnotizing her and he respected her intelligence, considering her natural mental limitations. She had the command of speech, and she had been articulate in her threats directed at him. He would use her. She showed promise.

She had fallen during the walk through the Seam, her hypnosis compromising her judgement and functions. The Seam had left its mark on her, and parts of her clothing and body were phasing in and out of existence, giving a holographic effect upon a ragged swath of her right side. The iridescent scar stretched across the kaith's face like a surreal tattoo, leaving Denloth to wonder about the state of her mind after interacting with the Seam so directly.

All that dared venture into the Seam, a state of warped reality, knew to never veer from what his people called the thread. It was a safe, narrow path that led from entrance to exit. Along the thread, all calls for reality as one knew it were off, and anything could happen. As a result, it was extremely dangerous to traverse, but the one rule all walkers had for their journeys through the Seam was to stay steadfastly on the thread. If one didn't do that, that walker was never seen from again.

"Come," Denloth commanded. For a moment, he worried his hypnotism spell had been broken, or degraded in some way, but a moment later, Wyld began to walk towards him, stopping before him, waiting for additional orders.

He smiled.

Though he had been bested by an anonymous band, he had one of their members under his control—a very powerful, ferocious member—and they would follow. And when they arrived to where he was headed, an army of the dead would meet them. Not a thirty-man detachment of their weakest troops, but thousands of newly minted true abominations that his master, Sha'oul, had personally risen, graphed, and chanted runic soliloquies of death and murder into.

"You lost control of the fort? How?"

"This one's friends stormed it midday," Denloth admitted, nodding to Wyld. "They are skilled combatants, and they also allied up with Dubix. They are headed here now. I have hopes to convert them to our cause. They would be powerful assets."

The two walked through a shaded canyon along the borders of the Imhotez mountains. They were only accompanied by a spellbound Wyld, who followed close behind.

"What happened with this one's...skin?" Sha'oul asked, unsure as to the odd optical illusion that scarred a good portion of Wyld's body and clothes.

"She fell in the Seam. It seems to not have affected my enslavement spell," Denloth replied.

Sha'oul continued his questioning. "These people, do they have any affiliations that you know of?" Sha'oul asked as the two made their way through the winding slot canyon. He seemed underwhelmed by Denloth's report thus far.

"None that I know of. There's only five in their group, if Dubix remains with them. My mammoth ape killed one of them. They seem to be specialists, however. They may cause trouble for us, but if they do follow him here, we will need to be sure not to underestimate their talents. Even with their small numbers, they could pose a nuisance to our plans."

Sha'oul stooped low to avoid a withered tree growing out of the cliff wall six feet up. Denloth followed, ducking his head slightly, much shorter than the giant man he followed.

"You may use whatever force necessary to snare this group—all I care is that they are out of the way for our march, be it through their deaths or their joining us," Sha'oul said, mostly unconcerned with the subject, but turning to Denloth and adding a menacing follow-up order, "Do not fail to this group a second time. If some random group of vagabonds can best you twice, you're perhaps less useful than I initially thought."

Denloth gave the threat time to sink in before replying with, "Yes, master."

The canyon opened up before them into a crag valley, arid trees pointing up like green spikes out of the hills on either side. The rain had granted a wave of new vegetation. The scene that normally would have been a lovely vista was marred by a spread of felled trees and the moaning lamentation of a pen of tribespeople, numbering more than a hundred, surrounded on all sides by a host of rotting arisen so numerous that most of their ranks were hidden deep in the tree lines stretching all the way back into the mountains.

"I have need of six strong souls. Find them there. Bring them to the tent of ash and meet me there. We've finished the slaughter of the mountain gorillas. I must finish the raising rites, and then I will see you in the tent," Sha'oul explained, then headed off up the hillside, leaving Denloth only in the presence of his tentative kaithian ally whose skin and armor glimmered a lustery opalescent as Wyld stared off blankly into the valley ahead.

"A ritual is afoot. Six strong souls is many," he said to his mindless companion, grinning at the thought of what was to come as he headed down to the moaning prisoners who cried one name over and over.

"Sha'oul! Sha'oul!"

"It seems our master is pleased with this people's name for him," Denloth mused sideways to Wyld. "I must admit, *Hell Raiser* is an appropriate name, one that he seems keen on permanently adopting for this war, at least. Come now, keep up."

Wyld hesitated a moment, wetness lightly brimming her one good eye, the other awash in dimensional matter.

The resistance ended as soon as it had come on. Wyld began to step forward, attempting to keep up with her dominator.

33

CLIFFS OF IMHOTEZ

Fin checked the strange marks in the scorched desert sands. An odd coruscating fluid had been scattered along the scar in the earth. It was like nothing he had ever seen before, and since he suspected magic at play, he had poked the substance with a twig instead of using his finger.

The twig, apparently agitating the liquid, disappeared, then the liquid itself vanished.

"It seems Denloth is headed for Imhotez Pass, employing some very strange means—magic of some sort. No idea when he traveled through here, but if the pass is where he's headed, we might want to trek up along the cliff walls to be safe. Would be bad if we come upon the arisen army while in the pass and not atop it."

Matt considered Fin's suggestion momentarily, then grumbled, "That's going to make travel for me a great deal more difficult, you know that? It's not exactly enjoyable to navigate a mountain range blind, boy."

Fin had no answer for Matt. After not getting a reply, Matt huffed, "Stumbling through the mountainside it is then. Wyld had better still be alive when we catch that son of a bitch, Denloth."

"Yes, and we had better pick up the pace," Malagar added, looking in the direction the strange scars in the sand led. "He may slip through our fingers if we linger too long. Every day that passes in his captivity increases her chances of sharing Cray's fate. I have known her for many years now, and I know how spirited she is. Unfortunately, I fear that may play against her this time. She may force her captor's hand before we can arrive to aid her if we do not hurry."

Hamui, half the height of everyone else, swathed in thick grey and red robes, stood silently, brooding under his wide hood. He had listened to their conversations, though hadn't contributed much most of the day.

"Right," Fin said, after looking over the group, analyzing where everyone was at, lingering on the quiet Hamui. "We head to the mountains then. It'll be difficult terrain to navigate at a quick pace. Keep your wits about you. I'll scout ahead once we hit the mountains and get out of this sand. Mal, you take lead for the group, I'll signal to you to halt if needs be, so watch for me—keep everyone at a good clip."

Malagar nodded, and though he expected to hear complaints from Matt, none came.

The group started their trek up once more with a bit more spring in their step, following the discordant scratch marks to the mountains ahead.

The day had come and gone along with an unhealthy amount of sweat from everyone, save Dubix, who labored effortlessly, even with his weighty armor he had salvaged at the fort. Whatever dark magics that kept his hinges moving did not wane in the least.

Their water reserves had suffered from the quickened pace they had set, and Fin had been keeping an eye out for pools of water to replenish their water bags.

Since it had been raining so often the last couple of weeks, it hadn't been hard to find standing water, but most pools were stagnant and thick with algae and not suitable, even with boiling, to drink. They still had time to be selective, so he had passed by quite a few watering holes already.

The striations in the sand had ceased a ways before they had entered the foothills. Footsteps had immediately preceded them and led straight into the vast canyon. Denloth had not made it hard to follow.

Cresting a peak, Fin scanned the next few mountain slopes ahead for signs of Denloth or the arisen horde. They were high up by that point, their ascent had lasted the better part of the afternoon, and though he had superb visibility down on the canyon pass, he saw that the way ahead, if they wanted to keep at the top of the canyon, was going to be arduous. The trip would not be easy for Matt to navigate.

Fin was just sitting down to await Malagar and the others when he noticed a small plume of smoke coming from a ways down on the other side of the canyon wall, in one of the many crags along the mountain.

He shaded his brow, trying to make out the scene that was nearly a half mile away. It looked like a small camp, and Fin made out what seemed to be a single figure. Surely it was not Denloth that he had spotted, having seen signs of a trail from time to time of Denloth and Wyld from his vantage point hundreds of feet above the canyon floor. They had kept to the valley. This figure was alone, and as of yet, Fin did not think aware of their presence.

Looking back to Malagar, who was now close enough to clearly see him, Fin waved for him to hurry up and keep low. Malagar whispered to the others of Fin's orders and the group approached Fin's spot within a matter of minutes.

"See?" Fin whispered, pointing to the camper deep in the mountainous region.

"I don't *see* like you mortals," Dubix hissed, getting an approving grunt from Matt, who was waiting for an explanation of the sight.

"Some lone wanderer. What are they doing way out here?" Malagar spoke aloud, answering the two companions that had not a keen eye, or eyes at all.

"How do you see, Dubix?" Hamui asked, breaking his day-long silence. Everyone turned to the two out of genuine interest.

The bleached skull looked down to consider the question and whispered to the small praven, "Patterns in the hexweave. All entities interact with the weave differently."

"How far can you 'see'?" Hamui pressed, the praven's natural curiosity kicking in fully.

"It depends on the complexity of the arisen. Some are barely aware of their surroundings at all. Others still have some connection to their senses they once held in life. I cannot see as far as you are pointing, the weave is too muddled for me further than a hundred feet or so. It is difficult to sort through all the chaos beyond."

"Curious," Hamui mused. He stroked his chin in the shadow of his cowled hood with his small hands, mentally chewing on the presented curiosity.

Fin noted the confessed information, distractedly moving the subject back to the lone wanderer below.

"Matt, you're with me. The rest of you, follow a ways back; let us approach first and back us up once we move to engage."

"Understood," Dubix answered for the others. Matt left the group, following Fin's lead as they made their way down the sloped hill towards the campsite.

34

AT A CAMP ALONG THE DUNES

"I'll rush back to let Bannon know we'll be stopping here for the night," Arie said, turning her dolinger around, spurring it into a trot to meet up with the troop that they had lost sight of after the last sprint of their journey.

"It seems we'll be sharing this camp, Sultan," Henarus quietly said as they continued to approach the desert camp where many tents had been pitched all around a central pit that blazed bright, even in the setting sunlight.

"Indeed. Reza, Henarus, come with me to entreaty if we may share this campsite with them. Perhaps mingling with their people would do our company good. The trade of information with locals could prove useful."

Reza and Henarus trotted up along with Metus ahead of the rest of the small group, leaving them at a distance as they approached the camp of around twenty-five people or so. A stocky man walked just out of the camp boundaries to address the three strangers that rode up along the highway.

"Greetings, travelers," the barreled-chested Tariganniean said in a thick accent. "I see you ride dolingers. Are you military? I see no banners or colors to guess where you might be from."

The man seemed pleasant enough, but as Metus looked over the camp more closely, he could see that the curious onlookers were heavily wrapped up, showing little skin. On the skin that was visible, Metus could see horrible lumps and bumps along flaking skin.

Metus must have been distracted by the observation for a moment too long. The man looked to the encampment, poignantly pointing out what Metus was wondering.

"Lepers, as you may suspect. I would not assume you would wish to spend the night in our camp, but there is plenty of good, flat ground in the area. We would not at all be opposed to having neighbors for the evening if your intention is to camp here overnight."

"It is rude of me to have hesitated. We have not seen leprosy in our state for many years."

"And where is this state of yours?" the man asked.

"The Plainstate," Metus simply answered.

To which the man replied, "Ah, yes. Though small, it is a prosperous and peaceful place, I have heard; at least those who are willing to keep well within the rule of law. I hear you are banished for the most basic of infractions there. Tell me, what post do you hold with them? Military I'd be guessing."

Metus nodded, considering his answer for a moment before agreeing, "Yes, military."

"Do you have a name, good soldier?"

"Adom," Metus replied, bowing his head slightly in greeting before introducing his two companions at his side. "This is Henarus Alabathe, a follower of Hassome, and Reza Malay, my right hand, and that is part of my attachment." Metus motioned to the others they had left thirty yards back.

"Very good. You can call me Darious. I hope to bring a measure of peace to these poor people, castaways from Rochata-Ung, doomed to exile. This camp belongs to the Traveler, as it has serviced thousands of weary wanderers over many centuries. Your company is welcomed to this area. If you plan to stay longer than a night, we'll be packed and moved out on the morrow."

"Where are you destined?" Metus asked, glad to have moved the focus of the conversation to Darious rather than on him, not wanting to give any more information about himself or his mission than was necessary.

"Surely you have heard of the enclave north of here along the Daloth crags? It is a town where all of Tarigannie's refugees, diseased, and other unfortunates are sent to."

"I have heard of the enclave, though, reports are sparse with details of its governance. Tell me, what role do you hold there, if any?"

"As long as you have no orders to interfere. I cannot think of any reason for a soldier from the Plainstate to care, but I'm what you could call an 'official' of the town. We have little in terms of governance, it's more a commune, but what order must be kept is kept by a few seniors, myself being one of them. The only credentials to my name are the number of unclean I have rescued from the slaughtering streets of the slums of Rochata."

"I respect your work, Darious. This is an honorable thing you undertake," Metus said, mournfully looking over the lugubrious group of lepers. A child and mother stood close to the outside boundaries of the tents.

The child spoke in a pidgin mix of old Tariganniean and callatum. Looking at Reza, whispering to her mother, she spoke the words, "Angel. That one's an angel."

Reza doubted Metus or Henarus could understand her broken words, but she had spent quite a few years in Rochata-Ung, and the bridge language between the lower class and the old natives had been used widely enough in the markets that she had, with her knowledge of ancient Tariganniean, picked up some of the cousin language through immersion.

Metus continued to talk with Darious, but Reza couldn't shake the bright blue eyes of the young girl. She could see the mother and daughter also suffered from the horrible, contagious disease. She had seen how awfully their kind were treated in the city. She knew little of the place they were destined for, but regardless of if they were accepted in the enclave or not, leprosy was known to ravage and eat away at its victims till nothing was left. She could not fathom that fate for such an innocent looking pair.

She quietly dismounted and started walking over to the mother and her child. The child held Reza's gaze, her conviction of Reza as an angel clear in her countenance; the mother, hopeful, pled for any miracle.

Darious, distracted as he spoke with Metus, looked over to Reza who was approaching the mother and daughter and warned her, "Girl, those two are unclean. Don't get too close,"

Henarus dismounted. He could tell what Reza planned to do, and he was there to aid.

Henarus' hands glowed a faint blue, striking amid the sun's dying orange light that shown along their upper halves. He softly spoke, chanting prayers to his god, pleading for clarity to endow Reza in preparation to her healing touch.

Reza felt Henarus' gentle hand rest on the center of her back, and she was filled with clarity of mind. She saw how far the disease had already progressed with the two, almost encompassing their whole body.

She decided to not call upon the ring for this healing. Leaf had given her strict warnings of misusing its power, and though she believed giving these two a second chance benevolent, it did not directly aid their cause in ridding the world of Telenth's corruption.

The healing would be draining, but she knew now, with the light of Hassome flowing through her, that she could manage healing both of the wretched illness. She would not be fit to be with Nomad that night, but she knew Arie and Cavok would care for him without reservations.

"Praise be to Sareth. Praise be to Hassome," Reza breathed, reaching out to touch both daughter and child. The two smiled with tears in their eyes as their skin began to smooth out and clear up, their wraps falling from their bodies, disintegrating into light.

Reza burned away all that remained of the disease and released them, falling back on Henarus for support.

"By the gods," Darious muttered in disbelief.

Metus had dismounted and now went to help hold Reza up as people from both groups gathered closer, seeing the glow and the crying mother clutching her clean daughter.

"Henarus, is she going to be alright?" Metus worriedly asked, seeing that she was dozing off in Henarus' arms now.

"Hassome wouldn't have sanctioned the healing otherwise. She'll be fine with some rest," he answered, hefting her up in his arms.

"Gale, go with Henarus and his priest and care for Reza. Cavok, Nomad, start pitching camp nearby for the night. Jasper and Terra, if you wouldn't mind tarrying with me a moment," Metus ordered. Henarus followed the sultan's guard along with Cavok and Nomad, who gathered the dolingers and hurried to find a suitable site nearby on the sunbaked sands across the trail to begin setting up the tents.

They got Henarus' tent up first to get Reza in out of the last rays of sunlight and removed her armor so that she could rest comfortably under his watchful care.

Darious' mouth was still agape, looking over the couple that he had come to know over the last week or two after having them released from the enslavement camps in the city.

"I have never seen such a marvel. Hassome, did he say? What favor must your two friends have in their god's eyes! And did my ears belie me, or did I hear her pray to Sareth? You travel with a saren knight? My friend, what company do you keep? Who are you?" Darious quizzed, elated at the healing that he had witnessed.

"Some discretion would be appreciated, Darious," Metus said, trying to calm the excitement that was beginning to grow through the ranks of the lepers that had gathered. "Reza is indeed a saren, but a young one, and one on a holy mission at this time. While I am happy to see you both healed of your disease," he said, smiling genuinely to the mother and daughter who had wiped their tears and stood nearby listening intently to Metus' words, "I do fear we cannot repeat that miracle, not here and now at least. To perform a healing of that caliber drains her energy greatly. And where we're going, we cannot afford to be spent upon arrival. The fate of many lives rest on the success of our mission. That is all I can tell you on the matter."

"Delain, Iris, come," Darious beckoned, inviting them to stand before Metus. "Where do you head next, if I may ask?" the barreled-chested man asked, a smile still creasing up the sides of his thick mustache.

"First, we're off to Rochata-Ung," Metus answered.

"It is not a far journey then, one more day of travel and you'll be there. These two," he said, gently patting the mother and daughter couple on the shoulder, "as far as you or I can see are healed. They were cast out of Rochata due to the advancement of their sickness. They don't need to come with me to the enclave anymore. Would you be willing to escort them home since you're heading that way already?"

"Of course," Metus replied without hesitation. He guided them to Terra, asking her quietly to show them to his tent, admitting that he'd most likely be with Reza and Henarus that night anyways, and to get them a change of clothes.

"I'm sorry we can't do more for you at this time," Metus announced, speaking to the gathered audience of lepers, looking on in longing at Delain and Iris as they walked away, cured and headed for a fresh start.

"We're engaged in a holy work. The lives of all Tariganneans are at risk. Once we accomplish our purpose, however, I will send representatives and doctors of the Plainstate to assess how we may be able to aid the enclave. What we can do will be done at that time, I'm only sorry that time is not now, however. I will make good on my promise, though, I swear it to you."

Heads turned, and the attention faded from Metus' speech as a group of riders raced at a gallop towards the camp along the highway coming from Rochata-Ung.

Everyone backed slowly to the tent line once more at the approach of the twenty horsemen. Darious' demeanor turned grim as soon as the lead horseman was in view.

"I've dealt with that snake before. He is a Rochata council member. Careful, he no doubt is here to stir up trouble," Darious whispered to Metus, eyes locked on the horsemen the whole time.

"Oh, I know him," Metus grumbled. Jasper stepped up beside his liege, the dark orange glow of a sun already set casting a dusty golden glow on the steely trio awaiting the riders' final trot.

"Darious, I did not give you permission to take these people from the stone sites. Plagued or no. You only have authority to take unclean from private investors, not from the city's workforce," the lead horseman snapped.

"*Workforce*? I see the council wishes to sooth the term *slave* to be more palatable to their sensibilities. These people are on the brink of death. Let them be."

The dust from the trail drifted off as the rest of the horsemen trotted up, forming two lines of ten behind their leader. The councilman gave an unpleased glare to Darious, answering, "The law is clear, and they will be coming back with me this night. There will be no sleep, no food, no water, no rest until they are back within the compound from which you stole them from."

"They have already served Rochata to the edge of their health. You would take them back for them to die and infect others. What good are they to you then? They would be a detriment, not a benefit."

The sharp-angled man was about to respond to Darious' rebuttal, but, glancing at Metus, his attention latched now solely on the sultan.

"What an unexpected surprise," the man crooned.

"Set. It has been many years. I hope time has improved that disposition of yours; though, by what I've heard thus far between you and Darious, I have little hope for that reality," Metus said, trying to keep as even toned as his emotions would allow him.

"My brother died by your hand, Metus. I cannot forget or forgive you for that. He did not deserve the fate you laid him with," the slender man on horseback coldly said, resentment clear in his voice.

Metus shook his head slowly, answering, "He earned his death, and you know it. His campaign of sedition was performed openly. The trial he stood for exposed his treachery against the Plainstate clearly. His guilt was unquestioned in the court of law."

"A court that was blinded by bias!" Set rejected.

Metus was quick to respond. "Biased to protect the state from collapse and treason, which your brother campaigned for."

The two men were becoming heated, and everyone else nearby stood in tense silence. The only movement was Cavok and Nomad as they slipped in from the approaching shadows of twilight, their cloaked figures menacingly haunting Metus' flanks like reapers ready to take any life that threatened their royal charge.

Set smiled, looking at the small show of force presented to his twenty cavalry. His wicked grin showed his thoughts. Even with both the unclean camp allying up with Metus' small troop, Set was confident that he could paint the sands red with the sultan and his people.

"You are in Tarigannie, now, Sultan. I would have advised you to watch your tongue with me, but it's too late for that. You speak falsehoods of my brother, Het, and invade our lands. Not only that, but we have an outlaw here, smuggling city workforce members from Rochata-Ung. We have the authority to trample you all where you stand."

Darious stood stern-faced. It was clearly a rotten day, but he had seen many of those. He clutched at the hilt of his dagger in his belt comfortably, ready to act at Set's move.

Metus looked to the horizon behind, seeing a glow of torch fire nearly a mile out. He turned back to Set with a smile.

"I am not alone, Set. My men ride dolingers, a hundred strong. If you plan to murder all of us here, you have mere minutes before you'd be overrun. I'd not advise it. This camp would be our shared grave instead of just mine if you do."

Set looked to the torch fire that was steadily making its way closer, and the size of the troop did seem to be as large as Metus had boasted of. A frustrated snarl began to appear on his thin lips.

Metus continued, "We come in peace, Set. I'd advise you to come to terms with your brother's crimes and not follow in his footsteps. I'll be seeking an audience in Rochata-Ung soon. Do not cross me. It will only end poorly for you. This is your only warning."

The Hyperium had begun to close the distance quickly at that point, their numbers clear now, all in a healthy gallop towards the large group at the camp.

Set eyed the approaching army momentarily, calculating a response. He no doubt had much to say to the man that had executed his brother, but the time was short. He pulled on his mount's reigns, ordering his twenty to clear out, galloping back the way they had come.

"We didn't need the Hyperium to take care of that rabble," Cavok gruffed.

"Agreed. Too bad they didn't test us—" Nomad added, cutting himself off from continuing his thoughts out loud. He returned abruptly to tend to the dolingers, leaving Metus, and even Cavok, concerned for their unusually dark comrade.

The Hyperium began to trot into the field, Bannon and Arie making their way to Metus to check in.

"We saw the horsemen and hurried here. Is everything alright?" Bannon asked, still mounted, Arie beside him.

"All is fine, though your timing was perfect. We'll need to keep relatively close from here on out. There are those who do not wish us here. Tend to your troop. Set camp a ways down the road, and I'll come visit in a bit after concluding my own camp's preparations," Metus said, breathing a bit easier after the lucky timing of Bannon's arrival.

Bannon and Arie bowed slightly in their saddles and trotted off to order the troop to begin preparations for nightfall.

"You did not tell me you were a sultan," Darious quietly said, some judgment at the edges of his tone.

Metus turned to consider the large man. "Pray forgive my precaution. It is not wise to announce my status to all I come across. I hope it is not taken as an affront."

"Perhaps not," Darious reluctantly agreed, nodding in approval after giving the situation some thought. Breathing deeply, having escaped a potentially disastrous encounter, the man bowed in thanks. "I wish well upon your journey, sultan. I've heard good things about you, and from what I've seen thus far, I am willing to allow myself to believe them, for now. But sultan, be careful in this land. Tarigannie is a harder land than your tamed Plainstate. If you do not guard yourself closely, her and her people will take advantage of any weakness you leave exposed. Luck will only get you so far here."

The stout man huffed out a sigh, only then relieving his hand from the hilt of his dagger as he shook off the stresses of the night before returning to the camp of lepers, leaving Metus with his people.

35

THE PRIVILEGE OF BLOOD

A roar ripped through the canyonlands, silencing all other wildlife for miles around as the eight-ton mammoth gorilla backhanded an arisen, one of a hundred corpses that had been tasked to tie down and restrain the cornered beast. The arisen blasted to pieces upon impact, smattering its rotten entrails along the large cave wall.

Spearmen moved in once the ropes were tugging tightly on the beast's limbs and neck. The phalanx of broadhead spear tips came in inch-by-inch, tens of points digging into the large beast all at once, causing it to thrash wildly, letting out another enraged guttural scream that boomed out of the cave.

The short skirmish saw ten more arisen blown apart by the gorilla's powerful hands, but more spears crept in behind, slowly skewering the creature, causing each outburst to lose steam.

A smile split Sha'oul's lips, showing yellow-black teeth. At his side, Denloth appraised the dark lord's mood.

"Terrific beasts, as are many of the creatures in this wild region. We will find few creatures, in such numbers, larger, more powerful than these. It is good that you had thought to come here to recruit their flesh to the master's cause. All to ash...."

"All to ash…," Denloth echoed, bowing his head in thanks from the praise from his lord as another gut-wrenching bellow resounded from the canyonland cave.

"Come," Sha'oul beckoned after seeing the strength fade from the giant mountain gorilla as more spears jabbed through its thick hide with less and less retaliation.

"Today is the day of visitation. The ashen moon rises high to the east," he said, pointing to the barely visible circle in the eastern sky.

"Sacrifices must be offered, or we shall pay the debt to our master instead."

Sha'oul's ruddy burlap cloak whipped about him as he headed off with Denloth in tow, the gusty canyon breeze tearing at their robes all the way to the large ritual tent.

The two entered the tent's open doors, two robed figures dropping the door flaps closed behind them.

"You have not entered the place of visions yet, nor seen the visage of our lord, have you, Denloth?" Sha'oul asked in a gravelly, hushed whisper.

"No, my lord," Denloth answered. He looked around the circular room, runes and symbols, some he recognized, some he did not, painted and displayed along the sandy floor.

Carved out husks of tribesmen were displayed, posing in various positions which he could only speculate as to the meaning of.

In the center of the room stood Sha'oul now, a ripple in the sand emanated from two pulsing black tusks, both taller than even Sha'oul.

"Bring them in," Sha'oul called to the shaman at the tent door. The cloaked, disfigured thing hobbled out, and Sha'oul dug out a long sliver of bone from the circle of teeth, tusks, and bones that encircled the rippling sand.

"All who witness his face must pay for the privilege in blood," he said, jabbing the spike of splintered bone into his massive forearm. He ripped it out, covered in thick blood, stabbing again and again, leaving three oozing holes in his bare left forearm. He clutched the spike with his other hand, stabbing three holes in his right forearm. Denloth saw no pain across his master's face.

Sha'oul held out the dripping shard to Denloth. Not a word was said, but Denloth knew what must be performed.

Each stab was painful, and though he winced, he held his composure as he self-inflicted egregious perforations along his arms. The price to underpay his blood tax would be too costly. He stabbed until Sha'oul held out a hand to collect the shared instrument.

Cries and wails of horror and sorrow filtered in through the tent doors as three men and three women from the Badlands tribes were prodded towards the two large tusks at the center of the tent, their bindings and leads making it impossible for them to resist and tear away.

Pushed ahead by the demented abomination of bones that somewhat resembled humanoid vultures, the chosen six came to a halt before Sha'oul's imposing frame.

He smiled, his black and yellow teeth promising nothing painless to the unfortunate souls cowering there.

He refrained from overly enjoying the bottomless well of despair from the strong bodied sacrifices.

"Each within his, or her, prime. The best of all six tribes, one from each, that we raided and harvested from. Their flesh is without blemish, at its height of its mortal performance. The potential each of these youth poses is boundless. Look to the moonless night's stars and their destiny lies among them. What might such fine mortals strive to achieve will now…never be."

The speech was not met with pause, as barely had he finished than Sha'oul plunged the bloodied bone spike into the stomach of the nearest stripling, wrenching it down through the young man's entrails, gutting him before the others. It sent the five into a frenzy, thrashing now for their lives to try and escape.

Sha'oul was fast to detain, slow to slaughter. Life after life, he drained with a bloodied shard. Every now and then, a dark glimmer of a smile stroked across his lips as he dug deep into each of their bodies, soaking the ivory several times over with different shades of blood.

The blood had soaked deep into the dusty sands, the rippling motions drawing the living liquid inwards. All flowed to the center, even the sacrifices' final screams and smell of death, all collecting in a bead in the center of the tusks, forming a small, perfect glistening sphere that Denloth could not help but to gaze upon in wonderment, even as the bloodbath continued.

A time had passed—Denloth had been too fully transfixed to correctly mark the passage thereof—a voice came from within the bead of gore, a growing whisper.

Sha'oul stepped up beside Denloth, holding his arms forwards, the holes in his forearms filled now with crimson liquid. Denloth followed suit.

A thin trail of blood flitted towards the blood sphere from all twelve of their wounds, the line linking fully from arms to bead now.

The whisper grew ever louder.

Denloth dared not look away at that point. The room darkened around him quickly, a lightheadedness brought on in heavy waves as the voices grew louder, trancing him into a chaotic haze. The blood bead was the only constant in his focus.

The whispers coalesced, and Denloth witnessed an image imprinted within the blood, consuming his mind with its vision.

He saw in his mind's eye, a withered giant, hovering before him. The figure's mortified skin was tattered and thin, ripe enough to split at the softest touch. His gangrenous flesh was black and purple, fading to festering, sickly, yellow-orange around its ribs and arm bones that held little tissue between them.

Its face was a pale yellow, ash seeped deep within the cracks in the skin, and a necrosis lined all around the area just around its closed eyes, mouth, and hole where its nose might have once been.

Denloth looked in wonderment as the giant's emaciated limbs began to spread out, its long arms hanging outstretched, hovering in the air before him.

"All to ash," he heard Sha'oul speak out, breaking him from the illusion that he was the only one witnessing the vast expanse of the ash lord's domain and vision.

"Blood to ash," came a voice in Denloth's head—no, not *a* voice, many voices, all speaking in unison. He felt as though the lord of ash was speaking through millions of mouths; perhaps of past followers or victims, he knew not, but all spoke with one intent—the ash lord's intent.

"Blood to ash," they both chanted back.

Sha'oul and Denloth stepped forward, both receiving the urge to come to the feet of the flesh totem that represented their god.

The closer they got, the louder the rippling whispers were, tearing at their thoughts, attempting to gain access to every corner of their minds. Denloth did not know how Sha'oul fared, but he felt fully violated, every sector of his brain laid open and exposed before the ageless entity. There was no hiding his thoughts from those hollow eyes. His aspirations, desires, hopes, goals, schemes, all lain bare before the all-powerful.

"Ilad Shukal, you have taken upon a new name—a given name from those that suffer under your hand. Sha'oul—Hell Raiser. This is good—it is a worthy title. Though you have seen a thousand years as Ilad, you shall now be known as Sha'oul from henceforth."

Sha'oul kneeled; even he trembled before the decree and praise of the Ashen One.

"All to blood, and blood to ash, and may the cycle continue, my lord god," he prayed, voice pale beside the omnipresent being.

"And you, Denloth the Waywalker, Pathfinder, Seamweaver. Many are your titles among man, and you also have lived many lifetimes over your natural allotment, always finding a way, through the weave, to outlast those around you.

"Your ingenuity and draw to power has led you to my servant's side, and after seeing within your mind, at his side you shall stay until all our purposes have been met. For we are all one, and all provide strength and power to the ash. The ash expands as the blood flows in its name."

"All to blood, and blood to ash, and may the cycle continue, my lord god." Denloth echoed his dark companion's reverent prayer, completely overtaken by awe in the face of such endless, ancient power.

"The ash is neither merciful nor cruel, only exacting. You both have a path before you now. Fail, and you will join with those whom you have sacrificed this day, sooner than later. They are one with the blood collective, soon to be one with the eternal ash within our realm. Fuel for the quickening of the realm's reach. You have gathered a sufficient army to take Tarigannie by force, which will grant you enough dead to wage war upon all of the Southern Sands.

"The flame of a movement is most vulnerable when it's an ember. Be vigilant. There are those who seek diligently to destroy this movement—a foreigner who carries me within him, and his comrades. They are no small threat, and if you fail to eliminate them, your campaign will end before it even begins.

"Give them no ground, for if we see you overlook their slights and schemes, you shall be rendered to blood and ash. There will be no second chances from here on out. Perform thy duties without flaw."

Both kneeling, they bowed their heads and answered with, "Yes, lord god," before the vision began to fade. Everything seeped out of their heads like a plug had been abruptly pulled, the red leaving their vision as their thoughts delinked from the ash and the communal hallucination.

They both continued kneeling for some time, collecting their wits, focusing on simply keeping balance as their senses began to come back under their control.

Sha'oul was the first to stand, and he in turn helped Denloth to his feet.

"You now truly understand who we serve. I am pleased for you. Rare is it those who join me are found worthy by the lord of ash. Often, they are rendered to blood and ash on the spot. You—he sees something in you, as I have. Welcome, Denloth—to the army of the arisen."

Though head still awhirl with visions of distant planes of endless corruption and ashfall, he nodded his thanks to his new companion.

This had been the endpoint of all his machinations and designs all these years. He devised methods to outrun death for the sole purpose of serving a lord of the Deep Hells in a meaningful position, and now, here he was, the end of his life's search—and yet, this really was only the first step as to where his future now led.

Sha'oul's previous words echoed in his head as thoughts of endless possibilities now stretched out before him.

*"The potential **this** youth possesses is boundless. Look to the moonless night's stars and **his** destiny lies among them. What might **this** fine mortal strive to achieve?"*

36

DESCENT UPON THE HAPLESS

A frosted white bottle went flying past Fin and Matt and smashed on the rock face behind them. Yozo cursed as he fell back next to his small fire pit, head whirling as he tried to regain his center.

Once he had righted himself, he grabbed for his longpipe, which had gone out a while ago. Drawing on the stem for a moment, no smoke coming, he turned the bowl over and dug his finger in it, finding the weed spent.

Tossing the pipe in the same direction as the empty bottle, he fell back in the sand once more and give up as he cursed whatever powers had cut him off from both drink and smoke at once.

Fin patted Matt, signaling it was time to make their move. Yozo still had not noticed them, even though they were close up behind some light bushes with not much cover.

"Hiro!" Yozo yelled, causing Matt to halt his advance. "Bastard…" he breathed, head lolling to the side, looking for his waterskin. He picked it up, putting the spout to his lips—the skin was bone-dry.

Fin knew of only one man better at stealth than him, and that was his master, Matt. Even well into his sixties, Matt made no mistake as he crept up to Yozo undetected.

Snatching Yozo's left wrist, he went for his other one; Yozo yanked it away from Matt just in time. Though the man was heavily compromised, his reflexes stubbornly went to work at fending off the attack.

He whipped out a belt dagger, slamming it towards Matt quicker than even the old veteran thought the drunk would have been able.

Matt secured the right wrist inches from his chest. Luckily for him, Yozo's position hadn't granted him much power in the thrust, or that would have been Matt's last mistake, but the old man twisted Yozo's wrists just so that he scooped the knife out and away from the two, the blade getting lost in the sand as the scuffle commenced.

Fin was moving towards the two now, but his pace slowed as Matt fell to his side, flinging Yozo around, digging his heels into the inner thigh of the younger man. He forced Yozo to spread his legs, locking his arms over and under Yozo's, greatly reducing the chance for him to regain his base and scramble out of the iron hold the old man had on him.

Fin stepped up in front of the man as he was trying to collect his wits. Yozo spat curses at the pair taking advantage of his dehydrated, inebriated daze.

"I thought so," Yozo spoke, loosening up a bit as he noticed the man that stood over him. "You're one of *his* friends. I remember you—wait—is he here? Where's Hiro?" the drunk man yelled as Matt weaved a hand around Yozo's neck, locking his arm over the man's neck to help quiet him from giving away their position in case any arisen were in the area.

"Last time I saw you, you helped us escape the woods, though you openly curse Nomad by his given name. I have not seen Nomad since that day. He's not with us," Fin said honestly, gesturing to the three crewmates that were now approaching their position.

Yozo jerked at the old man who held him tight, testing his restraints—there was no exit for Yozo. The old man's biceps flexed a bit, tightening up the choke until Yozo cooled down.

"I gave you a bit of information, now *you* give *me* some. When's the last you saw of our mutual friend? It'd be in your best interest to answer honestly—your position of power is quite compromised," Fin threatened. Matt accentuated Fin's point by squeezing the chokehold slightly.

Yozo coughed out hoarsely, "I brought him to Sheaf." Matt lightened up his hold a bit while Fin considered the information.

Yozo flailed, trying to throw Matt again, yelling, "Get off me! This is *my* camp!"

"Matt," was all Fin needed to say. Matt released his hold on the man who struggled to stay sitting upright after Matt let go.

"Don't give us reason to detain you again. Next time, Matt won't let go of that choke," Fin threatened, getting a scoffing chuff from Yozo.

Malagar, followed by Hamui, walked into the camp. Yozo looked around Fin to assess his enemy's strength. What worried him though was not the two that had walked into the camp, but the arisen that stood menacingly behind the two, choosing to remain on the outside of the perimeter.

"The walking dead…" Yozo mumbled, pointing to Dubix, a visible tremble in his flesh.

They all turned to consider their quiet companion. Fin turned back to Yozo with a tired smile on his lips. "Yes, the dead walk with us—for better or for worse."

Yozo froze, not paying attention to Fin's self-reflecting comment, and it was clear that he was no longer focused on Fin, Matt, or the others. They would get nowhere with questioning him as long as Dubix was there.

Fin knew how superstitious Nomad had been around the undead. He had gotten over his fright after some time of being completely immersed by them, but he had been rigid at the start of their journey. Fin guessed that it had to do with his people and their perspective on the dead.

"Mal, Hamui, Dubix, are you three up for continuing the hunt for your friend without me and Matt for a day or so?" Fin asked without taking his eyes off Yozo.

Malagar turned to Matt at first, but saw that Matt was content with sitting off to the side, allowing for them to make their own decision on the matter.

"We will," Malagar said firmly, looking to his two other companions for the road ahead. "Though, catch up as soon as you can. You know how powerful our prey is and where he's headed. The best we'll most likely be able to do is trail him until you two arrive."

"Wise man," Fin said, agreeing with Malagar's measured assessment. "Good, head out now. It seems our bag of bones back there is frightening Yozo, and I need him talking sooner rather than later," Fin finished in a mumble as he kicked Yozo's discarded, smoking pipe in the dirt.

Malagar slowly nodded, taking the hint from Fin's gesture. He knew the combination of being high and drunk often led to regrettable things said, suspecting that Fin wanted to take advantage of Yozo being cross-faded.

The three quietly kept walking, traveling past the camp and back up the rocky cliffs, heading the direction they had been going up until this point.

Yozo watched Dubix for as long as he could before collapsing back in the dirt, staring up in the bright sky.

"Foul sorcery and warlocks. You people walk with tethered spirits. You are cursed and those you visit are doomed. What evil have you brought upon me!" Yozo blathered out.

Fin stepped up and struck the gibbering man before he spiraled into a full-on breakdown.

"*I'm* going to give you information about Hiro, and *you're* going to give me information about him, alright?" Fin calmly said, beginning negotiations after Yozo had calmed somewhat with the smack across the face that had brought him back to the moment and out of his crazed hallucinations of walking bones.

"Matt," Fin said, getting the old man's attention. Mat had appeared uninterested in the irrelevant diversion to their main mission. "Get some rope," Fin mumbled under his breath.

"You're that scared of this guy?" Matt chuckled, patting the jittery man on the head. Yozo grabbed the old man's hand, twisting it and using it as leverage to hop to a squat, flipping Matt in the process.

Matt went with the throw, landing on his feet, snatching Yozo just before he was able to reach for his dagger in the dirt once more. This time Matt latched Yozo's limbs tight straightaway, straining Yozo's body's limits, evoking painful grunts from the man.

"Yeah, I am," Fin said, shuffling through his pack for a steel cable to tie the man up with. "If Arie says this guy is no joke, I tend to believe her."

Matt gave no further flippant remarks and instead allowed Fin to wrap the man's wrists and arms up tight around his torso.

In Yozo's eyes, Fin was like a spider wrapping up his caught prey in an unbreakable, thin thread, and so he writhed more out of fear than in defiance, but Matt controlled each part of his body to allow Fin to do his work while he restrained the limbs that needed controlling, the two working uncannily in sync with each other.

Yozo was beyond impressed with the two. He was genuinely scared out of his mind by the strange duo that had mysteriously descended upon his camp in the middle of nowhere with walking bones at their command.

"Devils! Spin your web, consume me, but I will not grant you the pleasure of breaking my spirit! Too many years have I been preparing for death. I fear it not!" Yozo shouted as Fin finished securing the wire tightly around the man's torso.

"We are not devils," Fin calmly said, sitting the man down on the ground, propped up by the boulder he had been sitting on when they first came across him. "We are…a diverse group of friends, but not devils in any way—well, aside from Dubix. I personally don't trust that one, but he has proven himself thus far as to trek with us."

Fin's voice seemed to calm the dazed Yozo slightly, and Matt sat beside the man as he was still having a difficult time sitting up without falling to either side.

"We're not on some demonic mission; in fact, we're the ones fighting the demons. Our friend was taken by a powerful agent of the arisen, a follower of Telenth. We are fighting for a *just* cause! Tell me, do you see us as demons now?" Fin questioned, overacting slightly to sell Yozo on their story as he could clearly see the man got swept up in Fin's tale.

"You bind me, and tell me you mean no ill?" Yozo spat, drawing himself out of Fin's convincing spell.

"We only bound you because you kept attacking us," Fin said, a fake hint of sympathetic regret on his tongue.

"I only attacked you because you invaded my camp by force!" Yozo continued.

Fin readily nodded his concession to the point. "Well, we could try one more time. Will you not attack us that we may share your camp with you to exchange information like civil guests?"

Yozo closed his eyes for a moment, thinking hard. His mind had rarely been so compromised. Every flinch, every facial tell, every syllable seemed loaded with ten or so different hidden meanings that led all different directions. He wanted them gone from his camp, from his life, but he also could not pass up the chance to garner information about Hiro. This he knew. He'd much rather them at least think him compliant and be unbound than otherwise.

He nodded his head and agreed to behave.

"Good," Fin said soothingly, moving to start to undo the wire from around the still dizzy man.

"You know, young man, you're quick." Matt paid compliments as Fin undid the binding. "With the right training, perhaps you could amount to something. Your grappling game is rubbish, but that can be developed. Your speed though; I could help you leverage that gift."

Yozo looked over for the first time at Matt, considering the old man, eyes clouded over.

"What could I learn from an old, blind man? I've survived alone from land to land with no help from the defunct. I've never lost a fight. All my enemies end up face down in the dirt," Yozo snidely returned.

"You lost to me," Matt said straightly, adding, "and it sounds like this Hiro fella isn't 'face down in the dirt' yet either. And I'm guessing whoever gave you those lumps on your face may be still walking around while you waste away here in the wilds. I'm not about training no pompous brats who don't know when their good n' beat, so I won't be pushing it on ya, but I know talent when I see it, and it might do you good to have some help in cleaning up your act for a change instead of lashing out at those who would be a helping hand."

Fin finished undoing Yozo's bonds just as Matt finished talking with the man, and Yozo, for the first time in days, let go of his scowl, reflecting upon Matt's words deeply instead of jumping to a counterpoint as he often did.

"Here," Fin said, gathering some water and victuals from his pack to give to Yozo. "Let's start this out right this time."

The sun lowered, and though Matt could see their situation was coming to a manageable tempo, he looked in the direction Malagar and Hamui had marched off in, hoping the same luck would be granted to his young pupils who were still quite green in the ways of the hunt.

He knew how quickly the hunters could become the hunted.

37

DIVISION AT THE GATES

"Sultan Metus and company, I presume," the gate warden questioned, stepping up to Metus and Bannon. The sandstorm made it difficult to hear him, even though he was practically shouting.

Metus looked back at his allies and troops. The sandstorm obscured his ability to see past a rank or two, but he could see that all his closest allies were near to him still.

"Aye," Metus replied, uneasy with the fact that even the gate guards knew or were expecting him.

"Your presence is requested before the council to explain your militarized arrival. You may bring a small company with you to the meeting, but the bulk of your troops must remain outside the city walls."

"I did not intend to bring my troop in with me to visit with the council, but surely you don't expect me to leave them without the walls to camp in the wilderness? Is there not space in the barracks enough to house a hundred soldiers? I come here in peace, as I always do. Never before have my men been subjected to remain outside the walls."

"I was given orders, Sultan. No doubt you've crossed many a

caravan on the roads as you've gotten closer to Rochata-Ung. It is a busy time of the season. We have merchants coming from all over Tarigannie to trade in the monsoon harvest market and festival days, and we have little room to house an outsider's troop at this time. Your men, save a few travel companions, are not allowed through these gates. Any act to force their entry will be seen as an act of war."

Metus looked back at the Hyperium one more time, whispered something into Bannon's ear, then nodded to the guard. "So be it. I will bring only my personal guard and escorts with me in that case. Oh, and two travelers we picked up on the road here. We have no connections with them other than we offered them safety on the road."

The warden looked out over Metus' company once more and then replied with, "When you are ready, my lord, I will escort you to a residence in the royal district. The council will be ready to hear from you this evening after your brief rest."

"Very well. Allow me to inform my troop of the proceedings," Metus said crisply, returning with Bannon first to the head of the Hyperium.

Hathos stood at attention as the two top-ranked men stepped up to him, shielding their faces from the blasting sands. His bronzed armor shone brightly, even though the sun was mostly blocked out by the wretched weather. His shorn head wore no helm, but a gold and black striped nemes, which was furrowed to help block the harsh sands currently. His head tilted slightly down, but his eyes locked fixedly on Metus.

The three men huddled close in the blasting sands, Metus explaining, "I did not anticipate this, but the council wishes— demands—the Hyperium to remain outside of the city walls. I'm afraid you will need to set camp somewhere out here."

"I would suggest along the foothills of Daloth's Spire, my sultan," Bannon cut in.

"Good. Yes, that should only be a mile northeast of the walls, if I remember. I cannot see it through this storm, but once it has died down a bit, make your way there and hold up until further notice," Metus finished, looking to Bannon to concur.

"Let Kissa and her two finest accompany me within the gates to keep a watch on you and Nomad's attachment, which I'm assuming you'll be taking in with you. If the Hyperium is needed, we can call for them as at that time."

Metus contemplated for a moment, then replied, "No. Kissa and her two I trust to somehow make entry into the city and shadow us, but you are not trained as they are for that sort of thing. I need you for another purpose. Stay with the Hyperium, and take Nomad, Henarus, and his priest and watch over them. Henarus should be able to help calm Nomad's mind. He has become more agitated these days. The curse is strengthening, he needs looking after, and I cannot deal with cracks in his mental state when within Rochata-Ung. Once within the walls, I'll instruct Cavok and Terra to go find Zaren and Jadu. That leaves me with Gale, Jasper, Reza, and Arie. Is all that understood? If there be any suggestions to the plan, speak them now."

Bannon gave Metus a disconcerting look, his hesitancy to allow his sultan to wander without him in Rochata-Ung clear.

"Understood. The Hyperium will see to your commands," Hathos said, saluting crisply to answer for his superior.

"Very well. Kissa will be watching from the shadows. Send word if need be. A white cloth from a window for distress," Bannon reluctantly agreed.

"Keep Nomad safe. I'll finish our duties in Rochata as quickly as possible," Metus said. Bannon and Hathos both bowed before heading back to the Hyperium.

Gathering Nomad's company around, Bannon briefly laid out their plan, everyone splitting up without much of a timely goodbye. Nomad, Henarus, and his priest headed out to tag along with Bannon and the rest of the Hyperium.

Everyone else hoisted their packs and looked to the city gates, which stood well over twenty feet tall. Rochata-Ung was a sprawling city, and most of it was open to the public, a vast network of districts, markets, and slums stretching out into the canyonlands and dunes nearby. But the central city itself was guarded behind its long, stretching wall. It was well-guarded and getting in without admittance was a feat for a real professional.

"Stay close," Metus ordered all in his group, approaching once again the gate warden. "We are ready," Metus spoke over the howling sandstorm.

"Follow me, my lord," the warden ordered. Two other guards on duty followed up behind them as they entered the gate into the expansive sprawl of buildings and bustling people.

The temporary resting quarters they were led to were more of a lounge than a private residence. Though there were partitions and beds comfortably placed throughout the large, extravagant room, it was very open, more than likely purposefully so, so that the guards could keep an eye on them during their brief stay.

Cavok and Terra did not stay long, though. After Terra freshened up, and Cavok took a quick sponge bath, they went to leave the lounge.

"Halt," one of the two remaining guards ordered as they went to pass through the threshold.

Cavok obeyed, but slowly turned his silent, intimidating glare the guard's way, causing the guard to stammer out, "Wha-what are you about? Your company is soon to be summoned by the council."

Terra offered an answer, seeing as Cavok only pressed his glare more intensely. "Our group is out of supplies from the long journey. While Sultan Metus is at court, Cavok and I are tending to some shopping so that we may leave as soon as our lord is finished with his business."

The guards looked to one another, considered the young girl's answer, and hesitantly waved them through.

"Jhans will go with you. Our orders are to oversee your company."

Cavok didn't miss a step at the slight hang-up of having a chaperone. One guard would be simple enough to lose. If he wasn't able to shake their follower, he knew he'd be able to make the guard disappear at the very least.

Jhans, the quiet guard with a mean frown, a scar along his jaw, and a visor slightly hinged down to block out the sun and sand, quietly slipped in behind the two, following them out into the court and into the streets from there. Metus and the others watched surreptitiously as the two left to complete the task of contacting Zaren and Jadu.

"That's one less Rochata guard rising in the morning, you know. Cavok is not delicate when it comes to reconnaissance," Arie whispered into Metus' ear, exasperation with the large man's brute ways of solving things clear in her voice.

"He knows Zaren and Jadu best out of anyone here," Metus sighed. "We need those two, Arie. Let's hope he deals with the guard discreetly."

Arie snickered darkly, murmuring, "Cavok, discreet?"

She grabbed a handful of fruit from the low-standing

refreshments table. Metus joined her, pouring water from the pitcher into a clayware cup, sipping from it while lost in thought about Cavok and Terra's departure.

It was a few hours later, after everyone had had sufficient time to eat, drink, rest, and clean themselves up, when the court master came with two more guards to lead them to the council's court.

Metus kept his company close. No one spoke on the long walk there, all slowly developing an ill feeling about the procession; after all, Metus had just threatened one of the leading council members the prior evening.

His message of peace and warning began to seem like little protection now that he was deep in his neighbor's capital.

Was he there to sound the alarm and save needless lives from an approaching foe, or was he walking into a fool's grave?

Part Four: Sands Soaked in Blood

38

CHAINS OF THE PAST

"So Nomad was healed in Sheaf?" Fin asked, restating what Yozo had just glossed over.

"To a degree. Not fully, though. As I understood it, it only bought him a bit of time," Yozo said, startling afterwards as he noticed Matt at his side for the third time in the last minute, even though Matt hadn't moved.

"Where were they headed from Sheaf?" Fin asked, snapping his fingers to bring Yozo's attention back to him.

"I think they were headed out to recruit some friends in Rochata-Ung, then head south to confront the arisen invasion," Yozo said, still side-eyeing Matt suspiciously.

"Friends in Rochata, eh? Could they be going for Jadu? Zaren was training him there last I heard," Fin mumbled, more to himself than to the others.

"Yes! Those were the names spoken of in the council," Yozo chipped in, adding, "They took a whole troop of soldiers with them as well. It's a large company, not just a few."

"How long ago was this, you say?" Fin asked, pleased with how willing Yozo had been in cooperating after they had calmed him down in his high daze. The alcohol seemed to smooth out his hard edges greatly.

"It's been no more than two weeks, maybe even just one. I don't remember. There was no reason for me to keep count of the days, so I didn't."

"They may already be in Rochata by now then," Fin thought out loud. "Thank you, Yozo, that's all I needed to know. You had some questions for me, did you not? I'd like to assist you if I could, seeing how you've been so helpful to us. I admit, though most of my friends seem to know you or have had time with you, I still know very little about you. I only got to see you in the dryad woods, and that was only for a fleeting moment."

Yozo took his time to process Fin's loaded question. Though Fin seemed comfortable enough with sharing his company, the rest of Fin's group actively thwarted his mission of justice. Indeed, his whole purpose even in being in this land was to kill Hiro, and so he admitted to himself, he did not know the implications of helping Fin as he had just done when Fin would likely take Hiro's side if he knew the full story of the situation.

Yozo brought his hands up to his face, feeling the lumps and crooked nose that had not set right from Cavok's beating. He had had migraines almost nightly since that night he had tried to kill Hiro and Cavok had caught him, and every night he was reminded of not only his hatred for Hiro, but equally now for Cavok. Though Fin seemed different than his other two comrades, he would still side with them, as the other, more level-headed ones surrounding Hiro had. When it came to it, Fin would defend Hiro, even if he were in the wrong.

His mood shifted, suddenly, slapping his deformed face hard as he bit out, "You lot portray that you're keepers of peace and fairness, but you're hypocrites! The only one you are true to is Hiro! All others be damned!"

Fin's eyes widened, taken aback by Yozo's outburst. Matt sat up, finally somewhat interested in the direction the conversation had headed.

"I've also heard much about this 'Nomad,' or 'Hiro,' or whatever the hell else you call him. Tell me more about him. It seems a great deal in both your lives centers around him," Matt ordered.

Fin looked to Yozo, not sure if Matt wanted an answer from the foreigner first or himself. Yozo's hesitation prompted Fin to speak first.

222

"I've known him for just a year now. He joined a reconnaissance mission I was a part of. We infiltrated Brigganden when the arisen army controlled it back then. We called him 'Nomad' because that's what he was at the time, a passer-through; that was until he started to form close bonds with our scouting party. After our mission proved a success, he stuck around, but an injury he sustained during the mission began to corrupt him. Some sort of curse had been placed upon him from the warlock we faced, and he had to seek aid from the saren monastery up in Jeenyre. I only saw him briefly in the Jeenyre region when Cavok and I went to check up on him and Reza."

"Cavok! He's another one I can never forgive! I have him to thank for this!" Yozo hissed, indicating the lumps across his face.

"Cavok would not have touched you unless you brought on his wrath," Fin said, discrediting Yozo outright.

"No," Matt said, holding up a hand to Fin. "You know as well as I that Cavok has a temper. Usually, you were there to help him simmer it, but the seasons you were not around him, well, he does tend to become feral. He's been known to do some…regrettable things."

Matt's interjection caused Fin to consider his dear friend introspectively a moment. Matt pursued more information on the point, asking Yozo, "May I feel, Yozo? I'm blind—can't see what he did to your face."

Yozo calmed a moment, fully expecting Fin's answer but thrown off by Matt's willingness and interest in hearing both sides.

With Yozo's permission, Matt brought his knobby hand to Yozo's face. He felt delicate features in most places. Matt was not accustomed to Yozo's kind, finding his bone structure to be quite interesting, but he could feel the places where bones had been broken and had not healed properly. Hematomas had clotted and scar tissue had swelled, and his nose was crooked. He had received one hell of a beating, Matt could feel.

"Cavok…did this?" Matt whispered, barely audible, but the sincerity of his pity very clear.

"And he shall die for it," Yozo huffed out, voice trembling with rage, on the edge of tears, emotions too strong for him to successfully fight off in his heavily compromised state.

"Oh gods, that boy. If you do end up killing him, can't say he doesn't deserve it. He's got so much heart for those he cares for, but those he don't, well, the man can be possessed by the berserker's spirit. Those that cross him have been known to end up face down in the gutter. It's a rough world out there; can you blame him for it? What'd ya do to cross him, boy? You must have done something to set him off."

Yozo attempted to compose himself, having the accusation abruptly turned back on him. His hesitation was not pressed as Matt and Fin waited in silence for an answer to the question.

"I...attempted to carry out justice on Hiro that night, and Cavok found me."

"Carry out justice? You tried to kill Nomad?" Fin asked to clarify what had happened.

"After what he's done, a quick execution would be considered a *light* sentence for his crimes."

"What exactly did this Nomad do?" Matt asked. "If he caused you to devote your life to following him across lands, chasing after him, well then, he must be some special sort of dirty bastard."

"Honestly, I've come across worse, many times over in my travels. It's not the severity of his crimes, it's his refusal to take ownership of them that disturbs me so," Yozo whispered, eyes closed, speaking as if to himself.

Opening his eyes, finding Fin and Matt still present, his voice changed as he added, "It is a long story. I do not see how it concerns you two to know the details of our family feud. Suffice it to say, Hiro, the one you know as Nomad, betrayed and neglected his family. Many in his line died because of his lack of foresight, one of them being his sister—my wife. Instead of dealing with his failures, he ran from them, from *us!* I shall never forgive what he let happen to us, the ones he said he loved more than any.

"Mayhap someday I will convey the timeline of events to you, but today is not that day. I simply wish to force him to answer for his sins. To force him to consider what he did to us. He left our family line in shambles—a line that graciously adopted me in and gave me a heritage, only to have it destroyed by his foolishness."

"Hmm," Matt rasped, sitting back comfortably. He picked up Yozo's discarded pipe, dusting it off as he continued. "Family strife. A powerful motivator for action. It has brought many kingdoms and would-be great tribes and organizations down into ruin.

"Feel not pressed to recount the tale. Oft times the details are biased and foggy. I doubt we'd get the true story from you anyways. It'd be jumbled with too many ill sentiments to be credible or useful to get a good judgement of the situation. You've got it in your head that he's slighted you and with that being your only driving factor all these years, doesn't matter how bad he crossed you at this point, you're just seeking closure, through his death, his admittance, or both—probably preferably both—no?"

Fin seemed a bit more concerned about the accusations than Matt was, listening to the conversation with a slight scowl as Yozo proceeded to slander his friend. "I'm not saying Nomad didn't do some regrettable things in the past, each man has his demons—that I appreciate—but Nomad is one of the more honest men I've known. His sense of duty is pure. I don't know of Hiro's past, but I know Nomad's present, and from what I've seen, he's hardly the person needing judgment in this region currently.

"The arisen lord is, effectively, at it again. He's created trouble in the area before, and by all accounts, he looks to overthrow the Southern Sands region, not just by replacing himself as its ruler, but by wiping out all citizens, raising them in a state of lifeless servitude. That, in fact, is the very cause Nomad is sworn to oppose. Surely your sense of justice would better be put to use by joining our cause rather than opposing those who fight for life and freedom."

Yozo side-eyed Fin as the man proceeded to attempt to dissuade him from a course he had been pursuing for years on end. Regardless of how convincing the man's argument was, for him to turn away from his goal now would undermine his whole existence from the day he set foot out of his country.

"So, you're asking him to take a break from trying to kill one man to kill another man, this *lord of the arisen* or whomever?" Matt asked.

Fin frowned at Matt's summary. "Well if I asked him to settle down to a peaceful life and tend a garden, I highly doubt he'd take me seriously. Yozo's obviously trained years in combat and survival strategies. It's gotten him from one side of the world to the other. A man with his skills, and in his prime still, would best be used and fulfilled by doing what he does best.

"You should know that better than anyone, Matt. It was you who trained me with a similar skill set. Your intent was not for me to enjoy a restful life, beginning anew with family somewhere in a sleepy hamlet. You trained me to be more lethal than my foes. That's the line of work Yozo is in, for better, or worse. My argument is that it would be for the better if he chose to join our cause."

Yozo was not happy with the two's underappreciation of his situation. "You don't know what he did to me all those years ago! You don't know how he forsook those he said he loved more than life itself—"

Fin cut in. "—I don't care how awful he was early in life! He could have been the *worst* of lowlifes for all I care! The past is dead. What happened years ago will never be rewritten. What I care about is what's happening here and now, and what I know of Nomad's present is that he's fighting harder than any of us, save maybe Reza, to put a halt to that tyrant, the arisen lord. He's putting his life on the line to save a whole nation's worth of lives. His current path speaks for itself; he's trying his damnedest to be a positive force in this world, making meaningful sacrifices for complete strangers.

"Meanwhile what are you doing with your present? Chasing around, like a dog, a man that's engaged in a worthy cause. Look at you—you're enslaved by the past. No matter the evidence presented before you to convince you of Nomad's present, you would ignore it and hold to whatever dusty memories you have of him. You're trapped in time, thinking all the while that if you can but end him, you'd end your imprisonment, and you'd finally be free of this torturous loop of suffering and sorrow of what happened all those years ago.

"Let me tell you, as someone who's gone through the same hell, killing that man—that ain't going to free you from those wretched memories. The only one that's going to do that is you. You, and you alone, have the power to relinquish the shackles of the past that hold you down."

"Aye," Matt concurred, stuffing Yozo's pipe with some of his own loose leaf, lighting it, and handed it to the silenced man.

Yozo accepted the pipe, absorbing all that was said, taking a draw as he reflected. The other two were silent, allowing him time with his thoughts.

"Sage?" Yozo questioned.

Matt answered, "Arnica."

The smoke smelled sweet and crisp. It lingered in the air as the three sat in silence while the day slipped by.

39

A SIMPLE EXTRACTION

Loose dirt and rocks slid down and over the cliff ledge the three scrambled along. Malagar looked back just in time to throw a hand over Hamui before the little praven, who had lost his balance, plummeted down to the canyon floor fifty feet below.

"Damn it, Hamui!" Malagar whispered out, cutting himself short on his reprimands as he realized now was not the time to berate his less acrobatically gifted friend.

"What, I'm fine. Let's get moving," Hamui said, shrugging off Malagar's frustrated concern for his safety.

Dubix followed the two in silence as they exited the tight squeeze of the ledge they had maneuvered past.

Motioning the two over behind a sizable boulder, Malagar waited for them to get close to talk softly to them, eyeing the encampment of arisen further up the canyon as some activity began to come into view.

"Looks like Denloth brought Wyld to the arisen's camp. That's not good."

"Oh, really?" Hamui sarcastically prodded, his annoyance with what he perceived as Malagar's over-cautious nature now on surface level.

Completely used to Hamui's lip at that point, Malagar shrugged the comment off, busy formulating their approach.

"Dubix. That sprawl of arisen is too massive for us to hope on finding Denloth or Wyld within it without being noticed by some sentry. Is there any way you might be able to locate Wyld? You sensed her life essence while we were in the jail. Can you sense it here now?"

Dubix remained still for a while longer, considering the request, attempting to feel through the masses of undead, locating the living within his range of perception…there weren't many.

"I do sense the living amongst the dead. Only a few. There could be more further within the camp. There." Dubix pointed with his skeletal hand, indicating a grove of wild cypress trees along the other side of the canyon terraces. "There's only one mortal alone in that grove, the rest I sense are cloistered together."

Malagar looked to the wide ledge far across the canyon, looking for a route for him to take to get there. The way looked rough and exposed—not an easy distance to travel, even for him.

"That's it then, our best chance at extracting Wyld from this wretched place," Malagar let out a sigh, preparing himself for some pushback. "I think it would be best if I went it alone from here. Traversing over to that ledge is going to be arduous to say the least."

"You think you can get over there without getting spotted? There's no place to hide crossing that canyon, not unless you backtrack and cross the canyon way back there, out of sight," Hamui scoffed, exposing the ridiculousness of his friend's foolhardy plan.

"That would take a good deal of time, and who knows how long Wyld—if it is Wyld—will be kept in that location? We've got to try it at least. I'll do my best to keep out of sight."

Dubix remained silent, but a shifting of his bones seemed to denote his discomfort at the proposed plan.

Hamui rolled his eyes at his companion's stubborn commitment to his path, looking to the thirty-foot gap that lay between them and the other side of the canyon, then down the fifty feet to the canyon floor.

"You think you could jump that gap if I gave you a little push? You'd only be visible to anyone looking this way for a split second instead of minutes with your plan."

"Jump that gap?" Malagar gruffed. "Even if the conditions were perfect for a long jump, that's a good thirty feet from ledge to ledge.

Not a jump anyone *I* know could make."

"I know. That's why I said I'd give you a push. If I conjure a blast of air behind you, you'll go flying. I can get you airborne over that distance, no problem."

"You want to send me *flying*?" Malagar incredulously laughed.

"It's our best chance at getting you to that ledge fast and undetected, and you know it. So why don't you stop arguing and get ready for a jump. I'm ready. We're wasting time going back and forth on this."

Malagar eyed the gap seriously, knowing that if Hamui was not good on his promise, there'd be no way for him to clear it, and he'd be left alone to face a fifty-foot freefall to the canyon floor. That distance would surely mess him up, if not outright end him.

Looking to the cypress grove and then to the army's encampment once more, he realized that there were too many arisen close by for his original plan to make any sense. The leap may very well be their best option.

"God damn it," he cursed under his breath, looking at the jump, mentally preparing himself for the tenuous journey. "You ready then?" he asked, checking with Hamui as he lined up his launch platform and landing destination.

Hamui began quietly chanting, holding his contorted gloved fingers and slightly glowing staff towards the ledge, a gust beginning to form along the cliff face they were close to. He looked to Malagar and nodded his approval.

Malagar's eyes fixed on the long ledge on the other side of the canyon. He imagined completing the jump in his mind, working through all the steps, watching himself as he touched down on the stone platform across the way.

Looking down at his feet, ensuring his footing was sound, he looked forward and bounded straight on, sprinting hard towards the edge.

He launched himself a foot short of the cliff, hurling himself over the canyon gap as a strong rush of wind lifted him a bit higher than he would have been unaided.

His flight was prolonged, the updraft floating him along, aiding his trajectory towards the other cliff's edge as he quickly closed the gap. He touched down cleanly on the other side of the canyon, tucking and rolling to help dissipate his momentum before he crashed into some bushes on the other side.

Malagar came up from the roll to look back on the gap he had cleared, only considering then how he'd be getting back once he'd found Wyld.

He looked up just in time to see Hamui flip him a rude gesture, presumably for not having initial faith in his abilities from the jump. The praven then went to take a seat with his back to the boulder they had been hiding behind, Dubix crouching down as well to keep out of sight of the camp.

"That's it then. I'm on my own from here," he whispered to himself, making his way along the cliff path towards the cypress grove.

His footsteps were nearly silent as he padded his way along the loamy sand. Though technically he was still in training, Matt had alluded to both him and Hamui that they were close to being ready for recommendation to the court, or private entities and the like. They had almost learned everything the old veteran had to teach, and Malagar made sure to keep his stealth game tight as he eased up to the line of wild cypress trees that blocked his view from the inner grove.

Wyld stood there, a streak of glimmering silver slashed across her side from the Seam. She was utterly still, looking off in the distance over the mountain range, unconcerned with the four arisen skeletons that stood beside her.

Each skull turned their empty socketed eyes towards Malagar as he hid behind the tree line, peeking in.

He raised his weapons, the surprise given away—though what he had done to give himself away, he was not sure. It didn't matter at that point anyways, and he cracked his knuckles, slapping his armor-plated leather gloves together as he leapt into the clearing to engage the skeletons who were forming a perimeter around the intruder between them and their captive.

As Malagar landed before the armed warrior, a sword chopped down at him. He effortlessly dodged it, slamming the protected ribcage of the arisen soundly, getting the foe out of the way, bumping it into the other arisen behind it.

As the two struggled to regain their balance, he was busy at work slamming the other two skeletons, knocking them in the skull multiple times, upper-cutting one so hard that its head detached from its spine, rendering it lifeless immediately.

Gripping the other skull with both hands, he pried it from its torso, popping it apart just as the other two skeletons came in at him.

A lazy sword thrust made its way towards him, but it was barely a threat. He deftly switched stances to grab its wrist, wrenching the sword from the skeleton's grip, breaking its fingers along with it.

He looped around behind the disarmed skeleton, the other smashing its comrade's ribs apart to get at Malagar. He thrust the disabled machination to the ground, throwing a high kick up and through the last standing skeleton's jaw, shattering it, launching its body into the sagebrush beyond.

A light breeze blew through the trees, the gentle rustle the only sound in the grove now. He waited a moment longer in a battle-ready stance to make sure the skeletons were not going to rise again.

The scuffle had been relatively quiet and quick; Malagar hoped quick enough that no one would have heard much, but if they had, he knew he needed to act now, and with all haste.

"Wyld," Malagar called out to an old friend that didn't seem interested, or even coherent, in the recent scuff.

Malagar walked up to his companion, inspecting the phasing, iridescent scars that had marked her body all up and down her right side. The patterns and otherworldly colors seemed somehow familiar.

What devilish magicks had done this to her, and what it had done to her consciousness, he knew not, but he knew now was not the time to investigate the matter in any detail.

Gently grabbing her left hand, he squeezed, and she reassuringly squeezed back.

"Good," Malagar breathed under his breath. "Wyld, I need to get you back to our camp. Can you follow me?"

She did not answer, or move at first, but as Malagar tugged on her hand to prompt her forward, she did follow, somewhat sluggishly at first. As he managed to guide her out of the tree line and back up the cliffside, she became less and less resistant to his beckoning hold.

Eyes, black as night, peered across the span of the canyon from the encampment along the western wall, narrowing as he watched the haltia male tug his hypnotized kaith along the canyon ridge until he crossed over it, out of sight.

Whispering dark speech to the wind, Denloth smiled, turning to consider his present company. Two blood-red bones, clad in sleek armor, covering most of their frames, helmets dovetailed down with golden wings flaring off to the sides, stood beside him at the ready.

"Follow. Bring me their bodies for repurposing. Fulfill your oaths," the robed man cruelly said, turning back to camp as his red warriors slowly began to march forth down the lonely canyon trail towards the falling sun.

40

OLD FRIENDS AND NEW ADVENTURES

"Here," Cavok whispered, handing Terra a few copper strips. "Grab yourself a sweet roll and coffee. I'll meet up with you in a bit."

Terra hesitantly took the coin, looking up to the quaint shop sign that read *Cream n' Brew Delicacies*, then looked back to where Cavok had been to only see Jhans, the guard that had been following them the last few minutes running frantically off down a side street, presumably after Cavok.

She had a bad feeling about what Cavok planned to do, and she stood there on the street corner, debating on whether to follow his orders and wait around for his return, or to follow the two and try to make sure Cavok did not do anything *too* regrettable. She knew they needed to lose the man, but there was a feeling in her gut that hinted at Cavok ending the man that was just performing his duty.

"I can't let him do that," she whispered to herself, taking off in the direction the guard had gone.

Cavok threw a strong arm out from around a corner, catching the pursuing guard by the neck. He threw him back into the alleyway, away from any witnesses.

Jhans coughed, trying to breathe, trying to call for help, but Cavok was on top of him in an instant, covering his mouth. Cavok took off his helm and smacked him across the face with it, knocking the man clean out.

Hooking his hand in at the opening in the guard's breastplate, Cavok started dragging the man further back in the alley, when he noticed Terra standing there, looking at him, worry clear in her countenance.

Cavok huffed and threw the man to the ground, harshly whispering, "I told you to wait for me back there."

Terra wanted to answer, but the large man scared her then, and all she could do was cover her mouth to hide her trembling lips.

He sighed again, looking off to the side, drawing his sleeve up to expose a network of tattoos along his arm which began to glow. Placing his hand on Jhans' face, he whispered a foreign string of words before picking the man up and sitting him upright against the side of the alley wall.

"He'll be out for hours, long enough for us to be about our business without too much trouble. But we'll need to be quick about finding the wizard and the little one," he gruffed, approaching the young girl who still looked warily at him.

"Come on," he said, a tinge of annoyance in his voice as he grabbed her hand, leading her out of the alley and off down the street to hunt down the wizard's school.

It had taken them only an hour to find the wizards' college to the northeast of the city borders. There had been little talk between the two the whole time.

"Tell the damn wizard that Cavok is here and to get his ass down here now," Cavok said to the stick-thin youth in robes at the campus gates.

"What '*damn wizard*' are you asking for?" the youth asked, cautiously disgusted at the brute on the other side of the gate.

"Zaren," Cavok spat, amending himself afterwards with, "No, get Jadu instead. Jadu will be more likely to hear me out. Is Jadu in there?"

"Master Zaren? Jadu?" the youth softly exclaimed, taken aback that this man might somehow know of the senior level enchanter and his star pupil.

"Yes, either one of them. Tell them Cavok requires their aid, and if I don't get it—" Cavok sneered, dragging his thumb across his throat, which sent the boy running for the college doors.

He let out a self-gratified smirk, shrugging his shoulders as he sat back and waited for the return of the messenger boy, hopefully to open the gates for them and allow them an audience with one of the two enchanters.

"You could have asked nicely," Terra said, upset with how Cavok had handled the gate boy.

Cavok's smirk quickly turned into a grumpy scowl.

"I was just teasing the boy, it'll quicken his step," he stated flatly.

"And were you just *teasing* Jhans back there? You were going to kill him if I hadn't had been there," she shot back.

"I wasn't going to kill him!" he said, lowering his voice slightly as he explained. "I was going to put him to sleep, as I did, even before you showed up to act as some pompous conscience. Why would I kill him? There was no need."

"You…weren't going to kill him?" Terra said, unsure about if her companion was leading her along or being honest.

"No," Cavok scoffed without hesitation, leaving the two in silence as they waited a few more minutes before the gate boy came scurrying back to unlock the gate for them and offer them to come on campus grounds.

"Come, Master Zebulon will see you," the youth said, locking the gate behind them, leading them along the brick path through the bright and blooming pinkish white cherry trees that shaded the grounds from the bright desert sun above.

The tall three-story building stood in front of them, red brick with white trim plaster, windows lining most of the façade. The three entered the main archway to the long, stretching university lobby.

Taking a quick stroll down the side colonnade, its many stone pillars casting long shadows upon the group as they walked down the quiet halls, they came to a large spiral stairwell, a green pool with dreary statues of mourning souls, naked and slumped, chiseled out of marble and covered in a thin layer of moss at the base.

They rounded the stairs, making their way up two flights before coming out into another side hall, walking along a wooden balcony. Cavok and Terra began to hear what sounded like furniture crashing and thumping about, the walls and floor trembling slightly, dust falling from the rafters as they neared the far wing of the building.

"Jadu," Cavok mumbled. Terra listened, a little worry evident in her step. "That one's always exploding something."

The boy knocked on the door at the end of the hall, another explosion rattling the hinges and shuddering the frame as he waited a moment before turning the knob and opening it, motioning for the two to enter.

Cavok strode in, and Terra noted the man was more tense and alert than usual, as if ready to react on a moment's notice. With all the ruckus that came from within the room, she supposed it was unwise to do anything but.

Before them lay a singed, small figure in thick robes in a room that was equally burnt, the tall windows either blackened or broken.

"You reek of sulfur, little one," Cavok said, dusting the little praven's shoulder free of soot after he picked him up and set him back on his feet.

The old enchanter tapped his finger along his thin jawline, sighing heavy before saying, "That one got away from you, Jadu. You have to contain the blast better if you wish to master that wand. They're more difficult to regulate than staves. Even though they hold less overall energy than a staff, they release their hexweave faster, as you hopefully just witnessed. We'll work on the same confluxation spell till you can master it. Try it with a different element this time instead of fire so you don't blow yourself up again. Maybe try water? Always going to fire right out the gate, you are. Like a moth to flame, I swear."

"I hate water…" Jadu grumbled, dusting off his robes as he righted himself.

His foul mood was fleeting though, as it ever was with Jadu. Seeing his old travel companion instantly lightened his countenance. Jumping up at the man, Jadu gave him a big hug, which Cavok openly welcomed, sweeping the robe-laden apprentice up in the air and around his shoulders.

"Oh, Cavok! What brings you here? Is everyone else with you?" the praven asked, looking over Cavok's shoulder to see a young girl looking quizzically back at him.

"Na, just me today, master brewer," Cavok said, putting the small praven back to the ground, patting his shoulder heartily.

"You come here to ask a favor, I assume? I don't recall you as the overly sentimental type. I doubt a friendly visit is your aim," Zaren gruffed out from the corner of the room, leaning easily on the side of the study table.

"Now that's not entirely true. I have sentiments for a chosen few," he said, winking at Jadu, which made Jadu beam even more, "but you are right about the favor. We have need of both of you. The arisen army is back. A war comes, and they arrive. This city, and every other, will be leveled if not contested. They only grow stronger the longer they are left alone."

"Ah, the insipid arisen once more come to end all life," the tall, old man scoffed and stepped up to the group, holding to his staff for support. "So let them come—try to take Rochata-Ung. It is a resourceful capital, after all. They have good odds of withstanding an arisen invasion, perhaps even completely ending that wretch arisen lord's reign completely."

Cavok crossed his arms, disapproving of the enchanter's flippant attitude towards the fate of thousands of innocent lives. "Good odds you say? And what if they lose that gamble?"

"Then the arisen move on to another nation," the old man said with a shrug.

"And this college? Your people? You'll be wiped out along with everyone else, Zaren," Cavok pressed, looking to the courtyard boy that had brought them there who hung around, listening intently at the conversation.

"You well know I can leave this land by many methods at a moment's notice. Myself and my possessions will be fine, and as for this school," Zaren said mockingly, "well, it's hardly a concern of mine. You think this is the metropolis of the enchanting arts? It's barely on the map. I brought Jadu here for the simple reason that he was causing issue with the new government in Brigganden after one too many explosions. We needed a larger campus for his training, and that is at least one thing the Blooming Lotus campus had."

"Cruel, old man," Cavok said, dropping his argument as he saw that he was going to get nowhere appealing to the enchanter's sense of honor. "You care about nothing but yourself—your things."

"He cares about me, too!" Jadu piped up, defending his master in his own way.

"You're one of his *things*," Cavok said plainly, letting out a sigh.

"Surely you can't mean to simply stand by and watch," Terra said, stepping out from behind Cavok's large frame.

"Yeah, you helped last time. What's so different about this time?" Jadu asked, easily switching sides and agreeing with the young girl he had yet to be introduced to.

Zaren considered the girl for the first time, reflecting on the matter before offering, "I surely *can* stand by and watch. And this time *is* different. All of my invaluable artifacts are safely stowed in vaults far from here this time. I have no tie to this land any longer other than to finish up your training," Zaren finished, giving a hard scowl to his diminutive student.

Cavok, seeing that the difficult subject was beginning to dampen the praven's feelings, offered to change the subject. "So, how do your studies go, Jadu? Are you close to becoming a master enchanter yet?"

"Close," he said, taking the bait. "I still have a thing or two to learn, but mostly all that awaits is my trial."

"What's this *trial?*" Cavok asked, not too surprised how quick Jadu had progressed through the enchanter's path. He had a quick mind, a dangerous curiosity, and an unhealthy passion for the work he was engaged in.

"I don't know yet; each student's trial is different. Zaren hasn't talked to me about mine yet," Jadu answered honestly, looking to the curmudgeonly enchanter.

Zaren, increasingly unhappy with all the pestering questions from everyone, answered shortly, "A trial is indeed unique to each student. It is a test of the student's studies in a live environment. Often, it's a lower priority task that would be a simple job for the professor but would test and prove the student. One such opportunity has yet to present itself for you, Jadu."

"Why not task him to overthrow the arisen king?" Cavok excitedly exclaimed, hopeful that they had just been hand delivered a reason to at least recruit one enchanter that day, seeing he was getting nowhere with Zaren.

"Are you mad?" Zaren scolded. "I'd be hard pressed to come out on top in an encounter with Ilad the Black. He's no pushover! He's even older than I am, and I've seen more years than all in the room combined, doubled over. That's a long time to collect information and locate powerful relics. If Ilad was actually trying, not like last time, then Jadu would be sucked dry of life essence in the blink of an eye. Giving him Ilad as a trial would be beyond cruel, it'd be downright idiotic!"

"I thought you said the arisen army was a boring matter? Sounds like there's plenty of challenge there for you," Cavok baited, smirking slightly to hear Zaren admit another might rival, if not outmatch, the supercilious grump.

"Powerful, he is. A challenge, definitely. That does not make one interesting, however. His aims are lackluster. It's the same old, same old story of a lust for power, domination, and rulership. His aims are the trite features about him, not his threat level."

Zaren finished by smacking Jadu on the wide-brimmed hat he wore, seeing that his student had become bored with the speech and had begun recasting the spell he had been working on all day.

Cavok looked to Terra at his side as she worked up the courage to challenge the old man. He didn't mind letting her speak, but he knew how hard the old man's heart was. He held no real hope for converting him to their cause by means of shaming him into it.

"Well, trite as you find his aim, the result of him fulfilling his goals are the same, destruction and suffering for thousands. The one he serves will not simply be content in holding Tarigannie, or even the whole of the Southern Sands region; he would go on to other lands and nations with a force as great as all the nations he's ravaged before. Wherever it is you call home, wizard, it is not far enough away if we do not stop this overlord early, before he's properly bolstered his army with fresh corpses."

Terra clenched her fists by her side as she spoke. All could tell how much this meant to her, perhaps more than any in the room cared for the cause, Cavok included. The three men were not ones overly concerned with the affairs of others, but her speech stirred something in each of them.

"We'll take care of the arisen lord. Ilad you called him?" Cavok stated. "Perhaps Jadu's trial could be a target more suited for him. Ilad had sentient arisen commanders last time in Brigganden. Lashik was one of them. Do you think tasking him to bring down one of Ilad's higher ranking commanders would be a suitable task for a trial of Jadu's caliber?"

Cavok hoped to capitalize on the somber tone that Terra had instilled in the room, and if he could at least recruit Jadu, he'd be happy enough. He never had cared for the old man with his tricks and frailty with no sense or care of kin.

"Lashik was still an accomplished warlock. I studied into him after our encounter. Squaring off with someone like that…would push Jadu to his limits. Normally I would say that's well above a student's trial level, but Jadu…he's advanced further and faster than any I've trained in the past, save for one. His trial does require extreme metrics. This—" Zaren said, hesitating, leaving the room in bated silence, "—might be agreeable."

Terra rushed to Zaren, abruptly hugging the old man.

"Thank you," she sincerely said into Zaren's robes. "Sha'oul's future is dreadful if we all don't play our role. I have seen you in my visions, and I was worried my dreams lied to me."

Zaren was stunned stiff at first, but his surprised expression slowly turned to a sour wrinkle. He stiffly patted her back as he grumbled, "A visionary, eh? All that means is more gods and goddesses in this whole mix-up. I'm not enlisting myself to your cause, dear, just my student, and that only for a very specific target."

"I have a feeling you'll be providing more aid than you say you will," she said, pressing her luck with the old man. She stepped back to stand beside Cavok again, a clear smile on her face.

Zaren cleared his throat sharply, looking to Cavok, getting back on topic.

"I'm sure you're not the one heading this ridiculous *quest*," Zaren said irritably. "Who's in charge? I need to have some questions answered before I can sanction this trial for Jadu."

Cavok slapped Jadu on the shoulder merrily, crossing his arms after, pleased with Terra's help. He answered Zaren with, "Reza and Sultan Metus are heading the mission. Come, pack your things, I'll take you to them."

"It will take the evening to pack, I'll not be rushed off without putting my things in order, or without getting a good night's rest. Boy, let the headmaster know I'll be departing campus for a while. We'll set out on the morrow," Zaren added to a group that was hardly listening, save the gate boy, who ran off down the hallway upon his new task along with his new juicy gossip piece for the campus.

Jadu shoved his wand in his pocket and clapped his hands together, quite excited at taking a break from his usual, brutally repetitive training routine. "Ah, to see Reza and the others again. You think she's missed me?" he asked Cavok.

Cavok let out a chuckle at the prospect of Reza having to travel with the inquisitive praven once more.

41

UPON DEAF EARS

The network of streets became more elaborate and confusing the deeper in the city they went. The districts they were escorted through gave them quite the sights. Somewhat familiar with the many splendors Rochata-Ung had to offer, they refrained from looking like gawking tourists, but the many patterns of paved, collared stone streets, gilded streetlamps, fantastic store and establishment fronts, and the general luster within the business and upper-class districts never ceased to instill wonderment in visitors.

The escorts had no desire for conversation, and other than the sounds of the city, the group quietly followed the guards into the judicial district, a place where Metus had been a few times before.

It looked the same as it ever had, much like the rest of Rochata-Ung. Little changed about the city itself, except those who briefly sat in the lofty seats of power and status. Few ever held on to authority too terribly long, the game of power abruptly ending those unfortunate enough to slip or make a mistake.

The court building was a daunting structure, pillars of marbled sandstone shooting up high in the stone arches above. They passed through the open threshold, were led down a long, flame-lit hallway

241

and into the large courtroom where a few judges sat, up along a row of majestic benches and tables.

"Sultan Metus," one of the shrewd looking judges said, voice sharp and direct. "You have crossed our borders with a rather large armed escort. I wouldn't quite call it an army, but nonetheless, this show of force is unusual, and we demand an answer for this lack of intent on your part."

"Might I know with whom I speak? I only know High Judge Cotious and…" Metus hesitated, unhappy with his presence, "…Set, that sits upon the council."

The keen-eyed speaker launched into brief introductions quickly, getting the pleasantries out of the way as quick as possible.

"On your far right, High Judge Uthman, then, as you say, High Judge Cotious, who is senior judge upon this particular council, then Circuit Judge Set, myself, High Judge Saahar, and lastly, Circuit Judge Hager. Does this introduction suffice," the judge more stated than asked.

"That should do," Metus shortly replied, seeing that the speaker was clearly on a schedule.

"Now then, to my initial question—what brings you here, Sultan Metus?"

Metus scanned the room, committing all judges' names to memory before he returned his gaze to the judge speaker, beginning an abbreviated version of his story.

"Not but a year ago, the Plainstate took to war with a warlord who had overthrown Brigganden. This warlord was a servant of the god of blood and ash, Telenth. We only knew him as the lord of the arisen at the time, for he commanded an arisen army, constructed of the corpses of his fallen enemies through dark magicks gifted to him through Telenth.

"You were all probably informed on the happenings through your sources, so I won't belabor a retelling of those events, but suffice it to say, we were not able to kill the man. He escaped the battlefield and headed into the Badlands, south of our state.

"We discovered a few months ago that he had been regaining his army through the slaughter of the nomadic peoples of the Badlands and Highguard. We also learned that he began creating arisen from the indigenous creatures in those wild lands. You know how harsh that wilderness is. There is plenty of wildlife to, if organized, create an issue for any peoples to deal with. More fierce predators in a land, you will be hard pressed to find.

242

"A month ago, Reza here, a saren knight and a longstanding ally to me and the Plainstate, as well as former citizen of Rochata-Ung, spurred me to action, bringing to my attention of movement and plans of the arisen lord's—*Sha'oul*, he has come to be known as—mobilization and intent of taking Rochata-Ung and the peoples of Tarigannie.

"Instead of simply sending a messenger to deliver this news, I wished to come to deliver this message, personally, and show my support in numbers, not just words. I have brought my most highly trained troop, the Hyperium, to help blunt Sha'oul's forces and to stand next to our ally's side in their time of need, for if you fare poorly in this coming battle, we will share your fate soon thereafter due to the nature of his necromantic arts."

"A messenger would have been faster," the speaker bluntly stated after Metus ended his speech, adding one last point to consider. "The council appreciates your intent, but we've known of this arisen nuisance for some time now. I can assure you, Rochata-Ung is more than well equipped to deal with any advances upon our lands without the need of a small token attachment of a hundred troops. If Tarigannie is this *Sha'oul's* target, then we shall end him and his army that has given so many others such trouble. We give no quarter, and with us, this war will end. We need no aid from other states or nations."

"This foe is beyond one state to put down. Sha'oul has the backing of a *god*!" Reza barked, completely done with how nonchalant the judge was treating the dire situation.

"You will be silent!" the speaker firmly ordered, pointing his nubbed gavel at her. "Sultan Metus is the only one permitted to speak to the council, or the lot of you will be thrown out."

The judge continued, "As for your Hyperium, see that they are out of Tarigannie's borders swiftly. Ally or no, we do not tolerate outside states leaving troops wandering our land for very long without seeing to those trespasses."

"Surely you're not serious?" Metus said in disbelief, looking to each of the council members. "A grave threat approaches…and you're turning away help?"

"Sultan Metus, you will see to it that your Hyperium troop is out of Tarigannie borders within five days from now, or it will be seen as an act of war. You, and those with you, may remain for as long as you wish, but as I see it was your intent to deliver this most important message of yours, seeing how it has now officially been delivered, I assume you'll be returning to your state shortly as well."

The speaker left little time for Metus to offer a reply, as he was still somewhat in shock at the degree of arrogance the council was displaying.

"Judges, are we in accordance?" the speaker asked. All offered an unconcerned, "Aye."

"This assembly is adjourned then. Guards, will you show our guests back to their quarters for the evening? They may stay there the night before heading off. I'm sure the trip here has been taxing for one of his status," the speaker said. Metus noted the offering the high judge provided him and his band at the end, not sure if it was a display of offhanded kindness or mockery.

"This land is doomed," Arie whispered as they were quickly ushered out of the court.

"Worse than doomed," Reza added in a voice loud enough for the old judges to hear. "Cursed."

42

CONFUSION AT THE GATE

"The sooner you answer to my call, the sooner your suffering will end," a whispered voice called to him in the guise of a million voices.

Nomad's mind was being flayed open, all his inner thoughts, all his deepest memories and emotions being exposed to the searing heat of boiling, angry souls that swam all about him.

The press of vitriolic entities swirling around him was suffocating, leaving him no space to come up for air to breathe and gain his bearings.

It was a familiar hell he found himself in. One that he had existed in endlessly not so long ago.

A chant began, no pauses between syllables—endless and breathless. They assaulted Nomad's opened mind cavities.

Nomad's control relinquished, and the orders that were being given to him in a language he had become very familiar with over the last few months, overrode his will. He was allowed one thought— *walk south.*

In the dead of the night, Nomad rose, getting out of bed in his fatigues, and began to head towards the tent door.

Henarus, asleep on the cot next to Nomad, awoke as he did so, calling to Nomad, who ignored the beckons.

Rushing out of the tent, he placed a hand on Nomad's shoulder, but Nomad continued his march with no acknowledgement of Henarus' presence.

The prophet studied the sleepwalker for a moment as the two walked out of the camp before realizing he was not going to be able to rouse his companion from his slumber.

Asking for Hassome to hear his prayer, he began to offer up supplications to guide Nomad's mind back to his body.

The chant was quiet, but soon, Nomad slowed to a standstill, and the two stood there in the open desert, Henarus' deep, soft voice comforting Nomad's restless limbs. Slowly, Nomad was able to begin to find a path back out of the labyrinth of misery that his dark master had wound around him, even if it was only a temporary measure.

Eventually, he let Henarus guide him back to their shared tent, getting him back into his cot to return to his slumber. Nomad seemed to sleep soundly after the prayers, but for Henarus, it was the start of a long, sleepless night.

Though the night was long for Henarus, the morning was longer still. It was well past breakfast already and Nomad still lay in a deep slumber. Henarus did not know Nomad terribly well, but he knew enough of the man to know that late rising was not common for him.

Figuring it best to allow him the extra sleep, he had stayed with him until the sun was well overhead, then decided to check in with the leadership, as he could see a gathering of Bannon and the other high-ranking officers on the perimeter of the camp.

Henarus strolled up to the leadership meeting, looking worse for the wear than all others there, but aware enough to pick up quickly on the ongoing conversation concerning Sultan Metus and crew and the worry they all harbored for their return.

"I doubt the audience with the judges took too long. I'm hoping they will return or at least send word by the end of the morning," Bannon said, looking to the other three leaders in the huddle.

Patting Henarus on the shoulder, Bannon smiled warmly. "Sleep evaded you it seems," welcoming the tired man to the conversation.

"When were we expecting Sultan Metus to be wrapped up with his tasks in Rochata-Ung?" Henarus asked, trying not to let a yawn out, his eyes tearing up a bit in the process.

"The two tasks they had were to relay the news of the arisen threat to the council of judges and recruit the enchanter and his apprentice. I would not assume that would take that long. By noon they should have had more than enough time to accomplish both ventures, or at the least have sent word of a delay to us."

A clean-shaven, blond-haired man in the circle spoke up. Henarus knew the man to be Hathos, the Hyperium Primus, otherwise commander of the Hyperium, only outranked by Bannon. Henarus knew little of the man other than his quiet but intense demeanor.

"I would have liked to resupply here. The Hyperium could use a few more rations for the road ahead, but…to be honest, I don't trust this city. Aside from that, I don't like the disposition of the governing body and how they are treating Sultan Metus. I do not think it wise to spend more time than necessary here. We could resupply in some of the smaller towns along our route if needs be."

Most nodded their heads in agreement. Henarus considered the serious concerns each of the men held with their current situation.

Looking back to the tent Nomad was staying in, he noticed through the open flap that the cot Nomad had been sleeping on was empty.

Making a quick scan of the encampment, he caught the attention of the group, each interested in what seemed to concern Henarus so much.

"Henarus. What is it?" Bannon asked, but an answer was forgone as the sounds of a scuffle out in the bush sprung them into action. They rushed to the sounds of the nearby brawl.

Looking through the tall sagebrush, down a knoll close to the main road, all recognized one of Kissa's Shadows, Naldurn, laying on the ground, getting up as Nomad turned. There was an evil in Nomad's eye and a snarl on his lips as he faced her, then turned for the road.

"Nomad!" Henarus scolded, shocked by the scene and the apparent hostility towards one of their own.

Nomad took no notice of the cry and continued his march away from the camp.

"Tend to the lady, I'll take care of Nomad," Henarus said, not waiting for compliance from the rest before scrambling down the crumbling caliche hill towards the man he had been given charge of.

"Nomad!" he called. He came close to the hunched man, hesitation grabbing him just before reaching out for his shoulder.

Nomad stopped but did not turn to face him.

"Nomad—" the prophet began, but a low growl cut him short.

247

The foreigner began slowly walking south once more, starting to leave, but Henarus, speaking in tongues, suddenly shot forth his hand, gripping Nomad's right shoulder. Nomad let out a roar so demonic, everyone present could have been fooled that they had stepped into a rift directly to a lower hell—the mourning, damnation, and anger of a thousand souls unleashing in one call.

Nomad snapped around, smashing Henarus across the face and sent him flying into the surrounding brush, at once unconscious.

Hathos was there in an instant, standing between the prophet and the wild man. Tau and Naldurn rushed to back him up.

Bannon was to Henarus' side quickly, but the man showed no response, clearly knocked clean out by the brutal attack.

Nomad turned his back once more, unconcerned that there were three warriors at the ready before him.

"Let him go, we don't have time for this," Naldurn said, still slightly winded from being knocked down earlier herself. "Sultan Metus and the others are in need! The Hyperium needs to be mobile immediately. Kissa is leading them to the gates, but there is no safety after that without us."

Bannon hoisted Henarus over his shoulder, seeing that he would not rouse, and ordered the others, "Do as Naldurn says. Ready the men. On my order, we head towards the city gate. Naldurn, with me."

Hathos and Tau lingered to make sure Nomad did not return to attack again, and then headed up the slope as Naldurn made her way to Bannon, helping to shoulder the unconscious man's weight.

Bannon turned and watched Nomad head south, knowing it was a bad move to let him go, but with their worries about the safety of the sultan verified, they had no time to lose another high-ranking officer in attempting to detain him.

"Damn this place," Bannon spat. He headed back to camp and ordered Naldurn to send a Shadow to follow Nomad and for her to fill him in with the details regarding Sultan Metus as they made their way to a medic and his priests to care for the unfortunate soul.

43

WHISPERS OF RICHES, WHISPERS OF DEATH

The night had been rough for Metus and Reza. The two stayed up most of it discussing their next move, having come off a crushing defeat of diplomacy, which they had not been expecting. They knew Rochata-Ung's leaders were shrewd and proud, but not to this level.

The two had not been expecting the Tarigannie governance to leave free help on the table, but then, to them, 'free' aid was not completely without strings attached. Even if other nations got wind that an arisen army attacked Tarigannie and they had accepted Metus' help, it could be seen as their nation not being strong enough to deal with the threat on their own, which might give surrounding nations a lesser view of their position of strength and military security.

Even without the issue of tarnishing their self-sufficient image, Metus doubted any of the judges wanted to, in any way, be in debt or favor to the Plainstate. Metus knew the leaders and people of Tarigannie had always seen the Plainstate as a weaker, softer nation. An ally in trade and desire to keep the relative peace, but Tarigannie had long derided the cleaner, freer way of life the peoples of his nation upheld in contrast to the harsh overlords that enslaved their citizens in all but name.

Metus had figured that they would have seen reason and accepted aid, but he had to admit to himself, and Reza, he had been naive to how stubborn and self-invested others could be.

The morning sun coming through the windows now, Metus roused Gale and Jasper, who had slept heavily that night since Reza was up to stay vigilant, while Reza woke Arie.

"I've been talking with Reza through the night, and though I would like to wait longer for Cavok and Terra to return, I feel with how we were received and treated yesterday, all haste in returning to Bannon and the Hyperium would be wise. Perhaps we can attempt to seek them out at the college. It shouldn't be too difficult to find. I hope their mission went better than ours," Metus whispered to the group once they were up and gathered. Though the guards were no longer at the doorway, prying ears were ever listening in Rochata-Ung, they all knew.

"I hope their delay in returning is not due to misfortune," Reza said, voicing Arie and the others' floating dread of the reality that their recent setback could easily get much worse.

"We will soon find out," Metus said, closing out the huddle. "Pack your things, we head for the college."

The streets of Rochata-Ung proved to be a small labyrinth for Metus and company. Reza helped to steer them in the general direction of the college, remembering the side of town it was on from her time as a citizen there years earlier.

Though she had the direction, she had never actually been to the enchanters' campus, and the press of the market and crowds made it difficult for the group to catch their bearings.

"There," Reza exclaimed, pointing over the commotion of the market they were in to a tall building with a blue-tiled roof, surrounded by pink cherry trees, in the distance through the long street ahead of them. "That's the college, I think."

Gale split the crowd in front of them as Jasper carried up the rear, ensuring that none got separated as they were pushed and steered from one side of the street to the next.

"We had to travel on market day," Metus murmured, cursing their luck as four large, rough-looking men stepped in front of the street a ways down, making a commotion, blocking everyone off for a half block.

"Street's closed, make your way around, by city's orders!" the largest man boomed into the disgruntled crowd. Some offered foul insults and threats while others went about turning down side streets or turning back, the crowd generally splitting up into smaller flows.

Reza looked to Gale, both with an unspoken look of vexation.

"Side passage, it's only a block," Metus shouted amongst the rancor of the crowd, prompting Gale to hesitantly guide the group down one of the residential alleys, away from the mass of congested merchants, farmers, and buyers.

"Never trust an alley in a city like this," Arie spoke in a low voice to Reza, attempting to warn her of their chosen path.

Reza had no answer for her. Her focus was solely on getting the group quickly through the detour and back to the main street that pointed towards the college.

The crowd thinned out further as they made a right turn along a side passage with tattered awnings, canvases worn and soiled from disrepair drearily hanging over them, shadowing them from the warm Tarigannie morning sun.

Gale slowed, looking to the side, then above along the balconies. He turned back, causing the rest in the group to look around on high alert.

Jasper drew his scimitar in a flash, grabbing his shield from his back as some of the crowd panicked from the aggressive action, while a few stayed, grim faces and weapons furtively appearing from cloaks and wraps of cloth.

Up ahead, a few more from the crowd turned around, drawing shivs and small blades, halting the group's advance, while the ones from the rear penned in their retreat.

"Above as well," Gale whispered back to Reza. Bowmen drew their strings, readying their aim from the splintered balconies.

"We want no blood," a thin, longhaired man said, stepping through the last of the retreating commoners, all at this point seeing they had found themselves in the wrong alleyway that particular morning.

"A dignitary of your position should have some amount of *financial leverage* on you. For you and your mates' sakes, I hope you do. It'll make this process much less…messy."

"I would prefer for things to go smoothly," Metus said, stepping up in front of Gale and Reza, facing the oily haired man.

"Good, that's good. I like your attitude. We might all end up having a good morning if that's the case."

"I have two conditions, though. If you can agree to them, what wealth I have on me, is freely yours, no hard feelings," Metus offered, his cool demeanor doing much to calm the tension on both sides.

"Let's hear it," the man said, his snakish smile easily showing his glee in the potential score.

"This ambush—it's too well planned. You must have had time to set it up, which means you learned of my presence here from someone. None of us are *dressed* like dignitaries, so tell me, how did you come to know of my position, presence, and path?"

The man considered the long-winded question for a moment, deciding on how much information was prudent for him to give up.

"Word gets around in this city. I can't rightly be giving up my sources, you understand, but I *could* say—well—power hates power, I suppose. There's reasons for some of them wankers in the judicial district to dislike ya. None my business, though. My business is more of a simple nature, with yer gold."

Metus let out a dismayed sigh, his worries seeming to be validated with the man's answer.

"What's yer second condition? Out with it," the man ordered, a hint of anxiousness showing as everyone stood waiting for Metus to lay out his terms.

"We keep our travel gear. Armor and weapons included. If what you say is true, you're likely not the only ones that'll be on our tails today. The wealth lies with my purse, not our gear anyways."

The man's gears were turning, and a gruff voice from a lookout down the alley called for the thin man to wrap it up.

"You got yerself a good deal today, mate. Hand over all yer purses and we'll call it a morning."

"Do it," Metus ordered. He handed the man his side purse and collected everyone else's loose coin quickly as possible, each group eager to be done with each other.

The man spent no time in checking the total, the heft and clink of the metal strips inside bespeaking the tidy sum for itself.

"Boys, outta here," the thin man said, twirling his finger in the air. The alleyway cleared as quick as they had appeared, the longhaired man strolling off down a side street whistling a tune as he went.

"We need to either get to that college, fast, or just start making our way to the city gates now," Metus said, breaking the eerie sudden silence of the alleyway.

"If the judges leaked information about our presence to thugs and guilds, we're in for a rough morning. That they would do that though, I don't see their reasoning in a betrayal…" Metus said, thinking through the quandary. An epiphany came to him. "Set. He's surely behind this. He's wanted me dead for years now."

"And he'll get his wish if we don't get moving again, Adom," Reza said, cutting Metus off from his line of thought.

"We head for the gate," Gale said, putting an end to the deliberations. "Inside city walls, we are vulnerable. Once outside, rejoined with the Hyperium, we'll be able to launch a detachment to extract Cavok and Terra."

"Lead the way," Metus agreed. Gale took point once more, moving the group out of the alleyways and back into the busy street.

Expectedly, the men that had been blocking the road minutes earlier were gone, and the traffic had once again begun to flow freely through the trade street.

"The city gate should be back the way we came, but if we keep fighting this crowd, we'll be at this all day," Reza said, calling to Gale, who struggled to make a path for them.

Gale cut to the curb, leading the group down a side street; and while not as busy, they were by no means headed down a shady alleyway like before.

Gale had taken executive control over the direction of the group, and though no one contested the move to a more manageable network of streets to make their way through, seeing that they were getting closer to the towering city walls, each turn they made away from the crowds they knew placed them in more and more peril.

"I don't like this, Gale," Metus said as they rushed down a nearly empty residential street. "Take us back to the main street. We've made plenty of ground. We can suffer through the markets a bit longer."

Gale nodded. He hurried along, cutting back into a tributary street that linked back up to the bustle of caravans that were on their way in through the main highway, blocking the roads with their beasts, wagons, and crew.

A bloody scream issued from the back of the group. Everyone turned around to see a man in leathers slashed open at Jasper's feet, blood dripping from Jasper's scimitar.

None had time to ask questions as Jasper called, "Watch your front!"

Gale tripped out of the way right before a man in a dark roughweave slashed his way into their ranks, lunging for Arie, knife point first.

Arie was no novice, however, and as the man came in, she snapped her hand against his wrist, snatching it and flipping the man over onto his back as Reza unsheathed her sword and stabbed the man through the lung as he impacted the ground.

"More!" Metus warned, pointing at the three bruisers headed their way from behind while three more came in from the main street.

They had quickly become outnumbered, and they backed together, closing their ranks for better protection, all centering around Metus.

Down from a rooftop came two figures, both picking a target that never saw the death plunging towards them from above.

Daggers came out just as they landed atop the main street thugs, dropping them quickly.

"Kissa!" Metus exclaimed, relieved at the unexpected arrival.

Gale snapped his scimitar back across the throat of the men closest to the main street that rushed the group, cutting him down with a bloody roar.

"Guards! Murder!" a voice shouted from the crowded street ahead of them. The main street began to break up at the sight and sound of the scuffle.

"Onto the main street, sheath your swords!" Metus yelled, pushing Jasper forward to get them moving away from the thugs.

They spilled out into a once overcrowded highway that had begun breaking up, city guards pushing against the crowd to make their way to the commotion.

A man stood atop a wagon, pointing at Gale and the crew, shouting at the guards that he had seen him slash a man open.

"The gate is there just ahead," Kissa called to the group.

"Get the sultan out before they lock down!" Gale shouted to Jasper, who wasted no time in grabbing Metus, bolting down the sidewalk towards the gate. The people there seemed curious as to the commotion but had not yet been privy to the assaults that were ongoing.

Kissa spoke quick words to her shadow, Eilan, and ran off after Metus, leaving Eilan there at Reza's side.

Reza ordered Arie to go with Kissa and Metus as well, leaving her there with Gale and Eilan to deal with the three bruisers that harassed their flanks, blocking their retreat.

The city guards had eyes on their group now, and Gale and Eilan made themselves as visible as possible to give Metus time to slip away in the crowd.

"Go with them," Gale called back to Reza, but it was clear to him she meant to stay.

"What's the plan?" she barked, slashing one of the brutes in the side street clean through his bracers, causing him to call out in pain, clutching his bleeding forearm.

"Halt!" the closest guard called, seeing the skirmish clearly by that point. The three bruisers finally retreated now that it was clear their prey had bested them.

Gale looked to Eilan and then to Reza, giving her a brief inspection up and down, sizing up her agility.

"You a good runner?"

44

THE OATHBOUND

"This is far enough for the night. Doubt my old bones could make it another mile," Matt grunted, calling a halt to the group's travels.

Malagar and the others had returned early into the night, and the group had decided to pack up and head out in case Denloth was keen on giving chase to them.

Now, deep into the night, most showed signs of fatigue, and though they had covered a great deal of ground, they were still within the Imhotez mountain range.

They shambled into a relatively wide, level shelf among endless Joshua trees, most gladly dropping their packs after the long night hike.

"No fire tonight, nor tents. Just—rest," Matt sighed, laying his head atop his pack, closing his eyes, and breathing deeply.

Hamui was face down in the dirt next to Matt, the two of them snoring within moments.

Wyld did seem tired, but still stood next to Malagar, who had not let go of her hand since scrambling through the canyon valley miles back before they met back up with the group. Malagar sat, exhausted, tugging on his inflicted friend to sit beside him, which she hesitantly did.

Dubix walked the perimeter, scanning the location they had chosen for rest to ensure its defenses.

Fin went to rest next to Yozo, catching his breath before asking, "How you feeling? Well—other than beat from the night hike. You sobering up yet?"

Yozo took a swig of water from the waterskin Fin had given him, refusing to answer Fin on the subject, giving him a sour look.

"Well, you were *very* compromised when we found you. *I'm* not the one that got you drunk and high, but it does leave me questioning where *we're* at," Fin said, motioning to Yozo and himself. "You're still with us, we didn't force you to pack up and head out. We'd welcome you on if you'd like," Fin continued. Though he did not enjoy the prospect of adding another questionable member to their team, he knew Yozo had potential. And at that time, he decided that potential treachery was a fair trade for quality manpower.

"I packed up with you lot out of necessity. I'm not waiting around in the arisen's territory after you just performed an operation on them."

Fin shrugged at his proposition being sidestepped. Yozo had at least not given him a *no* for an answer. He'd see if he could make it work for the two parties.

"The offer's there, mate," Fin said, getting up to check in with Malagar and the kaith they called Wyld.

"Any change with her?" Fin asked, waving a hand in front of the non-responsive companion, answering his own question by her lack of interest in him.

"She's only followed, and only when prompted to. If I release her hand, she stays where she's at. I had to practically push and carry her up the canyon back there before we found you guys," Malagar said disparagingly.

"That's not good. Who knows what Denloth did to her," Fin murmured under his breath. He inspected the dully glowing scars across her face, bringing up a hand to inspect the strange substance.

"Don't," Malagar ordered, drawing the attention of those that were not yet slumbering and caused Fin to halt just before touching a finger to her.

Malagar brought up his right hand. Fin listened intently but did not understand the connection just yet.

"I touched her…wound, or whatever it is that marks her face, already. I lost sensation in that hand when I did. It's slowly coming

257

back," Malagar said, wringing his fist out. "Whatever that mark is, it's dangerous. Perhaps that's what is responsible for her torpid demeanor."

Fin considered Malagar's assessment, not having a direct answer for him on the subject. Nodding his agreement that Malagar could be right on the matter, he replied, "Regardless of what afflicts her, maybe a night's rest will help give her ease and we'll see improvements from her on the morn."

"Let's hope so," Malagar agreed, unpacking a bedroll for Wyld to rest upon, trying his best to settle her.

"It's the mark of the Seam," a chill voice whispered. Malagar and Fin looked to Dubix who stood nearby, listening to their conversation.

"Mark of the Seam?" Malagar asked as he finished covering Wyld up with a blanket.

"What, is this some sort of arisen magic?" Fin quizzed, disgust clear in his tone.

None noticed Yozo smirking at the heated talks, slouched back among his belongings, flirting with sleep but still interested enough in the conversation to stay half awake.

"No. There are very few who can access that passage. Denloth, I know, was one of them. The striations in the desert days back, they are similar to these marks upon your friend. I think Denloth traveled through the Seam with her in tow, and she did not come out of that place unscathed it seems."

"I don't understand. You're saying this 'Seam' is a passageway or a place? I've never heard of it," Fin said, trying to make sense of Dubix's words.

"I see," Malagar uttered aloud, looking to Wyld's scars.

Fin looked at Malagar, lost in thought. A look of realization came to Malagar's face. He needed no prompting to explain himself.

"I—think I've been to this 'Seam' once, in the past. Maybe not *been* there, but at least witnessed its existence. It would make sense. I thought I had felt *this*," he said, flexing his numb hand, "once before. And those colors. Unbelievable colors, like some vibrant tropical bounty of fish, pearls, and liquid all spun together—blindingly beautiful."

"That's not helping," Fin said, his annoyance coming through as he pinched the bridge of his nose. "What the hell is this *Seam* place? Is it a location nearby?"

"It is no physical location that you can travel to—not without a means to allow you entrance. Are you aware of rifts?"

"Yes, of course. Portals to the realms of the various gods. Rare, but with the right means, connections, and favor with the gods, even us mortals can gain access to them. Are you saying the Seam is one of these rifts?"

"To not belabor your mind, you may think of it as one of these," Dubix said. Though his tone had not changed, Fin sensed that he was being patronized.

"Listen here you heap of bones. With Denloth still kicking around, we might have to deal with this stuff again. I need to know what we're up against, so you spill the details on this *Seam* right here, right now, or we're about to finish what we started that cursed night back in Brigganden," Fin hissed out, sounding almost as menacing as Dubix generally did.

"I might be able to help," Malagar cut in, seeing that Fin was about to lose it. "Within the monasteries, there is rumor of ascension to higher realms, and lower ones. If you delve deep enough through the levels of meditation, one can reach nirvana—a merging with the universal aether. Though none in my brotherhood call it *the Seam*, there are stories of a shattered existence. A place not here, nor there, but somewhere in between. It is a place of great chaos, and tumult.

"All monks gravitate towards the various gods, and as a result, commune and ascend to the various higher or lower planes of existence, but those who finally reach nirvana and find themselves in the shattered place either lose themselves or quit the faith, at least in an organized way.

"The same happened to me. I transcended not to find a welcoming deity to guide and teach me, but a broken place— unimaginably beautiful, but devoid of a creator's guiding influence— a place of utter chaos."

"It is…impressive that you have gained access to the Seam through willpower alone," Dubix said, humbly.

"Alright, so it's a confusing place. How does that explain Wyld's markings?" Fin asked, seeming to have begun to calm himself after Malagar's descriptive answer.

Dubix looked to the rent across Wyld's face and said, "It is no place for physical beings such as us. It is an endless webwork of splitting timelines, dimensions, and tares into nothingness, or everything that ever was. I have been walking Una for nearly three centuries, and in all that time, I have gleaned very little on the Seam. From what I understand, no one, not even the gods, can reliably utilize the Seam, and so only the mortals foolishly tinker with it—mortals that don't mind the odds of blinking out of existence at the random whim of the Seam's winds. To stray from the more stable paths in that place—" Dubix paused as he snapped his boney fingers together to emphasize his point, "—there would be the conclusion of your soul. I think this is what happened to your friend there, though, I cannot say for certain. This is the first time I have seen the aftereffects of the Seam.

"As I said, Denloth is the only one I have personally known to say that he walks the Seam, and even then, I figured he was bluffing, but it seems, perhaps he was not."

"Hmm," Fin exhaled. "Sounds like quite the place."

"Poor girl," Malagar said softly, looking newly upon the incongruent touch of the Seam upon Wyld. "If that is the truth of it, I wonder if there will ever be an answer to making her whole."

"Let's not think too much of it tonight," Fin said, patting Malagar consolingly on the back. "Perhaps some rest will do her good. There may be hope yet and staying up worrying about it won't do any of us any good. I'll keep watch tonight. You get some rest."

"You should both get rest. I do not require it. I'll keep watch," Dubix said.

Fin considered the animated skeleton standing before him, wearing a sword belt along with bits of old armor he had scrapped together from the fort before they had left, tatters of burlap rags hanging down over what wasn't covered by iron. Something glimmered around his neck, sparkling in the moonlight—a choker of some sort perhaps.

"What's your deal, Dubix? Why are you doing this? Surely the answer isn't you, an arisen, just happened to have a change of heart. You're incapable of that—you literally don't have one to begin with! The only reasoning I can come up with is this is all a ploy to draw our confidence in before betraying us to your master. I've allowed you to follow us for far too long in respect to our little one over there," Fin said, pointing to Hamui, "and Matt, who seems enamored by you, and Mal here, for that matter. Well, you haven't won my confidence yet. So tell me, since we have the time now, why should I think different than I do? Surely you can see why I hesitate to trust you?"

Dubix considered Fin's line of questioning for some time. The night air drifted a chill throughout the camp, causing Hamui and Matt to unwittingly cuddle up to each other as they slept. Malagar and Fin waited patiently for an answer from their dark friend.

Pulling down his raggedy shawl from about his neck, Dubix laid bare the bejeweled band he wore fixed about his spinal column. Fin immediately recognized its black and white gemstoned cast.

"You bastard. That's the bracelet I—" he paused, considering his word choice, "—*acquired*, from the wizard's tower which you stole from me that selfsame night."

Having said the words aloud, some of the anger that he'd harbored over the thieving arisen all those months ago dissipated, as he admitted to himself that he was just as guilty as Dubix had been in acquiring the ill-gotten gains.

"Yes, I did snatch this bracelet from you that night. It was this—" Dubix whispered, reflecting upon the memory as his phalanges slid across the white-gold band, "—that set in motion a great change to me in the following months. Slowly at first, but with a completeness that led me to leave the ranks of the dead to venture out on my own, away from the influence of my master, as his one domineering voice soon became an annoyance, and then a passing whisper in my consciousness, his hold constantly losing ground to whatever hex this artifact holds upon it."

"You're saying that bracelet broke the hold the arisen lord had on you?" Fin asked, clarifying the grim one's claim.

"Perhaps that, perhaps something more profound than even that. I didn't just detach from my master; I began to think—feel—differently than I once had. Repulsion became comfort, and vice versa. It changed who I was, unprecedented as it sounds; I bear witness that change did occur. Where once I sought your life, I feel compelled now to defend it. I do not attribute this change to myself, for I know I was a blight upon the land and would not have changed my ways. I was a mindless drone to facilitate evil deeds. I can only attribute it to this device. The fates have determined my course, and I am willing to walk the path they have lain before me."

Fin reflected upon Dubix's explanation for some time. Malagar tended to Wyld who had sat upright in her bedding, eyes open, Seam scars swirling slightly.

Fin had no immediate answer for Dubix's claims, nor time to discuss or question them, as Wyld stood up now, drawing everyone's attention.

"A foul presence approaches," Dubix hissed, drawing his sword and ordered Fin to awaken the others.

Yozo stood straightway upon the announcement, joining them.

Fin did as told and roused Matt and Hamui roughly, not sure why everyone was being called to arms but believing Dubix would not make a claim idly. Aside from that, being in the field for as long as Fin had, the charge on the air was unmistakable. He had, at that point, a sixth sense for danger, and that sense was backing Dubix's warnings.

"Which direction?" Fin whispered to Dubix after Matt and Hamui groggily stood up to seek revenge against Fin's rough kicks in their backs.

"There," Dubix hissed, pointing a bony finger upon the nearest ridge. There stood two silent, ironclad figures with dark, winged helms marching towards the camp still a hundred yards out.

"Beware, I do not know of this line of arisen—though—it reeks of Denloth," Dubix told the group, Matt and Hamui starting to understand the reason for the break in their short slumber.

Matt, wiping his eyes from weariness, nudged Hamui to attention. "Prep your strongest spells, boy," the old man commanded, in an unusually worried voice, a tone neither Hamui nor Malagar had heard the old man use until that point. It was a tone that scared the two more than the two intruders themselves.

Fin's frame trembled as well. Something told him and Matt, both seasoned warriors, that there was power headed their direction, perhaps more power than even they could deal with.

Yozo seemed cautiously confident, as he ever had when facing death head on.

The group stood ready for the two figures, waiting for their approach. The only ones rustling were Wyld and Malagar, who was trying to calm her.

Wyld twitched nervously, her limbs jolting from time to time, and Malagar could see a change come over her eyes. Where once there had been a soulless void, now tears—softness—shown through. A look of dread or regret racked her face in anguish as she seemed to struggle with her own body.

An insidious whisper slithered into everyone's ears, penetrating their minds. Harsh words that only Dubix truly knew, though Fin had heard more than once associated with the arisen.

"What's it mean?" Fin asked Dubix. He pried his eyes from the quickly approaching figures that were now in a dead sprint towards them for a moment to get Dubix's attention, knowing the arisen knew the fell-language well.

Dubix didn't directly respond to Fin's question, but instead called to Malagar, "Tie her up, now!"

Malagar hesitated for a flicker of a moment, faltering to fully latch onto Wyld's wrists before the kaith growled and ripped away from her would-be captor.

Fin looked to the wild woman. Her hackles were raised, looking as though she were scanning her surroundings for prey. He had no time to deal with her, though he knew she would need to be dealt with. How much of an issue she was going to prove to be was yet to be determined.

"Mal, take care of her. Everyone else, get ready for them. Hit them from range if you can, then be ready for a melee. Dismantle them at the seams, their armor looks sound."

Matt, Dubix, and Yozo stood at ready, swords and fists gleaming with bright steel and brass in the moonlight.

Hamui chanted softly, his crystal staff beginning to glow blue as he gathered a tight-knit clump of cloud vapor in the sky above them, darkening the scene dramatically as the charging knights drew closer.

Fin hefted four of his sturdiest throwing knives at the ready as he split his focus between gauging the distance between himself and the two knights and watching Malagar approach Wyld. She recoiled from his advances, looking ready to spring on him at any moment.

Wyld snarled, the rip of translucency across her face warping in and out just before she leapt at Malagar, claws out and forward. He was ready for the attack, however, and if any were going to grapple with the intensely strong and agile kaith, Malagar knew he was probably the best suited to do so.

He caught her wrists and locked his grip firm just as she lunged in with her fangs, attempting to go for his neck. Ducking under the bite and her right arm, he slipped around to her back, picking her up and throwing her over his back as he arched to attempt to suplex her.

Her ancestral reflexes activated, twisting mid-throw around in his grip, bounding off of him as he touched down on the ground. He attempted to recover his stance before she sprang out and back into the fray just as he got standing upright again.

The scuffle was fierce, and Fin sighed as he began to line up his first target, hoping that Malagar would be able to handle the unforeseen issue that their former companion was looking to give them.

Hefting the thick-handled throwing knife to his side, holding it at balance behind the middle of the shaft, Fin hurled the steel stake towards the closest target as though he was chucking a spear, releasing it with his index finger so that the hefty knife flung through the air in a low arc through half a rotation, punching through a slit in the gorget along the knight's neck.

The group took heart at the finely landed strike. A knife as thick as that sinking into the knight's armor would have felled anyone, but as the thing kept charging forward after the small setback, not seeming fazed by the blow, the realization that they were dealing with some arisen abomination sunk in firmly.

Fin didn't miss a beat with the ineffective throw, however, and he wasted little time in lining up his next shot, tossing his next heavy dagger at the same target, going right for the only other opening in the helmet down by the jawline.

Once more, the dagger landed true, this blow knocking the thing's head sideways as the tip slid through the binding hinges to loosen their opponent's helm slightly, showing a blood-soaked jaw beneath.

"Damn wretches, what hellish horror are they sending at us this time?" Fin murmured.

The one that took both knife points to the head lagged a moment, but it was only to let its partner lead the charge. The other one rushed in to work on closing the twenty-foot gap between it and the line of warriors that stood to stop it.

Hamui clenched his fist and slammed the staff butt to the ground as the heavens rumbled above them, charging the air above, their hair standing on end. Yozo's long, fine hair rose up just before a flash and clap of energy connected from the cloud to the tips of the golden wings atop the charging knight's helm, flinging it back several feet in a blast of pink light. It rolled to a stop as the other knight jumped over his lightning-kicked companion.

Fin landed yet another solid hit to the same knight that had eaten his last two heavy throwing daggers, this one completely dismantling the bottom half of its black sallet, exposing its fleshless blood-soaked identity. None in the group had ever seen skeletons that resembled these, except for Dubix.

Dubix was the first to step up, ensuring that he was the first to cross blades with the formidable foes. At the last moment, long, slightly curved sickles came out, and the dark knight brought one of the short sword-sized sickles to catch Dubix's longsword, slashing the other blade across Dubix's tatters which would have resulted in a disemboweling if Dubix had been living. Instead, the slash pushed him to the side, and the knight began to thrust in at Dubix's skull.

Though the attack jarred Dubix to the ground, its attack came to a sudden halt as Matt leapt in with a flying up-kick, knocking the winged helm right off its slick skull, blood speckling everyone nearby.

The shock of the moment, seeing the grim visage that faced them, was only surpassed by Yozo's swift blade, cutting in at a sharp angle, slicing the dome of the thing's skull clean off, bursting a magenta nova along its spine, producing a snap as it fell back to the ground, giving the group time to reform a line.

"Prepare yourselves. These are Oathbound. However many lives were sacrificed in their making is how many reanimations they're allotted. It may be a long night," Dubix hurried out as the skull's cap sickly slid back onto the open hole on its skull, the wet blood slicking over the cut while the other knight gathered himself, standing once more, small arcs of energy bouncing across its armor.

Fin hurled his last heavy throwing dagger at the now standing unhelmed Oathbound. The spike smashed through its face with enough force to punch through the other side, the same magenta light flashing as the hole quickly reformed as blood rushed to cover the gap. The eyeless warrior turned its focus to the dagger-throwing impaler who had caused it such trouble so far.

It jolted forward at blinding speed, ripping an iridescent tear in its wake, slamming into Fin, sickle point firmly embedded in Fin's shoulder. No one had time to react.

"They have the touch of the Seam!" Dubix hissed out the warning, readying his sword for the oncoming, fully armored Oathbound approaching them at a menacing jog. At the last second, it Seam-jumped several feet left, then appeared to the right as colorful tracer trails lined its briefly traveled path, rushing towards Matt.

Dubix stepped in front of the old man, bringing up his sword to point, attempting to gauge the approach, but as the Oathbound was just about within range to engage, it Seam-jumped through Dubix, stabbing at Matt who, either by chance or lightning reflexes, had brought his arm up just in time to take the blow which had been aimed for his chest.

Thrusting his other blade backwards, the Oathbound caught Dubix through the ribcage, flinging him, once again, to the ground as he ripped the sickle out of Matt, forcing the old man to the ground in the other direction.

Fin kicked the armored knight in the midsection away from him, and as the two separated, the sickle came tearing out of its fleshy sheath.

Fin saw blood squirting out of his periphery, and he knew that would need to be staunched quickly or he'd be dead within minutes. The Oathbound had other plans for his immediate attention, however, giving Fin no time to disengage further.

It came at Fin in a flurry of blade swipes and thrusts, each testing Fin's defenses, which were now greatly compromised. He did what he could with his left arm but parrying two blades with a stiletto while losing blood every passing moment allowed him to carry on through the assault for only a few seconds before the Oathbound scored another hit, slashing Fin's left forearm clean open. A smattering of blood sprayed both of them as Fin fell back against the hard ground in a cry of pain and exhaustion, feeling the end rushing in as his life essence gushed out.

Barely had Fin slammed to the ground than the red skeleton was thrusting for his throat. Fin rolled to the side, still aware enough to clumsily evade, and as the Oathbound brought up its other blade to deliver the coup de grâce, its head split in two as a dull pink flash erupted once more, blood mixing with the ample amounts that Fin already wore.

Yozo kicked the body to the ground away from Fin, taking the brief pause the skeleton needed to reconstruct its skull to tear off and toss Fin his thick scarf, seeing just at a glance that Fin was going to need something to staunch his wounds.

Yozo turned to the rising bloodskull, his hair tousled, but as his blade leveled, his deathly still stance gave the Oathbound a moment of consideration as it eyed him, dripping blood from the newly given slash to its dome.

Though Malagar could hear the melee going on within the camp, he had little choice but to block the plight of his friends out of his thoughts as Wyld kept him on his heels, ducking and dodging her claws and fangs. The two got further and further away from the encampment as they tripped and scuffled further into the canyonlands.

Snatching a stray wrist, Malagar pulled Wyld in, feeling the sting before the numb from gripping the phasing scar along her arm. Her mouth was on his forearm within a blink, biting wildly into his flesh. She wrenched free of his grip, but not without a blow from his elbow on the back of her skull.

The jolt roughly dislodged her, breaking a Seam-touched fang deep in him, its chill freezing his arm before going numb.

Shrugging off the tingling chill, he went back in, grabbing around her downturned head as she lolled there briefly from the head knock. He smoothly snaked in his wrist around her neck, forcing her head further inward as he locked his hands up around her, cranking inward and to the side.

She bucked, her senses coming back to her enough for her to realize she was getting in deep to a compromised position. Malagar did let go of his grip, but he quickly threw his arm over and around her arm, locking back up with the neck crank, squeezing it downward and in, forcing Wyld to go to the ground or risk having her neck snapped under the constricting pressure.

Malagar sprawled on top of Wyld in the dirt, and she began to thrash, but his vice-like grip was locked about her neck. As she struggled, he followed her with his secured grip.

Her slanted eyes were squinted in pain and strain, and her breathing was extremely labored as Malagar dug the blade of his forearm in deep around Wyld's throat, the knuckle of his thumb turned inward, cutting off blood flow.

She bucked wildly, her mobile spine helping her to twist around on her back, raking madly at Malagar, who released his grip on her throat. He knew he'd be torn to shreds within moments if he had decided to be stubborn on the hold. Instead, he spun around low on one foot, winding up a low, perfectly timed back kick, slamming his heel into Wyld's temple, knocking her in a heap against a large boulder, where she slumped motionless.

Malagar held his low, one-footed stance for a moment before approaching his unconscious friend to check her pulse to make sure he had not knocked the life out of her.

He got to work binding her before hauling her back to the battlefield with him.

Matt clutched his forearm, stepping back as the winged knight came in at him again with another stab and thrust combo. Matt easily dodged the two attacks.

The Oathbound lurched forward. Dubix smacked the back of its helm hard but failed to detach the protective encasing that was preventing mortal blows from being landed.

It turned, backhanding the unarmored skeleton across the skull, smashing Dubix's cheekbone into shards as it let out a hellish scream. It was immediately cast back as a strong gust of air from Hamui blew the knight over on top of Dubix.

Gripping the wings of the Oathbound's helm, he wrenched it off just as the Oathbound Seam-walked instantly around and behind him, gripping Dubix's skull with its gauntleted hands, ripping apart Dubix's jaw as teeth and bone shrapnel splintered the area.

"Now!" Matt yelled at Hamui. The Oathbound turned to look at the praven just as a molten bolt of plasma shot forth from his staff's crystal straight through the red skull, exploding chunks of blood and bone everywhere.

Dubix threw the Oathbound off of him with some effort, getting to his feet once more. Matt took the breather to find Hamui and stand between him and their foe as Hamui began chanting again in an exhausted, gravelly voice, preparing for the next spell. The crystal atop his staff, which once glowed a bright azure, now flickered a dull blue.

The thick blood reformed the skull on top of the suit of armor with demonic speed, each revival quickening in pace.

Dubix bounded back just as the Oathbound dashed forward, streaking a Seamline through him midair. It created diamond fractals in the surrounding area, splitting time and space.

The Oathbound warped to and fro, suspending Dubix in his back-peddling position momentarily.

The red skull locked its murderous gaze on Hamui, completely ignoring Matt, and rushed to him in blinding fashion.

As soon as the Oathbound jolted forward, Dubix's dimensional fractal chains broke loose, and he bolted for his sword on the ground, running to charge back into battle, his skull half gone.

Within a split second, the Oathbound was at the chanting praven and old man, giving Matt only time enough to step in front of Hamui, yelling, "Now!" again, praying his sacrifice gave the young talent a precious second more to finish his spell.

Two sickles jabbed into Matt's torso, snagging his innards as the knight ripped him viciously to the side. Matt landed in a bloody heap.

Hamui's hair lifted, his crystal flashing once, then faded out, another bolt of lightning coming down to strike the bloody warrior, blasting plates of armor off him this time, shooting him back in a flash of blinding pink light to Dubix.

Swinging his sword at the lightning struck Oathbound, Dubix chopped down through the opening in the shattered breastplate to cleave through bone and cracked armor alike. The magenta snap that followed blasted not only the armor apart but launched Dubix's sword off into the bush.

The Oathbound was unclad now, its iridescent bony figure fully exposed under the pale moonlight. It looked to Hamui, who had fallen from overextending himself, and started to warp the space about him, wrapping itself in a Seam rift.

Dubix rushed it, tackling it from behind, catching the Oathbound off guard, tumbling through image after dizzying image in his moment of impact on the Seam-walking Oathbound.

The two fell into a dimensional chasm, plummeting endlessly into the folds of the Seam rift, diamond-shaped cuts in space closing the tear soon after. The camp went dark and silent for a moment.

Yozo came in relentless, cutting and slashing the bloody stump that kept reforming as the Oathbound's head. Blood spilt in crescent shapes all about as he smashed the globule of blood and bone, a pink phosphorescence glowing constantly as he pressed his attack.

Blade struck blade, a sickle catching a sideways slice Yozo performed, then the other sickle came in to slap the sword down and away.

The skull had reformed, blood gushing up to consolidate it, but something was different this time; beneath the blood glowed a lustrous skull, translucent, pearl like. Through the cracks in its armor, it shot forth light, gleaming like the light through a stained-glass window. Yozo stepped back and sheathed his sword, waiting to see what this new change in the battle meant.

The Oathbound let out a horrendous screech at Yozo, its twitchy posture clearly showing frustration with the man. Yozo remained calm—still—waiting for the upcoming attack.

The space around the bloody skeleton split, a recess within reality fell in on itself. The skeleton's frame warped momentarily before it jumped, showing up ten feet closer to him than where it was a split moment ago, then it disappeared once more.

This time, Yozo made a move, drawing his sword blindingly fast, sidestepping as the Oathbound reappeared where Yozo had been, but now, only where his sword was slashing. His blade connected directly with the crystalized skull, smashing it into fractals that flung at supersonic speeds through the night sky, some inexplicably buzzing off hundreds of yards, some seeming to be caught in an invisible web, moving much slower than they should, while others blipped out of existence at different distances from impact.

"Matt!" Malagar called, putting down Wyld to rush to the old man's aid.

Hamui was up after a moment, hobbling over to the mentor, having witnessed firsthand how badly Matt had gotten it from the Oathbound.

Propping his head up, Malagar positioned Matt skywards, being careful with his midsection which had been slashed clean open, dark blood glistening like oil in the moonlight oozing out from his stomach and chest wound.

Matt gurgled, trying to speak, but blood shot out instead, his bloodied features winced in pain. Then...through bloodstained teeth, a smile, looking with his clouded eyes to Malagar, and then Hamui, a measure of peace falling on them, even though no words were said.

"Rest, Matt. Under the stars—" Malagar managed, seeing the light of life leave the old man even before he finished his statement, becoming the old adventurer's short, sweet eulogy.

Fin had, with Yozo's help, successfully staunched and bound his wounds, and both sat in silence as they watched from across the camp the passing of a legend, one that had played his part in shaping many lost souls into figures of change, or import—of good.

"Gods bless him," Fin offered a rare prayer, and even Yozo could feel the significance behind the old one's passing.

"Great respect we have in my country for the grey hairs that pass. I will stay with you to make sure he has a proper burial."

There was a movement outside of the camp, and Yozo stood at ready, hand on sword hilt, but as the figure stood, all could see it was Wyld, awakening from her impactful unconsciousness.

Malagar tensed, not sure if he could tussle with the kaith once more and come out on top as he had, his energy all but spent from the day's events.

"It was not just a dream, was it?" she softly spoke, looking around at her surroundings, her eyes falling on Matt last. She came forward to join the mourning.

"It's good to have you back, Wyld," Malagar whispered.

She sucked in a sharp breath, wincing and clutching the side of her head but seemed to recover after a second.

"You bastard, Mal," she hissed, feeling for a fang that had gone missing, her mouth and head throbbing.

"At least...you're alive to complain about that pain," Hamui said, looking to Matt, then to where Dubix had last been seen. He hobbled off into the dark, leaving the camp in silence once more.

45

AN ARMY IN PURSUIT

Kissa deftly lifted a folded stack of cloth from passing caravan's goods, tossing Jasper and Arie a dusty blanket each.

"Cover the blood. Cover the armor," she whispered to them both.

Gale had redirected most of the city guard's attention, and the one guard that still was pursuing them was calling ahead, but had lost his visual on them, shoving his way through the crowd that, just two blocks down, had little indication that they even knew something was amiss down the road. Most merchants were simply focused on ensuring all their merchandise stayed theirs in the busy crowd.

"Almost to the gate, don't look up," Kissa quietly said to the group as they made their way across the street, trying to merge with the small flow of exiting traffic.

The move made them stand out, however. As they pushed through the flow, the guard a block back saw them through the crowd and shouted up to the gate guards just ahead to shut the gate.

The guard's voice was lost in the busyness of the streets at first, but an off glance at the guard's waving hands piqued the interest of the watchmen at the gate, who received the message just as Kissa hastily guided the group into the shadow of the huge city gate.

Gears began turning, gate operators and watchmen above calling all traffic to halt as the portcullis began to slowly lower.

Most in the crowd either halted as ordered or moved hastily to get out of the way of the lowering spiked gate. Kissa pushed forward to break through the standing crowd line, allowing Metus and the others to run through. She followed up the rear just as the gate lowered overhead, and she had to duck to avoid the descending spikes.

"You lot, halt!" one of the gatemen called as Kissa, Arie, Jasper, and Metus all ran through the halted crowd, their cover now completely blown. They ran off along the dirt highway that led out into the open sands of Tarigannie.

"Let's hope Naldurn got the word to Bannon of our need. They most likely will pursue on horseback soon," Kissa shouted, the lot of them finally making their way through the bulk of the caravan traffic, jogging along the open road.

They sprinted a mile past the gate before Kissa slowed the pace of the group, looking back at the gate, squinting to see the portcullis begin to rise once more.

"Are they sending riders?" Metus asked, breathing heaviest out of the group. He was conditioned and in good shape but measured against the absolute athletes he was surrounded by, plus the extra armor he wore, the run was beginning to wind him.

"Not sure," she replied slowly, attempting to see details in the distance.

"Perhaps we should get off the road, it'll make finding us all that more difficult," Metus suggested.

"Not necessary, Bannon will be here within the minute," Kissa stated, pointing down the highway to a rising dust cloud as a few riders charged towards them.

"Thank the gods," Arie breathed, speaking for all of them that luck had, for once that day, been with them.

Bannon covered the distance quickly, trotting up with two empty dolingers at his side. Naldurn followed behind with two more mounts.

"There's the riders," Kissa stated, looking back to Rochata-Ung. Lots of them…" she slowly added. All looked to see a mass of mounted soldiers gather outside the city gates, making a formation, not yet in pursuit.

"The Hyperium is mobilized and is awaiting our return, Sultan,"

Bannon said, calling everyone's attention slowly back to the road ahead instead of the road behind.

"Reza, Gale…the others. We're leaving allies behind," Metus softly said. He was the only one still looking to the massive city behind them.

Bannon raised his voice, the urgency of the situation clear. "We would leave more behind as certain casualties if we do not press forward now. We must away from this place. That is a few companies worth of mounted troops amassing at the gates. I don't know what you did to kick the hornets' nest, but we need to get you to safety and out of Tarigannie. We are not in a position to start a war with the full force of Rochata-Ung."

"Retreat then?" Metus asked, turning back to Bannon.

"Unless you wish to instigate a war at a very inopportune time, or give ourselves up to Rochata-Ung's judges to answer for whatever you did to incur their wrath. We can settle disputes of this matter once we've returned safely to Sheaf, but you're giving a corrupt rulership easy pickings to deal with us on their terms if we stay here."

"How far are we from the Hyperium, and do we travel along the highway, or off trail?" Metus asked tersely, seeing their time was short.

"The Hyperium is awaiting us up that ridge. I suggest we move off trail. The Hyperium is fast, but we are not prepped to outpace a cavalry unit like that. We were rigged to camp and travel for weeks, not hours like them. If we stick to the highway, with their fresh mounts and soldiers, they'll likely catch up to us in the following days, if not hours, before we reach the border. At least with traveling the countryside, they'll need to slow as much as we are."

Metus reflected on Bannon's reasoning, wondering how their good intentions to help the people of Tarigannie went so south.

"Kissa, Arie, Jasper. Can I trust you three to split when we reconnect with the Hyperium and make your way back into Rochata-Ung and do what you can to make sure the others are safe? I cannot simply leave Reza and the others without attempting some type of aid."

"At your command," Kissa readily agreed, but Jasper, Metus could tell, was displeased with the order.

"My one duty is to protect you, as is Gale's. How can we do that apart from you?" Jasper asked.

"Your first duty is to obey my orders," Metus said in a firm tone, looking to the city walls where more troops arrived. He knew their time did not permit an open debate on the issue.

"Yes, my sultan," he agreed, seeing there was no room here to sway Metus from his path in sending him away.

"Due east, it is," Metus said, turning back to his general. "Lead the way, Bannon, to the Hyperium. Let's hope no more swords need to cross paths this day."

The desert sun took on an unusually red hue that day as it wore on, blaring down on the group as they rushed to reconnect with the Hyperium unit and moved to skirt along the foothills of Daloth's Spire, a spike of igneous rock that formed the main spire of the mountain range surrounding Rochata-Ung's natural northern barrier.

Kissa, Jasper, and Arie split after the meetup and went to lay low in the brush far out of the path of the approaching cavalry.

The plateau had granted them a good view of the size of the unit of cavalry that pursued them. The number grew to five companies of roughly one hundred men each, more than enough to cause great concern for all as they rode off through the sand and brush, seeing the pursuit was on in full force now.

By noonday, they could see the cavalry battalion slowly closing over the distant foothills two miles behind. By the time evening came on, the cavalry had closed the gap by a mile. They were able to make out details of the troops now.

"They'll be on us before nightfall at this pace, Sultan Metus," Bannon said in a voice only meant for with whom he spoke.

"I know," he said grimly, squinting against the sun to see if he could see who the lead horseman was. "I'm sure that's Set. He holds rank in Rochata's military. I have a feeling all this mess ties back to him."

Metus looked out over the landscape before them for any hope. There was a thin line along the dunes heading north that lined the low sandstone mountains.

"Is that...a road? I thought we were far north of the road to Sansabar," Metus said, confused by the appearance of the path a ways out.

"That does appear to be a road of some sort. We are far too north for it to be heading to Sansabar, though."

Looking back to the approaching cavalry, Metus said, "Let's see where it leads. With hope, maybe it leads to an old encampment or some fortification. It's about our only chance at establishing some upper hand with our pursuers at this point. A show of advantage might be our last chance at diplomacy before—" Metus left off, considering how far he'd let the hostilities go before deciding to surrender or fight.

"Looks like it leads into a canyon or something. Might be a dead-end," Bannon worriedly said, looking back to keep an eye on the approaching cavalry.

"At least we'd have our backs against a wall," Metus argued.

Bannon conceded the point and rushed up to the head of the formation, giving quick orders to his company leaders of their new destination.

The sun was low on the horizon as Bannon led the Hyperium in a charge up the old trail into a side canyon.

Before them stood a settlement, not terribly large or well kept, but one with sturdy stucco walls; it looked inhabited, and by its location, Bannon figured it to be the enclave of the unclean.

Ordering the rest of the troops ahead, he fell back to Metus, meeting with him once more along the side of the troops and told him of his suspicions. The both of them rode up ahead to stand before wooden gates of the fort town.

"Darious! Is Darious there?" Metus called out over the eight-foot-tall wall, which was just tall enough to keep him from seeing over it.

The troops had just begun to settle as a familiar face popped up over the structure. Darious stood on a platform behind the wall to address the sultan and his troops.

"Not that I'm unhappy to see you again so soon, Sultan, but by the looks of your haste, I should hope you do not bring trouble with you."

"We do indeed bring trouble behind us. Set pursues us with five hundred horsemen. You know Set well enough that without the clear upper hand, he will abide. Out in the open desert, I fear he will strike. If, however, we are allowed entrance into your walls, I believe negotiations may be possible. If I've got to give myself up to his judgments, so be it, but those terms will not be able to be made if he runs upon us out here in the open like I fear he would. Might we utilize your wall?"

"You can't *utilize* our wall without bringing the whole town into your clearly hostile affairs, Sultan. With all due respect, we stand nothing to gain and everything to lose here. How could you expect me to call myself a leader if I just let you drag my people into this?"

"True, and fair enough. What if I could offer your people a better life?"

Darious looked to the horizon in thought, watching the sun as it lowered closer and closer to the horizon. "I'm listening. What's your proposal?"

Metus looked to Bannon, quickly considering his options of what he knew he could deliver on. "You are forced into an unwanted, out-of-the-way canyon here in Tarigannie. No aid from your neighbors, healers, or supplies. There is no hope among your people, I have seen it at camp nights ago," he started, considering his solution to their problematic way of life carefully before continuing. "There is a land in the Plainstate—Barre, which was ravaged by the arisen earlier this year. The arisen have moved on, but now the town is in disrepair and desperately needs families, able bodies, to build it up once more, tend the land, and provide growth. We could offer you land there, supplies to begin anew for a renewed, relevant way of life for your people. We have the best healers in the Southern Sands, and as we healed that child and her mother the other day, we can start cleansing your people's sickness. You would all be given a new chance at life. But…first we need this one favor of you. Let us into your walls where we can begin discussions with Set."

Darious thought hard on the proposition. It clearly came with high reward, but at the potential cost of every life under his charge if Set came in his fury and was not only satisfied with simply eliminating his enemy, but also the enclave he had a grudge against for years now.

"You put me in a difficult position, Sultan Metus," he said, looking past the Hyperium to see a dust cloud behind them that indicated the approach of the horsemen.

"Your decision now, or we ride on," Metus said.

"Where'd ya be riding to? Up the mountain?" he said, on the edge of humor and frustration. "There's no other way out than through them now." Darious sighed, realizing they were all in this together at that point, regardless of if he wanted no part of it or not.

"Open the damn gates," he called down to someone on his side of the wall. "I'm caring to my people. You have the walls. I expect you to follow through on all your promises," Darious said, exasperation clear as he spoke. "And Sultan, I expect you to claim victory if it comes to it. If you fail and my people suffer due to your intrusion, you will have their innocent blood on your hands."

As the gates opened, Metus called to Bannon, "Lead the troops in." Bannon promptly did so, and Metus pulled up next to Hathos to confer with him as to their best options and chances at winning an encounter considering the odds.

"Five to one are not good odds," Hathos softly spoke, causing Metus to instantly regret all events and his choices that led everyone to this point today.

Hathos did not leave Metus lingering in his despair too long. He turned to look at the hundred men that entered the fort and said with a confidence that bespoke volumes to the faith he had in his men, "But the Hyperium have seen worse. Much, much worse."

46

THE SETTING OF THE RED SUN

Grit from the wide canyon's mouth blew against the stucco wall of the fort town as the remaining troops entered through the chambered gated entrance. Most of the Hyperium's leadership stood along the walled platforms, overlooking the horizon where the cavalry ominously stood, half a mile out.

Bannon and Metus conferred along the platform at the interior side of the city wall, speaking with Darious, who left as Hathos rushed up for a report to the two men.

"The wall remains a man-and-a-half all the way around the town, no exits other than the gate in," Hathos reported, the rest of the town busy about tasks to prepare for the worst-case scenario.

"As you saw, the entry gate has a short corridor before the second, sturdier gate. I fear that first gate will not withstand much punishment before breaking down. The second gate, however, is hinged better, twice as thick, and I think might withstand any punishment troops might offer without siege weapons."

Metus nodded, considering the report. "That is good. We have enough archers that even with five hundred riders at their disposal, they won't be able to remain within shooting range without losing troops and horses constantly. Their only hope would be to breach those gates and overwhelm us."

Bannon answered the gap in their plans. "Then we better make sure that doesn't happen. And if it does, we will need half of your Blood company there at the entrance with their spears to halt a trample and to defend against those who vault the wall, the other half positioned around the rest of the town's walls to defend against those that would make it over the walls on sides and back."

"What of the other companies?" Hathos queried.

"The Shield company will be joined with most of the Shadow company to provide ranged attacks. The Shields will be along the walls, firing their crossbows while taking care of any jumping the wall, while the Shadows will position themselves on vantage points along the rooftops. Darious pointed out buildings to me that they use as watchtowers. They have wood slats that will help act as turrets. We also have a hundred battle-ready dolingers if the walls are breached. Controlling them may be tricky in a melee, so we'll need to make sure we're organized. If those beasts are not properly handled, they can become more hindrance than aid," Bannon replied.

"What about civilians? Will they be in the way?" Hathos asked, looking around the small town as indeed quite a few townsfolk scurried from the buildings to retreat deeper into the village.

"Darious is taking them below ground," Metus offered. "They've connected tunnels that go quite deep into the mountain. They should be completely safe from any missiles coming into the town from the enemy."

Metus took a deep breath, a clear plan being laid out as they came to some quick conclusions about their tactics and aim. "All this being said, this is only if they press an attack without accepting any of my offers. If this is Set we're dealing with, negotiations may be difficult, but hopefully, he will find this town well defended and simply too much trouble to make a move on.

"If not, I'm willing to offer myself up as prisoner. Beyond that, we'll fall back to defend ourselves here and hope the skill and experience of the Hyperium will be up to the challenge of withstanding an assault from such a large troop. May the gods find favor with us this day."

"I disagree with allowing them to just take you," Bannon said, holding in that comment as long as he could. It would be a sticking point, he knew. "It's my task to keep you safe, and just to allow you to walk into the hands of the enemy...I don't like it."

"Bannon, your charge is not to keep me safe, it's to keep the people of the Plainstate safe. If they demand a prisoner instead of a war, more lives will be saved. The only reason we didn't attempt negotiations straight from the start is because if it truly is Set that pursues us, my life may not be enough for him. I've known him for a good many years now, and if there's one attribute that defines him, it is that he's an opportunist. He will take all that's on the table possible for him to take. He would look at the Hyperium as a simple numbers game. By the odds, he should be able to annihilate us. With no survivors, he'd be able to write history as he wishes, slandering our mission and possibly the motives of the Plainstate as well.

"I won't allow that to happen. However, if I am brought back to answer for what crimes they have chased us thus far for, then so be it. I will answer and give testament to our mission before their judges once more. Do you understand?"

Bannon looked out over the mass of troops along the entrance of the canyon and to the reddening sun beyond. He did not show expression often, but the disapproval was clear to Metus now in the light of the setting sun.

At length, after keeping an answer from Metus for too long, he begrudgingly said, "I understand, though I disagree."

Letting out a sigh, frustrated with the position they were in, Metus shrugged. "Let's hope a show of force is all it takes to dissuade them. Us behind walls puts a cavalry unit, even one as large as theirs, at a massive disadvantage. If he's not completely blinded by revenge, a total military imbecile, or has no regard for the lives of his own troops, it's an easy solution to not press an attack on a well defended troop."

"You listed all three reasons I worry for the worst if that is indeed Set up there at the front of that line," Bannon said, pointing to the line of horsemen.

The two stood, staring into the mouth of the canyon in reflection as Naldurn rushed up to Hathos, giving a brief report to him. As they waited for Naldurn to finish her report, Metus asked Bannon, "What of prophet Henarus? You say he was stricken by Nomad?"

Bannon sighed shortly. "Yes. Though it seems Henarus will pull through, he is quite dazed. Perhaps a concussion? His priest is tending to him, though he will be of no use to us in this encounter. It is too bad; we could use his blessing of clarity. We'll be on our own unless some watchful eye of a stray god happens to grace us."

Hathos stepped up, calling for Bannon and Metus' attention. "Ganlin is stationed on the tallest rooftop, there," he said pointing to a two-story building about a block back. Wooden pallets were propped up to create a barricade from projectiles, a strong-armed woman with an especially tall longbow comfortably perched behind the wooden wall.

"As our best sharpshooter, she'll be ready for orders to dispatch high-priority targets. Her effective range is about two hundred yards, three hundred with some deviations in accuracy on a human-sized target.

"Naldurn says the rest of her troops are in position along the rooftops, preparing for the first few volleys at your order. Most have good cover. Looks like they'll be in good shape to weather any return fire.

"The Blood company is barricading the gates and the main courtyard to inhibit a charge in case both gates are breached. After which, they'll hunker down behind walls.

"The Shield company is positioning along the front walls and readying their crossbows, setting up their station. If the enemy makes a move to encircle the fort, they will relocate as needed to fend off flanking maneuvers.

"The townsfolk have gone underground apparently; none are within the buildings at least.

"Also…" Hathos said pausing for a moment to let out a small grin, "before he left to shepherd his people, Darious pointed out two mounted heavy arbalests on both ends of the front wall. They're not quite as large as ballistae, but they'll rip through man or horse and keep going by the looks of them. They were covered up to protect against the weather when we entered, but I have two teams of two from the Shield company finishing uncovering them and loading them. It might be a show of power that could give our enemy pause."

Bannon looked to the two teams along down the walls at work uncovering the machines, stroking his chin in thought. "That's four men from the Shields. You believe a gain of two heavy arbalest operators worth the loss of four crossbows?"

"To lower the enemy's morale alone, yes, I think it already a worthy trade. That sort of weapon was built for armored cavalry," Hathos answered with confidence, getting an approving nod from Bannon.

"This is well. It seems all troops are in order, my sultan," Bannon saluted, followed quickly by a salute from Hathos.

"This is well," Metus spoke, sticking to Bannon's last words, attempting to convince himself that the upcoming situation might just work itself out in their favor this day.

"We will soon know. Look, they approach," Bannon ominously added, turning everyone's attention to the rising dust cloud as the horses rode forth.

"They are not slowing," Hathos pointed out, as the five hundred riders came clearly into view. Everyone waited for a speaker to approach alone to make demands.

Hathos slowly detached himself from the command group, giving prompt orders to Naldurn as the two rushed to their respective battle posts.

Bannon broke the silence between him and Metus, giving voice to their fears, "There will be no negotiations today, my sultan." Metus' countenance turned grim along with his commander as they watched the riders charge forward, battle cries sounding as they approached the town.

"May the red sun set its final time upon our enemies this night," Bannon reverently offered, his solemn prayer agreed upon by Metus with a nod.

"Men, to your posts! First volley, loose!"

47

THE GRAVE CANYON

Horse after horse hit the ground, throwing sand and dirt up in their wake, tossing their riders violently to their doom amongst the charge. Their yells and screams were cut short upon impact or drowned out by the thunderous trample of stampeding hooves moving forward over them.

The first volley of arrows hit the riders with devastating accuracy. Even with the first line of riders being stretched long, only two deep, their spaced-out formation still succumbed to the deadly aim of the Hyperium's skill with their respective ranged weapons.

For every two archers, at least one rider ended right there and then, and the first company of riders that moments earlier spanned the width of the canyon was now left considerably thinned.

A bit delayed, the heavy arbalests fired, one then the other, both hurling shafts as thick as spears, shooting much farther than the other bolts and arrows, ripping through the midline troops and causing an upheaval of horses, slowing the charge in the area slightly before the company could make their way around their downed comrades.

"Those arrows and lives cannot be taken back," Metus

announced, seeming to fully commit to their battle plan now that the window of negotiations had officially passed.

"Next volley, ready!" Bannon yelled down the line both ways. Most in the Shield company had already been hard at work cranking their crossbows back to load while the Shadow company nocked and drew their bows.

Bannon held his hand up, waiting for the last of the Shield crossbowmen to finish cranking.

"Aim!" Bannon yelled, adding, "Make it count," as bowstrings drawing tight all across the rooftops sounded. "Loose!"

Bolts and arrows, all in unison, hurled towards the fast-approaching army, felling even more this time, decimating the frontline troop. Horse and rider tumbled to their end, head over hoof, eaten up by the ferocious charge of those behind them, if not dying from the missiles outright, the stampede ensuring their demise.

The mounted arbalests launched again, careening through multiple targets in the mid-ranged group, spooking the horses, halting the charge for parts of the unit.

"Fire at will!" Bannon shouted above the roar of the approaching horde. A loose of arrows to flew skillfully at the two companies behind the remaining front line, the archers having enough collective warfare experience to know that if they didn't start thinning out the preceding units, they could easily be overwhelmed by the time the units arrived at the wall still fresh.

As the bolts started to click off, Bannon could see the two rear companies begin to fan out, moving fast to position themselves to take the flanks, rushing ahead, most likely to make for the sides of the town's walls.

"We've got our work cut out for us tonight," Bannon murmured under his breath before shouting to Naldurn, "Focus half of your Shadows on those two companies flanking! The other half, keep on the three center companies!"

Turning to Hathos, Bannon blurted out orders, "Head the breach they're about to attempt, get with Undine and ensure the Bloods secure the walls for those that vault it. I'll make sure Tau and the Shields keep the heat on 'em."

Hathos quickly saluted, running off to join up with Undine at the front gate.

"It begins, my sultan," Bannon said, taking one last look at the approaching unit only seconds away from arriving at the walls.

"Stay with me," he said, then shouted down to Tau a quick order to send five on each end to follow the two companies that were flanking.

A crash shuddered the front gate as a press of horsemen slammed against it, being rammed against it again and again by the horses behind it, all pressing on the main gate. The hinges failed within seconds as the wooden gate blew open and the horses trampled over those who sacrificed themselves as the first ones in the charge. Horses rushed to jump over downed allies into the gate corridor before being halted at the second gate.

Two squads on both sides of the gate lined up against the wall, standing on their saddles, jumping up to pull themselves over the barrier. The first to raise their heads over it were met with spear and sword tips, falling back off their horses in a gush of blood, beginning to litter the outer wall with corpses as the red sun began to fall beyond the horizon. The light left the grounds now, only illuminating the wall and the mountains behind.

Half of the Shadow archers that had been picking off the flanking companies were now joined by ten Shield soldiers, and slowly, their targets were falling; though not quick enough to keep up with the hundreds still incoming. The remaining horsemen were closing in around the side walls, and less than two dozen or so troops per side had been dropped.

"Bannon, we need support along the sides!" Naldurn shouted from the rooftop.

Luckily, Bannon heard her through the chaos and ordered four mounted Blood soldiers over to the right wall, rushing to Hathos, shouting to him to send four more to the other side.

Just as Hathos sent his four men off, the last gate lurched, another wave of riders packing into the corridor, pressing in, straining the heavy gate, causing it to buckle dangerously.

"Spears in!" Undine shouted at his thirteen men surrounding the corridor along the walls. Undine himself joined in, stabbing into the crowded pit of horse and man flesh, blood covering the walls and floor completely by that point.

Though the number of dead rose, so did the stacks of bodies along the floor, those horsemen rushing into the corridor now standing a bit taller, batting away the spears that were now level with them.

Javelins launched over the walls and gate; though they were being thrown blindly, it was making it difficult for the troops to focus on the task at hand, having to watch the skies constantly now.

"They'll be over the wall soon at this rate," one of Undine's lieutenants yelled at him, stabbing another rider that took his spear with him as he plummeted on top of the stack of bodies that continued to grow.

A sword slashed over the gate at the lieutenant, hacking in at his face, his helmet deflecting most of the cut. He fell to the ground, blinded by all the blood that seeped out of his deep gash along his face.

"Shadows! Focus on those entering the first gate!" Undine ordered, looking over the wall to gore the Rochatan soldier that had felled his lieutenant.

Looking at the first breached gate, he could see well over thirty horsemen attempting or waiting to squeeze through the space. The gate would fall, he could see. They needed to fall back now or risk having the gate breach before they were ready.

Naldurn's Shadows had kept picking off the second line of riders at a steady pace, but now they were at the walls, completely surrounding the front half of the town, along with most of the sides as the flanking groups rode up to the rampart, using their mounts as stepping platforms to hoist themselves up and over the ledge.

The heavy arbalests fired one more time, ripping through the closest troops, pinning corpses of man and horse to the sands. The Shields manning them quickly took up their lances, goring the Rochatan riders that rode up to the wall ready to leap over it, only to be met with lance points.

Riders were climbing over the walls at a growing rate, throwing javelins as they went, forcing the Shadows to take cover.

They came like rats leaving a flooding sewer, scrambling to simply make footing on the other side of the wall. Some were greeted with crossbow bolts and arrows as they breached, others cut down and speared as soon as they landed on the other side, but as the crossbows were being loaded less and less, and the number of riders vaulting the wall increased, the Blood and Shield companies were quickly being overwhelmed.

"Blood company, send your dolingers over the wall on the attack! Shadows, all focus on the gate!" Bannon shouted, his voice ragged from barking commands at the top of his lungs.

The gate was buckling, and men now spilled over the fortifications. Though the Blood and Shield troops were dealing with infantry, Bannon knew that if the gate fell, they'd have a flood of riders enter the battlefield, which could easily turn the tide of war in their enemy's favor. Rather than working on supporting the Blood and Shield troops, he determined their archers would be best used to keep focus on thinning the riders at the gate, holding them off for as long as they could.

Sultan Metus dodged a hack from a scimitar just as he noticed three men jump down from the wall. He parried another slash and riposted, hacking through the man's arm, sticking the belly of the second, then squaring off against the third.

Bannon caught the man off guard, slicing in from the flank, the man barely getting his falchion up in time before Metus cut into his exposed side. Bannon took advantage of the distraction and quickly ran him through as he recoiled in pain, falling atop his slain brethren.

Metus looked around the screaming, bloody, horrific scene that was unfolding all around him. The sight of war was overwhelming. So much death. The carelessness with which whomever had ordered the attack was disgraceful, the casualties on the enemy's side already stacking up to half their troops, mostly from the fire of the Shadow and Shield companies.

He did not doubt Set was on the other side of that wall. Metus knew no life that man valued, aside from that of his late brother. To him, five hundred lives meant no more than any other tool he used to make his way up the ranks of power.

"Naldurn!" Metus yelled, looking to the rooftops for her. She appeared and drew her bow in a flash, firing an arrow past Metus just as another rider leapt over the wall at Metus' back.

Metus didn't have time to thank her. "Your sharpshooter! Have her focus on the commanders! No one else till their leaders are dead!"

She nodded and vanished over the rooftop. Metus hoped that without orders, the enemy force might lose heart for the bloodbath.

"They're over the walls now. We need to fall back," Tau said, rushing up next to Bannon and Metus.

"Order all Hyperium to fall back to the left wall! Send the remaining dolingers on the attack at any that come over those ramparts," ordered Bannon. Tau ran off down the line to gather the troops on the ground and rooftops.

Thirty Rochatan soldiers formed up in the streets along the right side of town, the Shadows that had been keeping the invading troops at bay falling back upon orders.

The company captain marched through with twenty other troops down a ways closer to the front gate, joining up with the other thirty men, pushing back the already retreating Hyperium that had remained along the right flank.

Both sides merged into other groups of their allies as they traveled along the right side of the town, each exchanging attacks, both by blade and missiles, but with the Hyperium's tighter aim and better trained blades, the Rochatans were the ones losing on the advance.

Their captains knew well enough that the only chance they had at not losing the battle was to keep pressing until their enemies' backs were against a wall. They only hoped they had enough men to last through the brutal advance.

Ganlin scanned the warzone for high-value targets, loosing an arrow once or twice, taking out mounted soldiers moments before a horseman brought down would-be fatal blows on her comrades.

She grinned as she noticed a man, flanked by two others, off to the side of a troop of twenty riders. The man in the middle had dressed similar to the common soldiers, so did his two companions next to him, but she noticed he was sitting back, quite calmly, sending the other two to and fro, conversing with them upon their return.

"You wear no colors, eh?" she whispered to her newfound target, seeing through the common Tarigannie military custom to not dress up their commanders that made her job that much harder.

"No matter, my little man," she said, nocking an arrow. She drew the heavy longbow back, taking in a deep breath as she did so, holding it as she lined up her shot.

He was a good distance away, but not further than she could reliably shoot.

Her well-developed bow arm bristled with tension, the smallest quiver of a tremble as she loosed the arrow through the skies. It easily arced over the front wall, soaring towards her target, striking right between the man's legs, sinking deep into the saddle and horse's spine, dropping the beast at once as it was left paralyzed.

The horse collapsed with the man still hooked into the saddle, pinning his leg beneath the hundreds of pounds of horse.

The two men at his side sprang into action, dismounting, helping to lift the beast off of their senior ranking officer as Ganlin lined up her next shot.

Eyes emotionless, she let another shaft fly towards the panicking group of men. The arrow slipped straight through one of the aiding officers, dropping him on top of the man he was in the process of helping up.

She could see now the other man yelling up the ranks, and another leading officer heeding the call, looking to the horsemen that had just burst through the second gate, barking orders at them before rushing back to aid the two officers that she had centered on.

She drew her bow back again, waiting for a moment when the men's movements were less erratic. With the distance being so great, she had to know where her target was going to be a few seconds ahead of time, and now that they knew they were marked, her task had become that much more difficult.

The second gate exploded off its hinges, a grotesque wave of blood and corpses spewing out into the small courtyard. Frantic horsemen spurred on their mounts to make it through the sickening terrain, some horses losing their footing, getting trampled by those that were behind, champing at the bit to get out of the claustrophobic gate corridor.

Riders began to flood out of the narrow corridor and into the Shield company, who had formed a small phalanx, mixed within the barricades they had thrown together in the minutes before the battle.

Their long lances had been firmly planted, and as the riders bounded out of the mass grave that was the gate corridor, they sprang straight into the network of spears, all skillfully guided to end either a horse or its rider before it could break through their lines.

Down the street marched forty Rochatan soldiers, their troops thinning, but still pressing firmly the assault, squeezing Hyperium of all three stakes together, flanked between the incoming horses that were breaking through the phalanx and the approaching platoon of troops picking off lone soldiers one by one in the streets.

"Fall back! Form a line with Hathos!" Bannon shouted, his raw voice completely stripped, getting his men to maneuver around the incoming horse units just in time before the line broke, which would have cut off ten Blood and Shield troops that they could not afford to lose.

"Bloods! To the front!" Hathos shouted, everyone linking up now but a few Shadows along surrounding rooftops, still picking off troops as they were able, bombarded with javelins constantly.

Bannon, Hathos, and Metus made their way to the center of their troops, everyone converging in a section of yard between the outer wall and a longhouse the town used as a lodge. Now it was *they* who were trapped in a corridor, though this corridor was forty-foot wide as opposed to the fifteen-foot-wide gate entrance.

It gave them enough space to form up and reorganize themselves into a strong formation, Blood soldiers at the front, Shields behind supporting the front-line Bloods with spears and, the ones that still had them, crossbows.

The Shadow company was half on rooftops, but the other half, as they had lost ground in the town, had joined up with the other companies on the ground and now formed around the commander's huddle, ensuring them some degree of safety as well as being at good range to lob arrows over the heads of their allies into the enemy ranks.

Rochatan blocks of ten soldiers were splitting up through the streets, closing in on the main fight at the lodge yard, but the Shadows' constant arrow fire was making their progress through the streets slow.

The rain of arrows halved at once, and Bannon ordered Naldurn to get topside to find out what happened to their support from the rooftops.

The incoming rush of thirty horses quickly ate up what spears the Shining Spears had on the eastern flank, and the infantry made way for the healthy dozen riders to plow through the Hyperium's line, breaking into the heart of the force and creating an immediate problem for Bannon and his men.

"Close that gap behind those horses! Don't let the footmen get in behind their cavalry!" Hathos yelled, Bannon's voice now completely gone from constant shouting the whole battle.

A Rochatan captain shouted orders to get through the gap left by the horses, but Blood soldiers rushed in, slashing down those that tried to take advantage of their misfortune so ferociously, that even with the barking commands from the captain, the footmen failed to secure the advantage, falling back to form a line against the fierce Blood soldiers, keeping them at bay while the internal troops began the dangerous task of dismantling the fifteen horsemen that had rushed through their lines.

Forty Rochatan soldiers continued to press the east end of the yard, their numbers bolstering from more troops that finally made their way past some of the rooftop archers.

Seeing their sides numbers growing emboldened their leader to call for a charge. Sixty men rushed the small line of the ten Blood and nine Shining Spears that had been holding off the growing threat.

From behind, a pack of dolingers rushed them, plowing into their exposed backs, and ripped what troops they could snatch at with their maws before the rear line could recompose themselves to defend against the ferocious beasts.

A volley of arrows devastated the large troop in the midst of the distraction, felling a dozen men within moments. The Rochatan captain yelled orders for a unit of ten to face the seventeen or so archers that had snuck up along their flank, while the remaining forty men continued to focus on the charge, which had lost its steam all at once.

Naldurn was among that group, at the head of her Shadow sisters. Seeing the captain barking orders to reposition his men marked him as a clear target. His rank was on display now.

Lining him up in her sights, she loosed an arrow, immediately drawing and firing another, and another…and another.

Four arrows, only moments apart, stuck into the exposed parts of the captain's armor, two sticking through his skull, one in his neck, and one in his sword arm. He dropped, dead before he hit the ground, leaving the men he had been commanding panic-stricken as the Shadow Stake continued their brutal volley of arrows twenty yards down the street.

The east flank of Rochatan soldiers had dwindled quickly, shockingly so for the group that had been halved within a minute's span, the fight and steam for battle quickly leaving the group.

The horsemen that had broken through the Blood ranks had been halted by the spears of the Shields, three large dolingers backing them up. Once halted, the six Shadow archers guarding Metus and the other leadership had begun picking the force off.

They threw their hands up in surrender, dropping their swords and javelins. Metus quickly called for a cease fire from his archers and Hathos ordered an unconditional surrender to the east group of thirty soldiers as well, seeing the panic that had begun to set in amongst the enemy.

The troop attempted to retreat at first, but Naldurn's Shadows had relocated, blocking both alleys that would have been their escape.

"Drop your arms!" Hathos shouted, breaking through to the front lines so that he could be heard and seen.

With no captain, no leader threatening a death sentence for them and their family if they ran or surrendered, thirty soldiers dropped their weapons of war, holding hands aloft. They were ordered to move over against the wall, away from the weapons at their feet, to which they complied.

Undine ordered the riders to dismount and join the other prisoners, which they did readily.

"See to the others. I'll see that the Shadow Stake and a few Bloods will hold these in order," Undine said to Hathos, Hathos quickly moved to take all soldiers that were not guarding prisoners, rushing over to the west side of the battlefield, where battle still raged.

Hathos pushed and maneuvered his way to the front lines, finding the enemy troop falling before the Bloods much too quickly for them to even have a chance at winning this encounter at any odds.

Slashing an approaching soldier that rushed him, sidestepping to allow the Shield soldiers behind him to finish the job, Hathos heard someone in the enemy ranks ordering another charge.

He saw him, though; he was down the line twenty feet, too far to make it to.

Another wild swing came in at Hathos, his armor blocking the attack this time thankfully, then a javelin blew past him. He slashed his blade head height, slicing through the soldier's neck.

The man fell back, headless, and Hathos snatched the dead man's longsword, hefting it and hurling with all his strength up the line, through multiple combatants. It stuck in the captain of the unit through the ribs along the side, just under the arm.

The captain fell, and Hathos shouted just as a slight lull set in over the front lines, all seeing that they were now leaderless and losing badly. "Lay down your arms and you'll be spared. Keep fighting, and you die, every one of you!"

"There has been enough death this eve. Let us be finished with the bloodshed," Metus called, his voice stern, but with promise of reprieve if cooperation was their choice.

They chose cooperation. The twenty-four men still left alive on the western front began to drop their weapons as their captain weakly ordered, gravely wounded from the ground, "Arm and fight."

An anonymous arrow silenced the remaining captain.

Another arrow shot through the skies, taking everyone's attention, this one destined for far beyond the walls. They all listened as the arrow landed, the dying cries of a horse shrieking, adding its cry to the moans of the injured and near dead.

"Bannon, Hathos, six Shadows, find a mount. Ganlin's prey may not have escaped yet. If it's Set…" Metus left off, a dangerous edge of murderous intent lining his countenance.

293

The nine riders bolted past the rest of the Hyperium and prisoners they were corralling, horses leaping over the mass of bodies at the front gate entrance, landing along blood-soaked sands as the final light of day washed itself of the canyon. They rushed ahead. Metus saw another arrow fly over them, landing solidly in a soldier fighting with another over who claimed the only mount that had not been scared off or ripped apart by dolingers in the field.

The soldier finished the job, slashing the other one down, arrow in back, fatal cut in front, as the other laid down to accept his end, gasping for his final breaths. The soldier took the horse, mounted, and spurred it towards the canyon's entrance, Metus in fast pursuit with his posse to reach the anonymous rider.

Another arrow whistled through the air past Metus, ripping into the flank of the rider's horse, sending it toppling, throwing the man harshly to the ground. The man stood up right away, though his shoulder slumped, either out of socket or broken.

Metus rode up behind the fleeing man and kicked him hard in the injured shoulder, spinning him to the ground on his back. The two locked eyes. Set's eyes were full of pain and anger at first, but as soon as Metus' rage registered, the fear of death fell upon him like an angel of passing.

Metus said no words to him, but leapt from his mount, pouncing on the man that had plagued him so terribly the last few days, striking him with gauntleted hands, ripping slices in Set's face as steel gouged soft flesh. The blows landed, again and again, until Set no longer moved or attempted with his one working arm to squirm away.

The others rode up, watching their leader in his fury, none sure if they should intervene or allow the mutilation to continue.

Seeing the life draining from the one that so carelessly threw so many lives away, Metus stood, issuing out a hand, tersely demanding, "Rope."

One of the Shadows tossed him a hempen rope that had been lashed about the saddle. Metus snatched it, setting to work at tightly binding Set's wrists, finishing the knot so forcefully that everyone watching the enraged sultan's punishment heard bones snap like twigs along Set's wrists.

Taking the other end of the rope, Metus tied it to the horn of his saddle, mounted up, and spurred his horse back to the town at such speed, Set's broken frame was not long able to withstand.

Getting snagged along the dead that littered the battlefield, Set's hands ripped off, releasing him from his hellish leash. Metus threw off the rope from the horn, turning back around to continue unloading his anger on the man that laid very still in the dark of the battlefield, who blended in so well with the dead beside him that it took Metus a few moments to find him.

"Enough," a voice from his band hoarsely said, and Metus knew it was Bannon that had called him into check.

"The man's dead. If not, soon will be. Tarnishing your name and title will not make right all that he made wrong. We still have injured within the town to tend to, and prisoners to deal with," Bannon croaked, riding up to Metus, who listened as his eyes remained fixed on Set's unmoving body.

Trotting up to his sultan, out of earshot of the others, Bannon hoarsely whispered to his friend, "Collect yourself out here. Do not enter those walls still carrying this anger. Your people need a clear-minded leader, not one driven to madness in the face of the horrors of war."

They left their sultan in the midst of the field of dead, the moans from the dying the only sound to comfort him, and the inescapable ripe smell of hundreds of bodies open and lifeless overwhelming his senses.

Metus dismounted, staring off into the dark night. The stars began to appear in the heavens, Kale's green moonlight the only illumination of the slaughter that lay on every side of him.

He dropped to his knees, horrified at what had transpired that night. *Had he needlessly ended hundreds of lives? What could have been done differently? Why had Set not even attempted negotiations?*

Question after question bombarded his mind; though, no answers would be realized that night.

That night, away from all of his men, only seen by the hundreds of dead around him, he wept.

48

FAREWELL TO AN OLD FRIEND

The rare sound of birds chirping along the Imhotez mountainside accompanied the session of silence the group held over Matt's burial that sunny morning. A light breeze rustled the nearby sagebrush as the group paid their respects.

They had found a hewn slab along the cliffside, presenting a striking enclosed area that harbored a bit of verdant greenery not common to the arid region. They all agreed it was the perfect place to lay the old trades master to rest.

A long while went by, and slowly, some went back to the campsite. Only Malagar and Fin remained when Malagar broke the silence to say his peace.

Kneeling down beside the shallow grave covered with slate, Malagar offered a parting prayer.

"You've taken on many wayward souls throughout your years. I'm glad you took me on right at the end of your time. If I had not had you, Cray, Wyld, and Hamui to take me in once I was cast from the monastery…" He left off, stopping himself from continuing that line of thought, wanting instead to leave his old master with positive feelings of hope and renewed purpose instead of lingering on thoughts of what might have been.

"Lucky we are to walk this land, and you were blessed to walk it many days, inspiring the best out of others, helping forge wisdom out of youth. Within the days I still have left, I swear to do what I can to follow in your footsteps. I will aid in what ways I am capable in the war against this arisen threat, and then I will mentor others like myself, who are lost and seeking guidance. I will strive to be that stabilizing figure for those that need it. An anchor point for those lost in the storm."

Malagar bowed his head, saying his goodbye to his old master. He looked to Fin, nodded his condolences, and headed back to camp.

Fin waited until Malagar was out of earshot, then approached the grave and sat down next to it, letting out a tired sigh as he clutched at his painfully hot wounds Malagar had helped clean and mend the night before.

He looked out over the Canyonlands before them. The view was lovely. It was high up, allowing them a clear view of the vista of the foothills below. Though they couldn't see Brigganden from there, he knew it to be close by, just around the bend—he had seen the dim glow of it the night before.

"For once, I'm going to talk to you and you're not going to berate me in reply," Fin said, adding as a thought came to him, "Though, if you did reply, I'd only be so surprised. Always had to have the last quippy word in."

A bluebird swooped in, landing on the yucca bush next to them, bobbing its head this way and that as it inspected Fin and the grave.

"You'll have company here, looks like. The birds seem to like this spot—" Fin choked up, not able to continue his line of conversation with his deceased friend. Wiping his eyes dry, he looked back over the morning mountain scene, silently reflecting on his long-time mentor.

"Ghaa," Fin grunted out, "Cavok ain't going to forgive me for letting you die on my shift. Can't imagine how he's going to take the news."

He sat in silence for a minute, letting his thoughts and memories drift as they pleased.

"Ol' Mal there was way better at this," he laughed through some tears, wiping his face once more. "Well, guess that's why I waited till everyone left to do this. But…just wanted to tell you, Matt, to say it out loud to you once. I know we've had our fights and all, but no matter how mad I ever got with you—you were like a father to me—"

He choked up again, this time not able to regain his voice. Letting out a few more tears before getting to his feet, he looked upon Matt's gravesite once more, imprinting its location mentally so that he might be able to find it again someday; then, with a heart as heavy as he had ever felt it, holding his throbbing shoulder, he headed back down the cliffside to the others.

The little bluebird watched as Fin walked away, cocking its head sideways as he left, perching on the yucca branch until a grub crawled by. Swooping down, snatching it up, the bird flew up the cliffside overwatching the grove to its nest, feeding what it had to its little ones as the morning sun rose higher in the sky.

The camp was dour and quiet upon Fin's return, and Yozo, though respectful of Matt's passing, was packed, ready to head out, and Fin suspected, not in company with them.

"Yozo, you leaving us?" Fin asked, voice clearly expressing how drained he was from the sleepless night and just burying a dear friend.

Looking off over the canyonlands below them, Yozo turned back and nodded. "You have a mission before you, as do I. Both of us serve justice in our own ways, this I see now. I respect the sacrifice you lot are making for your land."

Fin let Yozo finish, but replied, disappointment in his voice, "Justice? Is that what we're doing in confronting the arisen? I don't know, maybe. It's a good cause I think, a noble one enough to die for. We're grateful for your help last night, but you…what is it that you're off to do? Are you off to kill Nomad? You think that's the work of justice? That's the work of revenge. They're not one in the same, Yozo. What you're doing is selfish.

"If you were a worthless vagabond, maybe I wouldn't care so much that you're wasting your skill, but I've seen your skill with the blade. This land could use your talent—*we* could use your talent. You could make a big difference in many lives—what a waste."

Fin turned to consider the other three who had paused while packing their things to listen to the reprimand. They all were tired, none of them getting sleep the night before, which made the quiet moment all the more morose.

Yozo had listened, though his back was turned. He stood there long after Fin's reproach, contemplating the roads before him.

"Yozo," Malagar called, stepping up beside him after a time, "Matt saw something in you. He's—well—*was* good at that. Though he was blind, he had a way of seeing past all the trappings the others get hung up on. He could tell the worth of a person better than anyone I've known. He wouldn't have allowed you to come along with us unless he approved of your company. There's something pure and strong in you.

"I don't know much of this grudge you hold for this Nomad, but what I have come to know is that the arisen that we fought last night, and the army that sent them to us, they will obliterate countless villages and peaceful peoples in Tarigannie and beyond if someone doesn't step up to stop them.

"I see now why Matt went along with Fin here, and I see now that you have a caring soul. You stayed and fought by our side, even though you did not have to. You owed us nothing, yet you risked your life in our defense. I don't know who you have as family, as comrades, but you have forged strong bonds between us last night. I for one, would be honored to have your company."

Yozo stood there, obviously mulling over the words and offer being presented, but giving them no indication on his standing. He slowly started walking, picking up pace as he headed down the cliffside, making his way out of the Imhotez mountains.

"It was worth a try, Mal," Fin said, coming over to the group of friends. "Though, I had my doubts about him from the start. Grudges can be hard to shake."

Hamui cinched up his sack, hefting his travel gear as the four of them allowed the peacefully quiet morning to roll by for a moment.

"Where to then?" Fin asked, knowing hints at Malagar's direction, though needing confirmation rather than assuming the man's intent.

"Indeed, where to," Malagar echoed in a mournful tone, hinting at more than just the question of physical direction.

"Cray and Matt are dead—as well as Dubix, presumably. Our rudders broke," Hamui mumbled in an unusually somber voice. Never had Fin seen Hamui so reverential.

"Wyld, you've been through more than most of us over the last few days. Do you have thoughts on where to go, what to do next?" Malagar asked, so tired he seemed out of breath.

The kaith sniffed the air, looking over the vista as she considered a response, lifting her lip to rub a tongue across her missing fang that was now either deeply embedded in Malagar's arm or somewhere in the dirt along the cliffside.

"This one," she said, pointing at Fin, "knows the stratagem of my captor. I intend to murder Denloth for what he did to me. You will help us plan an attack."

Fin, somewhat amused by the order, held back his smirk and replied, "I'm going after Denloth and his master regardless of being joined by you three, but if you would accompany me, well—" he sighed, "I would not hesitate to accept the help."

Malagar came out of his thoughts, looking to Fin. "Recovering Wyld was the main reason Matt brought us here, but I believe it was his intent to do what could be done to foil the arisen's plans. And as it was Matt's last undertaking in life, I'd like to honor him by continuing his mission and seeing it fulfilled, as much as I am able. Perhaps that will give me a measure of closure on the subject," he said, somewhat frustrated. "I don't know, I'm still at a loss with how things unraveled last night. One thing I know is that I agree with Wyld. Denloth cannot go unanswered for what he did to us. I usually do not promote reprisal, but he will hurt and kill others. He needs to be stopped."

"What about you, Hamui?" Fin asked, seeing now that the other two were set on sticking it through with him. Even if their motivations were different, their goals aligned.

"You all for murdering that arisen bastard?" Hamui said, looking up at them all, no humor at all in his countenance. "Then count me in."

"Well, Matt trusted you all enough to take you on as students. I'll do my best to get us close to Denloth to take him out. He does seem to be a big player in the arisen's forces, though the real threat is his master, the arisen lord. But we don't stand a chance at assassinating him, so we'll focus on Denloth—for now.

"I have connections of some renown. Sooner or later, I need to contact them and share the info we've gathered thus far. I suspect that's going to be the most useful thing we do out here on our own, but if we can take Denloth out, as far as I'm concerned, mission success.

"I guess we have plenty of time on the road to discuss the particulars of these matters, but I think step one would be to leave this place, just in case Denloth sends any other scouts to finish the mark he placed on us. Once out of these mountains, perhaps restocking and mending at Brigganden briefly, I say we once again approach their camp and establish a plan from there to catch Denloth vulnerable and separate from the aid of the army."

The three stared at Fin, and for a moment he wasn't sure if he had said something to lose the three's confidence.

"Well, get packed then. We're waiting on you," Hamui piped, hefting his rucksack, indicating to Fin's things still scattered about the camp.

"I—" a quiet voice called from down the way. Yozo walked back into the clearing. "—will lend my sword to your cause."

The foreigner's return heartened Malagar greatly, and Hamui and Wyld seemed pleased. Fin seemed perplexed by the return of the swordsman, but shaking off his bemusement, he jumped to gather his things, seeing that everyone was waiting on him to head out, adding as a welcomed smile now formed, "Sure beats taking on the undead army all on my own."

49

DARKNESS UPON THE HORIZON

They moved while we were in Brig that week. I don't know if we spurred them into action, or they had plans to pack camp and move the army regardless, but the arisen are on the move.

We needed the recovery time, though, no way around it. Some of us were in bad shape—myself probably most of all. My wounds were cleaned, properly sutured, and are mending well enough. It will be many months before a full recovery, though, and I'll be forced to watch myself, especially that right shoulder.

Brig sure has changed. Sure, a lot of the same people came back, but there's a new order there. Some stray sect of Elendium. They don't tolerate any slipups from out-of-towners, so we followed their decrees to the tittle while there. Making a note of that, though, in case we happen back sometime in the future.

Mal still has troubles with his arm. The Seam has entered his body through Wyld's tooth, which was never found or extracted. He has been lost in meditation more and more these days. I don't know much of the matter, but I sense the Seam is calling once more to him. Perhaps it is what the fates have in store for him—an unescapable draw or an endpoint from all converging possible paths he might take

302

in this life.

Wyld has had troubles with the Seam touch, more so than Mal. His is mostly a numbness and chill, but her—she's been blinking in and out of sanity since that night. Though I don't know her well, Hamui and Mal both tell me that this is not normal for her. She's becoming estranged to reality and her friends that she's known for years. Some days are worse than others. We will continue to keep an eye on her. Heaven forbid that she forgets one day who we are and if we're friends or enemies. And this is all not mentioning the strange…unweaving…of her scars at times. We're not even sure if she will be able to physically hold herself together for much longer. It is not looking good for her, to be frank.

Hamui, he's been grumbling about, well, everything, but I'm beginning to understand him a bit better over the last week of travel.

Then there's Yozo. He reminds me a lot of Nomad, though if I were to tell that to him, he'd likely kill me for even thinking such a thought. He does not talk much, but I did ask him why he returned to us that day. He said that he realized there's nothing, no one, for him out there. He was walking away from the only meaningful connection he's had in years and that, likely what Matt and I argued with him earlier about, once he killed Nomad, the empty void would still be there. He thinks that the cause we are engaged in is an honorable one, one that he could see his younger self being easily swept up in; he figures, at this point, his younger self seems like the better judge of right and wrong.

He decided he'd give us a chance to prove his original outlook wrong, but not to get too comfortable with his alliance as he alluded to still being undecided on the matter. It's the best outcome we could have hoped for, I guess. Regardless, having his sword on our side is a godsend. I would hate to have to square off with him otherwise!

We are investigating the Dolinger Crags on the morrow. The army went in, and I see no easy exit for such a large troop. Perhaps it is their intent to establish a war base there. It has its strategic flaws, but it is as central as they will get to Rochata-Ung without being easily detected with the size of an army as they have.

However it turns out, it is our intent to survey their whereabouts tomorrow and see if it is possible to locate Denloth. The boys are itching for his head. I have doubts that we're up to the task. I've got a bad feeling about that one.

I…still often think of Matt's end. Often have I lost friends, but it's been a while since I've lost family.

The clouds blazed orange on the horizon over the vast chasm before them. The sun, Phosphorus, was halfway set, lighting half of the sky, as Kale, the moon, hovered above it, lit clearly for them to appreciate.

"Dolinger Crags is called that for a reason, you know," Hamui grumped, sharing his people's distaste for the large, aggressive animals. They had, after all, been known to devour more than a few praven.

"I doubt even the dolingers are willing to come out of their canyon holes to scavenge while the arisen are nearby," Wyld solemnly said, her eyes fixed on something deep in the crags.

Fin watched as the sun vanished amidst heat waves along the horizon and uttered, "Well, at daybreak, we'll find out if that is true. I doubt traveling under the cover of darkness will do anything to further conceal us, at least according to what I gleaned from Dubix—while he was with us."

"We gonna kill that fucker tomorrow?" Hamui bluntly asked.

Fin replied in an uneasy voice, "We're going to survey the situation tomorrow, get what info we can about their combat readiness, size, and where their leaders are stationed. Once we have something to go off of, we can make plans from there. I'm not committing to throwing ourselves hopelessly at them if there isn't a valid path to an assassination."

He could feel their readiness to slaughter the one that was responsible for the murder of their friends, and he could understand their position, him being in their shoes not but a year prior, but he knew they stood very little chance at cleanly taking Denloth out and stood a very good chance of all of them being killed if they ran in there recklessly, as he could feel they wanted to do. What they needed right now was a bit of temperance and cunning.

"It's been a long day of travel," Malagar offered, breaking the tension. "Might be best if we all got a good night's rest and turned in early. There can be no room for slip-ups tomorrow."

Fin was grateful for the suggestion, agreeing, and moved to help set up camp, asking who wanted to take first watch as the night began.

"Who's that?" Wyld asked, everyone stopping what they were doing to notice the armored group leisurely approaching them.

"Who is that, indeed," Fin breathed. The pace with which the group approached did not bespeak danger to them and their little band, and a company so well outfitted more than likely would not be interested in robbing them. He put his things down and moved to greet the travelers, everyone else following Fin's lead.

They approached slowly, and as they got closer, both groups sized each other up.

Eleven females, all but three clad in heavy armor, rode on

horseback towards them. With their helmets off, Fin could see they all had platinum hair, and each wore a banner or sigil of some sort to signify their code.

"I know that sign," Fin announced as they approached within earshot. The lead woman in robes took point, pulling up short of Fin, horse flank exposed as she inspected him.

"What's a detachment of saren knights doing all the way out here? I have a hunch, but..." Fin trailed off, waiting for the older saren's response.

"We are not so well known throughout these lands that any commoner would know of our order's sign. Who are you, and how do you know of the sarens?"

As she spoke, Fin and the rest of the group became entranced, her voice commanding authority, measured and mature. Fin found himself wanting to explain himself to her, like a child needing to answer to a parent.

"A dear friend of mine is a saren knight. She...used to wear her sigil."

Fin could see the woman stiffen at his explanation. Thinking that she might know Reza, he continued. "Perhaps you know of her? Reza Malay."

She seemed to ease up a bit, even closing her eyes for a moment to consider the revelation, then answered, "Yes, I know Reza. I was her matron. I oversaw her development in her youth. So, you lot are the ones she's been traveling with these past few years?"

"No, only me," Fin answered, relaxing somewhat once he knew the woman he spoke with knew Reza. "They've never met Reza, but we share the same goal and have sworn to accomplish our mission at all costs. My name is Fin."

She considered the man for a moment before reciprocating the greeting. "I'm Lanereth," she said at length, adding, "and these are my battle sisters, the high guard and priestesses of the Jeenyre order of the saren knights. I have a feeling, Fin, we may be here at this location for a similar reason. I think it best to speak freely in regard to our purposes here at this desolate formation of crags."

Fin nodded his head in agreement, offering, "Sensible. We have nothing to hide, and I don't see how anyone would be opposed to our path. You know of the arisen army that's harried these lands over the last year, yes?"

"It is the reason we are here," Lanereth answered flatly.

Fin halted his exposition and cut to the chase. "This is our purpose as well. To foil their advances into Tarigannie."

Lanereth tilted her head slightly, showing a slight interest in Fin's stated intentions. "Why do you do this? Simply for the good of the people you serve? Forgive me, but your band does not look as though they are employed by any backing entity of Rochata-Ung or Tarigannie. What's in it for you then? Sareth herself has commanded my deployment in a vision. Who then ordered your aid?"

Fin considered Lanereth's reasoning for a moment, thinking about his group's motives, which were more complex than a simple answer as Lanereth had given him.

"We here," he indicated to Malagar, Hamui, Wyld, Yozo, and himself, "all have our own reasons for taking on this task. They're not as simple or clear a resolution as yours, my lady, but I can assure you, we're just as committed.

"The darkness down in that canyon must be stopped, or many more will pay a horrible price, and so far, few have stepped up to face it. Someone's got to, before it gets out of hand. We're here to do what we can, though I fear our small force stands little chance of truly making a difference in the end."

"Honorable." She nodded in approval. "You have a brave heart, or we would not have found you here. Perhaps, working together, your efforts will go further than you worry they will. Seeing that we're duty-bound by the same objective, would you be willing to work together?"

Fin turned to scan his companions, none seeming opposed to the offer. Seeing the reverential look for the knight troop on Malagar's and Yozo's faces, he guessed they'd be overjoyed to have help in the upcoming task of eliminating Denloth.

"That sounds agreeable. We were going to set camp for the night and scout through the canyon on the morrow. What's your plans with the approach?"

The saren answered, "We plan to ride along the crag wall tonight and get a visual on the army from above. We can set up basecamp after we have an idea of where they're at and what we're dealing with. Until then, few plans can be made."

"This is wisdom," Wyld voiced from the back, arms folded. Hamui nodded his head in agreement.

Fin didn't see the hurry in skipping sleep for another night in a row, but he could tell he was outnumbered on the matter. The smallest hint of weariness at the thought of another long night crept into his voice.

"We have no mounts for the journey," he pointed out, to which Lanereth offered, "None of you seem overweight, it will be no problem to double up with us."

Fin looked to the other women, high on their steppe horses. Putting aside thoughts that would likely get him in trouble, he agreed, "That would be much appreciated. Long have we traveled on foot. Too long…."

He turned, looking back at the glow that was a sunset a few minutes ago, and looked to the crags.

"We trailed the arisen. We know they're down in the crags, but where exactly along its stretch, we're not sure."

"Then let us help you find them again," Lanereth said heartily, offering a hand to Fin, helping to hoist him up behind her on the saddle.

Four other knights rode up to pick the rest of the group up. Fin noted the largest knight taking interest in Hamui, the strong lady picking the small praven up under his arms and plopping him behind her with a smirk of ownership on her lips. Fin wasn't sure whether he should be worried for the little praven or amused by the pairing.

It had just become true night by the time the sisters trotted to a slow gait, the edge of the crags slightly aglow in a ruddy red and purple light.

Lanereth made a hand signal to the others, as she came to a stop many yards from the cliff's edge, and they all dismounted, touching down on the cool, midnight-blue sands. The troop snuck quietly up to the drop-off, lying flat at the edge and slowly peered over to see the source of the unnatural glow deep within the canyon's belly.

A slow swirling mist covered the canyon floor, aglow in a royal purple hue. Hundreds of arisen stood at ready; other large platoons on rotted horseback strolled wearily through the canyon on an endless patrol, gleaming spears held high. Spectral blue wights stood at attention along the ruins of a large temple entrance upon the face of the hundred-yard cliff, entering the side of the canyon. There were many large beasts—behemoths of ash and blood—terrible creatures. Some were recognizable while some were simply monstrosities, pieced together rotted flesh and bones, not seeming to make anatomical sense. Lumbering, rotten cadavers, the reek of the hellish pit—all made looking over the edge all but unbearable.

"What in the hell…" Hamui quietly let out. All nearby agreed.

"Abomination…" Lanereth hissed, covering her nose and mouth

with her sleeve. Fin looked upon her and to the all-too-familiar sight that often haunted his dreams since the terrible events of Brigganden a year ago.

"Ever hungering for the sweetbreads of man. Only content to devour life and obey the will of the master. Miserable wretches," Fin sneered, his disgust with the display of twisted mockery of life.

"Each one of those...things...is a victim, murdered in the most horrible manner—and there's thousands of them," the priestess beside Lanereth whispered, horrified by the sight that stretched out before them.

"This army...this army is beyond us. There is no hope here— only death!"

Lanerenth looked to her priestess and waved for all to fall back, away from the sight that the group was getting lost in, returning to their horses that were more than a little uneasy.

"Few have beheld such a sight," Lanereth said in a somber tone, "so I will overlook your words," she said, looking to the trembling priestess. "But we know why we're here. And no matter how...beyond the veil our opponent seems, Sareth will outmatch them. She would not have called us here if not for providing a way for us to help end what blasphemy lies down there.

"I need all of you to take heart now. Fear will be your undoing. *Fear* is the substance that will take apart your armor, your defenses. Keep strong in your faith and we will find a path through this, but not if you allow even an inch of doubt to paralyze your stride. We are in this together, and Sareth *will* watch over us. All of us," she finished, looking to Fin and his group.

"We're here, and we're not leaving until Denloth is dead, or we are," Malagar said, conviction firmer than Fin had ever seen from the haltia.

"That old temple down there, he's in there, I can feel it. Where else would that pompous bastard reside. Not out with the riffraff, that's for sure," Hamui added, getting approving nods from those close by.

"I might agree with your assumption," Lanerenth said, hand to chin as she thought through the group's next line of action. "Within the ancient halls of the sun god, Dannon, our quarry lies. If we can execute the arisen leaders, the arisen army will no more be a threat. Their tie to this world is only held up by their connection to their master, so the records testify. We need to get in that temple, undetected by the bulk of the army. Once within, we need to find the avatar of Telenth, this Denloth you mentioned, and any other ranking followers of the lord of ash, and make our escape to avoid the fallout of the destruction of the arisen army's leadership."

"I know I speak for our group when I say, we're all in. Together, we might actually stand a chance at eliminating Denloth. If your order is anything like Reza, then the arisen are about to be pressed like they've never been before. May the light guide our path," Fin added, gaining a bit of hope for the first time in a long while.

Lanereth nodded her approval of it all, giving a commanding order to two of the sister knights, "Hassa, Gilding, you're on surveillance duty tonight. I want to know their schedule, sentry routes, headcounts, any information you can gather from up here. Stay hidden and safe; but keep an eye on them until I send the next shift."

The tall saren knight and the other priestess stepped up, bowing before the High Priestess, displaying their willingness to remain cliffside to suffer through the first shift.

"I'll join the sentry duty," Hamui said, waddling over to the saren that had given him a ride earlier. Fin and Lanereth did not miss the small smirk Hassa gave the little praven as he joined her side.

"Fin," Lanereth called, bringing Fin's attention back to the matriarch, "there is much to discuss. It seems you've been trailing this hellish troop for a while now."

Fin nodded, looking to the other three still at his side. "We all have."

"Come, we'll set camp a ways out from here. The night is still young, but we'll likely see it through filling each other in on what each party knows of the arisen lord. We prepare for a war like none of us have ever seen."

Though the stars were lit high in the heavens, the moon's light tinting the land a bluish green, the darkness seemed more oppressive than it should have.

Through it all, Fin breathed easier than he had in some weeks. They had help now, and a fighting chance, but more than that, he felt that win or fail, whatever the outcome, a conclusion to it all loomed nearby. And that, more than improved odds, seemed to lighten the weight from his shoulders more than any of it.

As they walked the horses a ways into the desert, Malagar's line came back to him, again and again.

We're here, and we're not leaving until Denloth is dead, or we are.

Continue the adventure with Reza, Nomad, Fin, and the others in book 3, Heart of the Maiden available on Amazon!

Hell is spilling out into the world...and only a few heroes are there to stop it.

The demonic warlord Sha'oul has risen to full power, threatening to open the portals of hell in the Southern Sands region. With the help of Telenth, the devil, Sha'oul is ready to summon demons from the planes of hell and wage war against the living world, with only a ragtag band of heroes led by Reza in their way to stop them. As the final hour approaches and the judgment of the gods draws near, the heroes must go up against Sha'oul and his army of the undead and face the darkness that threatens to engulf their world.

While they journey through treacherous canyons and ancient ruins, they encounter danger and challenges at every turn. They must confront powerful Oathbound, demonic greyoldor, and the treacherous Denloth, who has been seduced by the dark magic of Sha'oul. Will they be able to triumph over the forces of hell, or will the world succumb to the darkness?

Heart of the Maiden is the epic conclusion of a gripping dark fantasy trilogy rooted in dark magic, Lovecraftian horror, and the occult. Pick it up on Amazon and start reading today!

FROM THE AUTHOR

This move across country has been a bit of a rough one. I had planned on having this book out a good three years ago! Life sometimes has other plans for you, and though it has been hard, there's been plenty of opportunity for new growth in my life during this time. The important thing is that I kept at it and am proud to have continued this series.

I hope you enjoyed this book! If you did, make sure to leave a review on Amazon and Goodreads for me. After that, jump over and pick up the next book in the series, Heart of the Maiden!

Visit me online for launch dates and other news at:

authorpaulyoder.com

(sign up for the newsletter)

instagram.com/author_paul_yoder
tiktok.com/@authorpaulyoder
Paul Yoder on Goodreads
Paul Yoder on Amazon

Made in United States
North Haven, CT
31 October 2024

59672292R00193